THE LAST INNOCENT

R. J. STRONG

For Jake, who believed in me even when I didn't.

One may smile, and smile, and be a villain.

— WILLIAM SHAKESPEARE

I turn over the rocks these snakes slither under and let them burn in the sun until they know they're beaten. By me.

— LUKE MARSHALL

1

─────

504 River Side Lane
Savannah, Georgia
August 6th
0127 Hours

Luke Marshall never meant to hate him, but the dead man at his feet left him no choice. Sometimes justice is blind to the wrong things. Cade checked out the easy way and left all the wrong people to pay for his crimes.

Luke looked down at the dead man. A chrome-plated Desert Eagle lay next to the lifeless hand. Blood trickled from a hole in Cade's forehead to the bridge of his nose before dripping thickly onto the carpet. Blood speckled the imposing stone hearth but not a drop stained John Cade's crisp tuxedo shirt.

Across the room, Helen Cade's body slumped against French doors flanked by heavy drapes. A tangle of bleached hair straggled over eyes staring at nothing. Blood stained the chest of her red dress the color of a ripe black cherry. She kept her husband's secrets faithfully, but he killed her anyway.

Luke shook his head as the fog cleared and brutal reality tore at him. Those secrets were still lethal. They could bring down powerful men and destroy the woman he loved. Except now he couldn't protect her. Every cop in the house just witnessed what Cade said. The dead man had forced his hand, and Luke hated him for it. Luke felt his shoulders pinch.

A wisp of smoke curled in a slow lazy circle from the barrel of the gun in Luke's hand. The acrid sweet taste of lead coated his throat as the pounding in his ears dissolved into the pounding of feet.

Helmeted men in tactical gear swarmed behind him clearing every inch of the house. He dropped his hands but held onto his gun. Two SWAT guys cleared the room he stood in then dropped their weapons. Luke answered their muted suspicion with a glare but said nothing. Fuck them. He carried a badge too.

"Luke? You okay?"

At his partner's anxious tone, Luke realized his fist was clenched and his trigger still pulled back. He relaxed his hand and slipped the Glock into its holster.

Without a word Luke turned and walked away, through the massive foyer, past the dueling staircases, and away from his conscience. He shouldered through the heavy oak doors into the humid night air. It stole what little air his lungs still held. Every way he ran the scenario in his head, it ended up costing him everything.

2

———

4416 Interstate Drive
Atlanta, Georgia
May 19th
2000 Hours

Three months earlier...

The wipers swept rainy mist from the windshield as Luke drove. Dark warehouses lined the pitted road. Light from downtown Atlanta bounced off the low clouds bathing Bolton Industrial Park in a faint yellow tinge. Ahead a boarded-up house wearing a dingy coat of peeling white paint sat abandoned. A lone figure pushed a shopping cart, its contents sheltered by quilted garbage bags.

"Look, all I'm saying is if you're gonna toss out the hotties, at least throw 'em my way. You got my number. Hook a friend up." Thaddeus Aulden, Luke's young partner, tapped on his phone screen and chuckled at something Luke couldn't see.

"She's psycho." Luke pulled the black Impala to the curb between two semi-trucks and cut the engine. He ran his hands through his hair and eyed the homeless man heaving the shopping cart over the curb.

"You always say that. I could use a little crazy."

"Psycho's only fun for one night, Kid."

"Yeah, but what a night," grinned Thad. "She was smoking. This place, on the other hand, needs to be smoking." He leaned forward to look past Luke at the apartment complex nestled between two warehouses. He gave a low whistle. "Never gets any prettier."

"You seem pretty uncomfortable in the hood," teased Luke.

"Dude, racist much?" Thad grinned. "Man, I grew up picking collards and okra, and noodling catfish. I stick out like a blue tick in a hen house in the projects."

Irritation replaced the grin on Luke's face. He never could predict what was going to come out of that kid's mouth, but it was either funny or stupid. There was no in between. He shook his head and looked at the dismal sight as Thad grew serious.

"What was he doing here?"

"Let's go find out," said Luke.

In one smooth motion he opened his door and hopped out into the light rain. He strode across the street and jumped over a stream moving fast down the grimy curb.

Ahead, four multi-story buildings huddled together; residential holdouts in the heavy industrial neighborhood. Peeling brown trim bordered drab yellow brick. More shutters were missing than remained, and dying shrubs dotted forgotten mulch beds. A single pale blue rose on a sparse bush stood defiant against its monotone backdrop, but there was little else to cheer the eye.

Behind Luke, a muffled yawn dissolved into a loud curse as Thaddeus splashed through the dirty stream of water.

"Why do people have to kill themselves when I'm supposed to be in bed?"

"You weren't in bed."

"That's right." Thad pulled a face. "His fat ass has been ripenin for a couple of days."

Luke shook his head again. It happened a lot when Thaddeus opened his mouth. Thad was shorter and stockier than Luke, but powerfully built. His green eyes stood out from his dark skin giving him an exotic look. Thad had been Luke's partner for a year, and an agent for a year and a half. It was Luke's opinion that he would make an excellent agent with a little time and sense under his belt. He was a good kid, but Thaddeus was born with a defective filter. If he thought it, he usually said it.

"You're right, I was probably working," said Thad.

"Or partying."

"There's a difference?" Thad grinned. He hopped onto the curb and shook his wet shoe. His navy windbreaker matched Luke's. Large yellow letters on the back said FBI.

"So, he goes missing for two days and ends up here. What the hell was he doing?" Thad repeated, forgetting about his sopping shoe as he stopped beside Luke in front of the derelict apartments.

"I think that's the answer, not the question," said Luke.

"Huh?"

Luke started across the muddy grounds toward building 4416. The first '4' had lost a screw and hung upside down. Luke pulled open the metal stairwell door and the odor of twelve different kitchens hit them.

Thad wrinkled his nose. "Oh good, the curried fried chicken tuna casserole ala rotting flesh is on. When's dinner?"

Luke grabbed the peeling handrail and took the stairs three at a time. At the top landing, he stopped and approached the door marked 22. Two uniformed Atlanta PD officers and a grumpy looking detective turned.

The detective had a military style flat top that contrasted with his rumpled Columbo trench. The trio watched until Thad puffed up the last flight.

Luke pulled out his credentials and flashed them as the door to number 20 inched open. A sliver of face appeared between the door and jamb then it shut again. The five men glanced over but said nothing.

Luke turned back to the rumpled detective. "What's going on?"

"Thanks for coming out." The detective's voice was raspy from a two pack a day habit. "My sergeant's not going to touch this with a ten-foot pole. Did he give you the reader's digest version?"

"Enough to know it's ours."

"We got a noise complaint around two o'clock Saturday morning from the apartment below, but the door," he nodded to 22, "was locked and no answer. The officers didn't have probable cause to make entry so they left. A few hours ago, water starts running through the ceiling into the same apartment that called about the noise. The maintenance man goes in expecting a burst pipe, finds a dead body instead. Driver's license was in his wallet on the chair." Columbo gave a rattling cough. "Maintenance man didn't recognize him, thank god."

"What kind of noise?"

"Thumping or pounding. Downstairs tenants thought the unit was vacant and worried someone broke in."

"Alright, we'll take it from here."

Relief flooded Columbo's face. "Our caseload's a whore right now. This would bury us. What do you need?"

"Anything unusual I need to know?"

"You mean other than the fact there's a dead politician and some kinky shit in there? No."

Thad chuckled but Luke kept talking. "Alright, let's keep this quiet as long as we can." He glanced around at the apartment doors, but they remained shut. "As soon as I finish up here, I'll hand it off to our PR people and let them deal with the press. I don't want them showing up here."

"Yeah, that's why we waited to canvas," Columbo said.

"Good. Leave me these guys for a few minutes," he motioned to the uniformed officers. "We'll do that last. Anyone notify his wife?"

"Not yet."

"We're gonna sit on that for now." Luke turned to Thad. "Where's the Evidence Response Team?"

Thad popped his phone off his belt and started tapping the screen.

Columbo jerked his head toward the door. "Already here."

Without another word, Luke turned the knob and stepped into the apartment. It was cold inside. The hallway stretched the length of the apartment lit by an exposed bulb. It threw a yellow pall over the matted carpet and dingy walls. Cheap cabinets and a small fridge peeked out of the first doorway.

"Why are we here?" Thad shivered as soon as Luke closed the door. "This guy was a state senator. If he wants to check out, it's not our problem. Why isn't GBI all over this cluster?"

Luke flicked a raindrop from his forehead then grabbed the collar of his windbreaker and gave it a good shake. "He announced his candidacy for U.S. Senate three weeks ago. He's officially running for national office. Means we own it." Luke surveyed the dark hallway they stood in.

"Even dead politicians find a way to screw you," muttered Thad.

"Hot date tonight?"

"As a matter of fact, yes. With your mother."

"Not your best." Luke suppressed a smile.

"I know."

Luke walked the three steps to the kitchen doorway. Faded rooster border curled off the wall and three particle-board cabinet doors sagged on their hinges. A pretty young woman with a ponytail stood in the middle of the room holding a massive Nikon camera that dwarfed her tiny frame. A windbreaker like the men's topped her green polo and khakis, except hers read ERT. She offered a nervous smile when Luke entered. "Hi," she said.

Without answering Luke started poking around the room. She eyed him as he circled the kitchen, squinting and peering into cabinets and under the counter. He stopped in front of the refrigerator.

"The body is in...," she began.

"Did you get this?" Luke cut her off pointing to a yellow sticky note on the freezer door.

"Um, uh, not yet. I haven't made it over...." She trailed off as Luke walked out of the room through a second doorway that led into the living area. She was staring after him as Thaddeus rounded the corner.

"So, does this mean I don't have to vote...." Thad abandoned his sentence and threw his head to one side. Striking an exaggerated sexy pose, he propped his arm up on the doorjamb and puffed out his belly.

"Well, hello there, Meagan," Thad purred. "See any 'evidence' you wanna collect?" He rubbed his belly and shot her a mischievous grin.

Meagan recovered her composure and laughed. "Get the hell out of my picture, Thad."

"You better get it while the getting's good. I'm in high demand and I don't want to break your heart."

"High demand for what? Jenny Craig before pictures?"

"Ow, hey...."

Meagan pointed the camera at him, and he ducked back into the hallway and joined Luke in the living room.

The ratty hallway carpet gave way to worse in the living room. Large dark brown stains and small multi-colored ones dotted the once creamy white rug. It looked like someone set off a sprinkler of fruity sodas and never bothered to clean up. Dirty vertical blinds allowed in little of the weak streetlight. The room had no furniture except a heavy 70's era straight back metal chair with a pleather backrest near the kitchen wall. Two pairs of handcuffs hung from the rear chair legs.

Luke eyed the chair. He wasn't sure what he expected when he walked through that door, but this was bad. His simple assignment suddenly didn't feel so simple. Something caught his eye and he knelt by the wall to get a better look.

"Whew. Not the love nest I would have pegged for a senator," Thad said walking in behind him. "Saint Regis, that's where you take your hoes."

Luke popped up and kept moving. Beyond the living room, the hall led past a bathroom. Wet carpet squished beneath his feet as he approached. Luke ducked in.

It was dirtier than the kitchen, used regularly without benefit of regular cleaning. Luke opened the medicine cabinet first. Empty. So was the cabinet under the sink. A cheap plastic trashcan stood beside the sink with scraps of toilet paper in it. Luke leaned over and examined its contents. A pile of used condoms and wrappers lay inside. He glanced into the shower which had no shower curtain, then turned his attention to the toilet.

Clear water brimmed the top of the bowl. Floating inside was a hypodermic needle, a charred spoon and what looked like a blue scarf. The stretchy fabric had been too much for the plumbing. Small puddles pooled all over the floor out to the hall.

The door to the only bedroom sat at the end of the hall. A flash erupted from inside the room as they approached it. A tall, twiggy man stood in the far corner holding a large camera. His jacket also read ERT.

"Hey, guys." The man's flaming red hair clashed with his blue jacket and bumped up on the sides emphasizing his expanding bald spot. Freckles coated his pale skin.

"Hey, Sean," said Thad, "What's shakin?"

"Sean." Luke nodded in Sean's direction and reached into his pocket for latex gloves and pulled them on. Thad crossed the room and began talking to Sean. Luke tuned them out as he studied the room. If the chair gave him a bad feeling, it paled next to what this room inspired.

At some point in their history, the walls had been white. A newer but cheap mattress and box spring set lay on the carpet against the wall. A dark blue fitted sheet with several large stains covered the mattress.

Deck screws anchored two 4x4s to wall studs at the head of the mattress. Four heavy-duty eye hooks poked out of the posts at varying heights. Three of the hooks had long lengths of thick nylon rope tied to them. A leather collar, a length of chain and assorted scarves scattered across the floor. A vicious looking whip made of knotted leather lay tossed in the corner.

To the right, the closet door was long gone. A metal rod ran the width of the deep closet below an empty shelf. One end of the fourth nylon rope was tied securely to the closet rod. The other end dug into the ample neck of the late Georgia State Senator Cecil Twomey.

The rotund body had been there for a while. The dead man's face was dark purple, but his arms were the macabre yellow and gray fusion unique to decaying human flesh. His hands hung straight down and his forearms to his fingers were the same deep shade of eggplant as his face.

The dead man's tailored khaki pants were unbuttoned at his thick waist. His socked feet dragged out behind him, knees inches off the floor. Luke was amazed the closet rod supported the man's weight.

Crossing the room, Luke knelt beside the body. After all this time the fetid smell of dead human flesh still made his stomach lurch. He blinked hard then craned his head to examine the corpse. No wounds were visible, but thin pale lines circled each purple wrist. The dead man had sat in the living room chair before he died, cuffed. Luke reached out and touched a cold hand. The whole body swayed as though frozen solid.

"He's in full rigor and lividity is fixed. I'd say he's been here between twelve and twenty-four hours. I'd bet closer to twenty-four since the air conditioning is turned way down," Sean offered, not expecting an answer.

He got a "hmm" in reply as Luke stood and turned.

A pillowcase matching the bedsheets hung over the small window held in place by thumbtacks. Beneath the window sat another metal chair identical to the one in the living room. An expensive brown suede sport coat hung on the back, and leather penny loafers sat on the floor beside it. A small pile of items lay heaped on the seat. Luke approached the chair and studied it.

"Man, you gotta be one motivated sombitch to hang yourself when your feet still touch the floor," Thad muttered. "That's when you know it's bad."

"I knew it was bad when I heard Simon put him on this,"

Sean indicated Luke absorbed in the contents on the chair. "You don't bring in the Bulldog on just anything."

"Bulldog?" Meagan joined them and eyed Luke who was twisting on all fours to see under the chair without touching it.

Thad gave her a cheesy grin then dropped it when she scowled at him. "It's his nickname. Well, his unofficial nickname. He doesn't know we call him that."

"Why?"

"He'd hate it."

"No, Dumdum. Why do you call him that?"

"Cause he latches on and doesn't let go. If he's on your ass, you're not getting him off. Believe me, I know."

Sean bent forward so he could see both young agents. "Right before you two came on, he worked an organized crime embezzlement case where the suspect threatened to kill his mistress if she turned witness on him, which is exactly what she did. Anyway, when the suspect heard Marshall was the case agent, he turned himself in." Sean chuckled. "True story. Dude figured if he was going down anyway he'd get a better deal if he made it easy, but man did it ever backfire. Marshall crucified him. Loves a chase, that one."

"Is he always this...serious?"

"Yeees," said Thad.

"Has this been moved?" Luke barked across the room. He pointed to a manila envelope on top of a cell phone, wallet and keys. Irritated that no answer came immediately, he turned and glared at Meagan. When he asked a question, the answer better be close behind. "You are heading up evidence on this, right?"

"Um, yes sir. No, it, nobody's moved it," stammered Meagan.

"Also, he can be a little bit of a dick," muttered Thad out the side of his mouth.

"Photographed?" Luke turned back to the chair.

"Yes." Meagan looked at Sean, unsure if she made a mistake. Her partner's shoulders shook as he laughed silently, and she said nothing.

Luke picked up the envelope and opened it. He pulled two 8x10 glossy photos out. His brow furrowed as he looked at them. Without a word, he lay the pictures on the seat and walked to the bedroom door. Gazing out at the soggy carpet, he tugged on his tie to loosen it. He walked down the hall and squatted to look at the baseboard. He ran an index finger along the wall and rubbed it against his gloved thumb.

A camera flash erupted as Sean got back to work. Thad and Meagan's heads leaned together as they watched Luke move into the living room. Seconds later, he came back and stuck his nose next to the dead man's head then disappeared back to the living room.

This time Thad followed. Luke had his nose next to the chair backrest, then grabbed it and tipped it toward the wall. The handcuffs clinked on metal.

"What's the chair telling you, partner?" Thad crossed his arms.

Luke flung the chair upright again. Thad jumped when he actually got an answer.

"There's a chalky residue on the chair," said Luke. "It lines up with that scuff on the drywall. The chair hit the wall."

"He liked it rough....obviously."

"Why would she put it back up?"

Thad wracked his brain trying to come up with an answer. Luke was pulling himself out of his comfort zone to share his expertise and Thad appreciated it, but he was drawing a blank.

"She?"

"He was in it."

"How do you know that?"

"From the marks around his wrists, he had cuffs on not long before he died. And these are the only pair here," Luke nudged the cuff on the nearest chair leg with his foot. "Judging from the blackmail pictures he prefers women, so I doubt he was here with a man.

"Plus," Luke tapped his forehead, "he has a small abrasion right here. Maybe from hitting the wall when the chair fell over." Luke sat in the chair and tipped it again resting his head against the wall. "He could have hit his head when it went over." Luke jumped up and started pacing next to the chair. "There's a scuff in the hallway too, but who knows how that got there or how old it is."

"Maybe he wanted to clean up. It is common with suicides."

"Maybe." Luke stopped for a minute then resumed pacing. "But that's not right, is it? Twomey's MO is limos and five thousand dollar-a-plate fundraisers. Why would he come here, to maybe the most dismal section of town to end his life?"

"Well, he did have a lot to hide."

Luke pointed at Thad. "An unconventional sexual appetite explains this low rent love pad, but suicide is intensely personal. Every suicide I've ever investigated did it in some place that held meaning for them. Home, office, even their car."

"Maybe this place holds some meaning we don't know about."

"I doubt it." Luke turned and strode back to the bedroom where Sean and Meagan were lowering the body onto the floor. He walked past them and grabbed the photos he'd thrown on the chair and saw the smartphone underneath them. Something dawned on him.

"Stupid," he hissed. He darted down the hall into the kitchen. There it was, the sticky note he'd seen when he first entered. Four numbers were written in black ink and nothing else.

Zero, four, six, two.

He tapped them into the screen and the screen sprang to life. The word text application was already open. Luke read it fast and rejoined everyone in the bedroom. He handed the phone to Thad who read it out loud.

"Why can't they just leave me alone? I know I'm not perfect but neither are those raging faggots. They enjoy seeing giants fall so much they are probably toasting right now. I hope they're happy.
Now nothing is standing in their way. They ruined me. I am sorry to bring so much pain and suffering down on my family. If you can ever find it in your hearts to forgive me perhaps I will see you again in heaven."

Thad whistled and looked at the photos Luke offered. The grainy photo had been taken from far away, but the Senator's puffy face and signature thick silver hair were unmistakable. In the first photo, his arm circled the waist of a young woman in cheap revealing clothing. Thaddeus recognized the distinctive brick behind them. It was taken outside the apartments they now stood in.

The second was similar except the Senator guided a girl that looked much younger than the first.

"That is not his wife," said Thad.

"Luke," Sean called, "Come here for a sec."

Luke crossed to him and knelt by the body now lying face down on the floor. The stench had intensified since they moved him. The rigid corpse arched off the floor in the opposite position it hung from the bar. The head and legs pointed upward in a morbid U shape.

"You want to see this." Sean pointed to the back of the dead man's neck. On the skin, a vivid white line cut through the purple making an upside-down V that pointed up into the dead man's hairline. "Consistent with a self-inflicted." Sean settled into a practiced squat. "And look at this," he grabbed the body and rolled it over easily despite its bulk. The stomach reached into the air and the hands pushed parallel against the floor. "His left hand. You couldn't see it when he was hanging."

Something was written on the skin in faded blue ink. It was barely visible on the bright purple. Only an H and an A were legible.

"How do you say...the plot thickens?" Thad's fake Italian accent earned him an eye roll from Meagan.

Luke looked down at the body. Something was rotten in this room besides the corpse. Important people with secrets have important friends. Chances of them cooperating with an investigation were not good. He was going to have to step on some powerful toes. One corner of his mouth inched upward. Been a while since he had a good fight.

Luke put his hand on his knee to stand up when something caught his eye. He reached out and poked a lump in the dead man's right pocket. It was hard. Reaching in, he pulled out a second cell phone. He examined it as Sean pursed his lips and scowled at Meagan.

Without a word, Luke reached over and dropped the phone into an evidence bag and snapped off his gloves.

"Alright, let's get his hands bagged asap and you guys do your thing. Aulden."

Thad snapped from his conversation with Meagan. She

stole one last glance at Luke as he started barking orders at her academy partner.

"Have APD start their canvas, I don't want you doing it. Let everybody think this belongs to PD. Then hit up their vice unit and see if they can ID the girls in those pics. Prostitutes most likely."

"I'm sure they'll find all sorts of helpful people in such a nice neighborhood," said Thad.

Luke turned back to Sean. "What are you taking?"

Sean shrugged. "All of it."

"Good."

Thad looked up from his phone. "Luke."

"Yeah."

"You turned off your phone. Simon wants an update." Thad held his phone out.

"I'll brief him in the morning. I'm not doing it over the phone. Tell him to sleep well because he probably won't after tomorrow."

3

———

McAllister Mill Regional Park
Savannah, Georgia
May 26th
2036 Hours

Since the attacks happened everyone left before five if they came at all. She passed no one during her run. No bikers. No walkers. No runners. This was the most popular jogging trail in Savannah. Now nobody wanted to be here, especially after the sun went down.

"Not that they'd be out in this heat anyway," she muttered to herself.

She had hoped for cooler temperatures, but even at dusk, no breeze cut the heat. As the sun's last rays gave up, the smell of honeysuckle hung in the heavy air and the sound of croaking bullfrogs wafted from the pine trees flanking the trail. Deepening shade under the canopy made it seem cool and inviting, but she knew better. Even the faithful Georgia shade trees couldn't ease this oppressive heat.

"What's that, Tully?" A voice came through her

earphones. Sweat blurred her vision and it suddenly irritated her that music wasn't pumping through them. Just Phil's fat ass on the other end.

A drop of sweat dripped down her temple and caught on a deep scar by her left ear. It followed the line to its end at the apple of her cheek and broke free, dripping to her chin. She reached up and wiped it away.

"Thank goodness the operations bus has air conditioning. And cheeseburgers," Phil said.

"I'm gonna kick your ass," she growled.

"Yes, please."

She heard a chair scrape followed by a muffled grunt and Phil's loud laugh. Then her partner's voice came on the other end. "Tul, I think it's another wash."

"Awesome. Same time tomorrow?"

"No. You're taking tomorrow off. You need to rest."

"We're staying out here until we find them."

"Bring it in. We'll talk about it."

This wasn't working. Everyone avoided these paths for almost a month now. Yet here was a woman running every day for the last week, alone, down the same path where four women had been raped and beaten, one almost to death. It was hard to believe they wouldn't see her presence for the trap it was. Maybe the bad guys weren't as dumb as they hoped. Too bad. Idiots are easy to catch.

Then again, she volunteered for this op. She didn't really have a plan if these shit stains decided to make an appearance, and running shorts left nowhere to carry a gun. There were two of them and her nearest backup was a mile away. Maybe she was the idiot.

Tully picked up her pace anxious to go home. A straight week of runs had taken a toll on her hip. Lately, she hobbled around like an old woman. Tomorrow would not be fun. A rustle and a loud snap behind jerked her back to the present. She pulled up and stopped.

"Stand by. I've got movement." Tully turned expecting to see an animal crawl onto the blacktop. Instead, what she saw made her sweat feel cold.

Two men emerged from the bramble lining the jogging path. Like the victims reported, they hid in the pines waiting. Even with pantyhose smashing their features they looked more like teenagers than men.

The chubby one wore a black Bob Marley shirt a size too small for his pudgy frame. Sweat darkened the neck and the armpits and glistened on his plump, olive arms. The metal pipe in his hand twitched and his eyes darted between Tully and the other man.

His companion showed only hunger as he raked her body with his eyes. Vivid freckles stood out on his pasty skin and his dingy white t-shirt exposed the crude dragon tattoo on his right arm. He'd chosen a knife.

Here we go.

Tully bladed her body away from the men. "Well, well, well. If it isn't a description of the suspects. A brown fucktard and a white fucktard. With bad artwork." She glanced down at the white man's arm.

In Tully's ear, voices yelled, and chairs scraped as ten police officers scrambled into action.

The two men froze. The chubby one looked to his companion, panicked. Tully cocked her head at him. "Savannah PD, honey. You picked the wrong bitch this time."

Chubs stood rooted to the asphalt, his jaw slack. The white man hesitated then took off.

"One runnin' south," she yelled into her mic. Tully watched him for a moment, then looked back at Chubs. He moved toward her, eyes wide and the pipe cocked back. As fast as his flab allowed, he swung his hand aiming the metal piece at her head. Tully stepped aside and brought her hands up.

A stinging slap knocked his forearm across his chest and away from her face. She switched her feet and planted herself. The right cross connected with his nose, and he began to sputter as blood gushed over his mouth. But he didn't go down.

She backed up two steps, and he staggered after her raising the pipe again. This time she caught the halfhearted attack mid-swing and sent a knee into his wobbly gut. He doubled over with a soft "oomph".

Tully yanked the pipe to her waist and sank into a crouch throwing him off balance. As she felt him bend, she stood and again drove her knee up. It hit his broken nose with a loud crack. He let go and collapsed into a silent heap.

Forgetting to drop the pipe, Tully turned and sprinted after the runner. "Pete, we're headed south," she yelled.

Her partner didn't answer. Instead, she heard Captain Timothy, the operation commander. "Easton is coming to you. Everybody is." She heard sirens and ATV engines fire up through her earpiece and again in the distance an instant later.

"Do not engage him, Tully. The park's locked down, he's not going anywhere."

Her hard breathing answered him as she sprinted down the path.

"Meara? Meara? Tully, answer me," Captain Timothy demanded.

A hundred yards ahead, the blond man darted left onto an unpaved nature trail that turned into the woods from the jogging path. Bushes and fallen trees crisscrossed a small stream providing plenty of places to hide.

Tully yelled. The man glanced back. His shoe slid on the

loose gravel and he stumbled letting her close the gap. But she was still fifty yards behind, and she was spent. The suspect regained his footing and sped up.

"We're on the path to the old mill," Tully panted. Her lungs burned as she sucked in air, but the sirens were still far away. Dark was falling fast.

Metal.

Tully remembered the pipe in her hand. She hurled it at his sweaty back. It fell short but tangled between his ankles, making him stumble. With a manic burst, she caught him on a wooden footbridge crossing a babbling creek.

She slammed into him at full speed knocking him face first into the wooden planks. They rolled several times and a sharp pain burned down her arm. His knife skittered down the path.

She kicked out her leg and arched her back to stop their roll. The suspect stopped face down with Tully on his back cranking her forearms down on his head to drive his face down.

He writhed beneath her trying to roll her off, but she braced herself with her free leg. The other leg wrapped around his torso pinning his left arm. His free arm flailed trying to push himself up or make contact with Tully. He didn't seem to care which.

"Stop resisting," she yelled at him.

"Fuck you, bitch."

"Wrong answer." She boxed his ears then slammed his face back into the damp wood.

His free hand closed around her wrist. Trying to wrench it free, she released his hair. As soon as she did, he threw his head back and bucked hard. She could feel his other hand moving around beneath him.

Grabbing his thumb, she pried her wrist loose. Then she wrenched his hand behind his back. He howled as she yanked his wrist closer to his neck. Wriggling her leg out from underneath him she put her full weight on his back. His other hand kept moving underneath.

"Give me your hand."

"No," he screamed.

She slammed a palm into the back of his head bouncing his nose off the bridge, then yanked his arm until she heard his shoulder pop. He screamed and bucked again, but she hung on.

"Give me your hand," she yelled again. She had control, for now. But she didn't know for how long. This fight needed to be over. Ten miles and a sprint later, she was tired. Every second of this fight lasted an hour. He was stronger than her on a good day, and today was not a good day.

Sirens drew closer, but to Tully, they still sounded miles away. The approaching wail infused the man with energy. He rolled enough to free the hand under his body and pulled out what he'd been fishing for. Tully saw the glint of light on metal. Even in the gathering darkness she couldn't mistake the silver revolver as he brought it up and over his shoulder.

Gun.

"Oh." Her soft exclamation was drowned out by the report of the gun. Ringing filled her ears. She let go and threw herself into a roll away from him.

Blondie jumped up and sprinted full speed down the path. Tully pushed herself to her feet, hindered by her sore hip as her earpiece squawked to life.

"What was that?"

Tully couldn't remember ever hearing Captain Timothy sound scared. It was unsettling. She took off after her mark frustrated that her hip slowed her down.

"Tully, answer me." The panic disappeared. He sounded angry.

"He's got a gun," she said, breathless, "everybody watch yourself."

"Tully, stand down. We're almost to you," Pete's voice broke in.

"We're still heading to the old mill," she ignored him.

"Stand down," the Captain roared.

It was so dark now she could barely make out the white t-shirt ahead of her. A wide beam of light sliced overhead then flicked ahead helping her out. The chopper had arrived and was looking for them. In the quick light, she saw her quarry through the trees where the path bent back. Her muscles burned and she couldn't stop the limp, but she took off after him.

Rounding the curve, she found herself in a small meadow with the creek winding around to her right. The old stone skeleton stood on the sandy bank where it sloped down to the water. The chopper's floodlight pierced the hollow windows. Tully started toward it when she heard a clank to her left.

On the far side of the clearing, a tall fence marked the edge of the park. She saw a flash of white against the thick growth climbing the chain link. It disappeared through a gap.

"He went through the fence," she gasped when she was able to catch her breath. A few yards brought her to it, and she slipped through. A narrow stand of trees on the other side gave way to a weedy road. She stopped at the tree line and scanned left and right.

On the other side of the gravel road, a crumbling building stood on a small peninsula surrounded by the Savannah River on three sides. In both directions the road ended in the river. Rotten spires of once bustling piers spiked out of the dark water. Whatever World War era products the factory had produced were long forgotten. The tall arched windows gaped, nothing left to hold the glass in. Piles of brick lay beneath gaps in the façade that was two-football fields long. A loud crash came from inside the condemned building.

"He's inside the old factory," Tully whispered. She hunkered down in the tree line for a minute. He couldn't go out the back unless he wanted to swim. There was nowhere to tie off a boat. She doubted he had one anyway. She picked her way across the road and pressed her back against the decaying brick.

Whumping from the helicopter grew louder and light flooded the area. The sirens stopped and Tully heard brush and trees rustle and hushed talking as the team came through the fence. Close by a K-9 barked.

The smart thing to do was wait for everybody else. Or better yet, back the hell up to some decent cover. This maniac already tried to kill her once. But a perimeter meant one thing. A standoff. He'd made it perfectly clear he wasn't giving up, and letting this bastard check out with a bullet from his own gun was not okay. Every victim should get the chance to face their attacker.

Screw cover.

The faces of this man's victims swam into her head. If this rat died, those women would never watch him answer for the abuse and humiliation endured at his hands. She'd stood at every bedside and swore they would see that happen.

Monsters feared exposure; being on open display next to their deeds. Those swollen faces had turned up in bitter smiles at her promise. She had plenty of mistakes to redeem but breaking this promise would not be among them.

Captain Timothy was on the radio screaming, "Tully, post up. Do not engage. Tully? What's your 20? Tully?"

She slipped off the headphones and the radio from her

waistband and dropped them in the weeds. Through the window she spied a tall pile of railroad ties. She hopped through the opening, rolled behind them, and crouched listening.

Another loud crash and a curse told her he was about thirty yards ahead, but she couldn't see him. It was pitch black. Even the helicopter searchlight punching through holes in the roof didn't reach far enough to illuminate the massive space.

Tully could just make out several more piles of discarded material in the general direction of the last noise. She positioned herself at the edge of her cover and shouted. Her voice echoed through the void. "Hey, Blondie. You probably already know this, but you're surrounded. You got like two options. Handcuffs or a body bag. Douchebag's choice, but you better get to choosin."

She darted behind a small pile of bricks and listened. He didn't answer, but a loud clank told her he was moving. Toward her, it sounded like.

"Hey, Blondie...okay if I call you that? You can use it for your prison handle, I don't mind. You can tell everybody you came up with it."

She kept moving, speaking, then moving. In the darkness she saw a patch of white too bright to belong in the drab environment. It was working. He was moving toward her, picking his way across the rubble-strewn floor.

"Of course, you could come out here like you got a pair and give me your real name." She crouched behind a steel beam.

"I'm gonna kill you, bitch." His voice was deeper than she remembered on the bridge.

"I wonder if blonds are in demand in prison. Better work on that gag reflex." She darted behind a crumbled partition wall. "Then again, they might prefer someone with a bigger dick. Everybody said yours was really small."

Bricks clattered as he moved to find her, zig-zagging to avoid the searchlight.

"I wonder if Ripley's has a category for world's smallest dick." She tiptoed to a large pile of rubble.

A shot rang then burnt out in the cavernous space. Tully knelt but kept her head up watching the dark. Noise bounced around, but his muzzle flash marked him.

Outside, a bullhorn began barking commands at the man inside the building to come out with his hands up. He was surrounded. Tully glanced around to make sure they weren't breaching the building.

She looked back where she had seen the muzzle flash and felt a surge of adrenaline. Her distraction had given him enough time to move, and she didn't see where.

Shit. Where is he?

For the first time that night she suppressed panic. Feeling around, she found a brick and heaved it as far as she could. Two shots flashed in the direction of the noise.

Gotcha.

Blondie ignored the hovering chopper and the men outside, all his rage now directed at the woman mocking him. She would be his victim even if she was his last. And he had two shots left.

Tully heaved another brick. It clanked against metal. As soon as it left her hand, she moved to another rubble pile closer to the last muzzle flash.

Blondie no longer cared if he was quiet. He made his way toward the noise. Tully stalked him until she was right behind him. "Sup, Blondie."

He froze as a cone of brilliant light found them. Tully saw the man's shoulders flex and his gun hand whip around.

Enough. She was in pain, and from the way the Captain sounded, in big trouble, again. It was time to go home.

Her right hand caught the swinging arm at the wrist. Driving her left palm as hard as she could, she connected with the back of Blondie's elbow. It bent the wrong way and a jagged bone tore out of his bicep.

The revolver hit the ground. He staggered but didn't go down. Tully held onto the mangled arm and coiled her left hand across her body. A crushing backhand to his temple dropped him to his knees.

He uttered a guttural sound as Tully bent over and ripped off the pantyhose covering his face. "If you're gonna play in my town, you better be ready to pay up," she whispered in his ear. Then she planted her foot in his back and kicked hard. He hit the ground moaning, cradling his useless arm.

Tully flipped his gun away with the toe of her running shoe and squinted into the blinding light and waived. Soon yelling reached her ears over the whumping of the chopper. The pilot had radioed to the others. Backup was coming in.

She sat on a pile of railroad ties as uniformed and plain-clothes officers swarmed around her, all pointing guns at the whimpering mess on the ground. Without further ado, five of them pounced on the prostrate figure and cuffed him. When they touched his shattered arm, his screams pitched higher and he started fighting again.

With some sideways glances and a few grins at Tully, the group scooped up the bad guy not taking any pains to be gentle. Halfway out of the building he began screaming and kicking again. The party stopped for a minute and dumped him on the ground.

Tully couldn't see what was happening at the bottom of the pile, but she saw hands and elbows rising and falling. A few moments later they picked him up, hog-tied, and proceeded. He was still screaming, but now he couldn't move.

She laughed and looked at her partner. Pete drew his thick, muscled frame up to its full 5'5". He looked like a short, pale hulk, and he was furious. "What the hell was that, Tully?"

"What?" She shrugged and grinned. "He wouldn't stop."

Pete's nostrils flared. "Get up."

"Why?"

"We're going to the hospital."

"It's not my job to interview that jackas…"

"Are you kidding?" Pete interrupted. "As usual, I can't tell if you're oblivious or if you like the pain. You're bleeding." He pointed at her shoulder. "Again."

She looked down realizing her arm felt wet. Her left deltoid was laid open. Blood glistened all the way to her elbow.

"Ohh." She raised her arm to get a better look. "He fucking shot me. I didn't feel…."

Rubble bounced away from the boots of a stern-faced uniform marching toward Tully and Pete. As usual, Captain Timothy's mood was three steps ahead of him. And he was seething.

Smart comments lined up to escape Tully's mouth, but when she saw him shake his prematurely graying head and pinch his nose, she swallowed them. If poked too hard after the nose pinching began, the congenial Captain had a reputation for making life unpleasant. And after the stunt she just pulled, she needed to diffuse the situation.

Pete crossed his arms as much as their girth would allow, his expression smug. He was going to enjoy the ass chewing she was about to get. Tully narrowed her eyes at him as he nodded to Captain Timothy.

"Cap."

The red in the Captain's face dissipated. He slapped Pete on the shoulder as he passed. "Good work, Son." Then he turned to Tully.

The urge to yell seemed to have passed, but he leveled his steely blue gaze on her without his trademark toothy smile. She rounded her eyes to look more innocent, then dropped the act when his lips pressed into a razor-thin line. She was pissing off everybody today.

"Sup, Cap?"

It looked like he might pinch his nose off. "Tully," he said finally throwing a hand in the air, "you're killing me. You're gonna give me another heart attack. We've had this conversation before and here we are again."

"What conversation, Cap?"

One look made her back down. "I'm sorry." She lowered her chin and looked up at him, contrite, through her eyelashes. Randolph Timothy had been a father figure and mentor to her for many years. She was like his own daughter. Especially when he was yelling at her.

"Don't look at me like that. You better be sorry. And let's get one thing straight. When you're on the job and I tell you to do something, that's what you do. Understand?" His voice grew quiet. "I won't say it again."

She nodded. He always said that.

"You have got to stop this lone ranger crap, you hear me? I owe it to your father to watch out for you, and that's exactly what I intend to do. Even if I have to fire your backside."

"You're not gonna fire me," she teased. His face grew red again, so she added, "Sometimes you just roll with it. You taught me that." Her tone grew serious. "Cap, I couldn't let him kill himself."

"Dagnabit, Tully. You're in that ER every other month."

As hot-headed as the Captain was, she'd never heard

him cuss once in her entire life. She grinned. "It's been at least six."

"Stop it." He pointed a finger at her, but one look at her bloodied shoulder and his face grew soft again. "You're gonna have to make room on your trophy shelf. They'll be lining up to give you awards after this. But you gotta be alive to accept them." He put the finger in her face. "If you ever disobey another direct order, you'll never carry a badge again. You direct?"

"Yes, sir."

His head dipped to kiss her forehead, but he caught himself in time and squared his shoulders. "Don't make me bury another Meara." He squeezed the back of her neck and turned to leave. "Take a few days off. Ah, ah, ah."

She sat forward to protest, but he cut her off. "If I see you at the station before Monday, I really will fire you."

"So, you were just kidding before."

"Goodnight, Tully." He disappeared into the swirl of blue flashing lights.

"How's the hip?" Pete asked.

"My hip?" Her deltoid had nearly been split in half and he was worried about a four-year-old injury? She sat forward and arched her back trying to stretch it out so her limp wouldn't be so pronounced. "Fine," she said.

"Um hm." He never believed her anymore. Especially when the word 'fine' came out of her mouth. "Let's go." Pete pulled her up by her good arm. He was mad, and she didn't blame him.

She dropped her elbow, and pain seared to her neck as Pete helped her up and toward the waiting ambulance. The adrenaline high had blocked the pain but the sight of blood dripping down her arm undid it. Wincing, she clutched her arm to her body waiting for the tongue lashing she knew was coming. But it never came. She stole a look at Pete and saw his lips pressed together so hard they had turned white.

"Better than meatloaf and movie night, huh?"

"Shut your mouth."

Tully laughed.

4

Savannah, Georgia
May 29th
0940 Hours

"How's the shoulder?"

Pete and Tully stood in a tiny shaded parking lot. Bay Street was heavy with daytime traffic. The midday sun blurred through the clouds as though it could muster the strength to give oppressive heat but not brilliant light. The heat came early this year.

They leaned against a cruiser watching the bustle pass by. Pete nursed an enormous cup of coffee. Tully's water bottle was almost empty.

"It's really good, actually."

Pete shot her a withering look. "You're working too hard."

"Nah." She waved him off. "Trying to find something to do at home is working too hard."

"Three days is not enough time to heal. That was deep."

"That's what she said." Tully guffawed and nudged him hard in the ribs.

Pete shook his head. She saw his eyes flick to her bottle. Today's model was stainless steel. He knew what that meant, but she didn't care.

"Who pissed in your grits?"

Pete traced the rim of his coffee cup. "Just tired."

"How is the little nugget?" Tully was grateful for an opening to change the topic. "Shipping off to college?"

"Well, she can't roll over yet, but I guess it's never too early to research schools." Pete finally smiled. All it took was a reminder of why he was tired.

The way his eyes lit up when he talked about his daughter sent a spike through Tully's gut so sharp it physically hurt. She pushed away the thought and took a sip from her bottle.

"What are you doing next weekend?" Pete's sunglasses slid down his sweaty nose, and he pushed them back up.

"Nothing. You're not going to your dad's place?"

"Barbecue. My house. Melissa and I are having some people over. Nothing extravagant, just beer and my world-famous brisket."

"Cool, who's coming?"

"You won't know them, so you probably haven't told any of them to piss off yet. Old friends of mine from...."

"Uh-uh," she said flatly. "Nope. You're not setting me up with any more school friends."

"What's wrong?"

"Fuck off, Easton."

"Don't worry. They're cops, Tul. Some old buddies of mine from State."

"Nope. No more. It's always an unmitigated disaster when you try to set me up with someone and I'm not going to be a part of it anymore."

Pete threw his head back laughing.

"Keep laughing, you son of a bitch," Tully snapped.

"Your 'friend' CAME OUT to me. On a blind date. I can't believe you didn't know...," she stopped as it dawned on her.

Pete doubled over laughing and she aimed a punch at his kidney. Coffee sloshed as his hand clenched popping the top off the paper cup. He dropped it away from him as Tully massaged her stinging hand.

"You bastard. You knew he was gay when you set us up."

Pete backed away with his hands out as Tully bore down on him. "I wondered how long it was gonna take you to figure it out. That was payback for that little April fool's stunt," Pete gasped with laughter. "If it makes you feel better," he wiped a tear from his eye, "he was just as surprised as you. I had him believing you were a man. He set me up with a dude in college and I never paid him back. I guess we're all even now."

Tully threw her arm around Pete's neck in a chokehold and threw herself forward bending him over at the waist. "No, Pete, that doesn't make me feel better."

With her free hand, she was reaching back for her pepper spray when a young couple walked by with a double stroller. The twin girls in matching dresses pointed and laughed while Mom and Dad gaped at the two uniformed police officers fighting. Tully spotted them and let Pete go.

Pete coughed and started laughing again. At the sound of Pete's laughter, the man pressed his hand into his wife's back and hurried her and the stroller down the street. Tully put her hands on her gun belt and took a deep breath, glaring at her partner. The radio chirped to life dispatching them to a call.

"You better keep your eye open, Pardner. Payback's gonna be a stone cold bitch." Tully poked a finger into his chest then opened the passenger door.

"That was payback, Tul."

Over the roof, she glared at him. "Stone cold."

Pete mumbled into the radio and a few minutes later they pulled up to the Tasty Day Chinese Restaurant. An old Buick with faded brown paint and a primer trunk was stopped on the busy street. West Boundary Drive traffic snarled as cars tried to get around. Tully threw on the blue and whites as Pete called in the tag.

They approached and looked through the tinted glass. Trash covered the torn seats and a strong smell of cats wafted from the interior. It was empty.

Pete tried the door, but it was locked. Tully walked back to the cruiser to radio for a tow truck, while Pete positioned himself on the curb by the rear bumper to write a parking ticket. A minute later a wrinkled old white woman came screaming out of the restaurant.

Her gray hair was streaked with white, and she wore a thick blue cardigan despite the summer heat. Her hot pink t-shirt with a napkin still tucked into the collar clashed with her flowery purple skirt. Cowboy boots with metal toes completed her ensemble.

"What are you doing?" She yelled, eyes wide.

"Ma'am, is this your car? You can't park in the middle of the...," started Pete.

"Iiii," she gestured wildly, "am the light of the...the old...." She trailed off and stared at him with a shocked expression.

"What?" Pete looked confused.

"The car?" She sounded equally confused. She stood straight up and put her hand on her hip.

Pete looked at Tully then back at the woman who had now scampered to the front of the car. She pressed her cheek against the hood and started singing an unrecognizable tune. Tully slipped out of the cruiser and looked on in amusement. Pete was staring at the crazy woman in disbelief. He looked back at Tully. She planted her butt on the hood of the cruiser and grinned at him.

"Ma'am?" Pete reached for the old woman's arm.

"DON'T TOUCH ME," the woman screamed. She flailed her arms and ran around to the passenger side directly into traffic. Pete dropped his ticket book and rounded the car trying to get control of her. Traffic came to a stop as cars braked to avoid the crazed woman. Tully made no move to stop her as she ran by.

"Are you kidding me?" Pete threw his hands up. "Grab her."

With the agility of a pro athlete, the old woman bobbed and weaved to the opposite side. She never noticed Tully.

"I don't think I will actually." Tully crossed her arms.

The woman darted back around to the driver's door and yanked the handle. The door didn't budge. She forgot to unlock it.

"Grrrr." With a mighty grunt, Pete heaved his short beefy frame up and over the hood. He landed beside the woman, and she shrieked as he grabbed her and pinned her arms.

Tully sputtered with laughter when the woman started barking like a dog. She wiped away a tear as Pete wrestled the barking woman into handcuffs.

When they pulled into the station the clock read 6:15. Late as usual and the parking lot was deserted after the five o'clock shift change. A few cruisers and some unmarked cars dotted the parking lot behind the three-story headquarters. Pete put the car in park and looked over at Tully.

"You still mad at me?"

She smiled and shook her head. "Mad? Why would I be mad?"

"Truce." He stuck out his hand.

"I don't negotiate with terrorists," she grinned. "You going to Only's?"

"I'm heading home. Been a day, but you already knew that."

Tully chuckled as she headed into the station. "Ya did great, kid. You did great."

Thirty minutes later an irritated Tully left the locker room in jeans and a t-shirt. The tussle with Pete popped a stitch in her shoulder, and she had to apply a butterfly bandage and new gauze to her inflamed arm. She trudged down the long hallway toward her truck and the promise of an ice cube melting in whiskey. Doc could stitch her up tomorrow. They were waiting on her at the watering hole.

Her old rattletrap Blazer was parked on the far side of the deserted lot next to the dumpsters. She tossed her gym bag on the passenger seat and grabbed the door frame to hoist herself inside and a sharp pain tweaked her shoulder. She grabbed her left elbow to steady her arm and sucked in a few deep breaths, letting the pain ease. Movement caught her attention.

She squinted through the gathering dusk. At the rear of the fenced parking lot, Pete slipped through a small gate. It led to an alley running between headquarters and the high brick border wall of an old cemetery. He wore civilian clothes.

That wasn't right. Tully looked around the parking lot. Pete's jacked-up Silverado was still there. Usually, he went straight home, in uniform, and showered there. He only changed at work if he was going drinking. He shouldn't still be there, much less heading out the back gate in civies.

Tully hesitated. She shouldn't follow. He might see her. Or worse, she might find out where he was going. Then what? The hairs on the back of her neck pricked up.

Easing the Blazer door shut, she ran to the back of the parking lot and scanned her card to open the gate. She peeked through.

The narrow alley was empty. One hundred yards to the left it ended in trash cans and somebody's driveway. Oglethorpe Avenue was right. She headed toward Oglethorpe. At the sidewalk, she checked both ways.

Pete was walking through the iron gates of the cemetery entrance a block down Oglethorpe. Tully inched along the brick wall to the corner where it met the iron fence. The path was in clear view. Pete took it straight through.

On the other side, he cut straight across Perry Street and walked down Lincoln toward the cathedral. As soon as Pete's shoes hit the pavement, she sprinted down the gravel cemetery path.

Tully stalked her partner from two blocks behind, darting into an alley whenever she passed one. Pete didn't seem too concerned about being followed. His quick pace never slowed, and he never looked back.

On Harris Street, he turned right. She sprinted to the corner and stopped to watch. He walked the length of the Cathedral and headed across the street through Lafayette Square. Tully broke into a run to close the distance.

At the end of Harris, she skidded to a halt. He hadn't cut through the square; he was still there. Pete sat on a park bench under a tree. Another man was easing down on the bench beside him. Tully ducked behind a parked delivery van, her chest heaving. Inching to the front, she looked through the passenger window.

Her stomach dropped when she saw who he was meeting. That lying good-for-nothing snitch was not one of Pete's confidential informants. She and Pete worked everything together. They knew every detail of each other's cases. No way this was work.

In fact, the unwashed scum bag excuse of a man was nobody's CI, but a man with knowledge, nonetheless.

Nicholas Cummings had dirt on people. A fact he tried regularly to exploit for a get-out-of-jail-free card.

Too regularly. No one believed him anymore. That didn't seem to bother Pete as he sat on a bench with the man, deep in a conversation he forgot to tell her he had scheduled.

Tully had seen enough. Without waiting to see how the meeting ended, she turned and ran back to the station at a sprint. A limp formed as her hip grew sore. If she wasn't supposed to know about this, she needed to get the Blazer out of the parking lot before Pete made it back. Let him think she'd gone to the pub. He wouldn't check.

She drove the ten blocks home in a haze, dripping with sweat. She tried pushing the evening out of her mind but failed until she got home and grabbed the open bottle of whiskey on the counter.

The gym bag went on the bed and the bottle went to her lips. She let the liquid trickle into her mouth. It was enough to dull the screaming thoughts and her senses. Sweat on her body and the whiskey warming her chest made the air-conditioned room cold.

Slowly she peeled off her shirt, the dark gray nearly black with moisture, and tossed it on the floor. She unhooked her bra and let it slide to the carpet. The bottle went on the dresser while she shimmied out of her jeans and thong. She went into the bathroom and stepped into the shower. The bottle came with her.

Cold water hit her skin. As it warmed, she sank against the tile letting the water run over her breasts. They were cold like the rest of her. Steam rose as the water got hotter and her skin flushed.

She let out a contented groan. The pain in her hip eased and her mind calmed. She tried telling herself it was the scalding shower, but she tipped the bottle back again and felt better.

Flipping around, she propped one hand against the tile and let the water fall down her back and over the curve of her butt. The other hand hung down, wrapped around Jack Daniels' long neck. The water eased the aching while the whiskey dulled her racing mind. It felt good.

The feeling didn't last long. As her head grew fuzzier, she rested it on her hand. Now it was guilt she felt. It quickly dissolved in a rush of hate.

She hated herself for following him. For letting it go this far. For making him dance around the unflattering truth instead of letting him speak. Another swig nearly emptied the bottle.

That's how it had to be. She didn't want to hear what he had to say. Even best friends shouldn't know everything about each other.

She drained the bottle and stuck her head under the water letting drops patter her face. The glass bottle shattered at her feet and she started awake, unaware she had drifted off.

Ignoring the glass shards, she pushed her face directly against the tile. She would have stayed in there for an hour, but she was out of whiskey. Her old sweats and a fresh bottle would be just the thing.

As she reached to turn the water off, a loud crash came from the great room. She froze. Then scratching and a loud thunk.

Someone was in her apartment.

Letting the water run, Tully eased back the shower curtain, listening. Forgetting about a towel, she moved silently into her bedroom and grabbed the gun from her gym bag. Still dripping, Tully pressed herself against the wall by the door and pulled it open a few inches. Nothing. Whoever it was, they were quiet now.

Was it him? It couldn't be him. He never came to her house.

She strained to see into the kitchen, but she couldn't without opening the door further. She chastised herself for not setting the alarm. It was wasted money because she always forgot to turn the damn thing on.

The air kicked on. Her skin erupted in goose bumps as the register beside her spewed out cold air. Icy droplets let go of her hair and fell to the small of her back. They didn't warm as they crept down her exposed skin.

Planting her feet, she swung the door open and drove, gun first, into the living area. The moment she stepped through the door a loud crash came from the picture window that looked out to the courtyard.

He's outside.

Tully fell to the floor and crawled under the window. The curtain was parted enough for her to look through.

"Motherfuc...," Tully trailed off. She lowered her gun.

The neighbor's yellow tabby cat sat on the wide sill. He'd knocked over two terra cotta planters with wilted black plants Tully long ago forgot. He turned to look at her. His purring rattled through the window making her want to shoot him.

She sat back against the wall to let her heart rate come down. Then she realized she was soaking wet and naked. She took several long breaths as she put her gun on the end table and went to get a towel. Gradually she calmed.

Tully toweled her hair dry and slipped on her ragged blue sweatpants and a white tank top. From the medicine cabinet, she pulled a large gauze bandage and a prescription bottle. She re-covered her bloody shoulder and tapped two pills into her hand swallowing them without water. The prescription bottle went back into the cabinet next to three others.

In the kitchen, she grabbed a new bottle of whiskey from the cabinet. She was hungry, but all she wanted to do was rest. Settling on the couch, she lay her duty gun in the end table drawer next to her daddy's .386 Nightguard. A sepia toned framed picture of Sam Meara in uniform sat on top of the end table. She took a long pull from the bottle and sat it next to her father.

Tully clicked on the television and stopped on a cooking show. Easing a heavy blanket over her shoulder, she lay back against the cushions as the AC kicked on again. The pills and booze worked their magic on the pain and she drifted off.

BANG.

Tully felt something hard slam into her.

Two shadowy shapes stood over the prone figure of her father, still in his brown Sheriff's uniform from the day's shift. The hulking shape of Charlie Heyward pushed the smaller form forward.

"You ain't to take a Hayward to jail, Bobby." Tully could hear the huge plug of tobacco muddling Charlie's voice. "You make sure this pig learns it."

Tiny Bobby stumbled forward and dropped the shotgun muzzle low. Charlie shoved his brother and the pair forgot about the wounded deputy for a split second.

Sam Meara pointed his shotgun down the hallway and pulled the trigger. The blast sent Bobby reeling backward, arms flailing.

Through a crack in her bedroom door, Tully watched the red circle bloom on Bobby's shirt. He staggered back then fell. Tully saw the whites of his eyes in the moonlight pouring into the hall from a window. The hulking shape reached down to grab something then disappeared down the hall.

Crawling.

Tully watched again, frozen, as her father crawled to the wall and pulled himself up. A long smear of blood on the wallpaper followed Sam as he moved down the hall.

BANG.

At the living room door, he fired around the corner without looking.

BANG.

The blast came from the left. Yes, that was right. The left. Big, blond Charlie Hayward stood by the front door across the room from Sam's easy chair.

"Daddy?" Tully heard the words leave her lips. They cut through the thickness like a blade.

She opened the door. Rage took her and she flew at the man standing over her father, but her body wouldn't move fast enough. Furious, she kicked and scratched and beat on his thick leg with her fists. He was so big.

A beefy hand swatted her in the chest like she was a mosquito. She watched herself fly backward slamming into the coffee table in front of the couch. The glass top shattered and shards tinkled across the carpet.

She looked and saw her father's head flop toward her. Her cheek felt wet, and she wondered why she'd been crying. Wiping the tears away with her hand, she saw red running down her fingers. Her hand was so small.

Charlie stepped up to her father and aimed his gun at the fading deputy's chest. His ugly face was clear.

Crawling.

Glass tore at her arms and pink ruffled nightgown. Everything would be okay if she could get to him. She crawled to her father and lay her aching head on his arm.

BANG.

Tully's body jerked so hard that her arm slammed into the wooden coffee table. Her living room spun violently as she opened her eyes. Pain seared down her arm and up her neck, and she realized carpet pushed up against her face. She'd fallen off the couch.

Rolling to her back she grabbed her shoulder and felt sticky goo. The room seemed tilted and her head weighed a thousand pounds. She quit trying to lift it and closed her eyes again as darkness settled on her like a heavy blanket and she blacked out.

5

FBI Regional Field Office
Atlanta, Georgia
May 30th
1117 Hours

Luke and Thaddeus sat in the conference room of the Atlanta Field Office. The long table was piled high with boxes and bags sealed with red tape, delivered a few hours earlier.

"Newton said it. Not me. It's not some new-fangled idea I came up with just now." Thad stopped typing. "It's simple cause and effect."

Black mesh chairs lining the table twirled as Luke elbowed them.

"You're psycho pacing again," Thad said eyeing Luke over his laptop screen. He'd never been so happy to see an evidence delivery. For a week straight Thad listened to Luke complain about how long it was taking. Ten days was lightning fast for evidence processing.

"Why would he kill himself?"

Thad clicked the laptop shut. "He got caught in the hen

house. He committed political suicide, so he musta figured the best way to deal was actual suicide. That's all the evidence says."

"But that's not right is it?" Luke lapsed back into thought.

Thad wasn't having it. "Nobody cares about a dead politician. Right?" He tried goading Luke out of his haze.

When he got no response Thad pressed on, annoyed. Getting information was a full-time job when Luke got like this. "The evidence. You know, all this crap we gotta make sense of?"

Luke pointed at Thad like he made an excellent point. "It wasn't political suicide. There is no such thing."

"Pardon?"

"Politicians don't kill themselves when they get caught with their pants down. Literally or figuratively."

"What do they do?"

"They run for office again."

Thad laughed. Luke elbowed another chair into a spin. "Twomey's been implicated in several major scandals before, and he keeps getting re-elected. Three times if I'm right. Does the Lake Lanier incident ring any bells?"

Thad's eyebrow shot up. "That was him?"

"He was neck deep in allegations and still won that fall. Most politicians are Teflon coated, and he's no exception. This," Luke gestured to the pile of bags, "is just another day at the office."

"Somebody had pictures this time."

Luke waved his hand. "Somebody's always got pictures. Name one politician that committed suicide because he got caught in an affair." Luke dragged his hand through his hair.

Thad shook his head and shrugged.

"One other time Twomey was caught in an affair. The woman and her husband went quiet and fell off the radar."

Luke stopped and propped his elbows on the back of a chair.

"That was nice of them."

"Paid off, no doubt. It's a stretch that he would roll over at a simple blackmail threat. I'd bet a month's pay this guy has been down that road."

"I don't like to gamble. I always lose. Are you saying you think he was murdered?"

"No. I'm not saying that. I want to make sure we're not missing anything."

Thad relaxed a little. "Not much to miss. We've got definitive rope marks. A suicide note and a very good reason for him to be swingin from the rafters."

"There was a struggle," said Luke.

"He liked it rough. Doesn't mean foul play."

"I know. That's what bothers me."

"What?"

"Why was he tied? There's no way those tiny teenage girls were going dominatrix on him. It had to be the other way around. But there were marks on his wrists."

"Yeah that's a little weird," Thad admitted. "Then again, this whole thing is weird."

"And that crime scene was one of the cleanest I've ever seen. Everything in place. Staged. Wiped clean. Strange for someone who commits suicide on a whim to wipe the place for prints. And why bother putting a chair back up?"

"Unless it wasn't on a whim. People plan suicides, you know." Thad spoke slowly trying to emphasize his point. "It's common for them to clean up. So whoever finds the body will think better of them; that they weren't a slob. It's basic psychology."

"An image obsessed man kills himself in the shittiest apartments in Atlanta and leaves out the riding crop and the handcuffs. Sure doesn't seem like he was trying to control perceptions. I do agree with you though. Nothing's as consistent as vanity." Luke resumed pacing.

Thad closed his eyes and spoke deliberately. "And the evidence?"

"What about it?"

"Look, I know I'm the new guy here, but there's nothing to support anything but a self-inflicted death. This," he gestured to the pile, "is the equal and opposite reaction to the initial action or actions. That's why it's called evidence. Murder leaves evidence of murder, and suicide leaves evidence of suicide. Even tampering leaves a trail. That doesn't change simply because it doesn't answer every question."

"I'm not disagreeing with you."

"And yet you're still arguing," Thad muttered.

Luke spun and headed back down the carpeted aisle. "You were the psych major. Explain it to me."

"W...well," faltered Thad, "I don't really know why he would have killed himself there. Unless one of the girls holds some special meaning for him. Maybe he was in love with one of them."

"So he kills himself to spare a hooker the embarrassment of a scandal? Come on."

"Well, somebody obviously knew about them if they knew where to deliver the photos...."

"If they were delivered there," Luke cut in.

"There's no way he brought those with him. Maybe they were delivered while he was there. Maybe not. Maybe it was someone close to him. I don't know. Look, I don't have an answer for you. But it doesn't mean you can throw out the hard evidence because you have questions."

"I'm trying to get my questions answered."

"You're freakin' me out, Marshall. That's what you're doing."

"Who was the apartment registered to?"

"Some guy that doesn't exist." Thad flipped his laptop open, clicked a few times, and squinted at the screen. "Apartment was rented by someone named James Smith. Paid for a year in advance with cash. I got about four billion returns on that name in both Georgia DMV and CCH, but none with a matching birth date."

"So Twomey's people send in a ladder climbing intern with a fake id to rent this place." Luke stopped and rested his forehead on the backrest of a chair and hunched his shoulders.

"Nobody at the rental office recognized any of the campaign's people," said Thad.

Luke straightened. "Doesn't matter," he muttered. "Wouldn't tell us anything we don't already know." He leaned forward and rifled through a thick binder containing a detailed list. Something nagged at him all week.

He found it, then rummaged through the pile to find the corresponding item numbers. He pulled out the two cell phones, each secured in its own clear plastic bag and sealed to prevent tampering.

Luke held the phones side by side. One was a high-end black smartphone. The other was a cheap silver prepaid flip phone.

"I want a search warrant to dump this phone data." He held up the smartphone.

Thad nodded and made a note.

Flipping open his pocketknife, Luke sliced through the packaging of the cheap phone. He opened it and started punching buttons. Only two numbers were in the call history. "Find out where these numbers go."

"It's a burner phone. It probably goes to his pimp," said Thad without turning from his screen.

"Make sure."

Thaddeus looked up to see a cell phone hurdling toward his face. He snagged it before it smacked him in the forehead. "Dude, you need to relax. You're gettin my pressure up." Thaddeus went back to his computer.

Luke started pacing again. There were signs of a struggle, but that was easily explained. The toilet overflowed leading to the discovery of the body. Likely the prostitute's mistake. She woke up, found him dead and panicked. Thad was right. This was easy.

In the old days, gut instinct was his greatest asset. Hunting hadjis in the sandbox was less complicated than building a case. Instinct and experience made him good at hunting terrorists. These days it was less valuable. The American justice system had no use for his gut's point of view. Another in a long line of places he didn't belong.

"Okay, that's weird." Thad's voice broke through.

"What?" Luke whirled.

"Well, the first number I can't trace. My guess is it goes to another prepaid, probably his pimp. You know, like I said before. The other goes to a local business. Why would that be on his burner phone? Hang on." Thad tapped on the keyboard.

"Ok. One World, Inc." Thad scrolled down. "They are the largest environmental lobby in the U.S. Main office is in DC, of course, with a few offices overseas. The CEO is from Atlanta and it was founded here back in the '70s. They are mostly wetland preservation, anti-fracking and it looks like they might have had something to do with all those hippies stalking the whaling fleets. I'm reading between the lines here. They don't actually use the word 'hippie' on the website."

Luke stopped to listen as Thad continued.

"They are a celebrity darling, though. Apparently, B-listers fall all over themselves to be this company's spokesperson. I've seen their billboards. It's like PETA for mother earth, without the red paint and boobies. Too bad about the boobies."

"So, a conservative politician is calling a liberal think tank. On a phone no one is supposed to see." Luke resumed pacing.

"Shady," Thad agreed.

"Wait a minute." Luke went to the table and shoved some packages aside. He found a yellow interoffice envelope with sharpie scrawls all over the outside.

Thad watched him. "What's that?"

"Got this yesterday," said Luke. He upended the envelope and a plastic DVD case fell into his hand. Luke opened it and slid the disc into the player under a large flat screen TV mounted to the wall. He threw himself into a chair and clicked the TV on as Thad swiveled to watch.

"Two months ago, our dearly departed senator was involved in what turned out to be the town hall meeting to end them all. It was easy enough to find online, but it could have embarrassed Twomey's camp. I was afraid they would take it down, so I had Digital burn it for me."

Thad looked at the YouTube video title on the screen and did a quick search. "You're right. It's gone. Good job on not knowing how to do that yourself."

Luke ignored him. "I didn't think anything of it until you mentioned an environmental lobby just now. It was a debate in the low country against the man who would become his opponent in the Senate race. The topic was a little touchy. Guess what it was."

Thad shrugged.

"Environmental. Specifically, wetland development."

Luke hit play and the video blinked to life. The camera zoomed in on a man with a glistening bush of silver hair. His tailored pinstripe suit made him appear less well fed than he was. He stood behind a clear podium with a black microphone, his deep drawl booming through the speakers.

"My opponent is implying that I don't care about the environment. That I don't care about our protected wildlife areas. Nothing could be further from the truth. I was the loudest advocate for the bill that classified wetlands, farmland, and historical areas as protected. All while Mr. Onessa was still playing beer pong in college." Senator Twomey mimed swinging a paddle.

Laughter rippled across the gymnasium as the camera panned out. Behind the packed bleachers, a large gold and purple mural announced 'Home of the Hornets'. White fluttered everywhere indicating the temperature of the room. One proper madam ylelded a hand painted fan. Less prepared women made do with scraps of campaign literature. The men pretended they weren't hot as sweat rolled down their faces.

Twomey continued, his second chin quivering. "The environmental health of the great state of Georgia, and the nation as a whole, has always been of utmost importance to me and my record reflects that." He clasped the edges of the podium. "But like everything, there must be a wise balance."

A timer buzzed.

"Thank you, Senator Twomey." A poised Asian woman sat behind a white cloth covered table on the gym floor. It was fitted with two microphones. Her precise makeup and brilliant teeth gave the unmistakable air of a television personality.

"Senator Onessa, your reply," she cooed sweetly.

"Well, Lisa, I would like to go on record as agreeing with Cecil. He was indeed the loudest voice in the state legislature. And still is, I might add."

This time hearty laughter filled the gymnasium. Flashes bounced off the velvet stage curtain behind them as photographers jockeyed for a shot of the handsome young politician.

"But I say," Senator Onessa paused for emphasis, "that voicing an opinion is not the same as standing up for it." He brought up his fist with the index finger looped in the quintessential political gesture; emphatic but not aggressive. "We must protect our natural resources even when it is no longer politically or financially expedient to do so." He looked at the cameras.

"Even if that means erring on the side of caution. There are plenty of places to do business that do not fill up wetlands. I certainly cannot support it when it looks out for special interests." Onessa took a sip of water and stood silent. Whistles and loud applause rippled across the audience. Someone yelled something loud and unintelligible.

"Senator Twomey, your rebuttal," said Lisa Cho.

Twomey cleared his throat. "Prohibiting development around protected areas is not encroachment. This bill only further protects our priceless environment. I'm not even really sure why Henry is against the bill. He has a long history of environmental activism." Senator Twomey's sarcastic tone oozed out of the speakers.

"They weren't playing nice, were they?" Thad leaned forward glued to the screen.

Luke didn't move, his chin tucked down listening but not watching.

The camera attempted to cover both speakers but kept returning to the dark haired Onessa.

"I object to the 'clause'," Onessa bent his fingers into air quotes, "that benefits a small group of greedy people. Apparently, we are to protect our natural resources except when Senator Twomey's developer friends benefit. A gaudy sprawling tourist destination right up next to miles of intercoastal waterways and wetlands? That I cannot get behind."

"We cannot afford to fall back on paranoia and rhetoric when job growth is sluggish at best." Twomey wagged a finger at his opponent.

"This bill was designed to stamp out competition." Even on a 55-inch screen Onessa's six feet two were impressive. His green polo and khakis were a stark contrast to the Senator's pinstripes, even though Twomey had loosened his tie on seeing his opponent's casual garb.

Cheers and boos erupted in the crowd. Someone shouted in the back.

"Gentlemen," chimed the moderator, trying to regain control. The camera gave up trying to keep track of who was speaking and panned out to cover both men.

Twomey's round face went pink. "Commercial development will bring jobs and financial growth to the area. Tax revenue for schools and social programs that have been sorely hurtin' in these hard times." He finished with an emphatic head shake that made his chins jiggle.

A murmur of consent and a few loud "hear, hears" rippled through the crowd and scattered applause broke out. A few booed loudly.

"Yes. Jobs." Henry Onessa answered with a smirk. "A retail resort area will bring an influx of jobs to the area. Minimum wage jobs. I don't know that gambling our precious wildlife for employment that doesn't pay a living wage is a smart risk."

"Gentlem...." Lisa Cho was drowned out as she attempted to regain control, but the crowd was rowdy. Twomey seized his chance while she was distracted telling off some hecklers behind her.

"First, any development will certainly bring minimum wage jobs, but also corporate jobs. And havin' supported a young family on a cook's salary, I'll testify that a minimum wage job is better than no job at all. But I suppose if you went to Harvard, you don't have such worries like where next week's groceries are comin from."

"Gentlemen, please." Lisa raised her manicured hand trying to restore order. Applause and whistles ricocheted off the cinder block walls.

A stunned look appeared on Onessa's face for a moment, then he took a graceful step to the side of his podium and leaned against it. All noise ceased as he commanded the stage. Even Twomey leaned in.

"It is true, the citizens of this hard-hit area have felt the pinch, but so has everyone else in our state. And our nation." He brought his voice up a little. "But we must be slow to deal away what is most precious. If we are to protect our resources, then we protect them from every threat, even if that threat enters the highest bid."

Senator Twomey opened his mouth to speak but loud applause and whistles drowned him out. He closed his mouth and glared at his opponent as a bead of sweat broke loose and rolled down his temple. Half the crowd was on their feet. The other half sat stone faced.

Lisa seized her chance. "Gentlemen, that is time." Her voice cracked over the speaker even though five minutes remained on the clock in front of her. "We will now take questions from the audience," she said before anyone else could speak. Lines had already formed behind three microphones set up in the aisles.

A dark-haired woman in a business suit stepped up to the microphone labeled # 1.

"Microphone one, go ahead, ma'am," Miss Cho said.

"Yes, my question is for Senator Onessa."

Henry Onessa flashed his trademark smile and looked at ease, now holding his mic.

"Is this debate even relevant? You have both stated your intention to run for U.S. Senate. Will you have time to see this matter through to the end? And how will your campaign for the U.S. Senate election this fall affect your efforts on this bill?"

Henry Onessa leaned forward. "What's your name, ma'am?"

"Laura Randall."

"Well, Laura. We are scheduled to vote on this bill in two months. Until I am elected to Congress, I serve Georgia first. I have made it clear to my staff that while the assembly is in session, this, not my campaign, will be top prior...." He trailed off as two men begin shouting profanities at each other.

"This is where it gets fun," Luke said.

The camera swung back and forth trying to find the source. Thad squinted at the screen as it zoomed in on two middle-aged men trying to put each other in a headlock. Two beefy police officers pushed through the stunned crowd.

"He's right, you know," yelled an unknown man.

A chorus of boos answered him. Garbled yelling answered the boos.

The candidates looked at each other, all disagreement forgotten. The older man waved off Onessa's inquisitive look. Scattered applause crackled as some collected their things and tried to beat everyone else to the parking lot. Others held fast in the microphone lines.

A moment later shouting erupted and a woman screamed. A circle formed around two women shoving each other as the camera zoomed out. Thad's jaw dropped as the lens caught a middle-aged man aiming a folding chair at a group of teenagers taunting him.

Mothers grabbed babies from strollers and darted to safety as shoving matches broke out around them.

The video blipped to a news reporter huddled beneath an

umbrella against the same drizzle flicking onto the camera lens. "It was an intense town hall meeting that took place today at the Fleetwood High School Auditorium. A huge crowd turned out despite the weather to question their representatives about the bill that is up for a vote soon before the state legislature.

"Senator Cecil Twomey's brainchild, this bill would ban development within a several mile radius of protected land areas. The veteran Georgia state senator claims his bill will protect the environment. Popular Freshman Senator Henry Onessa opposes it on the grounds that the language allows for several key commercial developments within the protected areas, and that this language could benefit a select few developers and discourage competition.

"Both Senators are gearing up to run in the special election for the U. S. Senate seat to be vacated by Senator Roth following his cancer diagnosis. One of the key battleground areas is this southern Lowcountry region, home to hundreds of thousands of acres of protected wetlands.

"Polls show them neck and neck, so it will be interesting to see how this plays out. Tiffany."

"Alright, Susan. Thanks for the report and stay dry." She laughed at her own joke, and the soaked woman on the video monitor nodded and grinned.

The blond newscaster turned to her slightly orange co-anchor. "When is this rain going to stop, Paul?"

He flashed a neon smile at the wrong camera. "Soon, I hope. George, how about that forecast?"

The TV clicked off and Luke dropped the remote on the table.

Thad whistled. "Why didn't I hear about that? That's insaneballs." He opened his laptop and started typing furiously.

Luke eyed a group of suited men making their way down

the hall past the conference room. When they slowed to peer through the window at the pile on the conference table, Luke recognized most of them immediately. He swiveled so he could watch them.

As the most influential people in Atlanta filtered down the hallway, Luke sat slung back in his chair locking eyes with every man that walked by. Most looked away within seconds. The only man that didn't was the tall imposing city attorney. He held Luke's gaze so long that Luke wanted to pound him into his penny loafers.

"They're going to Simon to try to keep a lid on this. Sharks are circling. They can smell the blood in the water," said Thad, glancing from Luke's relaxed form to the window.

"He'll tell them to pound sand down a rat hole."

"I guess we'll see if Simon owes them any favors."

"Won't just be Simon. They'll call in every favor and get as many judges and lawmakers on their side as possible. Search warrants are going to be hard to come by in this town."

"You'd think they would want us to find out what happened in that apartment."

"Twomey's problems are over. They're in damage control mode now. All they care about is saving their skin and probably that bill."

"Which is gonna cost someone a ton of money," said Thad.

Luke pointed a finger at his partner. "Bingo."

"So, they'd squash an investigation about their friend's death because it might lose them money?"

"Welcome to politics." Luke held his index finger and thumb like a gun and pointed it at the door. He closed one eye like he was aiming. The Mayor's face appeared next in the large square of glass. He scooted away looking scandalized.

After they passed, Luke turned and sat forward. "That explains why he might call an environmental lobby. But why hide it? The bill's been getting some attention since his death hit the papers. From what I can tell, it prohibits development of any kind within, I don't know, a few miles from any designated protected wetlands lands or historical areas."

"Ten miles," Thad read off his screen. "Ten miles of some very desirable real estate."

"Of course, there are a few exceptions written into the bill."

Thad snorted. "No doubt benefitting the poor and needy."

"Very good, Grasshopper. A monster from what I read."

"Wilson Corporation," interjected Thad. He read his screen for a moment then whistled. "Their market share in Georgia alone is close to thirty percent of the commercial real estate market, but they're nationwide. The founder is one of Twomey's closest friends and forty-seventh on Forbes' wealthiest people in America list."

"The initial numbers for one of their proposed developments are a billion. Billion and a half maybe. Good thing you didn't take that bet," said Luke

"Come on," said Thad. "The day this shit doesn't happen you can strap on your ice skates and go to hell. This is standard political backscratching. The evidence, Luke. We don't have any evidence that supports foul play."

Thad shut his laptop and looked at Luke. "That said, either way, we need to be careful. A dead politician is shark infested territory, and you're swimming outside the rope by even thinking murder."

"He's calling prostitutes and environmental lobbies on his burner phone. I know why he's calling prostitutes...."

"Dinner and intelligent conversation?" Thad grinned to himself.

"Let's go pay the grieving campaign manager a visit." Luke stood and reached for his jacket.

Thad sighed, "Prostitutes or lobbies. Both are going to chum up the waters."

Luke pulled on his jacket and looked at Thad.

Thad sighed and clicked his laptop shut. "It's shark week." He rose and grabbed his own suit coat.

Luke's phone buzzed and he popped it off the belt clip. "Agent Marshal. Perfect. We'll be right there."

"Change of plan. The ME is ready for us." Luke tightened his tie.

"We should take her some flowers."

"You should let me do the talking."

"Don't bet on it," grinned Thad.

6

Office of the Chief Medical Examiner
Atlanta, Georgia
May 30th
1245 Hours

Doctor Berne raised a stern brow over her glasses as she watched Thad slouch in his chair. Her hair was pulled into a tight bun, its youthful blond tone contradicting the deep wrinkles on her face. Agitated pacing pulled her attention away from Thad.

"What do you mean the results are inconclusive?" Luke couldn't believe what he heard.

"I didn't say they were inconclusive. I said they were unusual."

"What's the difference?" Thad instantly regretted speaking.

Down went the nose and a harsh gaze shot over the half-moon readers. "Unusual means out of the ordinary. Inconclusive means," she leaned forward, "I don't know."

One corner of Thad's mouth turned up in a half smile.

Then he realized he didn't know if she was joking and cleared his throat.

Luke stopped pacing and exhaled. Sandra had never let him down. Sandra Berne was the best medical pathologist in the industry. She knew more about the human animal than most people do about their breakfast cereal. What she didn't know, she always found out. She liked saying that the distance to the truth was shorter from a dead man's lips.

"What did you find?" Luke sounded defeated.

"Well, the COD was definitely asphyxiation. The good Senator hung to death, there's no doubt about that. Nothing on the body was inconsistent with what you found on the scene."

"Then why aren't you ruling it a suicide?"

"I'm ruling it a suspicious death and not a suicide," she leaned back into her chair and touched her fingertips together, "because it was strange...."

"What was strange?" Luke cut her off.

Now she eyed Luke over her glasses. She waited a moment before she answered to make him pay for interrupting. Chastised, Luke cut short the tirade he felt coming on. If he pushed her too hard, she'd wind him up even more. Age hadn't softened her at all.

"What was strange was the large amount of narcotics in his bloodstream."

"Drugs are common in suicides, and there were needles at the scene." The words were out of Thad's mouth before he could stop them. He sunk deeper into his chair.

The doctor's eyes twinkled, and her nose twitched, but her face remained stern. "That is true, Agent Aulden, narcotics and alcohol both are very common in suicides. However, the long-standing rule is that alcohol is generally present without drugs, not the opposite. Especially when the vic is not normally a user."

Thad shifted in his seat.

Luke stopped pacing unaware he had started back up. "There was no alcohol in his tox?"

"None." Sandra pulled off her glasses and let them hang by the silver chain around her neck. "That's rare."

"How rare?" demanded Luke.

"Well, let me put it this way. I've been Medical Examiner for thirty-two years, and I have only ever seen that quantity of narcotics consumed without alcohol a handful of times. All were accidental overdoses in junkies with extreme addictions. Every other time large doses of drugs were present in the toxicology, so was alcohol. Every time. You simply don't see these results with any regularity."

"How much was in his system?" Luke turned to her.

"Enough to disorient him."

"Unconscious?"

"Possibly." Her eyes dropped to Thad who tried to make himself as small as possible. She spoke like a teacher addressing a class. "Alcohol lowers inhibition enough to make drugs seem like a good idea if they're presented. Drugs usually follow alcohol. The cart to a horse." She looked back up at Luke who stood rooted. "Like I said, nothing groundbreaking. Just a little strange."

"Strange enough to avoid calling it suicide," Luke said.

"There's nothing that speaks to homicide if that's what you're asking. I'm not one to dismiss things, but anomalies do happen. It seemed pretty cut and dry except for the blood work."

"Cut and dry," Luke muttered. He hated that phrase.

"What's bothering you, Luke?" Dr. Berne sounded motherly.

He raked his fingers through his hair and scowled.

"I don't have answers if you don't have questions," said Sandra.

"How was it taken?"

"Intravenously. I found a small prick mark in the crook of his right arm. Plain old crack. A little low brow for a Senator if you ask me, but maybe it's all his prostitute had. Have you found her yet?"

"The girls in the pictures have alibis," mumbled Thad when Luke didn't answer.

"What about the scrape on his head?" Luke asked.

"A small contusion. Can't tell you much more than that. It was clean. He probably hit his head on the wall. Or getting into his car. Or walking into a cabinet door." She shrugged. "I'm sorry."

She sounded genuinely sorry. Luke felt bad. Their friendship went back to the academy where she taught several classes, and he'd received his share of glares for speaking out of turn. He eased himself into the chair beside Thad and leaned toward her.

"You've failed me, Sandra." He smiled at her.

"Pssh." She waved her hand and smiled back. "Listen, I couldn't in good conscience list this as a suicide because of the strange tox results, but that's as deep as it goes. I know you hate wishy-washy answers, and I hope this doesn't spin you too much. Wish I had better for you. I really do."

She leaned back in her chair and put the well-chewed earpiece of her glasses into her mouth while she studied him. "You need to be careful, Luke. He," she gestured through a picture window at the large room with surgical metal tables and bright fluorescent lighting, "was a well-connected man. I don't know that even you have navigated this kind of jungle before."

Luke stood. Thad jumped up beside him relieved to get going. Sandra stuck out her hand to Thaddeus first who shook it firmly but didn't make eye contact. She winked at Luke.

"Oh, I almost forgot. 'doha' and 'chaud' were written on his hand. My UVIR camera was able to pick up most of it, but the last word is a partial. Ink is surprisingly hard to destroy, but this ink was too degraded to make out the entire word."

She took a folder from her desktop and handed it to Luke. "Here are the photos. Mean anything?"

"Nope." Luke grinned. "You're the best."

<hr>

A banner proclaiming, "Vote for Twomey, Vote for Values" lay on the floor of the campaign office. Two solemn employees wheeled a cart loaded with boxes over it. The upscale storefront office was mostly empty. Only a few soon-to-be unemployed staffers remained to pack up their desks.

The campaign manager closed the office door behind Luke and Thad for privacy. He seated himself gingerly behind a cluttered metal desk.

Bartholomew Duncan looked much older than his fifty-two years. Not that long ago his white-flecked hair had been brown. Purple bags hung under his eyes, and months of take-out protruded from his belt line.

On the wall hung several pictures of him and the dead Senator in hunting plaid during better times. Three more showed him smiling next to consecutive former presidents.

Duncan interlocked his fingers on the desk and leaned forward. "No, we never had a dialogue with One World. I'm sure we sent them some sort of correspondence as a matter of policy, or we might have called but that's it. Just so we could say we tried. We wanted the bill to be a bi-partisan victory, but they were pretty dead set against it," he said.

"So, you didn't do any business with One World." Luke

had sprawled in a guest chair immediately upon entering. He had one leg thrown up on the desk making Duncan visibly uncomfortable.

Duncan scowled. "They didn't want anything to do with us. We stand for conservative values. They're extremely liberal."

"Barty, why was the Senator at that apartment?" Luke abruptly shifted topics. At the same time, he snapped upright in his chair. The sharp movement made the older man jump.

The campaign manager scowled at being called 'Barty'. "I guess I didn't know him as well as I thought." He spoke so softly that Luke leaned in to hear.

"Really? That's Interesting." Luke stood and walked to the windows that lined the inner walls of the small office. He watched the movers loading furniture and electronics into the panel truck out front. "You mean to tell me that you've known Cecil Twomey for twenty years, managed four election campaigns, and you still had no idea he liked 'em young?"

Barty fell silent. Then he closed his eyes and sighed. "I always had my...I suspected something. Sometimes wisdom lies in ignorance."

"Wisdom? I think the word 'convenience' plugs into that sentence better, Barty boy." Luke moved to the edge of Duncan's desk and bent down well inside the man's personal space.

Barty flinched on cue. Luke stayed far enough away to keep the sweat off him, but too close for Barty's comfort. The best way to unnerve someone was invading their personal space. Luke liked his targets off balance. Nervous people made mistakes.

"Who took those pictures, Barty? How did they get to your boss?"

Barty slid down in his seat. He ran his hand over the bald spot on the back of his head, panting. "I don't...don't know."

"I know you have some thoughts on the matter, Barty. Nobody knew him like you. Nobody. Who was trying to bring him down?"

"Cecil is dead, okay. We lost a dedicated public servant. He killed himself for Christ's sake. Why can't you people leave him alone?"

"Because it's my job."

Every time Barty pushed back in his seat to get away, Luke leaned in closer.

"What else do you need to know? It's done. It doesn't matter now." Barty was almost hysterical.

"All that matters right now is what I don't know. For example, I don't know if you're going to cooperate, or if you're going to jail for impeding a federal investigation."

Any color left in Duncan's blotchy face drained.

"Now tell me again how you had no idea." Luke's smile was cold as he stood up straight and moved away.

Barty sucked in air like Luke released him from a chokehold. "I didn't know." The words were barely perceptible.

"Didn't catch that." Luke started leaning in again.

Barty leaped up and crossed to the room, anxious to put space between them. "I swear to you."

"You knew about the girls."

"Yes. I suspected, but I never asked. There are some questions you don't ask."

"Huh, you'd think a campaign manager would want to know something like that," Luke said to Thad.

"Unless he was doing it too," Thad answered.

Barty's eyes darted between them. "Everybody does it," he blurted out angrily. "Clinton, Weiner, Spitzer. They're just the ones that got caught. Do you have any idea what goes on behind the political curtain?

"It's not the secret you muckety-mucks seem to think it is," Luke said.

Barty mustered a little courage. "Look, these guys make this country tick. So what if they indulge in little pleasure? It's not my job to be their mommy."

"No, it's your job to lie for them," said Thad making sure Barty heard him.

Barty turned to Thad with a sneer. "Whatever. Everybody lies. I don't expect you to understand the complexities of governing."

"You know what I don't understand?" Luke advanced on Barty again. "Your behavior since your boy died."

"What?" The sweaty man's eyes rounded.

"People always drone on and on about how they never thought their friend would commit suicide. That they would *never* do that. I'm not hearing it out of you." Luke closed in, causing Barty to scurry back to the relative safety of his desk.

"What do you mean?"

Luke eyed Barty as he collapsed back into his chair and feigned boredom.

"I have no idea what you're talking about," Barty said like he was bored. "This sounds like desperation to me."

"Is that what you think?" Luke leaned in putting one hand on the desk and the other on the back of the man's chair.

Barty pressed his lips together. "My friend and colleague is dead, Agent Marshall. He killed himself. I don't know what you're hoping to accomplish here, but you should have more respect."

Luke straightened and studied him with hooded eyes.

"I wish I could help you more. I really do." Barty's voice

trembled as he tried to sound dismissive. "But I've got a lot of work to do."

Luke reached into his pocket and flicked a business card onto the desk. "I bet you do. We'll be in touch."

An oppressive blast hit the men as soon as they left the cool office. Luke yanked his tie off and scowled at the cloudless sky. God, he hated the heat.

"What do you think, Boss?" Thad threw his jacket in the back seat of the car and slammed the door.

"I think he's a liar."

"Why didn't you ask about the phone?"

"Never play all your cards at once, kid. Let's go back to the office and dig up every bit of dirt you can on Duncan, Twomey, and this One World outfit. I need a connection."

7

———

The Laughing Irishman Pub
Savannah, Georgia
June 3rd
1740 Hours

Tully walked by the dusty 'seat yourself' sign and past a long bar crowded with locals. She didn't slow. Not to let her eyes adjust to the dim or to answer the calls of congratulations and 'atta girl' coming from people she hardly recognized. She spent way too much time here.

European soccer flags, a chandelier strung with thigh-high stockings, and a taxidermy alligator hung from the hewn beam ceiling. Opposite the bar, police memorabilia covered the old brick wall. Photos of smiling police officers and friends rained down smiles and victory signs on patrons. Cigarette smoke curled past no smoking signs.

In the back, a group sat around several tables pushed together by the galley doors. They were all squinting up at an old man wearing a crisp white apron over a rumpled blue and pink Hawaiian shirt. His hair was white and his waistline thick, but his Irish accent had lost none of its vigor.

"...Sou then, three flies buzz right over and land one, two, three in each of the pints," he said. "Right, so the Englishman looks disgusted and pushes his pint away demandin' another. The Scot picks out the fly, shrugs, and takes a long swalla. The Irishman, now he reaches in the glass, grabs the fly and shakes him as hard as he can yellin, 'Spit it out, ya bloody bastard! Spit it out!'."

The group howled with laughter as the barkeep turned to watch Tully. A grin split his broad face. "Tully, love. How ware ya?" He grabbed her in a tight hug.

She wrapped her arms around his thick shoulders and squeezed. "Hi, Only. I'm fine. You?"

"I could be no better, now yare here."

"New material?"

"Gotta keep things fresh round here, love. Yare usual?"

"Double it up for me."

"Tough day, eh? You got it, love." Only hurried back to the bar. As he squeezed behind the polished walnut bar top, the rowdy group started pounding the table. Tully flipped them off with a smile and hung up her brown leather jacket. She wore a white V-neck tee, torn skinny jeans, and scuffed cowboy boots, her father's battered S&W .386 Nightguard nestled securely in the small of her back.

Squeezing Pete's shoulder, she slid into the empty seat. "Ya'll got here fast," she said turning to the huge man sitting next to her and bumping him with her elbow. "Hey, Jules."

"Hey, Tull." He bumped her back. "We didn't have a photo-op with every A lister in the city."

"That was the most tedious thing I have ever done," she answered.

"So, is it hard to walk with all those medals on your

uniform?" A brown-haired man on the other side leaned forward to address Tully.

"Shut up, Bret. You can't walk two feet without walking into something. Without any medals," the pretty brunette beside him snapped.

Tully grinned down the table. Bret and Jessica started a shoving match as Only deposited a tall glass of honey colored elixir in front of her.

"Not when her balls are bigger than yares," Only interrupted.

"Ouch. Ow, stop it." Brett stopped fighting. Jessica looked disappointed.

"Thanks, Only," said Tully. She drained half the glass in a single gulp then winced when the burn hit. Only winked at her and walked away.

"Why do you call him Only?" A young man on the other side of Jules asked no one in particular.

The huge Samoan man immediately slapped him across the back of the head. "Because he's the only Irishman in the city that hasn't kicked us out of their pub, Jimmy," said Julius. "If you're gonna hang with us, you better learn the important stuff, Rookie."

"Maybe somebody else should be his training officer then," Jessica shot at Jules. She winked at Tully and shook her dark curls. "What is that saying about the blind leading the blind?"

"That's rich coming from you, Jess," said Bret. "Your little protégé won't answer up for a report call even if it's next door. He parks his man-scaped ass behind the nearest shopping plaza and Netflixes all night. Maybe the next time you and your boy toy are making out, you could tell him to start pulling his weight."

Jessica grinned. "If I can pull my tongue out of his mouth long enough, maybe I will."

Bret choked on his drink.

"So, the mayor was really kissing your ass." Jules lifted his beer as he looked at Tully.

"Well, he had to tell me how much of a hero we are, and how he supports the police so much he amazes himself." Tully took another drink and relaxed a little more.

Jules snorted. "And by 'support' he means cut our pay and benefits."

"Just gearing up for the fall campaign."

"Obviously," said Jimmy.

"Shut up, Rookie," snapped Jules threatening to slap the back of his head again. "You've been a cop for like two minutes."

"Better than two centuries, old man." Jimmy dodged Jules' slow swing and laughed. "Bring it, old man. I haven't been in a good fight since last night."

Jules went back to his beer. "Whatever. That girl kicked your ass."

Tully laughed, grateful the day was over. The tightness in her back released as warmth from the whiskey spread through her muscles. The crushing media attention hadn't let up in the week since she caught the Stone Mill rapist and she was tired.

She drained her glass and caught Pete's eye. He'd said nothing since she arrived. She kicked him under the table. "How's the baby?" Awkward, but she had to say something. They'd said so little to each other over the last week.

"Still teething. I can't stay long," he said looking down at his watch. He rubbed his face. "If Melissa doesn't get some sleep soon, she's gonna divorce me. Or kill me in my sleep. Not sure which."

Tully saw the dark circles under his eyes. Pete never stayed long. He was always in a rush to get home to his family. She smiled. "Don't pretend like you mind."

Pete's eyes appeared above his hands, and he finally smiled. Tully felt a relief even the whiskey couldn't give.

"It's not like he had anything to do with catching them," Jimmy said deep in conversation with the other three.

"That's not going keep him from taking the credit come fall," said Bret.

"Anybody running for office is going to be all over this. It's the perfect platform. He'll claim he acted decisively to protect his constituents." Jessica shrugged. "I would."

"You need to knock it off with the big words. Constituents." Bret lit a cigarette and stuck it in her direction.

She knocked it away. "Crack a book, Bret."

"Didn't he know the family of one of those guys?" Jimmy asked.

"Nobody cares," said Jules. "A fart in the wind,"

"Bet voters won't forget so easily," Jimmy answered.

"Sure they will," Tully said as she tried to get the last drop out of her glass and set it down. It was immediately replaced with a full one by a beaming Only. "When it comes up, he'll distance himself from his friends. And they'll let him do it."

"Yeah, but everybody knows," Jimmy came back.

"It's not the Mayor's fault," said Jessica. "How could he have known his golf buddy's son was a violent rapist? As much as I hate the guy," she answered her own question, "that's not possible."

"That's pretty bleak. This job makes you that cynical?"

"Shut it, Rookie." Julius stuck a straw in his mouth like a piece of hay.

Tully leaned in so she could see the young man with sleek combed hair. "Cynicism is what everybody calls it kid, but when you're a cop it's observation. You don't ever really know someone. Cops are the only ones who'll admit it." She smiled at Pete. He hesitated, then gave her an uncomfortable smile.

"It's kinda hard not to when you have such a clear view of the carnage," Bret said, yanking Tully back to the conversation.

"Jules." Tully turned to her hulking friend. "How many times do you go to someone's house and they just know all these things about their family member? Their kid would *never* do that. Their spouse would *never* cheat on them."

"Once a week, minimum."

Jimmy pursed his lips but didn't say anything.

Jessica piped up. "One time I had a crazy chick swear to me her husband had been abducted, robbed, killed or whatever. He'd been gone for three days and she knew he was dead in a ditch somewhere. She 'just knew'," Jessica curled her fingers into air quotes, "that he would never leave her. She was offended when I hinted at it."

Tully tucked her left leg underneath and pushed down on her knee to stretch her hip. Pete watched and scowled but continued his silence as Jess spoke.

"He called us three days later from Vegas when it got back to him that his wife reported him missing. Turns out he was there with his twenty-two-year-old girlfriend who he'd been banging since she was eighteen."

"So? He's a good liar," said Jimmy.

"They were married for thirty years. If anybody could figure out when he was lying, you'd think it would be the person that knew him best, right?" Jessica said.

"Wrong," chimed in Brett.

"All that proves is people are idiots." Jimmy twirled his glass looking at the water ring on the tabletop.

"She was a Ph.D.," said Jess, "in physics. She taught at Tech for fifteen years."

"Oh," Jimmy said. His expression fell. When he couldn't think of a response, he chugged his beer.

"The point is, if someone is trying to hide something, you ain't gonna figure it out. Period," finished Jess.

"Are you going to let anybody else get a word in edgewise?" Bret swung the stump of his cigarette back towards her. She slapped it away again.

"Even the people closest to you can make you believe any lie they want. I take back what I said before. That's bleak." Jimmy sounded deflated.

"Why do you think I've been married four times?" Jules elbowed Jimmy.

"It's not really a lie is it?" Tully twirled the ice in her glass. Everyone looked at her except Pete who studied his beer.

"Sorry?" Jimmy leaned forward.

"They're not lies. At least not all of them. Just because someone hides something about themselves, it doesn't mean the rest of their life is untrue."

"Now there's a concept." Brett looked amused.

Tully ignored him. "Look, kid, you learn quick that only half of what you see is the truth. Everybody, and I mean everybody, has secrets. Things we don't want anyone to know about, but that doesn't make everything else a lie. It's usually something harmless, like Bret's third nipple."

Bret grabbed his chest and feigned horror. "I told you that in confidence."

"But it doesn't make you less of a stud, Bret." Jess rolled her eyes.

Tully continued, "Then again sometimes it's more serious. You remember the triple homicide last year?"

Everybody nodded except Jimmy, who shook his head.

"The two little kids and their mom shot in the house?"

Jimmy gave a nod of recognition. He'd heard about it. Everyone had.

"I got there first. I saw the twin eight year olds shot in the head, and mommy's throat sliced open. Dad was missing. We frantically tried to find him because we thought he was probably a victim too. Everybody we talked to swore up and down and fucking sideways they had the perfect marriage. Both the wife's and husband's families were ready to stake their lives on it. Right up until Daddy dearest shot himself in a cheap motel room in Charlotte."

Jimmy didn't take his eyes off her.

"I think he did love his wife and kids," Tully said. "I don't know how you convince so many people if it isn't true. But his demons were real, too. Unfortunately for his wife and kids, he was good at hiding them. Most of the time the two realities can coexist. Occasionally they can't."

"Like split personalities," said Jimmy"

"Not really."

"How is it 'not really'?"

"Look at the way we're raised. It's ingrained in our culture. We learn it at the same time we get potty trained."

Jimmy frowned.

"As children we're taught to project good and hide bad. Our parents and society both teach us that only certain things are acceptable, and everything else is to be locked away in secrecy. When you were growing up how many times did your mom tell you not to pick your nose or fart in public?"

"You're not supposed to fart in public? Owww." Brett said as Jessica pinched him hard on the thigh.

"Ok, let's assume you're right," Jimmy began.

"I am."

Jimmy adjusted in his seat to see Tully better. "How do you get to the point where you hide something like that? I mean, how does that work? Is that why people do horrible things? Because they hold it in?"

"It's not why they do bad things, kid. Only why it still surprises us."

"So, the entire population of earth is capable of murder?" Jimmy looked dubious.

"That's not what I'm saying. Abstaining from culturally agreed upon taboos is not deceit. It's manners. It makes society run smoothly. But everyone burps and farts even if we pretend we don't. Every now and then the secret is not so harmless, but people still don't talk about it."

Brett, Jessica, and Julius nodded in agreement. "Except for Brett's dick jokes, we don't talk about it," said Jessica.

Everybody sniggered except for Jimmy. Even Pete managed a smile.

"Picking your nose and farting aren't murder." Jimmy sounded desperate now.

"Murder is a cultural taboo, so yes, they are the same. But that's not the point. The point is that everybody's secrets are different. Secrets aren't always illegal or unethical, we even joke about most of them. I'm saying we're taught to carve ourselves up into different people. We all have a public and a private face. Neither is a lie just because one is hidden.

"Shoot, Thomas Edison deep fried the first man put in the electric chair. It was no honest mistake. Not even close. Edison tortured a man to death to discredit the competition. Awful, but it doesn't negate his contribution to history."

"So you're saying the lie is not telling?"

"I'm saying there is no lie. Everything is the truth, even if we don't know about it."

Jimmy fell silent for a moment and stared at his drink. He opened his mouth then closed it again. Finally, he found his voice. "That's what you figured out after years on the job?"

"Don't worry, kid. Tully makes everything sound depressing." Julius grinned at her. "It's not so bad. You just see a different side when you carry a badge. That's all."

"Is it hard to sleep?" Jimmy rubbed his hands over his face and sat back.

"No," said Brett.

"You better start developing some world class denial skills," added Jess. "In this line of work, you have to look at corpses, then go home and sleep like one. For everyone else it's personal. For us, it's business."

"She's right." Jules ran his finger around the rim of his drink. "They'll call you cold and callous, but it's the only way this job doesn't dismantle you. You've got a front row seat to the worst society can dish up, Rookie. You either let it go or eat your gun."

"If you can't?"

"Find another job." Tully took a sip.

"Preferably one where your co-workers don't call you a liar." Jules winked at her.

"You losers? You don't hold anything back. If somethin's bothering you, you don't pass up a chance to bitch about it."

"Hear, hear," shouted Bret and Jessica together. They raised their glasses and clinked them together.

"I'll drink to bitching." Brent slurred his words. Then he pointed his glass in Tully's direction. "And heroes."

"Then it's to you guys."

The table rattled as glasses bounce off and everybody except Jimmy gulped their drink. Jimmy sat quietly.

"It's alright, kid." Tully put her glass down. "You're gonna love being a cop. Best job in the world."

Jimmy gave her a weak smile.

Three hours later, the group walked out of the pub. This

end of River Street stayed quieter than the tourist packed side. At this hour it was deserted. Two cars and a motorcycle were parked on the street. A few yards past Only's pub, a steep staircase rose to Bay Street cutting through the stone wall.

"Night." Bret and Jessica called and walked off. They were holding on to each other, trying to keep from falling as they climbed the stairs.

Jimmy shook Tully's hand, but Julius grabbed her in a bear hug, then clapped Pete on the shoulder. Their voices faded as they disappeared down the street.

Pete and Tully walked in silence toward his motorcycle. Pete looked at her from the corner of his eye. "You alright, Tull?"

"I'm awesome." She pulled her leather jacket from under her arm and shrugged it on. When it touched her shoulder, she winced.

Pete picked up his helmet and twisted it in his hands. "You were pretty salty in there tonight. Quite the performance."

"Why, thank you," Tully slurred, and did a drunken jig.

"Even for a delicate treasure like you, it was a lot."

"Somebody had to hold up your end of the conversation," she grinned and hiccuped. He didn't return it. "Is that why you stayed so long? To watch the show?" Tully laughed. "Relax, I was just trying to scare the new kid."

"Maybe he should be afraid."

She squinted at her partner and oldest friend. "Huh?"

Pete swung his leg over the bike and stared at the gas tank for a moment. "I wonder sometimes, what this job does to us. What it turns us into. Jimmy wasn't that far off base." Pete's face darkened as Only shut off the pub lights. "You know, we're supposed to trust each other...," he trailed off.

Nope. Not now. Not ever.

Pete was nudging a conversation they would never have. She prayed it wasn't the topic she suspected, but it didn't matter. He might be her best friend, but even he couldn't hear what she was thinking. Especially not him.

She hiccuped and tapped out another awkward jig. "I do trust you, Easton. I just don't like you very much." She spun and meant to poke him in the chest but misjudged and rammed her finger into his neck.

He grabbed her hand. "Stop it."

"Stop it." She mocked him in a whiny voice.

"God, you're an asshole when you drink," said Pete.

Her fuzzy mind registered that he was sober. Pete could tie one on as well as the next cop. He always drank when they hung out on the weekends he didn't disappear to hunt. He never got irritated with her then.

"I didn't have that much. I'm just a terrible dancer." Tully straightened. She was pretty good at pretending to be sober. God knows she'd done it enough. Pulling her shoulders back she smiled to diffuse Pete's aggravation. The conversation was getting away from her.

"Yes, you did, and you know it." Pete continued to look annoyed. "Look," he trailed off as he thought about his next words. Then his eyes widened. His eyes flew to hers. "You've been talking to him again, haven't you?"

That topic he had no problem bitching about.

"Pete..."

"That asshole called you, didn't he? God. Or did he come over? You always get weird when he tries to get back with you." Pete gave a bitter bark of a laugh. "He calls and you trip all over yourself to do exactly what he wants. I tell you to stop chasing an armed suspect so you don't get shot, and you tell me to piss off."

"Pete, stop."

"No, Meara. I'm not gonna stop. When are you gonna

end this shit? How long are you going to let him do this to you?"

"I...."

"Tully, if he cared about you, you wouldn't need a Prozac and a fifth of whiskey every time he wants some. That's not how it works."

"It's not that simple," she replied softly to his tirade.

"What if I curb stomped the motherfucker, would that un-complicate things? It's a good thing you won't let us meet. If I ever do," he trailed off.

"It's not your responsibility."

"But you are." Pete lowered his voice. "You're my best friend, and frankly I'd rather you run into the woods alone after a bad guy. At least then I know you fight back."

Tully studied the damp cobblestone under her boots and said nothing.

"You think I can't see it, Tully, but I do. You don't have everyone fooled. The people who care about you want to see you happy, not keep you under their thumb. They're the ones that deserve you, not that ass clown."

"You're dumb." She tried to joke, but her voice wavered.

Pete exhaled and looked at the helmet clutched between his hands. "You ever say that to him?"

Tully looked away.

Pete tapped both thumbs on the top of his helmet then lifted it to his head. "You need to hear it, and from someone who cares enough to be honest."

"You worry too much, Pete."

He had no right. Some things were off limits even to him.

Pete tugged the chin strap tight. "Somebody's got to worry about you, Tull." He kicked his bike to life. "Cause you won't," he yelled over the roar. He held out his fist, and she bumped it and he pointed his finger at her as she backed away.

"Give the girls a kiss for me," Tully yelled, grateful the roar covered the tremble in her voice.

The bike lurched into gear. "Wanna ride?"

"Nah, I'm good."

"Okay. Night, Tull."

"Night." Tully watched his taillights shrink into the dark then turned and walked. She didn't want to go home yet.

Soon the bumpy cobblestones of River Street gave way to smooth brick under her feet, and the briny smell of the river. The Lowcountry humidity was the salt of the seasons, making everything more than it was. It amplified cold and sweltered every summer. Night gave no relief from its heavy presence. It even made the river bank smell muddier.

Tully stopped and watched a ship glide silently over the river. A tug hauled the twelve story, eight-hundred-foot-long container ship toward the Port of Savannah. The ship's massive engines were quiet; its presence announced only by ripples lapping the half-buried oysters on the mudflats.

In a few hours, this promenade would bustle with tourists, but for now it was quiet. She leaned against the railing and shoved her hands in her jacket pockets. Her fingers closed around something hard.

Tully pulled out a gold medallion hanging at the end of a blue satin noose. It felt heavy in her hand, and she could still feel the suffocating tug around her neck.

They called her a hero today, but they didn't know anything. They wouldn't call her that if they really knew her. Real heroes are strong.

She had felt like a hero last week, for a few minutes. But if running that jogging trail every day since couldn't bring the feeling back, a medal would do no better. Let it corrode at the bottom of the river where it belonged. Coiling her left arm, she flung it as far as she could over the railing.

Pain tore down her left shoulder, and she clutched at it. The barely healed gash throbbed and every muscle ached. Fatigue crushed down on her. Her apartment was five blocks away. It seemed more like five miles.

She slipped off her jacket so it wouldn't be ruined, hoping anyone on the old streets at this hour was too drunk to notice a blood-soaked arm.

Climbing one of the many staircases leading to Bay Street, she trudged for several blocks until she reached Forsythe Park. Sprawling Live Oaks lined the border of the city's centerpiece park; most of them older than the country.

When she reached Forsythe Park, Tully turned left onto E. Gaston Street. Antebellum row houses flanked the street, their brick staircases curving up to the formal entrances of the decaying grande dames.

At 309 she stopped and pulled out her keys. She shouldered open an iron gate creaking on its hinges and entered a narrow tunnel cutting under the house. The gate was never closed. She wasn't sure the ancient lock worked anymore.

The low vaulted tunnel stretched for sixty feet below 309 before emptying into a small courtyard lined on three sides by apartment doors. The old carriage house had been reclaimed for living space.

Four cheap fixtures hung on the tunnel walls, their gas lantern counterparts long gone. Two of the bulbs worked. Tully ignored the nest of mailboxes and pushed another decrepit gate open into the courtyard.

An algae covered fountain stood silent in the middle and patches of the starless night peeked through the canopy of oaks and moss. At each of the three apartment doors, another cheap fixture glowed. She headed for the red door marked "C" with her keys ready.

She went inside and checked the locks behind her. Then she limped into the great room that housed the living, kitchen, and dining rooms. In private her limp was more pronounced. No need to hide it here. She pried off her boots and kicked them into a corner.

Opening a cabinet above the stove, she pulled out a bottle of Jack Daniels and yanked out the stopper. Another cabinet gave up a highball glass which she filled halfway. She finished it in one gulp and poured another.

Only then did she look down at her sleeve. Blood had soaked all the way to the hem and smeared onto her bicep. But it wasn't enough to drip.

Taking her glass, she went to the bedroom. Her jacket and revolver went on the bed, and she walked into the bathroom and put her glass on the vanity top.

She took her shirt off and threw it into the trash, then her eyes flicked to the mirror. She hated the image that slid in and out of focus.

The scar had faded over the last twenty years. Now it was barely pinker than the surrounding skin. Her cheek was smooth, but the thin reminder puckered every time she smiled. So, she tried not to.

Even her mother hadn't been able to look at her without glancing at it. Every time Alice Meara saw her daughter's face, she lapsed back into her protective depression.

Mrs. Delany had called it a thorn in the flesh, like the Apostle Paul had. She never pointed to Tully making herself small in the back of Sunday School. Never said her name. But everyone knew who Mrs. D was talking about. Like so many well-intentioned idiots, she'd tried hard to make a marked up middle schooler feel noble instead of freakish. All she accomplished was making everyone look again.

It took two decades of denial, but Tully finally realized that fat bitch had been right. Her scar was her cross to carry.

Her brutal luck on display. She would never be rid of it or allowed to forget. Every time a stranger's gaze flicked to her cheek, she looked in that mirror. Every time a child pointed, she looked in that mirror. They wondered. She remembered.

Clutching the sink to steady herself, she turned on the water and splashed her arm. Watery blood spattered the countertop. She opened the medicine chest and slapped a new bandage on her shoulder not caring that it didn't fully cover the wound. It was the second time this week she'd popped a stitch. Doc had to keep sewing her up. But she wasn't going back tonight, not in this condition. She would have to deal with it.

She tapped two white pills into her palm and looked at them. Even in an alcoholic haze, she struggled to justify them. They were for pain, she told herself, and her shoulder hurt. And she needed sleep tonight.

Tully downed them with the rest of her whiskey. Staggering to the couch she lay down and readied herself for a dreamless night. If she was lucky.

8

Blaine Tower Complex - Building A
Atlanta, Georgia
June 5th
1425 Hours

Shafts of early afternoon sun cast crisp lines between the Atlanta skyscrapers. The tall buildings shaded all but long slivers of yellow. A glimmering modern structure rose in graceful bends as though made from fabric, not steel and glass.

Luke stood at the edge of a wide limestone plaza stretching around the base of the tall building. He stopped to gaze up at the newest expression of wealth and influence in Atlanta, then strode to the massive glass door and pushed it open.

A few minutes later, he was ushered into a small room behind the receptionist's desk, separate from the main waiting area of One World, Inc. The private vestibule of the regional vice president.

Rich cherry paneling covered three walls, and floor-to-ceiling glass made up the fourth wall. From the 25th floor,

Luke had a panoramic view of the city. He watched the cars race like ants along I-75 as the chemical smell of new carpet and paint assaulted his nose.

He'd come alone. Thaddeus had argued bitterly about being left behind. The kid was a good partner, and Luke knew Thad hated the thought of not having his back. But Luke needed to keep him away from this hornet's nest.

The end result of this meeting wasn't clear, and Luke didn't want to paint a target on his young partner's back. Thad's career was just beginning. Not the time to make enemies with powerful men. That was Luke's specialty.

The heavy paneled door behind Luke opened.

"Special Agent Marshall." The voice sounded more accommodating than he expected.

Luke turned. A middle-aged man with mousy brown hair and the slender physique of a runner advanced with his hand extended. "John Cade," he introduced himself.

Luke shook the man's hand twisting his own slightly to the top. Cade did not resist. "Mr. Cade, I appreciate you taking the time to see me."

"Not at all. Anything for the FBI," Cade preened.

Luke didn't buy the eagerness. He followed Cade into a large office with the same floor-to-ceiling windows and dark cherry paneling as the vestibule. A sleek desk of steel and wood and a judge's chair sat in front of the window bank. Opposite the windows, custom built-ins housed various ancient-looking artifacts.

John Cade sat down and gestured for Luke to take one of the tufted leather chairs opposite him. "How can I help you, Agent Marshall?"

"Do you know why I'm here?" Luke took a seat.

"I'm sorry, but I don't."

"I'm investigating the death of Cecil Twomey."

"Investigate? I thought it was a suicide," Cade said. His

eyes widened in disbelief. They were neither green nor hazel, but a swirl of both. Like his genes couldn't agree on a color.

"We still have to investigate." Luke gave him a wry smile.

"And a candidate for U. S. Senate, no less. Another one done in by lust and greed. Sad."

"Mr. Cade, did your establishment have any contact with Senator Twomey?"

John didn't answer right away, but his collar was suddenly tight.

Luke stood up but resisted the urge to get in Cade's face. Despite the compliant start, Luke doubted he would take a browbeating as readily as 'ol Barty. This guy clearly had a lot to lose. Instead, Luke unbuttoned his jacket and crossed to Cade's impressive collection.

The pieces were Asian and Middle Eastern in origin as best Luke could determine. They had to be very old, and very expensive, to merit such a display. The custom cabinets alone probably cost more than he made in a year. Luke paused at a museum quality display with dedicated filtered lighting. Crushed terra cotta had been re-assembled into the silhouette of a jar on a background of plush velvet. The label read 'Kartid Dynasty – c.1300'. He clasped his hands behind him and waited.

"Yes," admitted Cade after a long silence. "If it even rises to that definition."

Luke continued along the collection of pottery, spear tips, and a once lethal bow all housed in luxurious velvet and leather displays. That was easy. The veep wasn't exactly hoarding information, but Luke kept his tone casual. "Did he come here?"

"Yes. We had one meeting with the Senator. I did. It lasted about five minutes. But it wasn't supposed to be public knowledge."

"I don't think it is."

"Good."

"What did you talk about?" Luke turned and walked to the window. He positioned himself so he appeared to study the skyline while keeping Cade in sight.

"That silly bill of course," Cade said. "He came to us looking for support for his ludicrous proposal. He said his goal was bi-partisan support and felt this bill was worthy of it."

"You disagreed."

"What he wanted was an endorsement. The bill was the talking point, but his goal was having a prayer at the under thirty-five vote in November."

Luke didn't interrupt. He didn't need to. The vice president kept volunteering information.

"He was crazy if he thought we would ever endorse him. Or anything he thought was a good idea, for that matter."

"Why?"

This time Cade didn't hesitate. "We don't need him. We've got something better."

"Something better?" Luke turned to look at him.

"Do you follow politics, Agent Marshall?"

"Not if I can help it," said Luke easing himself back into the soft leather chair.

"Well, I'm sure you've heard the name Henry Onessa."

Luke nodded.

"He's it." Cade's voice had a note of finality. "He is the future. Sharp, talented, charismatic. He's the total package, and he happens to be a great friend of this organization. And its core beliefs."

"He worked here didn't he?"

Cade's friendly demeanor faltered as he realized Luke knew more than he'd let on. His expression became guarded, but he kept talking. "He started in our legal department fresh out of law school. Worked his way up to the head of the legal department faster than anyone thought possible.

"Whatever it is, he's got it in spades. We're proud to say he got his start here. He's a tireless champion for all the right things and lives the values Twomey blathered on about but didn't actually possess. Naturally, we back Henry."

"Naturally. When did Twomey come by?"

"About two months ago. Before he introduced the bill." John Cade drew himself up in his chair and puffed out his chest. "As I said, it was a short meeting. I told Cecil in no uncertain terms we would not be endorsing him or his asinine bill."

"How did he respond to that? I'm told he could be a little hot headed at times."

"He wasn't happy, but I don't suppose it came as any big surprise," Cade answered.

What the hell. Luke decided to see what would happen.

Luke stood and leaned across the desk far enough to violate John Cade's personal space, planting his hands on either side of the surprised man's desk. "Surely he'd figured that out on his own. Like you said, it was no surprise. Why come for the face to face rejection?"

Cade shifted in his chair and studied the paneling to his left. "I have no idea."

"Why is their camp denying that he came here at all?"

"You should ask them."

"And you never talked again?"

Cade pressed his lips together and shook his head.

"There was nothing else he wanted to talk about?" Luke pushed.

"We had nothing else to talk about." Cade was getting jumpy.

"You sure about that?" Luke scooted along the perimeter

of the desk getting closer and closer. He ended up propped on the corner causing Cade to lean away.

"If this meeting happened two months ago, why did he call you less than two weeks before he died? On a secret phone, no less."

"What control do I have over the phone he uses," Cade hissed. His face blanched when he realized what he said.

Luke grinned and leaned back giving the man some space. "So, you did talk to him again. What were you two kids gossiping about?"

John Cade mastered himself faster than Luke expected. "It was a desperate attempt to make us reconsider after he came in here acting like a buffoon. Like his attempts at governing. Feeble."

"Why didn't he call you on a normal phone? Was he trying to keep your conversation a secret?" Luke suppressed a smile. Sometimes his job was fun.

John Cade stood up ramrod straight and puffed out his chest leaving no doubt the interview was over. Luke stood, now nose to nose with Cade. Luke didn't blink.

Cade broke off and turned away. "I'll have the secretary show you out," he said.

Luke reached into his pocket and flipped a card onto the desk. "I remember where the door is. Thank you for your time, Mr. Cade. You've been very helpful."

Luke turned and walked to the door. As he closed it, Luke saw Cade snatch up his phone and punch a number into the keypad.

9

———

FBI Regional Field Office
Atlanta, Georgia
June 5th
1600 Hours

Luke had no sooner slung his jacket over his chair when Thad walked into his office.

"What the hell did you do?"

"What?" Luke massaged his temples and fell into his chair. It was after six and he'd hoped everyone was gone for the day, but Thad's entry dashed his hopes.

"Simon wants to see you. 'Yesterday' was the word he used."

Luke closed his eyes and sighed before heaving himself out of the chair.

"I'm taking your stapler if you get fired," Thad yelled after him.

"Close the door, Luke." The booming voice of the Atlanta SAC reached him before he got to the door. Luke glanced over his shoulder at the deserted hallway but shut it as ordered. He slouched in a chair and rested his aching head in one hand.

Steve Simon's desk and walls were covered with golf paraphernalia. A traditional banker's lamp cast a low light over the tidy desk. In his usual fastidious manner, the only items on Steve's desktop were a large desk calendar, the phone, and a glass bowl of gold foiled candy.

A large bookshelf occupied the back wall loaded with criminal law volumes and pictures of his grandkids. Steve's hulking frame covered most of the chair. Brilliant white teeth flashed against his black skin as he opened a piece of candy and popped it into his mouth. Usually, Steve was making bad jokes. Not today.

"Did you pay a visit to a Mister John Cade today?"

"Just got back."

"Now, why in the world didn't you tell me you were going over there?"

Luke shrugged. "Following the phone call. Didn't think it was a big deal."

"Not a big deal, huh? I would have agreed with you except I just got calls from two U.S. Congressmen and Assistant Director Long. They all wanted to know the same thing. Why were you grilling an executive of an organization with no link to Twomey?

"That was fast. 'Grilling' is a bit dramatic. And they do have connections to Twomey."

"No doubt." Steve leaned forward and put his beefy forearms on the desk. "But I also have the experience to know that Joe Long is a bad enemy to have. Tack some Congressmen onto that and you start to see a problem?"

"Joe still pissed that I said no?"

"Said no? You told the number three honcho at the FBI to go yank himself. Right after he offered you the entire counter-terrorism section."

Luke chuckled.

"Luke, you wanna tell me what in the sam hill is going on?"

"He wouldn't take no for an answer."

"With Twomey."

"Would you have told me not to go, Steve? It's an investigation. Same shit as always."

Steve Simon locked onto Luke with a gaze that caused many a man to confess back in the day. "Now, you know this is clearly not the same as always. Of course, I would have let you go, but I would have known you were about to stir the pot. I'm the one that fields complaints from these egotistical knuckleheads. And now Susan's mad because I'm late for dinner. How is it that you're the one antagonizing everybody, and I'm the one gettin yelled at?"

Luke smiled. "Sorry, Boss."

"Ehh, shut up." Steve sunk back making his chair creak.

"I push. That's why you gave this to me, isn't it?"

"Listen, I'm with you on this, Luke. You know that," he said. "But I'm afraid I might have put you in a difficult position."

Luke waved him off, but Steve kept talking. "I've been in this business a long time. I've seen it enough. Powerful people get twitchy when you start niggling around in their closets. Their skeletons are often more repugnant than everyone else's."

"Doesn't matter."

"Now you know it does matter."

"No. It doesn't. It's simple." Luke leaned forward. "I turn over the rocks these snakes slither under and let them burn in the sun until they know they've been beaten. By me." He pointed at Steve. "They don't get a pass because of who they are."

"There've been a couple of times you didn't think so." Steve's soft reply silenced Luke. "I never questioned your judgment, Luke. I didn't need to ask, and I never will. I defended you to anyone who came asking, including Joe Long. You're the best agent I've ever seen, and you're right. I put you on this case for a reason."

Steve grabbed another piece of candy and heaved his bulk out of the chair. He snatched his coat off a valet stand in the corner and looked out the window. "But there are people who would love nothing more than to see you brought down. So, if you're gonna bring it, you bring it hard, Marshall. You don't go halfway with a case like this. You either break it wide open, or you walk away."

"I will."

Steve faced him. "I know. But you need to think long and hard about the ending of this one. You've got my blessing to do whatever you feel is necessary, but for the love of all that's holy, be prudent. Ok?" Steve clapped him on the shoulder and walked out of the office. "And keep me in the loop. No more surprises. That's an order," he yelled over his shoulder.

Luke trudged back to his desk. He'd touched a nerve with Cade, which only brought up more questions. He ran his hand through his hair then ripped off his tie.

Thad poked his head in. "How'd it go?'

Luke told him about the conversation with Steve.

"Wow," was all Thad said when Luke was done.

"I don't know. Maybe I am way outta line on this." Luke locked his hands behind his neck and kicked his feet up on his desk. He didn't rattle easily, but a man he respected had pretty much advised him to walk away and leave the politics alone.

"Look, old man," said Thad, "you're the one that taught me to trust an instinct. I think you should follow your own advice. Besides, you'll wanna hear what I dug up."

Luke dropped his hands and saw Thad almost bouncing in his seat, laptop open. "Go."

"One World is a huge player. Like every other special interest lobby, they've been implicated in improper contributions to politicians through their PAC. You know, the ushz. It's the go-to charity for Hollywood types with an environmental bug up their ass. Well represented at elite political and social functions. They have a history of doing a little bob and weave with their moral position if it gives them an economic or political advantage. Again, not unusual for Washington.

"Here's where it gets interesting. I Googled the words Dr. Prince found on Twomey's hand. Chaud is French for hot so it sounds promising."

Luke gave him a withering look.

Thad missed it as he tapped on the keyboard. "Our choices include a clothing label out of India, a reporter, a couple of Canadian businesses, and said French translation. Maybe he was trying to tell us that he preferred French women."

Luke perked up. "A reporter?"

"Yeah, but he's a dead end. Literally. He died in Iraq while embedded with an Army combat support unit."

"When was he killed?"

Thad looked at his screen. "David Chaudhry. An embedded New York Times reporter. His unit was hit by an IED and small arms fire in March '08."

"Twomey had the name of a dead reporter written on his hand?"

"Yeah, half of it anyway. Random."

"I doubt it. What about the other?"

"That one's pretty easy. Doha...."

"Camp Doha?"

"Yeah. You know it?"

"It's shut down now, but it was a DOD multi-branch base outside Kuwait City. It was a major staging point for the initial invasion in '03."

"Uh, yeah. Were you there?"

"Me? No."

Thad waited. When Luke didn't say anything, he continued. "Found an article, blip really, that mentioned Camp Doha in a list of bases that instituted an environmental protocol plan or whatever. Something like that. I don't know exactly what that means. I'm pretty sure it's government pork."

"Never heard of it," said Luke.

"Not exactly nightly news material. Still isn't, but the Great Google further revealed that less than a year before the date of that article, our buddies at One World made a huge deal with the DOD to implement environmental protocols around military bases including Doha. One World was not mentioned in the first article, but it had to be them. No one else has done anything like this.

"Every major base in the Middle East and Europe implemented environmental reforms within a year. Every branch. At that time, it was something like fifty bases. For something that nobody seemed to care about, it was a massive deal pushed through in record time. In under eight months."

Luke sat forward listening.

"The contracts were awarded to several environmental service companies who wound up with fat government deals. One World was retained on a lucrative consulting contract. Put One World on the map. Guess who brokered the DOD deal.

"Cade."

"Boom."

"When?"

"About ten years ago."

"Around the same time he made vice-president."

"He was promoted three months later, actually," said Thad.

Luke jumped up and started pacing behind his desk.

Thad shifted in his seat with a satisfied look. "It gets better. Cade was the Middle East rep back then. He lived in Turkey and traveled extensively in that area."

Luke thought about Cade's impressive collection.

"About a year after he was promoted, one of their low-level employees was accused of blackmailing an exec. The newly minted vice president, Cade. I had to dig for that one. It got buried like a champ."

"What happened?"

"Nothing. The case was dropped. The employee was discharged and kinda dropped off the map."

"Dead?"

"Don't know. I can't find him."

Luke stopped. "So, Cade spends five undistinguished years as a lobbyist. Goes to the Middle East and suddenly has the talent to make Washington bend over backward for him. Makes vice president and gets blackmailed."

"And never gets promoted again." Thad drummed his fingers on the laptop waiting for it.

"You got plans tonight?" Luke grabbed his coat.

"Not anymore."

"Thatta boy," Luke grinned, "let's go pay Barty another visit."

10

Buckhead Commons Shopping Plaza
Atlanta, Georgia
June 5th
1825 Hours

Bartholomew Duncan ignored the half glass of scotch on the desk. Instead, he focused bloodshot eyes on the bottle clutched in his thick fingers. The table lamp on the console behind him cast the only light in the storefront. The dim light barely made it to the front door.

Barty took a long pull from the bottle. He spat it out when he heard something buzzing in the drawer next to him. With a shaky hand, he tugged the drawer open. A cheap flip phone vibrated across the drawer bottom. He pulled it out and gazed at it in horror. Liquor sloshed onto his desk as he slammed the bottle down. His gaze darted around the dark empty office. It snagged on the front door.

Luke watched him through the glass, the Senator's matching phone to his ear. He made a show of flipping the phone shut, savoring the panic on Duncan's face. Then he pushed the door open.

Duncan's panic turned to a route when he realized his drunk ass forgot to lock it. He jumped up looking around for an exit but gave up and cowered as the two men bore down on his office door.

"Hey, whatdoyaknow. That second number was yours," said Thad gleefully. He grinned at Luke who towered over Barty sweating in the corner of the office. "These little things are the best investigative tools known to man. I don't know how Sherlock did it."

The liquid courage made a last stand. "You don't know anything, you little prick," Barty smirked as the smile slid off Thad's face. His satisfaction didn't last long.

Now scowling, Thad posted his muscular frame against the doorjamb blocking any escape.

Luke tossed the Senator's phone onto the desk, his expression cool. The phone chinked against the liquor bottle. He took a step toward Barty who cowered again.

"Campaign manager, fundraising whiz, and pimp. That's a hell of a resume. No wonder you're so popular with the big guys. You've got all the right skills."

Barty looked like he was about to cry. He grabbed the windowsill and hung on for dear life. His gut hung out of his untucked shirt.

Luke looked at him coldly. "Why was your man calling John Cade on a disposable phone?" Luke perched himself on the corner of the desk.

At the question, Barty did start crying. A gruesome sight. "All we wanted was an endorsement," he whimpered.

Luke grabbed the bottle of thirty-year-old scotch. Barty covered his head and fell to the floor when it hit the wall next to him and shattered. In one swift move, Luke approached and grabbed him by the collar. Forcing the man around, Luke put his face inches away. The sweating, crying man reeked of booze.

"This is where you tell me what is going on and maybe, just maybe, I don't take you to jail for a half dozen federal crimes."

Barty threw his hands up to hide his face.

"You lied to me about meeting with Cade. Twomey knew he was never getting the endorsement. What was the real reason he went?"

"C...C...Cade's a piece of shit. He sucks off anyone who can benefit him and tramples everyone beneath him sh... show his superiority." Barty hiccupped every few words.

"I figured that out myself. Answer the question."

Barty began to blubber. Luke's right hand went to the man's throat, and he slammed the man down into his own chair. Barty coughed. Spit flew from his mouth. It was a moment before he could continue.

"C...Cade negotiated defense contracts by blackmailing the Chairman of the Ways and Means Committee. There were things going on around military bases that would curl your h...hair."

Luke slammed the headrest next to Duncan's head with his palm. "Like what?"

Duncan flinched and leaned away. "Human trafficking around U.S. bases. Mistakenly paid for by government contracts."

"A mistake? Cade blackmailed Congress with a mistake? You're gonna have to do better than that."

"They knew about it. Cecil found out about the whole thing. He said he had proof. Something that would win us the seat."

"What proof?" Luke growled.

"I don't know. I swear I don't know...please. He didn't share that with me. Please," Barty begged as Luke came nose to nose with him.

Luke said nothing. It had the desired effect.

Barty blurted it out. "Cecil had a couple of guys he used. Hackers. They got into Cade's personal server and found emails or something."

Luke straightened. Duncan breathed a sigh of relief.

"This is all very fascinating, but you're still being useless, Barty boy," said Luke. "This happened over twelve years ago. Long enough for them to deny it, and too long for anybody to care. That shit is way too old to be an effective play. What was Twomey blackmailing Cade with? What else did he have?"

"I swear to you I don't know," Barty whimpered.

"Get up." Luke reached for the handcuffs on his belt. The sobbing sweating man threw his hands up like he was fending off a punch.

"You're right. You're right. He never would have gone over if he didn't have something. Something big. About a month ago, he said he could get a One World endorsement and hit Onessa where it hurt. That we were unstoppable. I thought it was strange, but then I forgot about it. Cecil had a lot of dirt on a lot of people, but he never used it unless he needed something. I thought that's all this was. But I don't know what he had. What he found. Please, you have to believe me."

"I'm supposed to believe you didn't know everything he did?"

"I didn't know everything he did. I didn't. I swear to you. He hired me to do a job, and I did it. He was the one who got sloppy. And no, he didn't tell me everything. I didn't want to know. I swear I didn't want to know."

Barty's answers came quick now. Lies take more time to fabricate. Luke was satisfied he was getting the truth.

"You set up the prostitutes?"

Barty nodded.

"Who else knew about that apartment?"

"I used the same guy, always. No one else knew about it. At least that's what I thought."

Luke pushed away from the chair, ready to get away from the smelly drunken mess. "Still think he killed himself?"

Duncan shook his head. "No," he whimpered, dissolving into tears. "None of this can get out. It will ruin me. Oh god, this can't get out." He buried his face in his hands.

"Sorry, Barty boy." Luke grabbed both phones from the desktop. "Not my problem."

Luke and Thad left the distraught man and walked out into the hot night. "Cade keeps an apartment here, but he lives in Savannah," said Luke.

"So, we're going to Chicago?"

Luke looked at Thad.

"I'm kidding. Lighten up, Old Man. I'm packing, like right now."

"Pack for an extended trip. It's going to take a while to sweat him out."

"Okay."

"Get your caseload caught up. Be ready to go by next Monday."

"Can we make it a week?"

Thad never realized there were crickets in the city. "I'll be ready Monday."

11

FBI Satellite Office
Savannah, Georgia
June 8th
0845 Hours

Thunder rumbled behind heavy clouds as the men approached a brick two-story building on Bull Street. Fat drops began to fall, but Luke didn't bother shielding his face. Rain didn't bother him. He'd endured worse in the field for days on end.

Thad held the morning paper over his head in a futile attempt to stay dry. Halfway to the door, the bottom fell out and the news disintegrated.

Luke pushed through an unmarked brown door and climbed the carpeted stairs. At the top, the blue and gold seal of the Federal Bureau of Investigation hung in the small vestibule flanked by the American and Georgia state flags.

A pretty brunette looked up from the receptionist's desk behind bulletproof glass. Luke grabbed his collar and shook the water off his coat as Thad grinned at her. She smiled back.

"Luke Marshall and Thaddeus Aulden," said Thad. He leaned casually against the glass as he flashed his credentials at her.

"Oh, hi there. We've been expectin' you." She pushed a button under her desk. The heavy door unlocked with a click. She was already standing when they walked in, the slightest hint of cleavage peeking.

"Welcome to the Savannah field office. Greg is gonna be in a little late today, but I'll show you around if you like," she finished with a little flourish.

Thad looked like she'd offered him a million dollars. Luke glanced around at the small but modern suite of offices.

"My name's Susannah June, by the way. Everybody calls me Susie J, but you can call me anything but a bad name," she drawled, shooting sideways glances at Luke.

Thad grinned at her. Susie set off down a short hallway peppered with doors. Thad followed first then Luke.

They passed a break room with a green formica countertop and a large window that let in wet, gray light. Luke caught a glimpse of a deserted park sheltered by a sprawling canopy of trees.

The trio followed the hall until it made a sharp right and ended at a door. Susie pushed it open revealing a small office. Two modular desks faced the white walls. Desktop computers and phones sat on top of each and nothing else. There was barely enough floor space for the two chairs pushed under the desks.

It wasn't much more than a broom closet, but Luke was thankful it had a window. And he'd smelled coffee passing the break room.

Susie J's drawl answered him. "Ah just made a pot of coffee. Ya'll help yourselves."

"Why thank you, Miss Susie J," said Thad. His own

twang had grown considerably deeper in the last few minutes.

She smiled at him and turned to leave. "Let me know if ya'll need anything," she called behind her.

"I'll let you know...," Thad started to mumble at her retreating behind.

Luke cut him off. "Nothing but the best for company." He surveyed the broom closet. "Let's go unload the car and get to work."

Thirty minutes later the desks were piled with boxes and damp stacks of paper. Thad collapsed in his chair.

"I gotta be honest with you, Boss. I don't know where to start with this mess." Thad looked at the cramped office.

"Cade."

"What's that?"

"If we dissect Cade, we'll find something. Why we're here."

"Can't we write a search warrant on his house and be done with it?"

"He wouldn't keep anything incriminating in his house. Even if he did, the second he gets wind that we're in Savannah everything will get scrubbed."

"I still can't believe you found a judge to sign a closed warrant for his bank accounts."

"There's always an idealistic new judge ready to take on the world."

"Was it a woman?"

Luke ignored him. "I can't get into his offshore accounts yet, but his domestic accounts need some scrutiny. Cade is very philanthropic. He donates to people and organizations who can benefit him in turn. Academics, political action committees, re-election campaigns, and more than a few foreign third-world dignitaries. He's schmoozed royalty and procured god knows what for them. He's a slimeball of a human being, but he gets results for rich people who need a back-door provider."

"Um. Okay."

"I'm going through the bankroll to research the names on it. See what that gets us," said Luke.

He rifled around in a bank box and pulled out a ream of paper. Thad's keyboard and stapler bounced as the heavy stack hit the desktop.

Thad's eyes got big. "What's that?"

"Cade's phone records for a year. Cell and home."

"Um, where did you get this? The judge didn't sign a phone records subpoena."

"Cade would get wind of it. Patriot Act doesn't cover us there."

"But," Thad stopped speaking and squinted at Luke. "You know what? I don't want to know."

Luke smile. "Tried to get Twomey's too, but his account was flagged. I couldn't fudge that one. His legal team is top notch."

"Did you sleep with the phone company lady?"

"Didn't have to."

"I really don't know why women find you so irresistible," grumbled Thad. "They should spend an hour with you in a cubicle. That luscious hair wouldn't save you then."

Luke winked at him and whirled his chair to face his own computer. "Now I have to find a way into their personal servers."

"You know you're one of the good guys," said Thad. "You can't go rogue. And definitely no hacking into no damn servers. You're not in the Army anymore, Sgt. York. You gotta play by the rules."

"We don't need a warrant to window shop. We're just looking right now," Luke answered. He pulled more files out of a box. "They'll be plenty of time to play by the rules."

"So, what am I looking for? Exactly?" Thad leafed through the stack of phone number printouts.

"His wife and kid," came the reply. Luke was nose deep in his own stack, his feet kicked up on the desk.

"What's that?" Thad sounded irritated. It was impossible to keep up with Luke's lighting fast topic changes. That is until he wouldn't shut up about something.

"Start with his family." Luke flipped a page. "We're not going to find anything shady from the phone records themselves. Cade's too controlled for that. I'm looking for anything that seems out of the ordinary. It might not be much but look for anything that stands out. Excessive phone calls, calls at weird times, or someone he rarely calls."

"With his wife and kid?"

"Cade collects powerful friends, but the ones we're interested in will have a different contact pattern. Most of his friends are name droppers. They advance him socially or financially. The ones that aren't connected to his shady business dealings are the ones he'll let near his family. They may have kids at the same school, play golf with them, go to fundraisers. They'll be easy to eliminate.

"I want to know about the contact he hits up randomly or not very often. I'm going to compare that to the list of donation recipients I'm going to compile from his bank statements. Patterns should show themselves." Luke put the pile down and looked up. "And we need to find out what happened in Iraq."

"I hate to break it to you, but I don't know how to do that." Thad eyed his pile like it might bite him.

"I'll take care of Iraq." Luke stood and started to pace. He forgot how small the office was and nearly ran headfirst into the wall. He settled for leaning against it. "We need something we can use to put the screws to Cade. He's our big break, but he's smart."

"You think he'll cave?"

"They always do." Luke turned to look out the window. "If you push hard enough long enough. The secret isn't outsmarting the bad guy. It's outlasting him."

Thad looked dubious. "Okay." He licked his thumb and scooped up a page.

Luke gazed out the window. He would never admit it out loud, but Thad was right. They hurried over to this scrap of swampland to sift through a drippy haystack for a single slippery needle. They had nothing. Nothing except his flawed judgment.

He liked one thing about the broom closet. Despite an adjacent building that partially blocked it, the office had a commanding view of the best thing in this city. In spite of the gray dismal rain, the sprawling live oaks and brick paths of Johnson Square charmed him.

The city's tiny parks were as old as the historic city herself, and unlike anything Luke had ever seen. Bull Street split in two around it. An ornate stone pillar commanded the middle of the small park encircled by empty benches. The gnarled limbs of the live oaks dripped with Spanish moss and rainwater. He decided to see more of the city's squares on the next nice day.

A rap at the door made the men spin. Luke recognized his FBI academy classmate. Greg Lawrence cut an imposing figure at 6'3", and his pink face was smoother than Luke's lined one. It gave him a much younger appearance. The rack suit couldn't hide the generous layer of fat over considerable muscle.

Luke crossed the room and extended his hand. Thad watched as each man tried to crush each other's grip.

"Luke, how the hell are you? Been a long time." Greg's voice was friendly, but his green eyes were cold.

"Yes, it has."

Time had done little to ease Greg's resentment toward Luke. The academy had been one long fight with Greg coming in a bitter second to Luke in everything. Now Greg was in charge of a satellite office. A fact Luke doubted he would be allowed to forget, even if it was his to turn down first.

"So, tell me about the case. What kind of progress have you made?" Greg rested both hands on his hips and spread his elbows. He was a big guy, but he always tried to make his profile bigger. He'd done it since the day Luke met him.

Then he shouldered past Luke into the crowded office, forcing Thad to jam himself into the desk. Greg began rifling through the neat stacks Luke had organized.

"Just a few things to wrap up. We won't be here long."

"Oh, so you are going to wrap it up this time?" Greg smirked.

Luke wanted to choke him out. Instead, he briefed Greg about their investigation in Atlanta and the blackmail they'd uncovered. Greg hung on to every word.

"So, we have a dead U.S. Senate candidate and a juicy little blackmail scheme." The glint in Greg's eyes was bright. "Maybe we need to hold a press conference. Set up a hotline, gets some leads."

"We're not doing that." Luke sat down and kicked his feet up on the desk. It had the intended effect of coiling Greg even tighter. Luke watched with satisfaction as Greg's lips went thin. "We won't get anything useful, and it's none of their business."

"Let's get one thing straight." Abandoning any friendly pretense, Greg drew himself up to his full height. "I'm in charge of this field office, Marshall. I'll decide what...."

"Actually, this case originated out of the Atlanta office, and I report directly to your boss Steve Simon. We're here on his orders and under his authority. Basically, we're here to use your shitter and your copier."

Greg balked at Luke's dismissive tone.

"But I pinky promise we'll keep you posted on any developments. Okey dokey?"

Greg tried to recover his footing by sounding more pompous. "Well, I'll be talking to Steve and in the meantime, I'll expect you to keep me up to date."

"We'll do that."

Greg hesitated. Then he decided against saying whatever he was thinking and disappeared down the hallway.

Thad whistled. "Would you stop turning down promotions so those ass clowns don't end up in charge?"

"Don't tell him anything."

"Hadn't planned on it. He might be right about the press conference though. Could yield something."

"We'll do it when I'm ready," Luke snapped. "That donkey is not running this show. I am."

Thad faced his computer so Luke couldn't see him roll his eyes. The sharp trill of Luke's cell phone in the quiet made them jump. Luke snapped it off his belt and checked the caller ID.

"Hey, Sandra."

"Marshall?" The volume made Luke jerk the phone away. "Luke, it's Sandra," she yelled over a dull roar in the background.

Luke heard china clink. He put the phone back to his ear. "Is everything okay?"

"Oh, no, no, everything's fine. Listen, I'm at a pathology conference in New York this week and I ran across something you'll be interested in."

"What's that?"

"Well, I met up with an old medical school colleague of mine and your case came up."

"Tsk, tsk, you know you're not supposed to be talking about active investigations, naughty girl."

"Stop it, you. Listen to this. He tells me he heard of a similar case about five years ago. He remembered it because it was so strange. It was a case out of New Jersey. The doc that did the autopsy is retired, but he's a speaker. So naturally, I barged my way into the green room."

"Naturally." Luke couldn't help a smile.

"Luke, it was identical to your boy. The tox screen, I mean. The dead guy was a labor union big wig, and he shot himself after negotiations went south. But the guy shot crack like your senator even though he was wealthy enough to keep two mistresses and their kids in very nice apartments and was deathly afraid of needles. No alcohol."

Luke didn't say anything. He got up and strode to the window.

"You still there?"

"I'm here."

"Probably worth looking into. He's hooking me up with a copy of the reports. I'll email them to you as soon as I get them. New Yorkers love red tape so it will be a few days."

"You think it's a coincidence?"

"Why are you asking me that, Luke? You know perfectly well I don't believe in them. Why do you think I'm talking to your ugly mug right now?"

"Because you can't stand to be separated from me," Luke said. He saw Thad roll his eyes while pretending to study the screen.

"Umhmm," said Sandra, "I gotta run. If you don't have that in a couple of weeks, it means I forgot. Call me and reminded me."

"I will. You're the best."

"I know." She hung up.

Luke mashed the end call icon and his phone went black. He crossed to the door and threw the bolt.

"Whaaat's goin' on?" Thad said.

Luke exhaled slowly then turned to his partner. He told Thad everything Sandra had told him.

Thad's eyes got big. "There's more than one like Twomey?"

Luke grew solemn. This had turned into a bigger mess than he thought. "It sounds like an MO. If Twomey was murdered, we're looking at the possibility of a professional hit."

"Fantastic. A serial killer."

"No," said Luke, "A psychotic maniac did not kill Twomey. It was controlled. Surgical."

"A hit? On an American politician?"

"Why not?"

"Why not! That doesn't happen here. What happens if that's true? If you don't like someone's politics, you just bump em off? Chaos. Our whole system breaks down."

"It's worse than that."

"Sweet mother of Zeus, how can it be worse than that?"

"Cade is our only connection. His prints are all over this."

"Americans killing Americans?"

"Americans contracting on American politicians."

"Remind me not to run for office. You think Cade…," he trailed off mentally sifting through the mud Sandra's phone call stirred up.

"No," Luke said, "there's no way he's a world class hitman. He wouldn't get his hands dirty. Forget the phone records, I'll take care of those. I want you looking for similar autopsy toxicology results. We'll start on the eastern seaboard."

"Um, on what? There is no autopsy database. Or toxicology database."

"No, but death statistics are kept by most state health departments. You may have to backtrack to the individual police agencies from there for case info."

"Wait. The entire eastern seaboard? You know how many jurisdictions that is?"

"Concentrate on the bigger metropolitan areas first. Larger agencies will have electronic records so it will be easier. Smaller departments will take up most of your time. Start with D.C. and the surrounding jurisdictions all the way up to New York but focus on D.C. Narrow your search to drug positive tox screens, adult males over the age of 30 in the last ten years. Focus on suicides. I have a feeling you'll notice anything out of the ordinary."

"That could take months."

"Then it takes months. It's a place to start the investigation."

"Is that what you call this Piñata swing?" Thad muttered as he swung back around to his computer.

12

June 15th
1230 Hours

"Um huh. Yeah." Luke hunched over his desk with the phone to his ear. The fried rice beside him had cooled into a gelatinous heap. "I appreciate the call back. What's that? Not sure yet. Might be related to a case I'm working. Great. Thanks, man. I owe you one." Luke put the desk phone in its cradle and sat back.

"Who was that?" Thad slurped some lo mein.

"Army buddy of mine."

"Buddy? All you did was grunt."

It was an awkward conversation, and Thad noticed. Luke should have kept better contact with the men he'd fought beside but keeping his distance was easier. "He works for Spokane PD. He's head of the intel unit."

"Spokane PD has an intelligence department?"

"Unit. It's him, a secretary, and a filing cabinet. He knows his shit though. Local and federal law enforcement are the only ones doing anything about human trafficking these days. It doesn't fall under the military intelligence or Federal law enforcement umbrella."

Luke stretched in his seat and propped his feet on the desk. The last few days had blurred together. The rain was only now letting up. For hours on end, the only sound in the broom closet was rustling paper. Thad had made hourly runs to the break room for coffee and, Luke suspected, a quick conversation with Susie.

Luke itched to be outside. Nothing reset a stuffy brain like a hard, outdoor workout, and if it didn't dry up soon he'd have to do it wet. Savannah had nicer scenery than Atlanta, but they had terrible weather.

"He didn't seem surprised when I told him about the trafficking," said Luke, shaking off the distraction.

"Oh yeah?" Thad stabbed some lo mien between his chopsticks and slurped it.

"Can you not do that?" Luke snapped.

Thad dropped the chopsticks and fished a fork out of the plastic bag as Luke continued.

"Nobody gives a rat's ass about human trafficking. Chad's been trying to get his own agency to step up their enforcement, but nobody wants to spend the money. Nobody will throw the resources at it. Especially not cash strapped state and local agencies."

"Why not?"

"Doesn't affect them enough. More accurately, it doesn't affect the average citizen enough. The money gets funneled where the people cry foul the loudest. I'm not saying that's wrong, just how it is. Everybody's too busy making ends meet to care about some girl being forced to have sex in gas station bathrooms. It's not even on their radar."

Thad shuddered and put his fork down, appetite gone.

"Even the FBI has a single thirty-five-man unit devoted to a problem that involves over four million people in a given year. Four million within the United States alone. It's more prolific outside the U.S."

"I find that hard to believe."

Luke shrugged. "Chad said the numbers aren't a secret. They're common knowledge."

"Wow," said Thad.

"Inside the states, it's mostly pimps whoring out runaways. But cartels are starting to deal in flesh as much as they deal in drugs. Diversifying their income streams. Most of the massage parlors in America run on cartel provided labor. Chad's brought down ten of them in Spokane alone over the last couple of years.

"Okay. That's all fascinating and," Thad held his palms up, "frankly terrifying. But what does it have to do with our case?"

"When I brought up trafficking around military installations, he didn't skip a beat."

"What? He knew about it?"

Luke slumped back in his seat and scooted his Styrofoam container into the trash. "The government pays out billions in defense contracts every year. More during wartime. A huge chunk of the DOD budget goes to the administration of bases, both here and overseas.

"To maintain these bases, most of the auxiliary work is done by civilian contractors, not the DOD. Staffing stores, cleaning toilets, cutting grass, and digging ditches. Stuff like that. When these government contractors land the deal, if nothing in the contract prohibits it, they turn around and hire out the job to subcontractors. It's common practice. The DOD contractor subcontracts to the lowest bidder and pockets the rest. Nobody cares who's scrubbing their toilets as long as they get scrubbed. Lowest bidder always gets it."

Thad sat frozen, listening.

"Turns out you can put in a pretty low bid if you're using

forced labor. Most people think of human trafficking in the sexual context. But Chad says the use of illegal immigrants for manual labor is just as common, maybe more so. A lot of these subcontractors are nothing more than organized crime rings posing as legit companies. Most of them have ties to known cartels the world over. The new black market is in flesh."

"It's not exactly new," Thad muttered.

"The beltway bandits waltz off with millions for cleaning military crappers without even owning a company that cleans toilets. It's the perfect scam because it's legal. It's accepted practice."

"How do they keep them there? The people, I mean. If it's so bad, why don't they leave?"

"Most are illegal immigrants that got suckered by a sales pitch. Jobs and opportunity. They were promised freedom and a new life if they pay a certain amount. They get to their final destination, and their handlers take away their IDs and tell them the police will deport them or throw them in jail. Usually, these people are the poorest of the poor, and there is zero chance any of them speak the language of their new country.

"Their handlers keep them sequestered from the rest of the world and make them pay exorbitant prices for things like toilet paper and toothpaste or room and board. Any pittance they're 'paid' goes straight back to their handlers to cover basic necessities on top of their smuggling debt. They end up deeper in the hole and the cycle continues. At that point, physical violence and intimidation are all it takes to keep them in line. Six-year-olds sold for sex is only half the story."

"This happens in America too?"

"It's more prolific at foreign installations, but yes, it does happen here."

Thad looked sick, but Luke could see the wheels turning. "Your friend claims this is common knowledge. How did Twomey pull off a blackmail scheme with something that anyone with internet access and a morbid curiosity could tell you?"

"It wasn't common knowledge ten years ago. Awareness of human trafficking is only now beginning to gain any traction. Maybe the last five years or so."

"So, Cade found out about the trafficking at American bases and blackmailed Congress into his sweet deal? And then Twomey found out about this blackmail and blackmailed Cade with his own blackmail? My brain hurts." Thad shook his head.

"I don't think so," said Luke.

"You don't think what?"

"If that's what Twomey had, why wouldn't One World just deny knowledge, then make a show of investigating until it blew over? Congress would definitely plead ignorance. No one would be able to prove otherwise. Hell, they do that when someone finds the smoking gun in their glove box. But it's possible that most Congressmen don't know about the trafficking. Certainly not enough for Cade to pressure the Chairman of the Ways and Means committee to bow to his will."

Luke slammed a palm into the desk making the computer rattle. He jumped up and spewed a string of profanities when he hit the wall trying to pace.

"Boss?"

"You said the other word on Twomey's hand was a reporter?"

"Yeah."

"You said this guy died in Iraq when? The same time Cade made his deal?"

"Six months before. Give or take." Thad's eyes got wide. "Oh shit."

"Then he ends up written on a dead man's hand. And we're looking into trafficking around military bases. Was he at Doha?"

Thad shook his head. "I don't know."

"Cade didn't find out about the trafficking. He found something else. Something nuclear." Luke propped his hands on the windowsill, letting his head fall between his hunched shoulders. "What if Chaudhry was the one who found out about the trafficking? It would have meant much more than embarrassment. The war was at the height of its unpopularity. It could have meant a lot of money to the Washington elite. Billions maybe. If Chaudhry was about to break a story like this...."

"Luke, don't." Thad sounded hoarse. "American soldiers died in that attack."

Luke looked at Thad, then back out the window.

"Are you saying someone killed American soldiers to cover up the death of a reporter? Is that even possible? You think that's what Twomey found out?" Thad was almost whispering.

"That would explain some things. The powerful protect their interests," said Luke, his voice hard.

"Protect it how?" Thad said.

Luke knew he asked the question to keep from admitting the answer himself. Thad wanted to hear it from his older, more experienced partner. As if that would make the admission less horrifying.

Luke turned to his young partner. "We're going to find out."

Several hours later, Luke pushed away from his computer and rubbed his eyes.

The attack on the embedded reporter and his squad had

taken place between the allied controlled airport, and the so-called Green Zone in Baghdad. It was only one of many insurgent attacks in 2008. He hadn't heard of this particular attack, but there were too many to count. In those days, insurgent attacks had been clustered in the busier northern area of Iraq where he'd been operating at the time. Insurgents on a large scale that far south were unusual, but not impossible.

Luke yanked up the phone. He'd gotten all he was going to get from Google. Not every secret stayed in the sand. It was time to contact a more reliable resource. He needed to talk to Frank.

13

National Mall
Washington, D.C.
June 17th
1500 Hours

Commuter thought had turned to beating the traffic by the time Luke got there. Three hundred yards off Constitution Avenue, he leaned against an elm and pretended to scroll through his phone surveilling the rendezvous point.

Tucked away in the National Mall was a small man-made island in a shallow pond. Rows of granite stones carved wide grassy terraces stepping down to the water. Thick compact trees blocked the mid-afternoon sun for the few locals that knew about this place. Tourists never came to this empty corner of the mall.

It was unlikely he was followed. Still, there was a reason this meeting was in person, so he took no chances. He took his time evaluating every ingress and egress just in case. Frank's meeting place wasn't tactically sound, but it was quiet.

He crossed the wooden footbridge and picked a spot

away from the other occupants that allowed a clear field of view in every direction. To his left, the Washington monument dominated the tree line. The roof of the Lincoln Memorial rose above the trees on the right. It was particularly balmy for mid June. He took a deep breath and felt calm despite the angry honking on Constitution behind him.

He always liked Washington. Big enough to get lost in without the claustrophobic feel of the bigger cities. After ten years in the military, he'd spent two more haunting the streets of DC trying to find somewhere to belong. Which usually meant a bar filled with people as messed up as he was.

His cramped Atlanta apartment and his home state sprang into mind. Maybe it was time to request a transfer and finally go home. At least in Colorado, he could disappear into the mountains whenever he wanted.

A strong hand clapped him on the shoulder. "How you doing, you old slugger?" The voice was steely from a lifetime of leadership and gravelly from two packs a day.

Luke smiled before he turned. "Frank." Luke stood to greet the older man and stuck out his hand. Frank clasped it and pulled Luke into a hard hug. "How the hell are you?"

Frank's polo and khakis were crisp and sharp even at the end of the day. He made no effort to sand down his overt military bearing, from his graying high and tight to his rigid posture. The only thing that changed over the years was the amount of grunting as he sat on the stone beside Luke.

Frank rubbed his knee. "Wouldn't have anything to complain about weren't for this damn rain coming." Frank eyed the clear blue sky. "How are the peaches?"

Luke pulled a face. "Soggy."

"I have to admit I was surprised to get your phone call, Son. Been a long time."

"I know, Frank. I'm sorry."

"You up an' disappeared on me, Son. By the time I saw your discharge paperwork you were on terminal leave," Frank said. He pulled a pack of unfiltered Marlboros from his shirt pocket, tamped them against his palm, and stuck one between his lips. "Couldn't find you after that until you joined the dark side. How's that been for you?"

Luke shrugged. "Getting older." He tried to steer the conversation away from himself. "You?"

Frank obliged and perked up at the question. "Damn knee gave out on me. Had to get another one. Got five grandkids now. Them daughters of mine won't stop popping 'em out. Love those little crumb snatchers. Keep me young." Frank lit up and took a long drag.

Luke chuckled and shook his head. "I have a hard time picturing you playing Santa."

"I had to explain why Santa smelled like cigarettes to the oldest one last year. I think she's gettin' suspicious." Frank laughed and took another puff.

Retired Colonel Frank Longer had been Captain in the intelligence battalion that Luke was assigned to as a butter bar fresh out of West Point. They met again five years later. By then, Frank had made full bird colonel, and Luke had been an operator for three years. Frank took command of Luke's Delta Force counter-terrorism unit and became a mentor and a friend. There was no human being on earth Luke trusted more.

Military ran through Frank's veins. A member of the Longer family served in every conflict since the Revolutionary War; a fact he was fiercely proud of. As a young Lieutenant in Vietnam, a round shattered his knee. He could have stayed home like everyone else with a severe injury, but he charged back into the jungle as soon as he could walk. Even a bum knee riddled with arthritis couldn't slow Frank Longer down.

In his civilian reincarnation, Frank ended up at the Defense Intelligence Agency. Unwilling to let a man with Frank's expertise go, the SECDEF recruited him to head up the Joint Intelligence Center. Frank, unwilling to accept that the glory days were over, accepted.

"When you gonna leave those girly girls at the Bureau and come back to work for me?" Frank said.

"When are you gonna retire?"

"When I'm dead," Frank growled. "Ya didn't answer my question."

"You know the answer to that question."

"These pups I got working for me these days...." Frank shook his head. "You ever get tired of chasin' around train bandits and purse snatchers, you give me a call. There's always room on my staff for you."

"Sorry to disappoint you again," said Luke.

Frank chuckled. "The only thing that disappoints me, Son, is every single one of your post war decisions."

Luke smiled, then got to the point. "Were you able to find anything?"

"Well, most of it is still classified, but lucky for you, I'm golfing buddies with most of JSOC at that time. What's left of 'em."

"That's why I called you."

The crusty old soldier looked sternly at Luke. "Still keeping a mental file on everybody, huh? Glad to see you're keeping your skills sharp." He ground his cigarette butt on the granite.

"Learned it from you."

"Your request was a little unusual. I'm not often asked to dig up classified information on US operations in Iraq to give to the FBI. Especially on the down low."

"I know and I'm sorry about that, Frank. I wish there was another way. The normal channels would raise the suspicions of some people I'd rather keep dark right now. Powerful people."

Frank didn't seem surprised. "The shit always seems to find you doesn't it, Son."

"You ain't kidding."

"Alright." The colonel heaved his padded frame into a more comfortable position on the stone. "I did find the incident you were looking for. A three-vehicle convoy was attacked in Rasheed just outside Baghdad in 2008 like you said. Two privates, three corporals, a gunny, and a reporter were killed. No survivors."

"Were they scheduled to go through the area?"

"No, it was a combat logistics unit on a personnel transfer. Likely they were transporting the reporter to a new imbed unit taking a random route like they were supposed to."

"What was the reporter's deal?"

"He was to be attached to a unit out of Camp Hope near the airport. You were right. He spent a couple of months at Doha. He completed his training there before forward deploying with the 64th Armored Regiment."

"What happened?" Luke gave up trying to sit still and started pacing back and forth in front of Frank.

"Hit by RPGs and finished off with small arms fire. That is if anyone was still alive after the IED went off. It left a crater twenty feet wide."

"Seems like overkill. What was the frequency of attacks in the area?"

"By that time, it had died down in the region around Bagdad, but attacks still happened in random patterns. Just the fringe operators at this point, but it wasn't unheard of.

Attacks on either side were a couple of months removed from this one."

"Any of them use that much firepower?"

"Not even close. Most of the damage was on the convoy's left side, which was south facing. It was almost point blank. Definitely an ambush. They were hit from no more than fifty feet away, max."

Agitated, Luke sped up. "Did any of our boys return fire?"

"Their magazines were still full. I don't think they saw it coming."

"They were in APCs. How could they all die immediately?"

"What are you looking for, Son?"

"I don't know."

"Son, don't bullshit me. You're terrible at it."

"This is going to sound ridiculous, but do you think it's possible it wasn't an insurgent attack? That someone in the military or posing as military attacked the convoy?"

"I hope I heard you wrong. That's a very serious accusation. U.S. boys were killed."

"Why do you think I want to keep it quiet?"

"Well, I have to admit I'd given some thought to that."

Luke's pacing screeched to a halt. He snapped around to face Frank. "Why?"

"Judging by the wounds, they were hit by AKs after the initial blast. But no brass was found around the scene. No fresh brass anyway. They cleaned up. The responding infantry unit couldn't find hide nor hair of the attackers."

"Insurgents didn't do that, Frank. That country had 7.62 rounds for cobblestones. The last thing on their minds was spent brass."

"I know. I talked to Chaudry's editor at the time. Man

named Jenkins. He couldn't tell me much. He did say Chaudry's footlocker and bunk had been cleared out. He went to personally collect Chaudry's effects for the family and couldn't find shit. No idea when it happened or who took the stuff. No one could tell him anything." Frank pulled out another cigarette.

"Did he say anything about stories he was working on?"

"I asked him. Chaudhry had mentioned he was working on something other than his war correspondence but said he didn't want to discuss it then. Jenkins assumed the reluctance was due to his upcoming deployment. He was heading into a war zone after all."

"Do you know anything about human trafficking around military installations?"

"Sure don't."

"My source says it's a big problem."

"You don't say."

"You ever notice how most auxiliary personnel don't speak English or the host nation's language?"

"To tell the truth, no. I was busy all the time."

"They're slaves."

Frank looked thoughtful. "This have something to do with your case?"

"I think the reporter found out about it. A reporter dying in a roadside IED attack, no one would have questioned that."

"Son, you think somebody hired mercs to kill American soldiers?"

Luke glanced around then took a seat next to Frank. "Not just somebody, Colonel. Maybe DOD contractors. Tell me you found them. I know we tracked mercs and gun runners back then, even if it was spotty."

The wrinkles on Frank's face furrowed deeper and he thought before he answered. "Yes. There were several active in Iraq around that time."

"Good."

"What's next?"

"I don't know."

Frank pointed at Luke. "Luke Marshall always knows what he's going to do next."

"Is there any way you can get me a passport?"

"Absolutely not."

"Why not?"

"You're messing with me, right?" Frank flicked his unsmoked cigarette to the ground and stomped on it. "You cannot run a black ops incursion into fucking Bulgaria. I'm sure as hell not going to be a part of it unless you're on state's business, and you don't work for me, remember? And certainly not for some podunk Georgia carpetbagger."

Luke froze at the sudden block. He glared at his mentor and oldest friend. It was the closest he'd ever come to disrespecting the old war dog, but he held his tongue.

"Besides," Frank continued, "of the four teams I have information on, one entire group is either dead or missing. Two floating in the Dead Sea and the other four missing. All six were documented working together at some point in that five-year period. I'm guessing that's your dream team."

Frank had brought his A-game and Luke still had nothing. His shoulders slumped.

Frank threw his head back and laughed as Luke hunched over running his hands through his hair. "You haven't lost that fire in your gut. I'm glad to see that."

Frank was right. Of course, Frank was right. What was he thinking? He'd let it run away with him. Again. He tried to sound sincere when he said, "Thanks, Frank. I owe you one."

"I'll keep that in my back pocket for later," Frank grinned. Then he grew serious. "Can I ask you a question?"

Luke stiffened. If anyone else asked him that, his answer

would be 'no', but he and Frank went too far back. Luke owed the man more than he could ever repay. Especially after the shitstorm of his very last op. He'd let Luke move on without asking the one question Luke knew he wanted to ask.

"Yeah." Luke watched the ducks waddle around pecking at the grass.

"Of all the things I imagined you would do when you came home, white collar crime wasn't one of them."

"I don't just do white collar, sir. Unless it falls under a specialty unit, I take whatever comes up. It's why I'm stuck on this gaggle fuck."

"I'm a little surprised at the path you took within the Bureau. Are you happy down there?"

"Sure," Luke said. "It's not bad."

Frank laughed. "You are a terrible liar. It's probably a good thing you don't say much."

Luke looked at him and smiled blandly.

"Promise me one thing," said Frank.

"What's that?"

"If you ever get tired of those bureau bimbos you give me a call. I'd like to see you back where you can function optimally. You belong in intelligence. Specifically working for me. It's what you're good at. Not stuffed away in some over decorated building waterin your office plants."

"Sure, I'll do that," Luke lied again. He didn't mention his current office had no room for office plants. The men stood and embraced. Luke watched as Frank marched away. He sat back down and watched the ducks return to the water and paddle smoothly away.

What was he supposed to say to his mentor? That he'd rather scrape his own eyeballs out than go back to that life? Or make camp in a nest of desert vipers than go back to what he used to do? Hell, he'd rather get married and settle down.

No. He'd done his duty. And in return, he received a burdened conscience to haul around for the rest of his life. That's what he should have told Frank. He might not agree, but at least he would understand.

14

FBI Satellite Office
Savannah, Georgia
June 18th
0947 Hours

The next morning Luke rounded the corner onto Bull Street and almost ran into the back of a man wielding an enormous camera. A pack of local reporters had posted up on the sidewalk in front of the field office, their station logos emblazoned on the side of their cameras. They were waiting for him.

He stopped short as they turned and eyed him. In a flash, they surrounded him shouting questions at the same time. "Special Agent Marshall, I assume," a white-haired reporter with stains on his shirt bellowed, shoving a voice recorder in Luke's face.

"Tell us about the Senator's death," someone demanded as they jostled for position.

"Was Twomey involved in a blackmail scheme? Is that why he killed himself? Was he being blackmailed?" A redhead in a bright green blazer fired the questions at him while jamming a microphone under his nose.

"Agent Marshall, will your investigation affect the election in November?" yelled someone from the back.

More voices shouted over each other. Luke lowered his shoulder and forced his way through the mob repeating that he had no comment. He scanned his card and fell against the door slamming it behind him. He tried to compose himself as he climbed the stairs. It didn't work. He knew as soon as he rounded that corner why the reporters were there.

Special Asshole in Charge Lawrence had leaked it to the press.

Susie buzzed Luke in. He was about to demand Greg's whereabouts when he saw the morning paper on her desk. The front page had a full color picture of Greg standing on a dais behind a podium bearing the FBI seal.

Luke scanned the article. He was wrong. That son of a bitch didn't leak it.

The Savannah Tribune quoted SAC Lawrence as saying that Twomey's suicide was being investigated by his office. Anyone with any information was to contact his office or the Atlanta field office immediately.

Luke cringed at his own name mentioned several times in the article, as well as an alleged blackmail scheme that Twomey may have been involved in.

Greg had used all the right words - investigating, suspected, alleged. He had no facts to give them, and it was just enough information to drive the press mad with curiosity. No doubt his goal.

"Greg said he wasn't to be disturbed this morning," offered Susie timidly without Luke asking. She saw his face and shot a nervous glance at the closed door behind her. Without a word, Luke grabbed the paper and crossed to the door. He slammed the door handle down. It was unlocked. If it hadn't been, he would have kicked the door in.

"You called a press conference last night, you sack of shit." Luke slammed the paper down on his desk. "You squeezed it in before I got back so I couldn't stop you."

Surprise crossed Greg's face when Luke stormed in, but it turned smug. "I have to go," he muttered into the phone. He hung up and sat back in his chair. He seemed pleased at Luke's anger.

"You were in such a hurry to hamstring me you didn't even have the good grace to leak it anonymously," Luke accused him.

The smug look slid off Greg's face. "I'm in charge even if that doesn't mean anything to the agency rebel," he snarled. "I'm the final word on what happens here. Period."

"This is how you mark your territory? By fucking up my case...publicly."

"That's funny, Marshall. Me, fuck up your investigation. You're doing a great job by yourself. You don't need my help."

"Help. Is that what you're calling it these days? Luke sneered. "In the Academy, it was 'motivation'."

"You should be grateful. I have it on good authority that if you botch one more case you're out."

"You and Joe Long are buddies now, are you?"

Greg smiled. "It's good for you to get knocked off your pedestal every now and then." He sounded pleased again. "Besides, I probably got you a bunch of leads you didn't have before. Sometimes it pays to listen to your superiors." He emphasized the last word.

Greg leaned back as Luke leaned in. "You just hitched your wagon to mine, Lawrence. If I go down, I'll make sure you do too."

Uncertainty flicked across Greg's face before he could mask it with contempt.

Luke thumped him on the chest. "Stay out of my way. If you don't, I give you my personal guarantee that I will take you apart."

Before Greg could sputter a reply, Luke walked out of the room. Susie J stared at her ashen boss like she wasn't sure whether to get him some water or call an ambulance.

Luke stalked down the hall tugging on his neatly knotted tie. That miserable skulking brown nosing coward had always possessed a talent for screwing people over. Luke watched him do it to more than one good agent, and he was damned if he was going to let him get away with it now. At the broom closet door, he saw Thad focused on his computer screen. The Savannah Tribune article occupied the entire screen.

"Did you know about this?" Once inside, Luke kicked the door shut and rubbed his face.

It was clear from the look on Thad's face he only just found out why the reporters were outside. Thad tugged the paper out of Luke's hand and scanned it for a second before balling it up and throwing it at the wall.

"Chicken fucker," he hissed. "What are we supposed to do with this guy sabotaging us? You didn't tell me your arch-enemy was runnin' this joint. This is not good. Not good," he repeated.

Luke sat down. "It's done. He's done what damage he can, but he gets nothing else from us. From now on, anything we find is to go back to the hotel with us at night. It's not to stay in this office."

"Agreed. How'd it go in Washington?"

Luke scooted his chair to the door, opened it a crack, and peeked down the hall. The office opposite them was dark.

Satisfied no one was close enough to listen in, Luke closed it and threw the bolt.

"I was afraid you were going to say that," said Thad after Luke finished telling him what Frank had to say.

"More of the same inconclusive bullshit. This case has more than its fair share."

Thad looked at him almost pleading. "So, it definitely was the same reporter? I mean, I didn't really check to see if there was another David Chaudhry. But maybe..."

"It was him. Chaudhry had finished a training stint at Camp Doha. He told his editor he was working on a story but didn't tell him what it was."

"So it's true. Someone paid to have American soldiers killed so they wouldn't lose money."

"It's only true if you can prove it," Luke said. "But there's no way both of those names on a dead man's hand are a coincidence." He stood and stretched. He hadn't slept on the red-eye flight the night before. He was starting to feel it. "Twomey must have found something that looked like proof. A few days before he died."

"From whom?"

"His hackers. Maybe."

"Then the old coot went and told the wrong people," Thad's voice wavered like he didn't know if it was a question or a statement.

"Maybe. Maybe I'm talking out my ass," said Luke. He went to the window and looked toward the park. "If I could get into Twomey's server I could blow this thing wide open."

"How? We don't have a prayer at finding the hackers. And we don't have enough probable cause for a search warrant affidavit. Unless you got something else while you were on vacation in DC. Cuz a theory and phone records ain't gonna do it."

"It gets worse." He turned to look at Thad.

Thad's expression went flat. "Is that even possible?"

Luke pinched his nose. "Frank thinks the team that carried out the hit was killed off. One by one about eight years ago."

Thad visibly deflated. Luke felt bad. He was having the time of his life, but it occurred to him now that Thaddeus had stopped barking up this particular tree. Thad followed him out of faith that he knew what he was doing, but he was winging it.

Luke tried to ease the tension. "You're right about one thing."

"I am?" Thad's eyebrows arched.

"I can sit here and bellyache all day that Twomey is the pin in this grenade, but a lot of other people are involved, and that leaves a trail."

"A trail that, thanks to Lawrence, is being swept clean right now," said Thad.

"Can't help that. It will get back to Washington now, and people there have long memories. We're gonna have to be careful. Steve may get pressure to shut us down."

"Or have us killed." Thad's voice was strained.

Luke laughed.

Thad glared at him. "It's not funny. If somebody's bumping off politicians, you think they're gonna think twice about cappin' two FBI schmucks?"

"I know. I'm sorry."

"What is wrong with you?"

Luke chuckled again at his young partner's dismay. "Relax. They're only going to bring the heat if we find something concrete. Leaving a trail of dead FBI agents who don't know anything would bring way too much attention. If anything, Greg's little stunt told everybody we have exactly jack and shit. I'll think you'll survive this one, kid."

Thad sat quietly for a long time. He took several sharp

breaths, like he wanted to say something, but lost the courage. Finally, Luke heard him suck in air once more. "You really think there are others? Besides Twomey, I mean."

Luke walked back to his chair and sat. "Yes," he answered thinking of Sandra's call. "There are many reasons people kill, but politics and money are at the top of that list. Twomey wasn't the first. We can't get inside his head, so Cade is our all access pass to this party."

"I can't get you to go to a real party, but this. This is a party?" Thad was making a joke this time.

Luke laughed to be polite. He felt less guilty now that Thad had calmed down, so he faked a lighthearted tone. "I need some coffee. You want some?" He sprang out of his chair and Thad reluctantly followed him to the break room.

Luke eyed Greg's door, but it was shut. Probably locked now. Three other agents and a secretary hurried down the hall in a cluster without making eye contact. Luke ignored them and grabbed a mug from the cabinet. He filled it from the carafe then walked to the window sipping it.

Thad was pouring a large quantity of sugar into his cup when Susie poked her head around the corner. "Agent Marshall?" Her voice wavered a bit as he turned his head.

She rounded the corner when he didn't start yelling. Thad got over his nervousness and beamed at her as he slouched against the countertop. Even Luke had to admit she looked good today. Her pants hugged her curves, and her white blouse was opened low enough to hint at cleavage while managing to stay professional. He waited for her to speak.

"Um, there's somebody up front," she said focusing on Thad. "He says he wants to talk to the agent in charge of the senator's murder. I'm assuming he means you, but I don't really know what he...wants."

"A reporter?" asked Thad. Susie relaxed when he spoke instead of Luke.

"Ya'll wish," she grinned, "bring a bar of soap."

One look at Thad told Luke they were thinking the same thing. Neither Greg nor the paper ever mentioned murder.

15

Savannah PD Headquarters
June 18th
1850 Hours

By the time Pete threw the car into park the neon pink and orange sunset had faded to gray. The cruiser parking lot was empty. They missed the evening shift change. Again. Tully wondered if the two of them were really that dedicated, or if work was an excuse to avoid going home. It was for her.

Instead of throwing his door open, Pete left the engine running and stared out the windshield. He'd been unusually quiet all day. He was a piss poor actor when something was bothering him. She saw him reach for something in his breast pocket. He seemed to think better of it and dropped his hand. Tully braced for it.

"You know they can't fire you if you seek help," he said.

"Sorry?"

"If you seek help before brass finds out, they can't take any disciplinary action against you." Pete rubbed a hand down his face, then rested it on the steering wheel. His finger tapped the wheel and he avoided eye contact which was fine with her.

"It's not your fault, Tul." Pete's phone buzzed on the dashboard where he'd placed it when they pulled in.

"Your phone is ringing," Tully said flatly.

"Don't ignore me. You've got to stop lying. To me, but mostly to yourself."

She fell silent.

"It's worse, you know." He finally looked over at her. "You drink too much. And the pills." He threw up his hands. "Look, I don't know. You don't have to talk to me about it. That's fine. I get it. But you need to talk to someone."

Tully concentrated on the parking lot outside her window. The urge to run almost overpowered her. Away from this conversation, and the truth it threatened to unleash.

"I've been where you are right now. It's not a place you want to stay. I know you don't want to hear this, but you need to. I needed to hear it."

Tully's gaze locked onto his, her eyes wide. Turns out there were a few things she didn't know about her partner. He looked sad.

Encouraged by her attention, Pete twisted in the seat to face her. "I was lucky. I had Melissa in my corner. And I'm in yours. But if you don't do something soon, there may come a day when I can't protect you, Tul. Please don't make me watch that happen."

"Talk to someone?" Tully scoffed. "You think talking to someone will be enough?"

"It's enough to start."

"You don't know anything about me if you think meaningless words are enough," she replied, her anger rising.

"Why? Why is it never enough for you, Tully?" His own anger matched hers.

Pete's eyes opened wide. "That's it, isn't it? Nothing's ever good enough for you, not even almost fucking dying. It makes so much sense. The reason you push so hard is that you don't ever feel like you're enough. Look me in the eye and tell me I'm wrong."

"It's not that." Tully couldn't meet his eyes.

"Then what?"

"LEAVE ME ALONE." Tully exploded at him. "Why do you do this? Why do you have to push so hard? Just leave me alone."

Pete's voice softened as he said, "I have no idea how hard it was for a little girl growing up with that big scar. You must have grown up thinking you weren't good enough; that no one could love you. What that must have done to your confidence scares the shit out of me, Tully. It scares me that women feel that way. That my daughter might feel that one day."

He paused for a moment to let his voice clear. "It seems like you push yourself as hard as you feel bad about yourself. Like how much you punish yourself is equal to how unworthy you feel." Pete sat back. "I don't know. I don't have anything else to compare it to. What else would drive you to do the things you do?"

Tully looked out the window, willing the tears rimming her eyes to not overflow, but Pete wouldn't stop poking. Two big tears broke free and ran down her cheeks.

"You can't make it go away. You know that right?"

Tully didn't answer.

"It's taken me a long time to come up with the courage to say this, but I started so hear me out. Nothing you can do will make it hurt less. You can't outrun it and you can't outfight it. It's all back assward, but you have to let someone in. You have to let someone care about you. Let someone love you."

She kept her head turned away from him. Her hair was pulled back into a bun and she had nothing to hide behind. No camouflage to shield her soul from her best friend.

The phone buzzed. Melissa was calling again.

Pete picked his phone up, his finger hovering above the green button. "I'm worried about you. I love you, Tul. I would storm the gates of hell with you. And I see it sometimes, you let your guard down around me, and you're...." He paused and rubbed his nose awkwardly. "You're beautiful, Tully. You think you're unlovable, but take it from me, it isn't true."

The lump in Tully's throat wouldn't have let her say anything even if her mind hadn't frozen with dread at how tuned in he was to her pathetic little life. She needed to get her shit straight.

Popping the trunk and her door at the same time, she got out of the car without another word. She snatched the rifle case out of the trunk and headed to the entrance on the other side of the parking lot. She wasn't in the mood to hear snippets of their nauseatingly perfect marriage.

Inside the door, a blast of cold air raised goose bumps. Arms full of equipment, she headed down the long hall. Her sweat soaked undershirt clung to her skin beneath her body armor.

In the armory, she slammed the light switch up with the end of the rifle case. Racks lined with guns and stacks of equipment flickered into view. Her heavy gear bag hit the floor with a thunk, and she hoisted the rifle case onto the long center island.

Tully took a long pull from her water bottle and wished it wasn't water. Then she set the bottle on the counter and opened the gun case.

Lies are more powerful when they're kept quiet. The deeper the hurt a lie protects, the more unbearable to hear it out loud. But Pete was right. The chilly truth was the ship was sinking. It was time to get off.

She'd never admit it, but the thought of hurting Pete was the most unbearable. Her mistakes would not leave him unscathed. He would be marked too. If she could change, a big if, that would be the reason, not her job. Like she cared about losing this fucking job.

Tully thought of Melissa on the other end of the line with a cute story of something the baby did, and the little chuckle that came from Pete almost every phone call these days. Relentless sadness threatened to drown her. Maybe she would never have that but damned if she was going to let her bad decisions ruin their shot at happiness.

Forgetting about the loaded rifle in the case, she leaned forward and propped her elbows on the countertop arching her back, and kicked out her knee to stretch her hip. How she didn't know, but she would work on it. Somehow, she would make this right.

Tully's radio chirped to life. What came over the air was not the bored tone of a dispatcher, but the garbled sound of a fight. She cocked her head trying to hear better. Looks like they'd be going back out.

"...units...," the voice broke in and out "...armed..." The radio went silent and ice spiked through Tully's veins.

It was Pete.

Time lost its grip in one agonizing moment. Already moving for the door, her fingers curled around the rifle grip. As she yanked it out, the case spun launching her bottle off the counter. Five steps to the armory door seemed like fifty as Tully bolted to it.

Like a dream, something held her back when she needed speed. The clip-clop of her plastic bottle hitting the floor did not register. She flung open the armory door and started down the hallway, but it was gone. There was nothing but a door she needed desperately to reach. It was miles away.

Run.

Her mind commanded every movement. A strange calm settled on her. Calm trained into her so that panic would not override decisiveness. Obediently she placed one foot in front of the other. She was running, but the door didn't seem to get closer.

Get to Pete.

Every piece of knowledge she ever possessed was forgotten as her body shut down all unnecessary activity. Adrenaline allowed only what was needed to meet the threat. Blood flooded her muscles readying them for action. Thoughts dropped into her brain, concise and solitary. Like numbered lottery balls rolling down the chute as their unlucky audience waits.

Faster.

Voices came over the radio, but she did not hear what they said. They were only voices and no use to her right now. Her mind was tuned for one sound. Her partner's voice. It never came.

Not alone.

She exploded through the door and sprinted to the far end of the parking lot where she left her partner talking on the phone only moments before. Cruiser after cruiser clicked past, and anger seared across her mind that she hadn't reached him yet. Then, after an eternity, she was there.

Gun up.

Tully knelt behind a cruiser and obeyed. She drew the rifle to her shoulder and flipped off the safety in one smooth motion. Rising, she stepped out from cover, the weapon in a rigid line, eyes searching for Pete.

What she saw should have stopped her. It should have

knocked her to her knees, but her adrenaline-fueled mind still issued commands.

He's got a gun.

The driver door was open. Pete sat on the blacktop propped against the rear tire. His shoulders slumped and his head lolled back and forth like he was having trouble keeping it up. His eyes blinked straight ahead, and his mouth moved, but no words came out. A red stain grew above his belt.

Standing over him was an emaciated, disheveled man Tully recognized instantly. Greasy hair hung limp around his gaunt shoulders. Needle pricks in various stages of healing ran down his arms. His pockmarked face showed shock and dismay as he gazed at the officer on the asphalt. He brought the small black gun in his hand up to eye level, his mouth gaping.

The parking lot melted away. Only the scene in front of her existed. She stepped toward him, forgetting to speak a command. On the second step, her footfall alerted the man to her presence. His head jerked toward her and a look of horror flashed on his face. Tully didn't hesitate.

Kill him.

Her brain didn't let her blink as she squeezed. A muffled pop hit her ears and the muzzle flash flared and faded in the dusk. Her target jerked as a round slammed into his left shoulder. His hand still clutched the gun, but he wasn't paying attention to it. Nick Cummings was looking at Tully.

Kill him.

Tully fired again. And again. Each step she took she fired, and the man jerked.

Nothing.

It was deafening, the quiet. The gun in his hand fell onto the pavement with a thud no one heard. Cummings fell to his knees and pitched forward coming to rest at Pete's feet, eyes wide open.

He's dead.

Pete rushed back to her mind. Refusing to admit what she knew she would find, she released the rifle. It clattered on the pavement. She fell to her knees beside Pete, but misjudged the distance and crawled the last three feet to him. The approaching sirens cut out and tires squealed as she reached him and pulled him onto her lap.

Footsteps pounded on the pavement and everything sped up. Noise crushed her as a wall of officers descended on them. Tully cradled Pete in her arms and rocked him back and forth.

"Pete," she pleaded. "Pete, stay with me. Stay with me, please."

Except for his tan skin gone gray, he might have just been tired. His eyes drooped and he blinked sleepily. She rested her forehead on his, rocking him. He opened his mouth then stiffened. His eyes emptied and he didn't move again.

"No," Tully whispered. "No." She cupped her hand around his cheek and rocked harder. "No, no, no, no."

His body became dead weight in her arms and his head flopped onto her chest. Now panic and confusion burned up her mind. Something wasn't right. This wasn't right.

"Pete. Pete." She slapped his face hard trying to wake him up. Doubt shielded her from the truth, but it didn't hold for long. She curled her body tight around his.

Rough hands grabbed her shoulders and pulled her back. She fought them, but more joined in and dragged her away. A strong hand grabbed her jaw forcing it around, and she realized she was screaming.

Captain Timothy's face came into view. He wrapped her in a bear hug and pulled her away. She twisted trying to get a view of Pete, but white shirts and bright red medical bags swallowed him up.

———

S he didn't hide. It seemed fitting that she stood out from the dark-clothed crowd. It seemed fair. They should all know it was her fault that Pete was dead. But even the gawking wasn't enough penance. They couldn't possibly hate her as much as she deserved.

Under the dripping oaks, black umbrellas huddled together in the haunted old cemetery. Except for her. She stood exposed to the weather, and the faces, in a blue sundress.

When she put on the uniform that morning, she vomited. So she put on a dress instead, but she didn't own a black one. After her mother's funeral, she threw it away. She vowed she would never wear another black dress; that she wouldn't bury anyone else. Yet here she stood. At least she wasn't wearing black. She kept that promise.

"Amen." The crowd murmured the last words of the prayer together, but no one sitting under the green canopy looked comforted. A thin woman in a black sheath dress sat in the front row, her hands folded in her lap. She didn't speak the prayer. She studied the flag draped coffin in front of her. Fatigue had etched fine lines into her young face. Her brown eyes were dry. She had no tears left. An older woman next to her clutched a sleeping baby and wept.

Lines of uniformed police officers stood among the endless maze of headstones. Raindrops and tears dripped down the faces of hardened officers. A few clutched the hand of the one next to them.

Jessica, Brett, and Jules all stood next to each other in the massive uniformed formation. They hadn't spoken to her today. They knew better.

The minister cleared his throat twice as he turned a page in his Bible, studied it for a moment then closed it on his carefully edited notes.

"To be perfectly honest there are times I hate my calling," his voice cracked. "Times like these, when words are hard and tears are easy, anything I say runs the risk of sounding cheap and trite. We speak of comfort, but I can't call it into existence. We look for comfort, but we don't find it. So what do I say to you?

"Do we look to God? Certainly. That is the first place we should look. He promises to comfort us in our time of grief, and I can assure you today, He will not fail in that promise.

"But is there anywhere else to find relief? Is there something tangible to ease this terrible pain?" He paused to compose himself and a distant chirping reached the silent crowd. A few trees rustled, and the far-off roar of a jet was a cruel reminder that the world hadn't stopped to mourn with them.

"I submit to you today that there is. I am here today to tell you that one of the greatest healing powers given to us by an almighty God is already inside of each of you. It is your memory. Your memories of a loving husband and father," his voice cracked again as he looked at Melissa. "And they have never served you like they will now." He stopped for a moment to wipe his nose.

"No one lives forever. Everyone we love will leave us at some point. We know this, and yet we still love. Carelessly. Recklessly. Why? We love because any pain is worth the memories we build. Our tears are the toll we pay for loving these borrowed angels. And a terrible toll it is, but how much worse to never have loved them. Only that would be a true tragedy. If we refuse to mourn his death, and instead celebrate his life, in time you will be healed."

Tully had heard enough. The Preacher had no idea what he was talking about, and she wasn't going to stand around while he blathered on like an idiot. She made her way to the top of the small hill behind the crowd and past the dozens of honor guards standing at attention on the small cemetery road.

As she passed the open hearse emptied of Pete's body, a dispatcher's voice came over a loudspeaker. She was saying Pete's call number. But he didn't answer. He would never answer that number again.

She walked faster. Commands were shouted far off. She jerked as three volleys of seven shots cracked through the air, but she kept walking. Then the bagpipes screeched to life. When they died down nothing would follow. Just emptiness.

Without meaning to, she turned to catch one last glimpse of the casket and something caught her eye. At the back of the crowd, Tully saw a man standing alone. He was dressed in a neat modern suit, but his tie hung loose. She stiffened and picked up her pace.

His back was turned to the ceremonial pageantry. He was watching her.

16

FBI Satellite Office
June 24th
1400 Hours

Luke sat in the broom closet, his jacket hung over the back of his chair drying. He'd stood for two hours in the rain at the slain officer's funeral. Nicholas Cummings had been quietly buried the day before. Luke went to that funeral too but left when only three old ladies showed up to the service. For the umpteenth time that week, Luke opened the video footage from his interview with Cummings looking for what he'd missed.

Six days ago, Nicholas Cummings showed up at the Savannah FBI office to talk to him. That night Nicholas Cummings killed a cop. He missed something. Something big.

Luke clicked play. The interview room in the video was bathed in cold yellow from the fluorescent light reflecting off the beige carpet and walls. Onscreen, Cummings took a seat at the table opposite the camera hidden in the light switch. He was instructed to sit there and did so without a fuss.

Nicholas Cummings was a nervous junkie with track marks up and down both arms, some of them still bleeding. He wore a stained canvas fishing vest over a rumpled black t-shirt and jeans. His hair was a long mess of frizz except the scalp, where unwashed grease plastered it to his head. On the monitor, Luke saw himself and Thad come in and take their places at the table.

The man hadn't said much, Luke remembered as he forwarded the video through the introductions. He'd come to talk and then didn't talk. But as he hit play, Luke knew that assessment was wrong.

"I...I think I know who killed your Senator, there." The man leaned forward trying to get close to Luke so he could speak quietly. His voice was still caught by the microphone hidden in the power outlet by the man's chair. He looked around nervously, his left hand compulsively rubbing up and down his right arm.

"You do?"

Luke winced as he heard his condescending and dismissive tone. Preconceptions were the undoing of an investigator, and he had passed judgment before a word passed between them. No wonder the man bolted.

Everything gets attention, no matter how small. Now he had to watch his smug self breaking that rule over and over on camera.

"Mr. Cummings, do you mind telling me why you think the Senator's death was a murder?"

"I got 'em...I got 'em. The drugs, see. Wanted the good stuff. Good enough to make him sleep, see." He spoke in staccato tones and short bursts. Even now it grated Luke's nerves, although not as much as his own indifference.

In the video, Luke and Thad glanced at each other for a

split second. Luke could see the man's awareness of drugs used in the Senator's death had bothered him greatly at the time.

Greg's press conference had been three minutes long and stated only that Twomey's death was being investigated by his office. He gave no details about the case beyond a scant reference to the trafficking connection. Even Greg wouldn't cross that line. He was just trying to put Luke in his place.

Twomey's camp had been vigilant to keep any mention of drugs out of the press coverage. They couldn't cover up where his body was found, but the evidence, including the ME's report, had not been made public. It would not be until Luke's investigation was complete. Assumptions could be made, but it didn't sound like Nicholas had been making assumptions. He sounded pretty damn sure.

An international conspiracy and a local druggie was the one with his finger in the dike. Figures.

"Mr. Cummings, can you be more specific? Who were the drugs for?"

The man on the video grinned. His rotten teeth had turned Luke's stomach. "For your boy in Atlanta."

"My boy? Mr. Cummings, do you have any specific information for us?" Again, Luke cringed as he heard his superior tone. He hit pause and ran his hands through his damp hair then clasped the back of his neck. He messed this up big time.

The handle clicked and Thad pushed the door open. Luke's hand went back down to the mouse. He let the cursor hover over the play button until Thad shut the door.

Thad knew what Luke's expectant look meant. He threw the bolt and held up an envelope. "I got it."

"Good." Luke held out his hand and Thad gave him the white envelope.

Thad took a seat in his chair and started tapping on his phone screen as Luke hit play. Like Luke, he knew the tape by heart.

Cummings' voice quivered through the speakers. "He wanted an eight ball. He said it was for him, but I knew better. He paid me double. He always paid me double, to keep my mouth shut, see."

"Mr. Cummings, who bought it?" Luke saw himself lean forward hoping for a name, the first real interest he'd shown since the man came in.

"He said," the man trailed off and stared at the wall, his eyes unfocused.

"Who?" Luke prompted.

Suddenly Cummings' face grew distraught. He began shaking his head. "I can't. He'll kill me."

"Mr. Cummings, you need to tell me who you're talking about."

The man looked wild-eyed at Luke. "Can you get me out of here? I don't have any money. The FBI can get me out, right? Set me up fresh somewhere new? I need money."

Onscreen Luke sat back and studied the junkie in front of him. "I can't do that unless I know you have something I can use. I can put you in witness protection, but I need to know that your life is in danger and that you have information vital to prosecuting this case."

Luke had lied. Witness protection would never be authorized in a suicide investigation, even if he had something they could use. Luke said it to keep him talking.

It didn't work. The man clamped his mouth shut and started shaking.

Luke watched as his onscreen self looked away and exhaled loudly, annoyed at the man across the table. Cummings' sat with his arms crossed and palms tucked under his armpits. He began rocking back and forth blubbering that he was going to die and that he never should have come.

Then Luke watched his screen self lose all patience. "Mr. Cummings," he roared at the pathetic mess across the table. Both the man and Thad jumped on the screen. "Why did you come here?"

Nicholas Cummings began to move his head back and forth. It was halfway between shaking and twitching. It was a repugnant sight with, Luke remembered, a smell to match.

"I shouldn't have...shouldn't have come here. He'll find out."

"Not if you tell me who you're talking about. This investigation is confidential."

The man gazed at Luke as though something had occurred to him. "He probably already knows." Then in a quick movement, Cummings pushed his seat back and moved toward the door. "I need to leave. I need to leave. Shouldn't have come."

The microphone picked up his fevered words repeated over and over. "Need to leave." He rushed to the door and scratched at it like an animal in his haste to leave.

Luke had let him go. He'd gotten the man's information, including the homeless camp he lived in, with a plan to follow up with him later. Maybe.

Onscreen Luke waved a hand to Thad, who rose and showed the man out. Luke saw his legal pad on the table with only the man's name and birthdate written at the top.

He shouldn't have let the man leave. He should have made him stay and tell everything. He should have promised that dirtbag whatever he wanted.

But video Luke hadn't thought Nicholas Cummings knew anything of value. That he was some junkie who saw a headline and thought he could capitalize on it. Video Luke had been dead wrong.

Luke snatched up the rumpled Savannah Tribune from Sunday. The page header was the official photo of a police officer in uniform. The caption read, "Decorated Officer Slain in Police Station Parking Lot."

He'd memorized it, but he read it again. The doubt that had taken hold the past week blossomed into dread at what he would see on the disc Thad brought.

The Savannah Police Department released the name of the police officer killed in the line of duty on Friday evening. The officer was ambushed while returning to the station at the end of his shift. The officer succumbed to his injuries on the scene after being shot in the parking lot of the Historic District Station.

At approximately 7:00 pm on June 19th, the officer, now identified as veteran Officer Peter Easton, 38, was approached by the suspect in the parking lot. The suspect pulled a gun and fired at the officer hitting him in the torso, below his body armor.
The suspect, identified as Nicholas Cummings, 46, of Savannah, was killed by responding officers after he refused to drop his weapon. Cummings has a significant criminal record and no known permanent address.
Officer Easton is survived by his wife and six-month-old daughter, mother and father, and two sisters. Details of the funeral and memorial service will follow.

Luke threw the paper down and ripped open the envelope Thad delivered. The funeral announcement was not the only thing released that week. As it always does in the days following an incident, information began free flowing from the PD as their investigation wrapped up. The security footage was released yesterday, the day before the funeral. Another video Luke knew he would watch on repeat for a week.

"I can't believe that stinky bastard would go and kill a cop. I've been thinking about that all week. He was a piece of work, but a cop killer?" Thad swung around as soon as Luke hit stop. "I'm still having a hard time with that one."

"It gets worse." Luke inserted the disc into the desktop. It whirred to life.

"You keep saying that. I hate it when you say that."

The cursor hovered over the icon that popped up as if Luke didn't want to touch it and speak at the same time.

"Peter Easton called Nicholas Cummings on his personal cell phone about two weeks before Cummings showed up here."

Thad raised an eyebrow. "Your girlfriend at the phone company tell you that?"

Luke ignored him and double clicked the icon.

The parking lot blinked onto the screen in black and white. The footage was clear, but the vantage point was far away. The camera was attached to the building at the far end of the lot.

Luke and Thad watched the gate slide open and a marked cruiser pull into the lot. A shadow darted around the back fence and slipped through the gate before it slammed shut. No one had noticed then. It was painfully obvious now.

The car pulled into a spot in the middle of the lot. The occupants did not immediately get out. They stayed in the car for over four minutes according to the clock in the lower right corner. It read 18:55 when the trunk popped, and the passenger door slammed open.

A woman in uniform got out of the car. A little too fast. Luke wondered if they had fought. She seemed upset as she retrieved a long rifle case and black bag from the trunk then headed into the building at a fast clip.

It was her. Easton's partner. The woman at the funeral standing so far away from everybody.

She grew larger as she approached the door below the camera. The bottom of the screen flashed silver as the door opened and she disappeared inside.

Easton had been driving. He was still in the car on the phone with his wife. They knew that now.

In the top left corner of the screen, Cummings stepped timidly from behind the dumpster and moved toward the cruiser. Easton must have seen him now because the driver door sprang open and he got out, phone still to his ear. Easton ducked his head and tossed the phone on the driver seat, the line still open. They knew that now too. His wife heard the shot that killed her husband.

Easton faced the approaching trespasser with a hand out, but with no particular alarm. Luke noted that Easton didn't even reach for his gun.

Luke watched the junkie for anything that looked like fear. The man's terror seemed real enough when he spoke to Luke. Why else would he take a gun?

Cummings appeared anxious and most likely high, but it never approached what he displayed in the interview room. The man in the parking lot looked more determined than afraid. He looked like a man with a goal. In less than six hours, Nicholas Cummings seemed to have grown a pair.

The men spoke, more like argued, for several moments. What they said was lost forever. The security camera had no audio.

Then the footage showed Cummings trying to go around Easton toward the 'authorized personnel only' entrance where Easton's partner entered the building. Cummings had made no attempt to get in through the main door on the other side of the building.

Easton moved to block him, placing his beefy frame

between Cummings and the building. Cummings tried to push past, pointing urgently at the building.

That's when the suspect pulled out the small black semi-auto. The police report said it was a Lorcin L9, a cheap gun readily available on the street. He clearly had no idea how to handle it. He was jumpy and shuffled his feet as Easton reacted to the sight of the gun. The officer raised his hands and tried to talk the assailant down when Cummings stepped too close.

Easton grabbed the wrist holding the gun and pushed it to the side. The men struggled, locked together as Easton chose to reach for his radio instead of his gun. Luke wasn't the only one that underestimated Nicholas Cummings.

The footage blurred as the action onscreen sped up. Nicholas Cummings was stronger than he looked, common with people high on certain drugs. Luke's stomach hurt as he watched the men locked in combat, the gun somewhere between them.

Then he saw Easton twist. There was no report. Not even a muzzle blast onscreen to indicate the gun had gone off. It was pressed into Easton's torso. His body jerked and both men stopped fighting in an instant.

Easton staggered back and hit the car he had exited moments before. He fell against the vehicle and slid down to the ground, arms limp at his sides.

Cummings staggered back, the gun still pointing at the fallen officer. He looked at the gun in his hand with a stunned look.

A silver blip flashed in the lower right-hand corner of the screen as the door below the camera slammed open. Pete's partner had run from the building.

A few frames later, the woman, Tully Meara, came into view. She moved through the parking lot with quick decisive movements. Crouching while she ran, she used the parked cruisers as cover while she stalked the shooter with her AR-15 rifle at low ready.

Luke watched her kneel for a split second behind a cruiser and admired her ease with the weapon. He saw the flex in her forearm indicating she switched the safety off. A scant movement separating life from death.

Rising from her knee, she stepped into the open, her gun pointed steady at the shooter. He turned to look at her but did not drop his gun.

She didn't hesitate. This time he saw the muzzle flash and the suspect's instant reaction to it. He jerked. Then another flash and he jerked again, and the gun fell from his hand. One last burst and Nicholas Cummings became the late Nicholas Cummings.

Thad turned away from the computer, and Luke heard him sniff as he shuffled through some paper.

Feeling like he wanted to throw up, Luke watched Easton's partner fall to her knees and crawl to him. She didn't try to revive him. She clung to him like a child to a teddy bear. None of the combat effectiveness she displayed survived the sight of her bleeding partner.

A few hours earlier Luke had stood in a drippy cemetery watching her for the first time, soaking wet from the rain in her civilian clothes. Like she was desperately trying to be there but remain separate at the same time. She should have been up front with the family and her fellow officers for support, not in the back. But he knew why she was there.

"I need to talk to her," said Luke.

"Who?" Thad sounded suspicious.

"Easton's partner. Meara."

"Why?"

"What do you mean 'why'?"

"Why do you need to talk to her? We can look into this guy on our own. You don't need to go to the local 5-0 and tell them you think their dead hero is a goddamn assassin. I'm beginning to see why people think you're not right in the head."

"First, I'm going to be doing the talking." Luke glared at Thad. "And two, that's not how I'm going to approach it. She may know more about Cummings."

"Right." Thad didn't bother to hide the sarcasm.

"I don't want to go barging in there any more than you do, but we don't blow off leads when they're unpleasant," Luke said, thinking of the first video. "Every lead gets vetted. I'm not making that mistake again. We'll wait a while, of course. We're not going tomorrow."

Thad opened his mouth to speak but swallowed it. He turned around and said nothing else.

17

Savannah PD Headquarters
July 2nd
1305 Hours

Luke sat at the conference table staring through the glass wall at the CID cubicle field beyond. He wondered which detectives' torrid love affair made this fish tank of a room seem like a good idea.

One look at the faces milling around the cubicles and his smirk disappeared. No one was really working. As ordinary as that is on a normal Friday, the faces of every Savannah PD employee marked this Friday as anything but ordinary.

Almost two weeks had passed, but the sadness was as tangible as the wood table propping up Luke's elbow. Every few minutes, the receptionist dabbed her kohl-rimmed eyes with a Kleenex. Grief smothered the building like a wool blanket in the Georgia summer, the same taunt expression on every face. The dead officer had been well loved.

And in swoops the FBI. Luke steeled himself for his unpleasant task.

The Captain had been accommodating on the phone, but he didn't know the questions they were about to ask. Luke got the distinct feeling his visit would not be well received. The week he'd waited out of respect didn't seem long enough now, judging by the suspicious looks thrown his way.

Thad faced him at the other end of the table tapping away on his laptop. He glanced sideways every few minutes gauging the dirty looks, then went back to his screen.

Luke crossed his arms and met each glare as it came. They all looked away when he didn't. He didn't want to be here any more than they wanted him here, but that didn't matter. What precious few leads he had weren't yielding much, and his most promising lead was dead. He had no choice but to pull on this string. It would hurt a little more this time.

The click made him turn. He rose to his feet as the door swung open. A man in his late fifties entered in full dress uniform and took off his five-point hat. His thick silver hair was combed lightly over the thinning spot on the back of his head. Dark bags under his eyes made him look as tired as he had sounded on the phone.

"Captain Timothy." Luke held out his hand, and the Captain grasped it firmly, nodding.

Captain Timothy turned to introduce the woman following him, wrapping an arm around her shoulders. Luke didn't miss the protective gesture.

"This is Pete's partner, Tully Meara."

Luke's breath snagged in his throat. At the funeral, standing in the rain, she'd looked bedraggled and awkward. Now that he was close, awkward was not what occurred to him. He was sharply aware of her.

She was pretty enough but in another scenario, some random bar scene, he wouldn't have noticed her. Wavy blond hair fell around her face and dark jeans hugged a fit body that looked underfed. The simple blue shirt she wore deepened the blue in her eyes. Like the Captain, she sported dark purple rings under her eyes.

What Luke noticed was the veneer of control that everybody around her, even the Captain, seemed to buy. It was missing in the cemetery. But now, cleaned up and removed from the emotion of a funeral, this woman was trying to act like it didn't bother her and no one seemed to notice.

To Luke, the hard look in her eyes telegraphed desperation, not strength. But then she just buried her best friend. He knew what that felt like. And the unconscious cruelty of grieving people looking to someone as empty and broken as them for strength and hope, he knew what that felt like too.

His eyes lingered on a long scar on her left cheek. It was barely visible but her hair on that side was slung forward and wavier like she was trying to hide that too. It made her seem vulnerable despite her icy bearing.

For the first time since he walked into that seedy Atlanta apartment, Luke felt his resolve falter. He cleared his throat and extended his hand to her.

Her hand inched up as she squinted at him. Then Luke saw the recognition register. She'd seen him at the funeral.

She yanked her hand back and threw her chin up. Stalking to the middle of the table, she made sure to put space between them. When she turned her back, Luke saw the print of a gun in the small of her back beneath her shirt. Her weapon.

She slumped into a chair, studying Thad under hooded lids. Captain Timothy trudged to the other side and sat across from her.

Luke yanked on his already loose tie and took his seat. Tully's pursed lips parted, and she refused to look at him. Luke caught himself staring at her mouth.

He cleared his throat again. "I'm um, I'm Luke Marshall. This is my partner, Special Agent Thaddeus Aulden." He gestured to Thad who gave a quick wave then went back to his laptop. "Thank you both for seeing me. I know this is a difficult time."

The Captain acknowledged him with a tired nod. Tully studied the wall with a stone face.

"I have a few questions related to the shooting last week," Luke said.

Tully broke her silence, her voice dripping with disdain. "Why is the FBI here about a police shooting? It's not federal jurisdiction. The FBI has no reason to be here." She made a show of addressing Captain Timothy, not him.

"I'm afraid I do," answered Luke keeping his voice even. "But I'm not here about the shooting exactly. I'm here about the suspect, Nicholas Cummings."

Tully drew her shoulders back and dropped her chin but said nothing. She still hadn't looked at him. He pushed ahead. "Do you know why he was here that day?"

"No." She finally focused a chilly stare on him.

"Any guesses?"

"Well, he brought a gun. I dunno, maybe that's a clue."

Luke ignored her sarcastic dig. "Does he come to the station a lot?"

Tully smirked. "Not unless he's in handcuffs."

"So, you do know him."

Tully took a deep breath and swiveled her chair around to face him. She leaned back and crossed her legs, resting her left arm on the table. Luke saw her eyes flick over him as she sized him up.

"Everybody knows Nick Cummings, Special Agent Marshall." Her eyes flicked back to his face. "Everybody."

"Tell me about him."

"A low-level drug dealer. His own best customer, if you know what I mean."

"Did your partner know him?"

She leaned forward and jammed her index finger into the wood. "You find me an officer in this town who doesn't know Nol Prosse Nick, and I'll give you a million dollars. He gave new meaning to the term frequent flyer."

"When did you see him last?"

"You mean before I killed him?"

Luke couldn't stop a smile. "Yeah."

"It's been a while," she said, drumming her fingers on the table.

"Did you ever arrest him?"

Her eyes fluttered shut and her neck contracted as she swallowed hard. "Are we gonna play verbal ping pong all day? Or are you gonna start asking the questions you came to ask?"

She didn't play around, and he liked it. Time to rip it off. "Nicholas Cummings came to me last week. He said he had information about a case I'm working. A possible murder."

A derisive laugh came from Tully. "Well, that's unfortunate."

The Captain threw her a reproachful look as Luke's eyes narrowed.

"Why is that?"

"What the hell is a 'possible murder'?"

"Why is it unfortunate?" Luke prompted her.

"Nick Cummings, as an informant, is not the most reliable source of information. And that's being kind. He's tried to sign on as a paid CI in five," she wiggled the fingers of one hand for emphasis, "local jurisdictions including this one. Nobody will work with him because he's unreliable on a good day. Every other day he's a pathological liar. Ask any of our vice guys, they all know him too. Let me guess. He asked for money? Relocation?"

Thad and Luke looked at each other. She saw it.

"He'll say anything you want to hear if it pays for his next hit."

Luke pushed ahead. "How well did you know your partner, Peter Easton?"

Tully's chest rose sharply. When she spoke, it was through gritted teeth. "We worked together for six years. He's my best friend."

"Security footage shows...."

"I've seen it," she interrupted him, but he wasn't giving up the floor. She was getting agitated and out of habit he pounced.

"Then you saw them talk for over a minute and a half before Nicholas pulled out his gun. They seemed to know each other. Their discussion seemed a little...heated."

She flushed. As the blood rushed to her face, the scar stood out; a silvery pink line cutting through her red cheek. "They did know each other. Anything else I need to repeat?"

"It's hard to deny that it looks like he came looking for something or someone. He tried to get inside, and he seemed intent on something."

"Yeah. Killing a cop. I'd say he accomplished it."

His calm was agitating her, so he lowered his voice even more. "It didn't start out as a fight."

"The fuck?" She was yelling now. "Did you watch the whole tape or just what was convenient for your little theory?"

"What theory?"

"Do you think I'm stupid?" Her voice dropped to a whisper.

"What were they talking about?"

"I. Don't. Know. But in my line of work, if somebody

brings a gun to a police station, he ain't here fer the donuts," she spat out. "Who he fixated on probably wasn't even here. It doesn't matter. Pete was the only person in the parking lot. If he came here to kill the Chief, he would have run into Pete first."

"Shooting a random cop seems like a little bit of a stretch with his history. Cummings doesn't have any violent crime on his sheet."

Luke watched, impressed, as she mastered herself. The red in her face drained and she turned icy again. Her eyes seemed to darken as she grew angrier, but when she spoke her voice was low and even. "It sounds an awful lot like you're callin my dead partner bent."

"No, I'm not," said Luke. "What I am saying is that Nicholas came to me with information that, by all accounts, he shouldn't have. He was afraid he would die, and now he's dead." He leaned in, "Go on, you tell me why."

Tully seethed in her seat. Suddenly her fist crashed down, rattling the table. "Pete's body is barely cold, and you come in here dragging his name through the mud based on the word of a strung-out dope dealer?"

She was shouting again. He'd pushed the right buttons. The veneer was cracking. Paper rustled behind her, but she was so focused on Luke she'd forgotten about the other agent in the room.

Thad muttered under his breath, "He's just asking some questions."

Luke tensed as he saw her face contort. She shoved her chair back and whipped around to face him.

Thaddeus registered shock as he saw her advancing on him with her right hand cocked back. He scrambled to his feet sending paper flying.

It took Luke a split second to realize what was happening and rise from his chair. Two swift strides brought him up behind her. In one smooth motion, he grabbed her coiled arm with his left hand and spun her around.

Her eyes looked nearly black now. They rounded with surprise when he forced her face to face. If he thought his iron grip would take the fight out of her, he quickly found out he was wrong. She just switched targets.

Her hair whipped out as she whirled. Without hesitating, she yanked her wrist back pulling his hand to her chest. Then she dropped low trying to throw him off balance. In a flash, she straightened, and her free elbow came up and around, aiming for his jaw.

Luke snapped his head back barely avoiding a direct blow. Her elbow grazed his chin. Enraged, she grabbed his thumb circling her wrist and yanked back, almost breaking his grip.

She was quicker than he anticipated. Luke barely got his other hand up and around the arm trying to knock him out. He forced her arms up over her head, taking away her leverage against his superior strength. Furious, she gave a guttural growl and tried to break free. He pushed her backward, using her own tactic of throwing her quarry off center, but her foot slammed into his instep and tripped him.

Momentum sent them reeling into the clear wall behind them. When Tully's back hit, Luke heard the ping of metal from her off-duty weapon slamming against the plate glass, fracturing it. The ear-splitting crack sent heads popping up above cubicle walls.

Tully gasped in pain but threw a knee at his crotch. He kicked it to the side and pushed his body against hers pinning her to the glass. Her chest heaved against his.

His warm breath hit her temple, and he caught the faint smell of sweet gardenia and spice he couldn't identify. The urge to brush his lips down her neck barged into his head.

Instead, he placed his cheek next to her ear and whispered. "Calm down, Tully."

Once he took away her leverage, it was easy to overpower her; he was a hundred pounds heavier. Still, she bucked at the sound of her name. Her effort only succeeded in rattling the glass.

"Tully." The Captain's stunned voice behind them made her body relax in his arms. She stopped fighting and Luke released her. She shoved him away and stood shaking with her fists clenched, glaring at him.

"My partner's right, that's all we're here for. Not to accuse anyone." Luke rolled his shoulders to straighten his suit. His voice was gentle, but his sparring mate flinched at the sound.

Considering the hell she went through last week, he shouldn't have pushed so hard. He thought about putting his hand on her shoulder, but he thought it would start another fight.

"Then depose me," Tully whispered. Her gaze now hovered on Thad who stiffened. She ripped it back to Luke. "Because this conversation is over."

Her shoulders slumped. She moved to the door giving the Captain a tormented look. With her hand on the knob, she paused.

"You want to know why your star witness is dead?" She looked at Luke. "Because that's what happens when you kill a cop."

The door slammed open and she strode past their speechless audience.

18

———

FBI Satellite Office
July 2nd
1558 Hours Local Time

Thirty minutes later Luke slumped into his chair and raked his hands through his hair. His head was whirring with questions that had nothing to do with his case. What the hell just happened?

Thad immediately sat down and began tapping on his phone screen. He stayed mercifully quiet on the ride back from the station. Maybe he was finally figuring out when to keep his cavity shut.

Luke propped his feet up on his desk and focused on the wall trying to sort out his tangled thoughts. The dull thump of a phone case on Formica interrupted him. He looked over.

Thad tapped the corner of his phone on the desk. "So that went well," he said when he caught Luke's eye.

Luke stood up so fast his chair flew into Thad's. "I'll be back."

He could only assume Thad wanted to talk about it, but

he couldn't do it. Not right now. He needed to think, not talk. He would hate to have stopped Meara from punching Thad senseless, only to do it himself. It was best for everyone, and Thad's nose, if he left.

Thad gaped after him as he hurried out without another word. Luke took a left out of the front door away from noisy Bull Street.

The square he'd seen for weeks from his window lay a block ahead. He made for it walking fast. The sun had finally come out, but it was cooler than the first weeks he'd spent there. A soft breeze fanned him, and he suddenly felt friendlier toward the old city. When she wasn't trying to boil him like a crab, she was a pleasant place.

The marbled shade of the square felt even cooler. Most of the park benches under the sprawling oaks were occupied by men and women in business attire, the last of the lunch crowd. The rest were occupied by camera toting tourists.

Sitting wasn't what Luke had in mind. He stayed on the brick path that cut through the square. He needed to move.

Their visit to the station went as he expected. Except for the cage match. He didn't see that one coming. Or her.

He smiled as he thought about her gunning for Thad. Luke knew no less than ten people, mostly women, who would love to fatten Thad's lip, but she was the only one who actually tried. The look on the kid's face was priceless.

Her scent wafted into his mind. He wondered if the rest of her was as soft as her cheek and tripped over a root pushing up the sidewalk. He looked up.

To the left and right grand old row homes flanked the tree-lined street, double staircases curling down to the sidewalk. Luke turned right and walked, drawn by their nostalgic beauty.

Soon he came to another square, this one with a

gurgling fountain in the middle. Again, every bench was dappled with sunlight and filled with people. Luke slowed to look.

Bells from a church on the other side of the square chimed the quarter-hour, and a street performer broke off his out of tune flute solo. As soon as the bells died down, the man started his halting version of Twinkle Twinkle Little Star again. Luke chuckled as he made his way through the square. Then he spotted a bar.

He ducked inside and ordered a beer to go, silently thanking the old city for her liberal public drinking laws. As soon as he went inside, he decided he was going to do some drunk sightseeing. It was a beautiful Friday and this place had caught his attention.

A tattooed redhead behind the bar eyed his business attire and returned his smile. Minutes later he emerged with a plastic cup of stout. He preferred something stronger, but historically bad decisions followed whiskey, so he stuck to beer.

He made it through two more squares before his beer ran dry. He detoured to another bar, then continued his aimless wandering with a fresh cup. No matter which way he turned, he found another city square. This place had more than her fair share of beautiful parks.

They called Savannah 'the beautiful woman with a dirty face'. That seemed unfair. With every passing step, and sip, he was more offended for the old gal. He liked her hair down, partying ways.

This place was a contradiction at every intersection. Grand mansions stood next to trash-filled alleys. Majestic oaks older than the nation graced trailer parks outside of town. Everywhere he looked, Luke saw hard reckless defiance that rendered labels meaningless. The city defied any classification put to her. She was what she was, damn what anyone thought.

Luke's phone buzzed as his third beer ran dry. It was Thad.

"Yeah."

"Are you comin back?"

"What do you want?" Luke tipped the cup to get the last drop.

"Whoa. Easy. Remember how I was gonna drive to Atlanta tonight? For the long weekend?"

"Yeah, your hot date."

"Well she's not that hot, but it is a date. But I'll stay if you need me. It's not a big de…"

"Get outta here," Luke cut him off. "We'll pick it up on Tuesday. Happy Fourth."

"It's only two."

"Beat it. You're gonna hit traffic anyway."

"Word. See you Monday." The phone went dead.

Luke envied his partner. Thad recovered easily from nearly being walloped by a girl and bounced right back to his irritating norm. Luke's head, on the other hand, had been scrambled by a pair of blue eyes. Right now his thoughts were pinging around like a busted pinball machine, and the curve of her neck was driving him insane. He should never have gotten so close to her. Luke tossed his cup in a trash can and started looking for another pub.

Three hours and four beers later, Luke found himself on Bay Street without knowing how he got there. He crossed the busy avenue and followed it until he spotted a stone staircase beside an old cotton merchant building; one of many that lined Bay Street. He took the stairs.

At the bottom, an uneven ballast stone nearly caused him to roll his ankle as he walked between the buildings to River Street. He decided the stairs were a good choice as he looked out on the Savannah River and Hutchinson Island. In the distance, Talmadge Bridge spiked into the blue sky. Luke took a deep breath and stood for a moment, enjoying the sight.

River Street cut left and right, lined on one side with the backside of the merchant buildings, and water on the other. Unlike their fancy facades on Bay Street, the basement floors were made from rough brick and hand-hewn timbers. The wide arching doors once gave easy access to ware-houses filled with cotton, tobacco, and other plantation exports. These days they held shops, restaurants, and expensive loft apartments. To his right, Luke saw crowds of tourists milling around stands selling cheap souvenirs. He turned left.

The buildings on this end hadn't been restored to the same extent. It had a seedier feel that made him feel more at ease. Even the street hadn't been fully uncovered. Stone wove in and out of pitted blacktop.

Luke had a vague plan to circle around and get back out to the main part of the city. River Street wasn't all that inter-esting except for the view, and he still had over half the squares to hit. Although he wasn't sure how many more he'd see if he kept drinking at this rate.

He thought about driving back to Atlanta in the morn-ing. He'd been away for a while and things at home could use some attention. None of it seemed important at that moment, and an empty apartment sounded like torture, so he decided to stay. This place was better than the ATL, and there had to be some single women somewhere in this city.

Ahead, past a bank of windows with seeded glass, an alley cut into the bowels of the building. A dim gas lantern flickered at the end and Luke saw a sandwich board with the pub name worn off. It had one happy hour special written in unreadable chalk scrawl. The rest of the squares would have to wait, he decided as he headed in.

Inside Luke felt the sweat on his forehead dry. The heavy walled, low ceilinged room stayed comfortable despite the windows flung open to the warm day. A breeze off the water blended with slow ceiling fans making it feel cool despite the lack of AC. The late afternoon sun blazed off the water, but in here it was dark and cool. His kind of place.

His eyes hadn't yet adjusted by the time he made it to the bar. He took a seat on the far end so the door was in view. Out of habit, he studied the clientele. Three people sat at the bar and two booths were occupied. It was a quarter past five and the place wasn't busy yet.

Behind the scuffed bar, a white-haired man in a tacky Hawaiian shirt and apron talked to a woman sitting in the middle of the bar. She hunched over a glass staring into it. It took a moment before the old barkeep sauntered over to him.

"What can I get ya," he asked with a thick Irish accent that caught Luke off guard.

"Ah. A beer, please. Whatever you've got that's dark."

The old man nodded. Then Luke changed his mind. He felt like he'd made friends with the old city today, so he decided to tear a page out of her playbook and let it all hang out. "You know what? Fuck it. Give me a whiskey."

"Haha, good lad," grunted the old man, pleased at the change of order.

By now Luke's vision had adjusted to the darkness. He saw the woman look up from her glass. He glanced at her and did a double-take. There was no mistaking the blond hair covering the side of her face like she was trying to hide behind it.

Meara sat at the center of the long bar paying no attention to two male patrons eyeing her from their end. She wore the same clothes he'd seen her in at the station and her shoulders were bowed low.

"Tully Meara."

When he spoke, her head jerked up and snapped in his direction. In the dim light, it looked like fear on her face.

That was his fault. What was he thinking when he went there? He should listen to Thad more often. The kid had good instincts. Not that either of them could have predicted her. Seeing her sit there slumped over made him feel especially bad. He wanted to make it right.

Luke saw a muscle twitch in her neck. She swung her knees away desperate to turn her back. Southern breeding prevented her from being too rude, and she ended up looking straight ahead. He slid off his stool and approached her.

"Of all the gin joints, right?" He sat and smiled hoping it would have the effect it usually had on women.

"Thfuck do you want?" She rounded on him.

So much for southern breeding.

"Are you following me?"

"No, I...."

"Why are you here?" She demanded, swiveling her seat so she could get in his face.

"I saw you and, um, I just wanted to make sure I didn't... You're not hurt are you?"

"You come to my station and accuse my dead partner of being crooked, and you're worried about hurting me? That's what's keeping you up at night?" She slurred her words a little. He opened his mouth to speak, but she didn't let him. "Save your apology."

"I'm not apologizing."

She glared at him.

"Not for that, anyway. You were about to punch a federal

agent for god's sake. Did you think I was going to let you? I wanted to make sure you're not hurt."

"Fuck off."

"I'll take that as a no. And you're wrong, Tully." He watched the muscle spasm again when he said her name. "I wasn't accusing your partner of...anything."

He nearly said, "accuse your partner of murder," because he was buzzing, and his mind couldn't keep up with his mouth.

"But I should have handled it differently," he admitted. "For that I am sorry. I get carried away sometimes. Bad habit. I knew Cummings was a scumbag, but I should have been a little more...."

"Yeah. Yeah, you should have," she said, locking those brilliant blue eyes onto him.

The second he met her it was clear she wasn't capable of halfway, even when she wasn't punching someone. But the quiet pub and peaceful river backlit the chaotic passion oozing from every word. At her angry outburst, the men eyeing her suddenly became interested in their beer.

Luke wanted more. "Please believe me, the last thing I would do is smear a fellow law enforcement officer without concrete evidence," he said.

"I should hope so." She turned back to her drink.

"My partner was right. We were just there to get some questions answered. It was me that got carried away. I overplayed it. If you still need to pummel someone it should be me."

"Overplayed? Is that what you were doing?" The apology must have worked. Her anger had subsided. Now she sounded annoyed.

She cupped her glass with both hands. "It doesn't matter. Everybody's moved on anyway. People barely remember that a cop died two weeks ago. They're all back to their comfortable lives. You showing up is…."

"People care more than you think," he cut her off softly, placing a hand on the back of her stool.

A stiff gust of wind whipped through the windows and flipped her hair. A strand snagged on her eyelash. Luke's hand twitched as he stopped himself from brushing it back.

The old bartender had been hovering nearby watching the two of them. His demeanor toward Luke became much cooler after Tully's initial reaction. He slammed down an empty glass in front of Luke but didn't fill it. Luke was sure he was about to get kicked out when Tully called him off.

"It's okay, Only."

"Sure, Love?" The old man eyed Luke up and down like he could take him.

"Yeah. I'm fine."

"Alright, Love." With a withering glare, Only poured Luke's glass half full of Jack Daniels and shoved it forward.

Luke picked it up, hoisted it in the air to thank him, then downed it. The burn felt good.

He turned back to Tully. "I swear I didn't know this was your watering hole. I happened to run across it."

"Right. Look, I don't know if I should even be talking to you."

"Oh, we definitely shouldn't be talking." He grinned at her and this time it worked. She parted with a tiny smile. "Can I buy your next one?"

She thought for a second. "That's a bad idea."

"God, I love those." He motioned for a refill. "What are you drinking?"

"Same." She indicated his glass.

"Two then," he said as the old man scowled, but refilled their glasses.

Luke twirled the brown liquid so it coated his glass in

dripping ribbons. "Listen, I really am sorry about earlier. That...whole thing was messed up and it was my fault. I can never seem to get what I want without being a jerk."

He meant to make her laugh. Instead, the tortured look on her face grew. Suddenly she remembered the glass in her hand. She put it to her lips and Luke watched her kill it in a single gulp.

"Wow. You should probably slow down. You're kinda small to be throwing that much liquor back."

"I can drink you under this bar, G-man."

Luke raised an eyebrow. "I believe it."

She slammed the glass down. "So, what do you want?"

"I wanted to see...."

"No. What do you want? Why did you come over here?"

Luke studied her face without answering. She could handle herself in a fight, that was abundantly clear. Even she could tell he wasn't worried that he hurt her. He just didn't know what else to say.

"He was a good man." Tully's look was pleading.

He nodded so she would keep talking.

"I've never met a better officer or family man." She blinked and the strand fluttered. Luke's hand twitched again.

"They just had a baby, you know. He and Melissa were married for six years, and they tried to have Katy for five." She gave a little laugh and hiccupped. "I couldn't get him to sit still for a week after they found out."

Luke turned away and focused on the rows of bottles behind the bar. The timing of the shooting was too perfect to be a coincidence, but he didn't have the courage to say it to her face. That the man she respected so much was probably involved in some very bad things. She wanted to hear him say that he believed her partner had been nothing but the upstanding man everyone thought he was.

It was the look. He'd seen that look from friends and families of the men he'd put away, the day they learned betrayal doesn't come from a stranger. She never saw it coming. Good people who love bad men rarely do. The agony on her face in that conference room cut deep.

Now he endured it a second time, inches away listening to her talk about her partner. The pain mimicked her soft southern accent, stretching and wrapping itself around each slow vowel. Only appeared and their drinks refilled. Like any bartender worth his salt, the old man was a firm believer in liquid therapy.

Luke wanted to say that this whole thing was screwed up, and he was sorry he made her sad, and would she come home with him. "I'm sorry," was all that came out.

She said nothing, and Luke shook his head. "Why would he go to the station after he came to me and claimed he's afraid for his life? And with a gun. It doesn't make sense. Is he known to carry one?"

Tully shook her head.

"And the camera footage...." He saw her stiffen. "He was looking for someone. Maybe it was bad timing," he finished.

"You know," she twisted her fingers together, "if you showed up and asked me about anyone else in this town, you would have me wondering too. But not Pete." She shook her head again. "Not him."

"Do you think Cummings really had anything?"

"Maybe. Or more likely he was spinnin' a yarn. He knew how the public snaps to when people start spouting off at the mouth. Nobody can resist a crooked cop theory. He knew it well. That shit sells."

Luke leaned back. "He never mentioned a cop. We never would have met if your partner was still alive."

She looked at him, surprise on her face. Then she shook it off.

"Trust me, you'll find a dead Nick Cummings works out for the best. It's a defense attorney's wet dream to see someone like him on a witness roster. Any case you cobble together on his back is over before the prelim, my friend."

"Of course it is," said Luke as he rubbed his face. Like everything else in this dead end he called an investigation. At least it wasn't a total loss. Her anger was subsiding at the same rate she threw back whiskey. The fact that she wasn't yelling felt like a victory.

He dropped his hands when he realized she was studying him. "Where does this leave us?"

She smirked. "Us? I think you mean 'where does this leave you'. And with Nick Cummings as a lead, it leaves you with precisely dick."

The strand of hair had worked its way loose from her eyelash and rested on her cheek. Luke surrendered and brushed her hair behind her ear. "That's not what I meant."

She flinched and a hand flew to her scarred cheek. Flustered she dug her hair out from behind her ear and smoothed it back over her cheek. "What?"

"You forgive me?"

She wouldn't meet his eyes.

"Tully, I...."

She turned back to her glass. "I'm not gonna be your little snitch, G-man. Pete was my friend, and he was a good man. Don't insult me." She slurred more now.

That's not what he'd been thinking. Not even close. He was thinking about the way her lips parted when she was mad like she needed more oxygen to fuel the fire. He was thinking about taking her clothes off and feeling her hot skin next to his. He was thinking about how much he didn't want to be alone.

"No. That's not...," Luke stopped. He was already at three whiskeys, the point his judgment usually took a detour to

Shitsville. Taking her back to his hotel was a terrible idea. Especially when she was drunker than him.

"Not what?" Her eyes bore into him, cloudy but still accusing. "Not why you came here? Why are you here then?"

He needed to get a handle on this. "I should go," said Luke realizing the glass he emptied was full again. He swallowed it and reached for his wallet. "You were right. This is a bad idea."

"No." She grabbed his hand. "You can't come in here then just leave. You have to tell me what's going on." In her drunken state, she twisted too hard and made him wince, but she didn't notice.

"It's a routine investigation."

"Bullshit," she said, a little too loud. "Why are you asking about Pete. Why?" That familiar passion radiated. Or was it desperation? She leaned in, twisting his arm further. "What do you know?"

"Ow," he said, trying to right his arm.

"Sorry." She released him but continued to lean in. "What do you know?"

All she needed to do was lean in another inch to make him tell her everything. A hint of cleavage peeked out from her V-neck, and she was so close he could hear every rustle of her clothing. Luke turned to the bar to put some space between them. "Nothing," he said, defeated. It wasn't a lie.

It seemed to satisfy her. "You're wrong, you know. You're so wrong."

Luke gave a noncommittal nod and waived off Only, who was about to refill the glasses. "I think maybe we should switch to beer, huh? Something a little lighter?"

Tully pulled a face but didn't argue.

The whiskey did its job, and the conversation became easier. Luke told her about Atlanta and the blackmail scam.

He left out the part about the murdered reporter, the soldiers, and the hitman. He wasn't ready to tell her that. The night was going too well. As they talked, darkness gathered, and the pub began to fill up with its usual night crowd.

A car sped down River Street too fast. It seemed to jerk Tully back to the present. She looked out the window at the dark street, then around the bustling bar in surprise. She checked her watch. "It's ten?"

"So?"

"We've been here for five hours?"

"You have somewhere to be?"

"Um, n...yeah." She started digging through her pockets.

"I got it." Luke cut her off and slapped a hundred down on the bar.

She staggered a little as she slid off her stool. He reached for her, but she had already righted herself. Luke was impressed. As much alcohol as she consumed, she should be on the floor.

"Bye, Only. I'm going home," she called to the old man. He was at the far end of the bar.

"Lemme call ya cab, Love." He reached for the phone sitting next to the polaroids of people banned from the pub.

"I'm good." She blew him a drunken kiss.

"I'll make sure she gets home," Luke told the Irishman who scowled.

Luke wrapped his arm around Tully's waist, returning the glare. They walked out the door. Only turned and picked up the phone anyway.

"I don't neejour help," Tully slurred and yanked herself out of Luke's embrace once they were outside. To avoid a scene, she waited until they left to push him away.

Luke smiled. She was nicer drunk than sober. "I bet you don't," he said.

"Duz that mean?"

"You make this trip a lot in this condition?"

"Fuck you, Marshall. You think you can jusshow up in my town and start judging everyone. And I'm s'posed to be fine with it because you're...," she stopped as he looked down at her and gave her a little smirk. "FBI," she finished lamely, then burped.

Like him, over the past several hours she had a hard time hiding her interest. She would realize she was staring only after he caught her, then look away pretending she was interested in something else. She got worse at it the more she drank.

Tully whirled and walked toward the steps to Bay Street. She went first, hanging on to the handrail to help herself up. Behind her, Luke didn't have to hide that he was admiring her well-formed ass ripple in tight jeans. Luke forgot everything but the scent of her perfume, he was so tuned in to her. He swallowed hard as the carnal thoughts barged into his mind again.

At the top, she turned right, and they crossed over Bay Street at the next light. Her pace quickened, and it was obvious she knew where she was going. Maybe she would decide for both of them and take him home. He wasn't sure, and she said nothing so he kept following.

Soon they crossed a quiet street and the largest park, Forsythe Park, spread out in front of them. Ahead he could see the centerpiece fountain of Forsythe Park. The circular path around the fountain was lined with benches. Only two were occupied.

Tully walked up to the wrought iron fence around the fountain and propped her elbows on it. Her movements were fluid and natural like she stopped there all the time. Probably a habit on her way home drunk from the bar. Luke stood beside her feeling the cool spray on his face.

She lowered her head. "Why is this happening? This

can't be happening." She said it so softly he nearly missed it over the rushing water.

Then it hit him. It felt like someone doused him in cold water. She wasn't thinking about sleeping with him. She was thinking about his boneheaded questions and her partner. He wasn't going to argue with her drunk. He wasn't going to argue with her at all.

Luke put a hand on her arm. When she didn't fight, Luke reached around and gently turned her to face him. Either he moved in or pulled her too far because suddenly they were closer than he meant.

Tully pulled away so their bodies didn't touch, and she refused to look at him.

Luke placed his hand under her jaw to lift her face when a door slammed nearby.

A gigantic man with a bald head and dark skin emerged from an illegally parked truck on Drayton Street. "Tull? Tully, where are you?"

At the sound of her name, Tully pushed Luke away. The man left the truck running and bore down on them fast for someone that big.

"Tull, are you alright?" He approached Tully and sized up Luke. "Only called me. He said you were acting funny."

"I'm fine, Jules."

"Come on. I'll give you a ride home." He said it looking at Luke.

The two men squared to each other.

"No, Jules. I'm two blocks away. I'm okay."

"All the same. C'mon, Tull." Jules placed his bulk between the two of them and slung his arm around Tully's shoulders. "You're drunk and walking around with strangers. You're not fine." He glared at Luke.

Luke took a step back, chastised. He'd started feeling protective of this woman he barely knew. But his fleeting notion of protecting her from some unsavory truth withered next to that of a close friend protecting her without the ulterior motive of getting her into bed.

He watched as they walked to the beat-up Dodge. Jules helped her in and slammed the door shut. As he walked to the other side, Tully gave Luke a sad look from the safety of the cab.

Luke turned and walked into the shadows of Forsythe Park without waiting for them to drive away.

19

—————

July 3rd
0412 Hours

Luke reached out to the nightstand. The light spiked into his eyes, and he slammed them shut. Squinting, Luke read 4:12 AM on his phone. Once the alcohol wore off, sleep became dodgy. He rolled over and kicked off the covers that had tangled around him as he tossed in bed.

He went to the sink for a glass of water, then lay back down. After another twenty minutes of racing thoughts, he gave up and slung his legs over the edge of the bed. He tried to rest his face in his hands, but his back was so tight that pain spiked up his neck. Instead, he stood to stretch, then began to pace.

Before long, he pulled on wind pants and a wrinkled t-shirt. If he wasn't sleeping, it made no sense to stay in his dismal, sterile hotel room. He could pace at the office and get some work done.

Luke slipped on his sneakers without tying them and grabbed a tattered leather briefcase. It held every document he and Thad had deemed sensitive. Anything they wanted to keep from Greg went in the briefcase and back to the hotel each night. A discouragingly small amount of paperwork.

He took the stairs three at a time and pushed the door open into a warm Lowcountry night. Even a party town like Savannah had settled down by this late hour. Or early hour. The traffic on Bay Street had dwindled to nothing but an occasional taxi. The streets took on an eerie feel. Without cars whizzing around, the city had a different aura. Street lamps were the only technology competing with the ghosts.

Luke walked two blocks to the office entrance and swiped his card key. Productivity was looking good for the day. No one else would show up to work on a Saturday morning. Greg would be golfing, and Thad was in Atlanta. The rest of them didn't matter. With the exception of Susie, they hardly talked to him anyway. Given the choice between Luke and Thad, people usually talked to Thad.

The scanner beeped again and the door by Susie's desk clicked open. Luke left the hallway lights off and walked to the break room. He flipped on the light and put his bag down long enough to start a pot of strong coffee. Then he continued to the broom closet.

Leaving the office door open, he threw his bag on Thad's chair and sat down in his. He closed his eyes listening to the whoosh of the air conditioner and the whir of the computer booting up. For a moment it was soothing. Until it wasn't. He usually liked the quiet, but this was a little too quiet. Thoughts get louder when nothing drowns them out.

The fact that she bothered him so much irked him. She was nothing special. There were plenty of other women to occupy his time. More beautiful and successful than Tully Meara. He never had a hard time finding a date, but there was never a woman he couldn't forget.

That woman clung to his train of thought like moss to a

river rock. Every useful thought was interrupted by one of her.

"Shit," he said out loud, needing to say something, anything. He stood and stretched, then went to the break room. He came back with a full mug of steaming black coffee and put on some old school blues to drown out the distracting thoughts.

From the bag, he pulled out a stack of manila file folders. He pulled his own working folders from the bottom. One contained a spreadsheet with five years' worth of cataloged phone calls between John Cade and a collection of friends.

It was a who's who of businessmen, lobbyists, and politicians. Saying John Cade could sniff out power players was like saying Pele could kick a soccer ball. Cade knew his business, and he knew it well. And his business was not saving the environment.

Except for a hand full of celebrities, the entire list had one thing in common. They preferred to stay low key. Powerful elite that shook hands and steered the world from behind closed doors. The most influential centers of government and commerce were represented. New York and Washington, although LA had a fair representation as did the South.

Congressman Jonathan Noble had recently been appointed to chair the Ways and Means committee. Senator Raymond Schiatta was favored to win the upcoming mayoral election in NYC. A 9th Circuit Court judge, three Fortune 500 CEOs, and a musician not famous enough for Luke to recognize him without Google's help, but popular nonetheless. Cade didn't swim in the shallow end.

Luke clicked through a few more pictures and saw Cade with President Obama at a fundraiser. A few pictures later he stood smiling with Henry Onessa, a man many saw occupying the White House in a few short years.

Gala after gala, Cade and his wife walked the red carpet with the biggest names in business, industry, and entertainment. Pictures of him with politicians were not as readily available online. But the phone numbers in Luke's folder left no doubt they existed somewhere.

Luke imagined the walls of Cade's luxurious riverside home filled with pictures of him in expensive hunting gear, posing next to the more discreet on the list. All of them tolerating his sycophantic fawning because he could deliver whatever unsavory request they had.

Which meant something illicit. Rich, powerful people had staff to cater to their every whim. Cade delivered something that they couldn't have their yes-men do. Anything is for sale if the right price is on the table. John Cade just brought the table.

"You need something, you go see John," Luke muttered to himself.

Cade's time in Istanbul had been his start. He must have discovered his talent for connections and decided to make some money. The culture of secrecy in the good ol' boys club worked for Cade, and he exploited it. Luke felt a flicker of respect for the man. There was no way he was as dumb as Luke thought. Cade was deliberate and careful.

Respect was soon replaced by repulsion when he thought about Twomey. Lucrative government contracts and political favor were one thing. A politician killed by opposing interests, by a hitman so professional the cops didn't look twice, was something else entirely. Covering up the murder of soldiers, that was unforgivable. Luke vowed he would burn for it.

Luke crossed off the celebrities and musicians. This case

had a distinctly political feel to it. Satisfying illegal sexual desires or befuddling the IRS didn't seem like the right place to spend his time. The CEOs and judges would bear a look, but it wouldn't take much to eliminate them. Shocking secrets were never buried that deep. Just ignored.

They all had deep pockets. Every pocket Cade was in was deep. Very deep to pay for his well curated connections, but Luke wasn't interested in the pockets. Luke wanted the provider. The other side of the penny. He pulled out a highlighter and turned to page 12 of 204. It was going to be like drilling and blasting inch by inch, but that's how he would find them.

Thad had imported his fragmented, emailed document into an electronic spreadsheet. Then he had attempted to teach Luke how to use the spreadsheet. After Luke made the lines go all squiffy one time, he printed it out and went old school highlighter on it. He'd pay more attention next time Thad tried to teach him technology.

An hour later, Luke's coffee was cold, and the lines of numbers and names kept going fuzzy. He began to regret his decision to come to work. While he was tossing and turning, work sounded like a relief. Now that he was doing this mind-numbing work, tossing and turning sounded nice. At least then he could think about her without distraction.

He decided he'd give it one more cup of coffee before he quit. See if he could clear his head enough to keep going. Come morning, he would be exhausted, but he had nothing better to do than sleep all day. Then he'd be ready for another night of drinking in his new favorite party town. The July 4th weekend scene would be lively.

Luke reached for his mug. In his sleepy haze, he misjudged the distance and knocked it over. Brown liquid shot across the file folders, pooling on the paper.

He cursed and jumped up. He grabbed the folders by the spine to shake the coffee off onto the carpet. In his haste to save them, a clump of papers flew out of a folder and scattered across the floor.

He ripped open Thad's top drawer and pulled out the take-out napkin stash. It wasn't the first mess they'd made in the broom closet. With the napkins, he sopped up enough of the coffee to run to the break room for real paper towels and a spray bottle to clean up.

Ten minutes later the office still smelled strongly of coffee, but he had the mess in the garbage can. Luke knelt to retrieve the papers he'd dumped on the floor. They were from one of Thad's folders, and Luke didn't remember seeing them before. He flipped through.

They were police reports. Different formats indicated they were from different jurisdictions, but the information on the front of each report was similar. Victim blocks, suspect blocks, addresses, dates, and all the basic information. He pulled one out and looked at it.

It was an incident report for an unattended death ruled a suicide by the medical examiner. Luke pulled another out. Suicide. Another, overdose.

Son of bitch. The kid had actually been working. Luke shook his head and smiled. Here he thought the kid was flirting with Susie all the time, but he was actually pulling in cases for them to review. Luke decided to tell Thad he'd done a good job when he got back. Not directly. The kid would never shut up about it.

Luke counted the stapled bundles. There were thirteen. He had no idea how far Thad had gotten in his queries, but the fact that any jurisdictions had sent reports was heartening.

That reminded him. He opened his email and pulled up

the incident report Sandra had sent and hit print. He'd forgotten all about it. It went on top of Thad's pile, then Luke went to refill his mug. His cross-eyed highlighter orgy was about to take a different direction.

When he sat back down, he pulled out a fresh legal pad. Carefully avoiding his mug, he pushed everything to the side except the stack of police incident reports and the legal pad.

None of the police reports, including Sandra's, seemed interesting. Nothing notable stood out and the investigations appeared to be well conducted and written out in detail, per typical agency policy. Nothing to see here. But nothing was what he'd expected to see.

In the left-hand margin of the legal pad, he wrote a column with every report date. Fourteen cases spanning a period of roughly ten years. He highlighted everything within the last five years. That trimmed it to nine cases.

Luke turned to his screen, hesitated, then clicked on the 'date' column. He pumped his fist when the spreadsheet cooperated and ordered itself by date newest to oldest. He could narrow his search quickly now.

Energized, he flipped a page and wrote the date of the senator's untimely demise at the top. The second date also got its own page. Soon he had nine pages with a single date at the top. Luke randomly decided to look at a three-month window on each side of the police report dates. Every name called within that range went on the page, except for the numbers Luke knew by heart now. Like Cade's wife and his lawyer.

He started with Twomey. Luke flipped back to the first page and scrolled down to his preselected date range. Luke felt confident that after Twomey sent a blackmail threat along with whatever 'proof' he had, any professional hit would have been carried out with relative quickness.

Assuming Cade used his phone to communicate that is. If they met in person, maybe travel related credit card charges would yield some information, but he hoped it wouldn't come to that because he probably wouldn't get a warrant for it. Email would be even harder.

When he was done, he sat back and dragged his fingers through his hair. He had over two hundred names to background check. Or in this case, Google, because anything else would alert Greg. Plus, he didn't have enough probable cause to start pulling criminal histories on all these randos. Google it was.

He grabbed his mug and realized it was empty. The sky was brightening, and a big yawn wracked him. For two hours now he'd been engrossed in his work, hunched over his desk. Bed sounded good. Then something occurred to him.

"Idiot," he hissed at himself.

His fingers went to his keyboard, then he paused. Luke typed Pete's number into the spreadsheet. Nothing. He exhaled in relief before he realized he had been holding his breath. Did he not want to find out? Or was he barking up the wrong tree entirely with this whole Easton thing?

Whatever the reason, he was relieved to find that connection did not exist. At least not today. He pushed his chair back and took his mug to the break room only to find out the coffee pot was empty too.

Luke did pushups and burpees in the hall while a new pot brewed. His muscles were stiff from stooping at his computer. Outside, the city was waking up. A panel truck rumbled down Bull Street, and he saw a jogger stretching in the corner of the park that he could see from the break room. Maybe he'd go for a run later. He refilled his mug and got back to work.

Over half of the list were businessmen that had ties to

the surrounding states. Their businesses ranged from multi-million-dollar corporations to a small company that reupholstered boats.

Several calls went to charity organizations Cade had known ties to, most running some sort of vague medical sounding research. The CEO of a pharmaceutical company got a star next to his name. There were a few calls to the private school Cade's son attended, and multiple calls to a prestigious golf country club Luke knew Cade belonged to. He might have to get in there at some point to see who Cade met with.

Two professors caught his eye. Mainly for the fact that they were the only professors on the list. Natalie Roone was an authority on art history. She was head of the School for Modern and Contemporary Art at Princeton, an NEA board member, and a personal friend of the Vice President's wife. She was also eighty-three years old. Luke crossed her off as a player.

The other professor was fifty-four-year-old Alexander Wynn. Wynn was a prominent psychologist, although prominent was an understatement. He dominated the field. An in-demand speaker and lecturer, Wynn had authored six books, two of them graduate level textbooks.

Wynn grew up in a state housing project in North London, and scrapped his way up to number one in his class at Cambridge. A classic rags to riches story. A cursory internet search revealed a plethora of photos of the distinguished Wynn.

Luke found only one photo of him with Cade at yet another red-carpet function promoted by One World. Cade had his arm around the doctor's shoulders with a broad smile like they were fast friends. Alex looked bored.

The next snapshot showed Wynn with his arm snaked around the waist of a young model, looking considerably less bored. Wynn had traveled extensively after quitting his position as head of the clinical psychology program at Johns Hopkins. Then he took a part time position with the small local South Eastern University. He'd lived in Savannah for over fifteen years.

How convenient, thought Luke. He checked the phone list. Cade called Wynn four times in five years. The call always came from Cade. The first call happened four months before a case out of DC. Fourth one down on his legal pad. Over the next two years, the men talked twice. Neither of those dates corresponded to any of the police reports. The fourth call came after a two-year gap. This call occurred thirty-seven days before Twomey died.

Luke spent the next hour trolling through every psych medical publication he could find for a mention of Alexander Wynn's name. On an old website with a green background that hurt his eyes, he stumbled across a downloadable document of Wynn's first graduate thesis. Published in 1982, it was titled The Evolution of the Common Man. Luke downloaded it and printed it out.

By three o'clock, he had the stack of paper dog-eared and crumpled papers with large sections underlined. Luke paced feverishly in the tiny office.

He would never admit it to Thad, but Luke needed him to come back from his revelry in Atlanta. He needed to run this new disturbing information past a set of fresh ears. Luke broke free of the office and began pacing the empty hallway, his mind overwhelmed with what he read.

All traces of tiredness had evaporated. Luke decided to go for a run then hit the gym. That should clear his head enough to get back to work. It was a nice day again. Soon the rain would move in for the Fourth of July weekend. He left everything but his scan card in the office.

Two hours later and freshly showered, he headed back

to the office buzzing with endorphins from his workout. He felt more energetic than he had since they got here. Now he was starving and on a mission to find some southern comfort food. Luke stuffed the folders into the briefcase. The last one rested on his phone. When he moved the folder, he saw he had missed a call.

The number was local, but not one he recognized. Quickly he finished stuffing the paperwork into the bag, grabbed the thesis and headed out the door before dialing the number back. The thick stack of paper did not cooperate, and several pages drifted to the sidewalk as he pulled the door closed behind him. He snatched them up as the line rang.

He wedged the phone between his shoulder and his ear still trying to cram the offending thesis into the bag. The phone stopped ringing. Someone had picked up the line, but no one spoke.

"Hello?" he said, irritated.

"Agent Marshall?"

He knew that voice. He passed out drunk the night before still hearing it. "Oh, hey. Hi, Ms. Meara. How...how are you?" Luke juggled the briefcase and the stack of paper he still hadn't managed to stash while trying to bring the phone closer to his ear.

"Are you busy?"

"Nope," he replied without hesitating.

"You look busy."

Luke's head snapped up. Tully stood a few feet away looking at him. She looked amused. She looked perfect.

"Hi...hello," he breathed.

She gave him a cautious smile. The night before was still fresh, and they both stood in awkward silence for a few moments. Then Tully nodded toward his arched shoulder trying to keep his cell phone from hitting the concrete.

"You need some help?"

"Nope. Got it." Luke muscled the paper into the bag feeling it crinkle and rip. There would be some straightening out to do come next week.

20

July 3rd
1731 Hours

"What are you...I mean, why did you call?" Luke stumbled over his words.

He hoped his dumb question wouldn't scare her away. He should've asked why she looked so good. That was stupid. He rolled his shoulders back and acted cool, painfully aware of the frayed sweatpants he'd thrown on after his shower.

She didn't answer. She didn't need to. It was clear why she had come. It was an attempt to convince him of her partner's innocence. Or maybe she was campaigning on his behalf. Luke didn't care.

"I was wondering if we could talk. Again. Maybe sober this time," Tully said. She seemed to struggle with what to say next.

Luke felt like he needed to fill the silence. "Oh, okay. What did you want to...."

"I'm sorry about last night," she blurted out. "I'm a miserable little shit when I drink."

True to character, she just ripped it off. Luke laughed.

She must have known that blue was her color because she was wearing it again. Her blue tank top exposed toned arms and made her eyes bluer. Tight, ripped up jeans showed more leg than jeans are supposed to, and her high, messy bun frizzed a little in the humid air.

Luke looked down. Her shoes caught his attention. Next to her casual garb, the strappy heels stood out. They were patent leather, and so high he had trouble looking away. Then he remembered his shame the night before and cleared his throat. "Can I change first?"

"Sure." A small smile made her scar pucker ever so slightly.

The second his eyes flicked to it, her smile vanished. He cleared his throat and turned toward his hotel. Tully fell in step behind him.

They walked in silence. In the lobby, he fished in his pocket for his room key.

"I'll wait here," she said, not looking at him.

Luke nodded and bounded up the stairs. He couldn't wait for the elevator; it would give her too much time to change her mind.

Deciding what to wear was an aggravating chore since he had no idea where they were going. A collared shirt seemed wrong next to her casual look, so he settled on his favorite pair of tattered jeans and a t-shirt. It didn't matter what he looked like anyway.

He checked the mirror as he passed it. There was no time to shave so he'd have to rock the scruffy look. He spiked his hair, splashed a little cologne on, and decided it would do. Luke sprinted back down the stairs.

At the bottom, he peeked through the narrow door window to see if she was still there. Tully stood gazing out the windows without really seeing anything. She picked at the corner of her large clutch, the tension in her body telegraphing across the room.

Luke pushed the door open. At the noise, Tully swung around. As he closed the distance between them, he could see her uncertainty. She was having second thoughts about coming here.

He grinned and felt like an idiot but went with it. Anything to put her at ease. "I hope you know a good place to eat, otherwise it's gonna be a hamburger."

"What do you like?" She didn't relax, but no longer looked like she might bolt.

"Food." He smiled at her. "I haven't eaten much today."

"There's a place further down Bay Street. Southern Fusion."

"Perfect." Luke pushed open the lobby door and held it as she passed. "Do we need the car?"

"It's three blocks," she gestured down the street. "And parking's terrible."

He motioned for her to lead the way, and she headed for the crosswalk like she was on a mission. She strode across Bull Street without looking. Luke looked for both of them and hurried to catch up with her.

"Hey, slow down." He hooked his fingers into the crook of her elbow and immediately regretted it.

She flinched and pulled away from his touch. They stopped outside a brewery with loud country music pumping from the dark interior.

"I'm sorry," he said, yanking his hand away. "I'm sorry. You seem a little...."

"It's fine," she stated, her voice flat.

Luke shoved his hands in his pockets so he wouldn't touch her again, but he had to keep talking. This was not going well. He needed to keep her from realizing this was a mistake. Which it was.

"And don't worry about last night. You don't have anything to apologize for."

Luke meant to keep talking, but the words stuck in his throat when he realized any conversation led to her partner. It was the only reason he even knew her. Figures. The first time he met a woman he actually wanted to talk to, that was the topic they had.

He'd meant what he said last night. They shouldn't be talking outside official channels, but the thought of not following her to that restaurant was unacceptable. Simple as that.

Simple. Really? How was jeopardizing the case that could salvage or destroy his career, to see a woman, simple? In the past twenty-four hours, Luke ceased to recognize his own behavior. He was risking his investigation for a pretty face.

If he lost concentration now, he could kiss his job good-bye. The Assistant Director slot was never going to happen after the bridges he'd torched but never mind that. He wouldn't be employed if he dropped another case. The reason wouldn't matter.

"Are you okay?"

Luke's head snapped up and he saw Tully studying him. She looked suspicious. "Is something wrong?"

"Yep. Probably why we get along so well." He gave her a cheesy grin.

She turned her scarred cheek away, but he saw her smile. "Yeah, right."

"Well, until you try to punch me, I'm declaring victory."

She started walking again. Luke walked beside her, keeping his distance. Thad would have a solid month of material if he ever got wind of how flustered Luke was right now.

Soon they approached a centuries old storefront.

Chunky white molding updated the aged brick and distinguished the restaurant from the Civil War era warehouse it was attached to. Black gooseneck lights curved over the heavy oak door splashing light on the word TIDEWATER in sleek black font.

Intimate candlelight glowed through the seeded glass, illuminating diners in leather booths. Laughter and the clink of silverware drifted out when Luke opened the door. The smell of a grill in full swing made his mouth water.

"You sure they can get us in? It looks busy." Luke craned his neck to see the dining room.

"They'll find a spot," Tully said. She approached the young man at the podium who smiled and chatted with her.

When he saw Luke scowling at him, the man became engrossed with his smeared dry erase map.

Ten minutes later, they slid into a corner booth and the conversation lagged until their waiter came to fill their water glasses and take the drink order.

After he left, Luke cleared his throat. "Listen, I really am sorry about yesterday. That whole thing was screwed up."

"Stop apologizing. I shouldn't have...," She paused as the server set two whiskeys in front of them. "Your partner is an ignorant pup, but I probably shouldn't have tried to punch him." She grabbed one and took a sip. It seemed to calm her.

"He inspires that in people." Luke grinned at her and took the other whiskey. "You're not the first."

She gave an emphatic nod. "No doubt."

Luke laughed. "So, I guess now I have to ask you about yourself. And you reply with how many siblings you have and where you fall in the age order of said siblings, and how you feel about long walks on the beach. All the shit nobody cares about, but you have to ask to be polite."

"Don't do that. That sounds like a date." Tully fished the

small ice cube out of her whiskey and crunched on it.

"Yeah, it does."

"This is not a date." She pointed at him.

"Then why did you wear those shoes?" It was a joke, but Luke saw her shoulders hunch forward like she was suddenly self conscious.

Luke began to doubt his initial assessment of her trying to manipulate him. She was a contradiction of determination and indecisiveness. He changed his opinion of her as often as she looked away from him. "So how many siblings do you have?"

She choked on her ice and chuckled in spite of her discomfort.

Luke smiled. "How many years have you been a police officer? Do you like it? Is it hard being a female cop? Blah, blah, blah." His easy tone seemed to work.

"What? You're not gonna ask how old I am?"

"Hell, no. You have to keep it nonpersonal."

"Nonpersonal? I thought my shoes made this a date."

"You can't suck me in," Luke said. "If I ask how old you are, you'll say, 'how old do you think I am?'. Then I'm the shmuck because if I guess too low, that will imply that I think you're immature. If I guess too high, then you're old and weathered. Either way, I lose that round."

Tully's shoulders released as she drained her glass and held it up to the waiter. He nodded from across the room. It seemed they couldn't talk to each other without copious amounts of liquid courage. "That's a cute little speech, but we both know it's horse shit."

Luke almost spat out his whiskey. "Pardon?"

"You don't have to ask do you?" She leaned in. "You already know."

Luke's stunned silence answered her. He wasn't convinced she wouldn't start fighting him again.

Instead, she sat back and said, "Hit me with it."

"You're pretty blunt."

"I don't like games."

Her expression was halfway between annoyed and fascinated. It was exhausting trying to figure out her motivation for showing up tonight. He finished his whiskey and settled back. This was going to be fun.

"Okay then. I did look you up. You're a decorated 16-year veteran with as many reprimands as you have commendations. A loose cannon with a tendency to blow off whatever you don't like in favor of something you think is better. I didn't research that, by the way, that's strictly observation. No doubt you've thumped your share of garden variety bad guys within an inch of their lives."

Luke grinned at her. "You are thirty-six years old, and in '09 you took a bullet in the line of duty. I see a catch in your step every now and then, so I'd say it still bothers you. Oh, and you drink too much."

"Very good, G-man."

"Stop calling me that."

"What should I call you? Asshole?"

"Luke," said Luke.

"That's right. This is a date."

"As for your scar." Luke could tell that was a topic he wasn't allowed to bring up. "I don't know what happened. And frankly, it's not my business."

Surprised and visibly pleased at his easy candor, she opened her mouth to speak but the waiter stepped next to the table and delivered two more whiskeys. They spent the next few minutes looking between the waiter and the menu.

When he left, Tully set in on her second glass. She settled back into her seat with a sigh of pleasure. "A loose cannon, huh? That's a little harsh."

"It wasn't an insult."

Her smile was beautiful but awkward. Like she wasn't used to using it. "The decoration was me and Pete being stupid."

"And the reprimands?"

She ran a finger around the rim of her glass but didn't answer.

Luke shrugged. "Sometimes stupid is the right thing to do."

"Stupid or not, I at least have the grace to accept civic recognition when it's given to me."

Her smug look spread as his surprise registered. "You're not the only one who did their homework." She leaned in. "Why does someone turn down the Congressional Medal of Honor?"

Now it was Luke who drained his glass. "Didn't deserve it."

"Well, that clears things right up."

"I didn't think that going into the desert with eight men and coming out with three merits any positive recognition."

She raised an eyebrow but let him talk.

"It's scrap." Luke studied the wavy glass in the paned window. "Medals are society's way of making themselves feel better about sending others to dodge the bullets. For sending young men to be cannon fodder while they sleep on thousand thread count sheets. Nothing more than a giant middle finger to those the powerful view as unimportant enough to do a job they never would. You should know that better than anyone." He couldn't keep the bitterness out of his voice.

"That's not true." She scowled, but her prickly demeanor softened.

Luke looked back to see her studying him. "Trust me, it is."

"The Congressional Medal of Honor is not just any

medal. And it definitely isn't scrap. What happened?" Not a trace of sarcasm or anger. Just curiosity.

Luke shrugged again. "We walked into an ambush. Five of my men, including my best friend, were mowed down. It was my team, my op. And they were my responsibility. I failed them. That doesn't deserve a slap on the back. It's really not complicated."

"You can't ensure anyone's safety in war."

"Doesn't take away our responsibility."

"Yes, it does," said Tully. "That's a lie we tell ourselves. So we can postpone thinking about a dead friend. People die in war, but we say it won't happen to us if we fight hard enough. It's an illusion as old as war itself."

"Like heroism," said Luke.

"No. Heroism is real. It just masquerades as guilt." She laughed bitterly.

"Can you go one hour without starting a fight?"

"I'm not starting a fight," Tully said. "It never ceases to amaze me how good men take on the responsibilities of evil men. It's not your fault they died, but you volunteer for the blame."

"It's not that simple," said Luke softly.

"I know. I'm just sayin." She fell silent.

"Failing to protect the innocent isn't something you should be rewarded for." Luke tipped his glass forgetting it was empty. He frowned at it.

"Oh?" She looked around the room, thoughtful. "Huh."

"What?"

"That's an antiquated notion."

"What is?"

"That anyone is innocent."

Luke's brow furrowed. "Not everyone is guilty."

"There's no difference," Tully said pursing her lips.

"What are you talking about? Of course there's a

difference.”

“No. There are three types of people. Those that need to go to jail. Those that don’t need to go to jail. And the people I actually care about. But no one is innocent.”

“Oversimplification seems to be your wheelhouse.”

“It’s true,” she insisted.

“No, it isn’t. What about everyone else?”

“There is no one else. You wanna talk about an illusion. It’s innocence. It doesn’t exist, it never has. All of us are rotten at our core. At any point, no one is more than a couple of bad decisions away from being society’s worst. The only thing distinguishing good from bad is that some fight their nature, and some are consumed by it. We view it as guilt or innocence, but it’s choices we make. No one is innocent.”

He studied her for a moment. Restrained ferocity stretched her eyes wide. Her chest rose and fell like she was out of breath. She sat forward, her hands clenching the edge of the leather seat. Clearly, he’d brought up a touchy topic. He didn’t mean to. Conversing with this woman was a minefield.

“That’s not how I see it,” he said.

“How do you see it, G-man?”

Luke held her gaze for a moment before continuing. “I’m not talking about perfection. By that definition, you’re right, no one is innocent. Everyone agrees that children are innocent, but a schoolyard bully doesn’t really fit your definition.”

“I’m almost certain you’re trying to make a point.” Her voice dripped with sarcasm.

“Some people get what’s coming to them and we call it justice. And some get crushed by circumstances they didn’t create. That isn’t justice. All I’m saying is, not everyone earns the fate they draw.”

The sarcastic expression died on her face. She avoided his eyes and studied the brick wall behind him. "Like bleeding out in a desert," she said in a low voice.

"Or a police station parking lot," said Luke. "The Captain told me about the ambush when you got shot. I know what Pete meant to you, Tully. I do."

She flinched when he said her partner's name. It took her a second to speak, and when she did her voice was thick. "The first round shattered my hip. I was pinned down next to a three-foot cinderblock wall. I couldn't move. Pete low crawled to me and carried me out with bullets flying all around us." Tully twisted her hands in her lap. "And when he needed me, I wasn't there."

"See, you blame yourself too."

Something snapped, and her eyes flew to his. They were dark. "I know you think he killed that senator, but he didn't. I know that's why you're here and you're wrong."

Luke stiffened waiting for the attack, but she stayed calm. It disturbed him how calm she was.

She continued, keeping her voice down. "I don't care about you, and I don't care about some dead politician. I can't stop you, but Pete's not here to defend himself, so know that I will."

Luke couldn't help but smile. "I'd be disappointed if you didn't."

The waiter saved Luke by showing up with their food. Spicy steam reminded them how hungry they were as he set the large bowls in front of them. A mound of rice floated on creamy gumbo crowned with golden fried okra. As they ate, the conversation drifted to the mundane.

Tully had said what she came to say, and they soon reached an unspoken agreement to change the subject they were both weary of.

21

———

Drayton Street and York Lane
July 3rd
2045 Hours

After dinner Tully and Luke wandered back through the historic district. Savannah seemed to give him the same urge to stroll aimlessly as it did her. She didn't know why, but it made her feel better about him.

Countless nights she'd roamed these streets, most of the time too drunk to see dawn. But the nights. She owned the nights in this town.

Dusk was falling and the streetlamps projected pools of orange light onto the sidewalk and up into the oak canopy. Lightning skittered across the thick clouds. The storm was closing in.

Then he did it again. He always had to say something when it got quiet.

"I'm pretty sure I just got robbed," Luke chuckled.

"Sorry. I thought it would be better." She rewarded him with a little smile. It was what he wanted. He kept trying to make her smile like she was some ditzy co-ed.

"You've never been there before?"

"No. But everybody raves about the place."

"Damned hipsters." He gave her side eye, hoping for another smile.

Tully knew his type. Sullen and morose macho men. Guys like him didn't say much to begin with, so it was strange the way he kept trying to fill the silence. The G-man couldn't bear any quiet between them. It was sweet. And naive.

So she smiled at him. Not sweet or coy, that she couldn't muster, but she humored him. It made him look happy. That wasn't what she intended when she went to see him. She didn't want to laugh, and he was terrible at small talk. The sparks flew when they talked about deep shit, but his cracks showed when the talking stopped.

But she had no choice. He was coming after her friend, and she was going to stop him. Anything she wanted to know she couldn't ask outright. She couldn't be that obvious. After years of working the street, she knew nervous talking was a gold mine of information. And if he kept blabbering, she'd find out what he had on Pete. She wouldn't need to ask.

Lightning flashed again. Tully hadn't known what she was going to say when she got Agent Marshall's contact from the Captain. And she really didn't know why she was standing outside of his office before she even dialed the number.

The man that walked into the station yesterday was not what she expected. The first minutes of their conversation, he'd poked around to find her button. And find it he did. His questions unnerved her so much she lost her cool. Lost control.

It happened again last night. She spent the better part of

fifteen years making sure she wasn't caught off guard, but Marshall kept doing it. She almost took him home last night, and today she walked to his office. Now he was trying to make her smile, and she was playing along.

Then again, someone stumbling around as drunk as Marshall when he showed up at Only's last night must be as fucked up as her. Or maybe she was lonely. She didn't know anymore.

When he ambushed her at the pub, she'd been so drunk she couldn't remember half of what he said, but she remembered his desperation. He looked sad when he talked about Pete. At the time she was grateful. The next morning, she convinced herself it was a calculated play to earn her trust.

Now, as she watched him bumble around trying to make her laugh, she knew it was her play.

"It was glass." The words were out of her mouth before she knew it.

Shit. That last whiskey had loosened her tongue. She meant to reel him in, but not like this. Revealing herself to this stranger was dangerous. He was already primed to go to bed with her. Why did he need to know this?

"Pardon?" He sounded surprised when she spoke.

Too late now.

"It was glass. A broken coffee table. I was seven." Tully brushed her scarred cheek with her fingers. She kept walking, and silently thanked him when he looked anywhere but at her.

She told him the story of the night her father died, deliberately downplaying the man that destroyed her family. She wasn't ready to talk about him. 'Some local hick fuck' was the only description she gave when Marshall asked.

Every time she recalled her father's death, it was the

sounds that she remembered. The sound of wood splintering. Panic in her father's voice. The final shotgun blast, and the ringing silence after. She'd never figured out why she couldn't remember touch or smell.

"Pretty gruesome, huh?" She looked at him, searching for a reaction.

He didn't give her much of one. "That explains a few things," he said softly.

"Ancient history." She waved him off.

"Our own histories are never ancient. God, what a relief that would be."

She stopped and turned to study him. The hardboiled federal agent waiting for her in the conference room yesterday was nowhere to be found. Now he was awkward and off balance.

She pushed away the urge to tell him more, her whole ugly story. Even he wouldn't be that understanding.

"I don't tell many people," she continued in a hurry to cover up her hesitation. "It's too much, and they start feeling sorry for me. Pity is the most unbearable. It's why I moved here. Whispers are always loudest in a small town. I had to get out. So thanks for not saying you're 'sorry'."

"You mean you don't tell that story to all your dates." He sounded amused.

"I don't go on a lot of dates. Too much of a bitch, I guess."

"Noooo."

Tully punched his shoulder and heard herself laugh. He was sucking her in again, and she forgot herself. Not that he had to work hard at it. She was supposed to hate him but had trouble doing it. Had he been in town for any other reason, she would have gone home with him last night without a second drink.

"Come on." He was smiling again. "You're not a bitch. Possessed by determination bordering on insanity, maybe. But not a bitch. That's the only story anyone has on you."

"I attacked your partner," she reminded him.

Marshall laughed out loud. "I told you. That's a normal reaction to Aulden. For a second, I thought about letting you do it. But if anyone was getting into a fight with the likes of you, it was going to be me."

"The likes of me?"

She could tell he thought they had been wandering. He looked surprised when she made an abrupt turn by a columned mansion onto Gaston Street. His eyes flicked to Forsythe Park behind them and he realized where he was. This was farther than she brought him last night. It dawned on him that she had a destination.

"You almost had me." His voice softened.

"Whatever. I wasn't much of a match for you." Tully couldn't keep the shame out of her voice.

"Says who?" He sounded surprised. "You almost broke my face."

Lighting ripped across the sky followed by a thunderous crack. She stopped in front of a scrolled wrought iron gate. The number '309' marked a brick tunnel through the basement of two conjoined row homes. She saw him glance through the tunnel at her courtyard buried deep in the city's grid.

Their eyes met and held. This time he didn't try to fill the silence. A chubby raindrop hit Tully in the face, and she flinched. "I'm, uh, I should get going. Thank you." She turned to leave.

"Can I see you again?"

She turned back. Marshall had hesitated to ask the question, and she didn't know the answer.

Then her eyes fell on a green mud-splattered '82 Blazer parked on the street, and memories of her and Pete working on it crushed down on her. Or rather, of Pete working on her truck while she and Melissa drank beer in camping chairs on the driveway.

Her head dipped as she steeled herself. "You need to stop, Agent Marshall. Whatever it is you think you're going to find here, you won't."

"What?"

She squared off with him. Face your opponent. Never expose your back. "You need to stop investigating Pete."

"Tully, I give you my word, if there's no evidence your partner was involved his name won't even go in my report."

"Not good enough."

"It's the best I can give you."

"No, it isn't," she hissed at him. Marshall's reply was a harsh reminder of why she shouldn't be around him. He affected her too much. Even halfway sober she was about to invite him in. "Goodbye." The sprinkle steadied into rain as she whipped around to leave.

"Tully, wait." He placed a hand on her bicep.

She knew it was a reflex, but it felt like an attempt to hold her there. Just like at the station, she felt pleasure from his touch and fury at his attempt to control her. She knocked his hand away and glared at him.

"Tully, please." He was begging now. Strong, intimidating Agent Marshall reduced to wide-eyed entreaties. All because he wanted to get some.

"I'm not convinced the drug dealer was that good of an actor."

She backed away. "He was a piece of shit."

"I know, but he was scared. And if he was there looking for a cop, I need to know who it was and why."

She faced him in the low light of the streetlamp. Anyone else begging like that would have earned her hate, but Marshall clearly wasn't accustomed to begging. He was terrible at it. It sounded like an order, which made her prickle.

Tully stood rigid and unyielding as he leaned in. If he was trying to intimidate her, it wasn't going to work. "You won't get that from me," she said defiantly.

"That's not what I want from you."

The rain fell heavy now, but neither noticed. The storm was overhead now, lightning and thunder coming at the same time. Luke took her hand and pulled her into the shelter of the tunnel. The exposed bulbs at either end cast a flickering glow as the rain pounded outside.

Tully threw off his hand. "Then what do you want? This whole circus has been nothing but you pushing me around." She could smell his cologne in the steamy night. He smelled like sawdust, pine needles, and whiskey. It made her angrier.

"That's what it's all about, isn't it? Make a name for yourself and get laid," she sneered. "You sling a good line, and I almost bought it."

He just stood there and let her tell him off.

The sadness on his face only stoked her fire. He was faking it. He couldn't help why he was here, but he didn't have to pretend he cared.

"Well, you're not going to get that. Not from me," she sneered.

"I already have."

She balked. "What?"

"I can tell a lot about a person by the people they surround themselves with. Why do you think I went to dinner with you? I wanted to know what Peter Easton was like. I needed to know what his best friend was like. So yes, I got what I wanted from you."

Tully took a step back, reeling from his answer. On one hand, she'd pleaded Pete's case, which obviously had some effect on the FBI Agent. On the other hand, he'd manipulated her, and she hadn't even realized it, she was so distracted by her hormones.

She needed to stay away from this man. He was dangerous. But even as she thought it, her body rebelled against the idea of leaving. "Why do you keep coming at me sideways."

"I'm not coming at you sideways, Tully." He took a step toward her. "I mean everything I say. If you don't believe anything else, you can believe that." The conviction in his voice soothed her ragged mind.

"Then why are you still here? If you got what you came for, why don't you leave?" She wanted him to leave. He needed to walk away, not her. They couldn't do this, and it wasn't fair that she had to make that choice.

He closed the distance between them in two strides, his hand up. He brushed away a droplet running down her jaw. Then she felt her damp hair brush away from her face, exposing her cheek. She flinched. A strong hand snaked around the back of her neck.

Tully felt herself shaking. She tried to tell herself it was from confusion, not fear. But the truth was, she was terrified. Terrified of how he made her feel. Of how easily he slipped past her guard. Terrified of how fast he would leave if he knew about her past.

Gently, the hand cradling her neck pulled her closer. He seemed to be fighting the same battle in his own head, but neither of them cared anymore.

The rough, cool brick disappeared behind her back. The only thing she could feel was him moving closer. The rain pounding outside made no sound. The only thing she could hear was the rustle of his shirt.

Locking his arm around her waist, he pulled her roughly against him, and she let him. He kissed her hard, uncertainty replaced by hunger as she fumbled for her keys.

22

---

309 E. Gaston Street #C
July 6th
0815 Hours

A loud buzz broke the sleepy fog. Luke forced his eyes open and saw his cell phone vibrating on the small desk on his side of the bed. Luke had left his phone unattended once and Thad installed the Superman symbol as his caller id. Now it flashed on the screen. Luke saw 'Tuesday' under Thad's name.

"Shit." Luke flipped over and came face to face with the elbow that woke him up three times last night.

Tully's naked body was tangled in the soft white sheets, an arm and a leg sprawled onto his side. The bright morning light bounced off her blond hair fanned over the pillow, wavy from drying as she slept.

The holiday weekend came and went, and they never left the apartment. Sunday they drank whiskey and ate nothing. Monday they ordered food in so they didn't have to leave the house, or each other. That night they spent an hour together in the shower then passed out from exhaustion, finally satisfied. He couldn't remember much after that.

A smile lifted the corners of his mouth as he thought about the last forty-eight hours. He'd lost track of time. Of days.

Luke ignored the phone and swung his legs over the edge and pulled on his underwear. Padding to the window, he stretched and tried to stifle his yawn. For the first time, he hated the thought of going to work. Work kept him occupied. Today it would keep him from doing what he really wanted to do.

Behind him, Tully stirred with a moan. She patted his empty pillow and lifted her head to look around. Spotting him by the window, she gave a sleepy smile and flipped over pulling up the sheet to cover her bare chest.

Luke took the two steps back to the side of the bed and looked down at her.

"Hi," he whispered.

"Hey, G-man," she murmured, tugging the hem of his boxer briefs.

Before Luke knew what happened, his face was buried in the velvet curve of her neck and her fingers traced the outline of his back.

The phone clunked onto the carpet still flashing a large red "S".

———

By the time Luke got back to his hotel, showered, and changed it was ten-thirty. Without a word, Luke walked into the broom closet and threw his freshly pressed jacket on the back of his chair. His collar was buttoned, and his tie knotted tight.

Thaddeus sat slung back in his chair with his feet

propped up, scrolling on his phone. He sported dark circles under bloodshot eyes and looked like he hadn't slept in days. When Luke opened the door, a mischievous smile spread across his face.

Luke sat down and faced his computer. Saying nothing seemed like the best course of action.

Thad's throat clear was loud. "How was your weekend?"

"Fine. You?"

"Pretty epic actually, since you asked. I was going to tell you about the twins, but in my humble experience whoever gets to work last had the best weekend."

"Grow up, Kid. You're not in college anymore."

"And you're not a virgin anymore."

"Funny."

Thad's eagerness withered. "Really? No details? Nothing?"

Luke's phone vibrated. He tapped the screen quickly and set it back on the desk.

Thad's eyebrows almost disappeared into his hairline. Luke's impatience with anything of a cellular nature was legendary in the Bureau, and the butt of many jokes, most of them originating from Thad. He'd never seen Luke send a text.

Thad let it go. "Alrighty then, I'll go first. Thank god we had Monday off. Monday was the worst day of my life. Saturday and Sunday however, is another story...."

Luke booted up his computer and watched it blink to life. Thad's voice faded as he tuned his young partner out.

He wanted to believe she was just another blip on his radar. But the scars he saw refused to sanction his self-imposed isolation. She had kept fighting. He could too.

Ten years ago, he came back from the war and started looking in a bottle for what he left somewhere in the desert. Bar brawls, panic attacks, and one-night stands with women he wouldn't spend thirty sober seconds with burned up two years of his life.

He'd lost track of the number of times he pressed his 9mm to his temple when he hit bottom, again. He didn't dry out until an old Army buddy convinced him to join the Bureau. A fresh start, if there was such a thing for men like him.

Some powerful people were disappointed when he refused to join the counter-terrorism division. It had been expected of him. It was the only reason they gave a booze-soaked Delta with three assaults on his record a chance. Luke was the best at what he used to do. But he wouldn't go back to that life no matter how much he sucked at this one.

No. There were wolves out there that didn't remind him of his own past, so he chose to hunt them instead. It would never pay back what he owed, but it satisfied his demons. Try as he might, he would never make it off that tightrope, and he'd made his peace with that.

So, he reordered his life and made sure it was a fortress against anything that might compromise him. It held for eight years until she brought it crumbling down. He craved the raw, bleeding mess under that fiery husk because it looked like his. It felt familiar, comfortable.

Every day since he poured the sand out of his boots, he wondered if it was possible to move on, or if a temporary distraction was the best he could hope for. Was Tully just another way to forget for a few sleepless minutes?

She was a witness. He slept with a material witness, and worse, he wasn't going to stop. He rubbed his hands over his face.

"And she was all, 'Oh, really? I've never seen one of those...'." Thad stopped and eyed Luke. "You okay, Boss?"

"Great." Luke yanked his tie loose and directed the

conversation away from himself. "You look a little hung over."

"Another night might have literally killed me. I'm never drinking again."

"Never or the weekend, whichever comes first." Luke finally smiled. They had this conversation every Monday and it normally annoyed him. Today it made the broom closet feel more like home. Something normal to soften this uncomfortable territory he found himself in.

"How is the autopsy search going? Are people giving you any trouble?"

"Not really. Some of them are skeptical, but no one has told me to step off. Not yet anyway. Most of the record keepers are ladies, and you know how irresistible I am." Thad grinned. "Bigger agencies are getting back quickly. The smaller ones take a while. None of them have updated record keeping systems. They have to go through boxes of paper reports. Those are rolling in much slower."

"Don't let up now. Stay on it." Luke said.

Thad nodded.

"Good work though. Keep it up." Luke reached into the briefcase for the thesis to hide a smile as Thad's grin returned. At least now he had a second brain to run his thoughts through. He smoothed the crinkled stack as Thad watched.

"What's that?"

"Those phone records and your handy dandy police reports yielded something interesting."

"You don't say."

"A guy by the name of Alexander Wynn is a colleague of Cade's. He's a shrink. Ol' Johnny boy called him not long before Twomey died."

"No way." Thad leaned in listening.

"This is his first doctoral thesis, written in '82."

"First?"

"He has three earned doctorates, one of them from Cambridge, and two psychiatric fellowships. He's been published in every major medical journal that I'm aware exists. Guy's a certified genius."

Thad whistled. "I barely made it through grad school." He grabbed the stack that Luke offered and flipped through it.

Luke sat back in his chair. "He ended up teaching at South Eastern in the late 90's and early 2000s. He must like the south because he never left. He's English. He has no family here."

"The Cambridge?"

"Yes. Now he lives outside of Savannah, although he travels extensively. He has a thriving practice here and in Charleston."

"What makes you think he's involved, other than him being Cade's friend."

"They're not friends. They hardly talk despite living within an hour of each other. Cade called him about a month before the senator died. And," Luke paused to make sure Thad was listening, "several months before the case Sandra gave us. No other calls on recent records."

"Okay wow. That doesn't seem like a coincidence."

"And then there's that." Luke motioned to the dissertation Thad was skimming.

"Oh." Thad bounced his palm off his forehead. "That's where I know that name from."

"What?"

"My senior year I offered to tutor this freshman. You know, 'cuz she was really hot. I was trying to get some, so I offered to help her with a psych paper. It was one of my majors so I figured I could 'pump'," he made air quotes, "a little benefit out of it. Worked like a charm."

Luke glared at Thad who shrugged. "You wanted my input. Anyway, the class we were in had one of his textbooks assigned. I remember it. It was four inches thick and thirty pounds if it was an ounce."

Luke ran his hands through his hair and left them covering his face as he waited for Thad to say something useful. The wait was excruciating but short.

"It was personality disorders if I remember right. That's the one Amber did her paper on. I don't remember much about it, except it was weird."

Luke peeked from behind his fingers. "Amber?"

Thad grinned. "Some of his theories are a little, well, controversial."

Luke dropped his hands and straightened in his chair. "Controversial is not even close. He doesn't shy away from an unpopular line of thought. Some of his treatment methods are, well, they're throwbacks. Like dipping schizo patients in ice water and electroshock therapy. But nobody's shutting him down. His patient roster has a waiting list. Hell, he's even worked for us a few times," said Luke.

"Controversial means somebody likes what he's doing."

"But that's his day job. His real obsession is criminal psychology."

"I'm a little confused about how you spent your weekend," Thad said.

Luke ignored him. "Wynn might be a certifiable genius, but he's also a nut job. His views on criminal behavior are as far out as I've ever seen. That thesis," he gestured to the paper in Thad's hands, "is called 'The Evolution of the Common Man'. He outlines why he considers the common street criminal more evolved than a law-abiding citizen."

"Clearly he holds a higher opinion of them than most," snorted Thad.

Luke propped his feet on his desk. "He claims the

average criminal is in better physical condition and sharper focused than the average citizen. Growing up and surviving in an unforgiving environment develops skills and toughness the average person lacks. Although he admits that this so-called advantage hasn't lofted them to greater heights than boosted cars and drug rips. Check out page 124."

Thad flipped through the pile. Luke didn't wait for him to read it.

"He comes straight out and says that anyone with a basic knowledge of forensics, that can also master the physiological effects of guilt, can become an invincible force. I guess crime doesn't pay only if you get caught."

"That's kinda true," said Thad.

Luke went on. "He says knowledge isn't the key though. Behavior is. Guilt or fear always manifests in a physiological way. It's the fight or flight response as applied to criminal behavior. When adrenaline is in the system, involuntary things happen. Anything from running, stuttering, and stammering, to increased heart rate and sweating. Polygraphs are based on this principle, but you can see the signs in anyone if you're paying attention." Luke nodded toward the paper in Thad's hands.

Thad's mouth gaped then he read out loud. "Any action executed by an expert at abating the mental strain of the consequence of guilt and detection would be sui generis. These unique actions would lead to altered trails of evidence that would be nearly untraceable to authorities." Thad looked at Luke, his eyes wide.

"Wynn's got a whole noble savage thing going on. He argues that despite lower average grades, the common street criminal is better at adapting and surviving when faced with unfavorable circumstances. Strong survival skills make them more fit, therefore stronger. Wynn calls it the 'great leap forward', a true evolutionary feat independent of the laws of man and nature. He seems genuinely disappointed that such a person doesn't exist."

"We already call that kind of person a sociopath." Thad studied the paper.

"No, he differentiates. He argues sociopaths simply don't form attachments or observe social norms. His so-called missing link is average but has the ability to suppress or control the body's reaction to adrenaline. It's not about a lack of empathy or attachment per se. It's about remaining calm when anyone else would panic.

"He tries to make it seem like it would only apply to bank robberies and insurance swindles. He even throws in a few positives like infiltrating terror cells and intelligence gathering. Not very convincing though."

"There aren't too many uses for someone with no conscience."

"I can think of one," said Luke.

"Knocking off politicians," muttered Thad.

Luke stood and started pacing.

Thad spoke slowly. "Except that society would crumble if criminals are left unchecked. Criminals only survive by leeching off the accomplishments of others. How can he see them as evolved when all they do is destroy?"

"He accounts for that. He admits the whole idea is a long shot, and the average criminal is still average in every respect. The theory is that one in a billion might possess the ability. This 'great leap forward' would blend the survival instincts of a street rat, and a smart, educated, genteel even, criminal."

"Sounds like some mad scientist shit."

"Funny you say that. The President of the American Psychology Association called his thesis the work of a crim-inal Frankenstein. They've been feuding via medical journals for the better part of two decades. Personally, I found it persuasive."

Thad frowned. "Sounds like you think he found it."

"Just trying to get my questions answered."

Thad plopped the stack down and leaned back in his chair. "I mean, is it even relevant? It looked like suicide. Do you really need to be an evolutionary anomaly to set that up? All you have to do is watch Law and Order. Or get it off the Internet."

Luke shook his head.

"Then what?"

"TV is not reality. Second-hand fictional accounts are not going to cut it. To be successful you'd have to know what police look for at these scenes, and how to avoid raising suspicion. Cops know human behavior better than anyone. Anything that would even raise a question has to be avoided. Like you said, even tampering leaves a trail. That kind of nuance would take more than cursory knowledge."

"You mean Easton?" Thad sounded sober.

"Maybe," said Luke.

"The fact that he was out of town that weekend doesn't look good."

Luke stopped pacing and his head snapped up. "What? How do you know that?"

"I was talking to one of their dispatchers last week. You're not the only charmer in this room." He answered Luke's look with a wink. "Sorry, I kinda forgot about it with the holiday weekend and everything. Anyway, it's a pretty small group around here. Everybody knows everybody. Easton's family has a huge tract of land up in South Carolina about four hours from here. He hunts up there on the regular. He always goes alone."

Luke said nothing but started moving again.

"In fact, their little clique broke up that weekend. They

usually go to some bar, and she goes sometimes. That week nobody went. Everybody was busy."

"Doing what?"

"She didn't know about the rest of them, but Easton was going hunting. He was talking about it to his," Thad paused, "partner. She only remembered because they seemed to have a little tiff over something."

"They fought?"

"More like a disagreement from what Mary said. She couldn't hear them. Luke? You alright?"

Luke moved to the window while Thad talked. He stared outside not really seeing anything. "Nicely done, Aulden. Not exactly our smoking gun though is it?"

"No," said Thad. "But it doesn't look good."

Luke's phone buzzed on the desk. He picked it up and looked at the caller ID. "Hello?...Hello, sir. Thank you... Yes...We're on our way. Thank you very much, sir." He hung up.

Thad pushed the thesis to the side. "Where are we going?"

23

July 8th
1020 Hours

"That was Captain Timothy. He gave me the go-ahead to look at the evidence collected at the shooting scene. It's ready for us."

"Wow, he's letting us look at it?"

"I may have overemphasized our interest in Cummings, so don't blow it when we get there. I doubt we'll find much, but I'd rather not burn that bridge right now. I think he just wants us out of his hair."

Twenty minutes later, the men walked into a converted 1960's textile warehouse near the courthouse. The lock buzzed open, and Luke pushed the peeling paint on the metal door and swung it open to let Thaddeus pass first.

At the far end of the small room was a large open window and counter with chipped wood veneer. A bright fluorescent light cast a blue tone over the aging vinyl floor and drab paint. A metal desk with a computer and a large table with the same chipped veneer sat along the left wall. A white-haired man perched on a stool behind the computer on the counter.

"Hi there." The man addressed Thaddeus with a deep southern accent. "Are you Agent Marshall?"

Thaddeus pointed over his shoulder. "No, sir. He is."

Luke stepped up to the counter and reached across to shake the man's hand. "You must be Gary. Thank you for helping us out. Can't tell you how much we appreciate it."

Gary took Luke's hand and shook it hard. He was stoic and unvarnished, likely a former cop that landed this cake job as a retirement gig. His skin was wrinkled and pocked marked.

Luke's misdirection must have worked because Gary was pleasant despite his gruff manner. "Well, Cap'n said to let you handle whatever it was you needed. Ya'll lookin into the fella that shot Pete?"

"We are," said Luke. "Again, let me say how sorry I am for your agency's loss. I know he was well respected and liked."

"That he was, Agent. That he was. One of the finest officers I've ever had the pleasure of knowing."

Thad shifted uncomfortably next to Luke. Luke silently willed him to keep his mouth shut as Gary went on.

"I pulled these for you." He swiveled on his stool toward two large boxes on a dented metal table behind the counter. "This is what we have. Everything except the suspect's gun. Nothing else went to the lab. Wasn't much need for it since the suspect was put down. Would you mind?" Gary gestured to the boxes. "They ain't too heavy, but I got a bum L3."

"No problem," said Luke a little more chipper than he intended. This was going better than he thought possible.

Gary slid off his stool and opened the door next to the window. He held it open as Luke and Thad went behind, each grabbed a box, and went back out to the waiting area table. "Ya'll let me know if ya'll need anything," Gary said and closed the door. He motioned to a bell beside the computer, then disappeared into the rows of shelves housing boxes and bags of evidence.

"Thanks," Luke called after him already opening his box.

Inside were tightly sealed clear plastic bags containing various items of evidence. Luke could tell the items in his box were taken from the slain officer. A uniform shirt lay on top. The bloodstains looked more black than red on the dark fabric. Luke ran his hand across the plastic. Beneath, he could feel the blood dried to a hard crust. A texture he wished he wasn't so familiar with.

He pulled it out quickly and set it on the table. Under it, a white T-shirt revealed the blood in blunt contrast. It covered the entire torso and lower portion of the chest. It too had dried. Luke swallowed hard and placed it beside the first bag.

Beside him, Thad was digging through his box. He pulled out clothing too but much dirtier and rattier than the officer's uniform.

Luke looked over when Thad pulled out a pair of jeans. They had no blood on them. The suspect's shirt had a small circle of blood in the dead center, front and back. The suspect's wounds had been grouped in the middle of his chest. Luke thought about Tully wielding the rifle and suppressed a smile.

Item after item they pulled out and examined in silence until they both had empty boxes.

"Anything?" Luke looked in Thad's box.

"Nada," said Thad.

"Alright. We can check it off the list at least." He turned back to his box. As he reached for the items on the table, his elbow bumped the corner. The box slid a few inches on the table, and Luke heard a small swish as something kept moving after the cardboard stopped. He looked inside.

At the bottom of the box, the corner of a small bag was visible from underneath the loose inner flap. Luke pulled it out. Inside was a small piece of white paper soaked in blood. Luke checked the handwriting on the outside of the package. It was found in Easton's uniform breast pocket.

Luke squinted at the small type. About half of the print was obliterated by the deep reddish-brown stain. It meant nothing to the detectives investigating the case, but what Luke saw made his stomach sour. It couldn't be.

The receipt appeared to be from a gas station, although the items purchased were long gone. It was the date and address Luke couldn't look away from. The gas station had an Atlanta address. It was dated the day before the senator died.

"What? What is it?" Thad saw him freeze.

Luke pivoted so he faced the security camera in the corner, forcing Thad's back to it. He handed the receipt to his partner.

Thad's eyes grew wide and his mouth dropped open, making Luke glad he had positioned this way. "I guess we know where he went that weekend," he whispered.

"Holy shit," Thad said out loud.

"Keep your voice down," Luke murmured glancing over his shoulder for any sign of Gary. "We can't take it right now, and god forbid it should go missing because someone finds out we're interested in it."

Thad nodded and Luke saw him swallow hard. Luke placed the receipt next to several other pieces of paper that he had no interest in and snapped a picture with his phone. He made a big show of also photographing several of Cummings's clothing items. No doubt Gary was in the back, watching them on the monitor.

Then Luke motioned to Thad to put his items back in his box. Thad did so mechanically, looking over his shoulder like he expected Gary to come roaring out and grab the evidence out of their hands.

Luke packed his box, careful to put everything in neat but random order. The plastic bag with the receipt he tucked next to a bag with other pocket contents, although he doubted anyone would look that closely. SPD's investigation on Cummings was closed.

He and Thad hoisted their boxes up on the counter and Luke rang the bell. Gary shuffled down the aisle and typed his password into the computer. As he began checking the items back in, Luke leaned against the countertop in a nonchalant pose.

"How long do you typically keep items of evidence? In case I were to need any of Cumming's clothing again for lab work."

Next to him, Luke could feel Thad physically draw in, cringing. He kept going. Gary didn't seem to notice anything wrong with the question.

"Typically a year after the case has cleared court so any chance of appeal has passed. In this case, there is no court. It will be a five-year hold since it was an officer-involved incident."

Luke nodded. "Good to know. Thank you for your help, Gary." They turned to leave.

"Whatcha investigatin that dead asshole for? He got a federal rap sheet?"

Thad's face displayed panic, but Luke turned and gave the man a broad easy grin. "You got it. Just trying to clear out some cases. Same as you."

Gary gave a brusque wave and turned to the boxes on the counter. Thad was the first one out the door.

"Why would he keep it? Why would it be in his pocket?"

Thad blurted out the second the car doors slammed shut. "None of this is making sense."

Luke started the engine and pulled onto the street before he answered. "I don't know, Kid. But it does explain why Cummings would have come to see Easton."

"You honestly think that scuzzball is involved in a hitman scheme?"

"Easton got the drugs from somewhere. Why not the neighborhood meth head that nobody believes? Or maybe he provides the prostitute bait. Who knows."

Thad shook his head. "Okay, I can buy that. But a receipt in his pocket? Over a month later? You keep saying this guy's an expert. But this is, like, the third time he hasn't acted like one. It's not jiving, boss."

"I know. Twoomey's phone. Now the receipt. It's sloppy and not the kind of mistakes a professional would make."

"So you're saying it's not the cop? Or not a professional?"

"I'm saying we can't believe anything we see."

"Well, we gotta believe something. Did Easton and Wynn ever talk to each other?"

"Not over the phone, but they wouldn't need to. Wynn lives close. I'm starting to think that's not by accident. There is some good news though. That little piece of paper is enough for a sealed search warrant on both Cummings, Easton, and Cade. At least now I can get into their accounts. Even an evolutionary leap needs to be paid."

The next week went by in a blur of phone calls, drives to Atlanta for the search warrant, and arguing with the IT team about the best way to harvest account data without leaving a trail. Six days later, Luke had the financial statements of all three men on his desk. By Friday they had a small amount of paperwork to sift through. Only Cade seemed to have any money to speak of.

Luke's phone buzzed. All week Tully had texted him. It

didn't go unnoticed. Luke caught Thad watching every time he typed a reply. Thad never said anything, but he got a big stupid grin on his face. Luke ignored him, but he felt bad. Thad had a right to know, but not now. Not yet.

The texts were surface, lacking any romantic context, but Luke could feel the undercurrent of desire. Or maybe he was reading into it. She wasn't used to reaching out, and any effort to do so said volumes.

So did his own behavior. He'd spent every night that week at her place, although he was careful to make it to work on time to avoid questions. Every day she asked, and every night he found himself knocking on her door. That first night was a shameless dig for information, Luke knew that. But something had changed.

She stopped asking him questions. In fact, she never mentioned his investigation again. It surprised both of them; their similarities an unlikely salve. Against the odds, they fit together somehow, content for hours with little conversation.

Now he faced the prospect of discrediting himself or outing her partner while hiding his indiscretions from his own partner. Luke's frustration at the slow pace of the investigation was cushioned by the growing threat to this new relationship. This investigation was the only reason they met, but it would end up screwing one of them. Luke just didn't know who yet. It wasn't fair.

Luke pushed his chair back and threw his pen against the wall with a low snarl.

"What?" Thad swung around.

"Nothing. Absolutely nothing."

There was precious little information in any of the bank statements. Cade's charitable donations were prominent, as Luke expected, no doubt for the tax benefit. His salary from

One World was respectable but didn't put him anywhere near the one-percenters he hung out with.

He was a board member of several environmental services companies and owned a consulting business that brought in over half his sizable yearly income. There were no abnormal expenditures around the time of the two target dates.

Nicholas Cummings had not held a bank account since 1996, and had no debt. He received a small disability check each month, delivered to his dead mother's derelict home on the wrong side of town. He cashed it at a check-cashing place. That's where the money trail ended.

Peter Easton carried a relatively high amount of debt. Nothing extraordinary, but enough to make things difficult. Public servant salaries were public record, easily viewed with a few keystrokes. His wife's heavy student loan balances, a couple of car payments, the house, and three credit cards were bound to make ends hard to meet on a cop's salary.

"Another dead end that won't allow us to take any decisive action," mumbled Luke. "I don't have enough to even name a suspect, much less clear out the case. Holding Cade responsible for any of this monkey business is damn near impossible."

"What if the transactions happened from an offshore account?"

"That's likely," Luke admitted, "but we can't touch those. They're completely legal, and even if our court had jurisdiction to subpoena an offshore bank, the accounts are numbered. It's virtually impossible to build a case on an offshore account because it's so hard to definitively link it to one person. No one's been successful at it without teams of people working on it for weeks." Luke stood and shrugged on his jacket.

Thad huffed. "Which we don't have." Then his look turned suspicious. "Wait, where are you going?"

"I'm gonna go hear what he has to say."

"Who? Wynn?"

Luke didn't answer. He picked up his cell phone.

"I know that look." Thad's voice fell flat. "Luke, I'm not questioning you, but you know damn well you don't want to hear him out."

Luke straightened his tie.

Thad didn't stop. "And you're right, this whole thing stinks of murder. But you're dragging some of the biggest names in...in anything into this investigation. An investigation that by the looks of it," Thad gestured to the mess on Luke's desk, "we'll never be able to close. The potential here for a career-ending mistake is off the charts. Greg is gunning for you, and he's the least of your worries. If you keep picking fights with powerful people just to chase down a hunch we can't prove, we're fucked."

"Keep working on the autopsy reports," said Luke.

Thad threw up his hands as Luke walked out the door without another word.

24

July 15th
1530 Hours

A large painting hung on the wall next to the receptionist's desk. The young man sitting there cast disapproving glances at Luke's rumpled back as he studied the painting. Only muted gray and taupe covered the canvas, but the color was where the tame ended.

The distorted head looked small compared to the gaping mouth that filled the canvass. Hundreds of tiny human shapes marched in lockstep along a wide road into the inky abyss of the mouth. Crudely drawn warts and pockmarks on the grotesque face formed craters and valleys of the mountainous head. A tiny lone figure stood on the top of the tallest mountain. The uplifted head made the figure look defiant despite its featureless shape. Small figures that did not survive the climb littered the side of the mountain.

Luke tilted his head and squinted at the canvas. Modern art irritated him. He was pretty sure the painting was trying to say something, but it was so distorted and vague that it could mean any of a dozen things. Still, he leaned in. A twinge of satisfaction hit him as he saw one figure still crawling up the steep slope. Luke felt a little better about the painting.

"Provocative, isn't it?" The smooth voice had a sophisticated British accent. Luke turned to meet the speaker.

His features weren't exactly handsome, but Alexander Wynn was certainly impressive. At six feet he was two inches taller than Luke, and thick dark hair grayed around the temples. He wore a tailored suit with his shirt collar casually open. Crossing to Luke, he offered his hand.

"Doctor Wynn." Luke shook it.

Alex turned to study the picture himself. "One of my patients painted it. I've had it for ten years and I have to admit, I'm still in awe of it. Every time I think I have it figured out, I see something new that contradicts what I thought earlier. Like the human mind. Fascinating." The doctor's tone was sincere but measured.

Luke immediately hated him.

"Please come into my office."

Luke followed Alex into a lavish, richly paneled office. It looked a lot like John Cade's. Or, Luke suspected, John Cade's office looked like Alex Wynn's. A tufted leather couch sat in the corner with a leather chair next to it. The three-hundred-dollar-an-hour corner.

Alex settled into a judge's chair behind a hand-carved desk. He smiled but it stopped short of his hazel eyes. "What can I do for you today, Agent Marshall? Michael said it was urgent."

"It usually is when the FBI comes calling." Luke settled into the chair on the right making Wynn adjust slightly to see him. "I'm investigating Senator Twomey's death."

"His suicide, you mean?"

"Of course, Doctor," Luke smiled. "His suicide."

"Please call me Alex." Wynn stood and propped his hands on the desk. "Would you like a drink?"

It was only one o'clock, but what the hell.

"Yeah, thanks."

Luke watched him walk to a paned picture window that looked out on a large lawn shaded by oak trees. Beneath the window, a custom cabinet hid a small personal bar. Wynn lifted the panel and raised the lid of an ice bucket filled every morning by his preening assistant. He tossed an ice cube into two glasses, then he took a bottle of Scotch out. Plucking the cork from its hole, he held it to his nose and inhaled deeply.

"Forgive me if I'm stealing your thunder, Agent Marshall, but I'm getting the distinct impression you reject the notion of suicide." He poured a small amount into two glasses and set one in front of Luke.

"Very good." Luke had a hard time masking his disdain.

"And now you're here." Wynn twisted his glass on the polished desktop as he sat. "I'm sorry, but I don't consult with the FBI anymore."

"Oh, I'm very direct about that. You made it perfectly clear you were done. Front page of the New York Times clear, if I remember right."

Alex chuckled. "Then why are you here?"

Luke drained his glass in one drink and leaned forward. "Because you don't think it's suicide either."

"People kill themselves all the time and for much less reason than he had, Agent Marshall. Why would I doubt it?"

"You're the psychiatrist."

Alex studied him through narrowed eyes. "You're right, I am. But I study personality disorders, not the despaired depression of a life spiraling out of control. Although to be honest, I'm doing less and less of that these days." Alex put his glass to his lips.

"But you are an expert in criminal psychology, right?"

"How does that apply to suicide?"

"It doesn't."

"I'm sorry?"

"Cecil Twomey was murdered."

The glass stopped halfway to Alex's lips and he lowered it back to the desktop. "You keep saying that, but what evidence do you have? If you can't prove murder, then it wasn't murder."

"Interesting observation, which of course is factually incorrect. Besides, how do you know I can't prove murder?"

Alex sized up Luke for a moment before speaking. "Well, without the facts of the case, I couldn't say one way or the other, but I assume you would have made an arrest already."

"Not having probable cause to arrest a suspect is a different topic entirely. That, and multiple arrests take more time to put together." He watched Wynn's face twitch then return to calm. It was on. "How well do you know John Cade?"

The doctor's face was icy. "I see. You're not here for a consultation gratis."

"What about Peter Easton?" Luke sat back, his gaze as cold as Wynn's.

At the officer's name, Alex looked surprised. He took a sip then settled back in his chair and laced his fingers together. "I don't know any Peter Easton. John and I studied together at Cambridge many years ago. We've kept in touch over the years. But only just," he added.

"You called him two months ago."

"A general catch up kind of talk. The kind I trust you had a warrant for."

"What did you talk about?" Luke picked off a scrap of paper stuck to the bottom of his shoe and dropped it onto the carpet.

Wynn smiled coldly but did not answer.

"Doctor, the Senator was murdered by a professional hitman." Luke stood and walked to the bar. He picked up the crystal decanter and refilled his glass. Before he put the stopper back, he ran it under his nose and breathed in the aroma. "I see you know Scotch as well as you know criminals."

"Very subtle, Agent Marshall."

"Oh, you're too smart for anything else." Luke turned to face him. "Tell me, this super criminal you wrote about all those years ago. Does he exist?"

"You read my thesis."

"Yes."

"Well, as I said, there is an exception to every rule. If he existed, he would be that exception. Ordinary criminals are one-dimensional and boring. The real danger is the one that is not."

"You mean the real accomplishment."

"You got me, Agent Marshall." Alex threw his hands up in mock surrender. "I am fascinated by such a concept. If this person existed, they would be remarkable."

"They wouldn't be that remarkable. Criminals are motivated by two things – greed and fear of getting caught. Always. And always in that order."

"Are you so sure?"

"I haven't been wrong yet."

The smile on Wynn's face darkened. "For someone who hunts criminals, you have a dull-witted view of the human animal. Especially disturbing for someone in your profession."

"How's that?" Luke leaned forward.

"You leave no room for change. Only those who adapt make any progress."

"Adapt?"

"You've never been proven wrong because truly exceptional people are so rare. Even with all your accomplishments, you have followed the same path as the rest of the dinosaurs at the Bureau. Any new thinker will run circles around you."

"Ignorant?" That threw Luke. Shouldn't he deny this? Instead, Alex boasted about it.

"You law enforcement have a boxed-in view of the bad guy. You were a soldier, were you not? You have the bearing of one."

"Yes."

"In the desert, you shot them down. That was 'justice'. But you can't do that here, can you? So you reduce the human mind to a set of fixed rules that make you comfortable. Most of the time it works. Occasionally, though, they slip through your grasp, do they not? There is a reason for that. You are a prisoner to your own rules if you fail to see one important difference."

"What's that, exactly?"

"It's inconceivable to you that a criminal might be justified in what they do, even if it seems twisted to us. What we call criminal behavior is simply an altered viewpoint. His motivation comes from experiencing circumstances that normal people never have, so his natural perspective is different than ours.

"The most influential people in history have been rule breakers and outcasts simply because they had a different point of view. Why is it so far-fetched to apply that principle to criminology?"

Is. Present tense, thought Luke. "Spoken like a true intellectual," he said.

"Have you not learned to look beyond the expected?"

"Not from a professor."

"I agree with you there, Agent Marshall. Life is a much

better instructor. If there's one thing it has taught me, it is that you cannot corral a mind. The infinite possibilities of the human mind are untapped. We have yet to see what it can do. Your own mind is narrow, Agent Marshall. You may have met your match this time."

"My match," said Luke quietly. Alex's face grew hard making Luke smile. "Doesn't sound very hypothetical."

Alex's sneer was dark. It was clear to Luke that any hatred was mutual, but Alex seemed to be enjoying himself. "But it is hypothetical, an exercise in maybe. I was merely commenting that you are convinced of murder and have not made an arrest."

"So you don't know anything about crime syndicate slave trade around military bases funded by the DOD? Washington's dirty little secret."

Alex didn't answer. He glared at Luke who didn't flinch. Neither man looked away.

"Oh, that's right. You're a forensic psychiatrist. You wouldn't know anything about that," said Luke.

"I no longer consult for the FBI," said Alex standing and buttoning his jacket.

"No." Luke stood too. He didn't offer a handshake. "You've gone into business for yourself."

"You know the most incredible thing about the human animal, Agent Marshall?"

Luke stopped.

"Its ability to surprise. Never assume anything, especially about yourself."

Luke walked out of the office. The heat blasted him when he stepped out of the air conditioning and walked to his car.

Alexander Wynn was about to undergo some very serious scrutiny. Even if he couldn't get anything on the prestigious doctor, Luke vowed he would make things as difficult as possible for him. He smiled as he thought of serving a search warrant on that office and ripping it apart. Wynn would know that he too could bleed.

Luke's phone buzzed in his pocket. He pulled it out and looked at the screen and hit the answer button. "Hey."

When he hung up, he had forgotten all about his feud with the doctor. He threw his car into reverse then dialed Thad. It was early on Friday, but Luke needed to tell him he wouldn't be back in the office until Monday.

25

July 16th
1600 Hours

The brim of his stained Rockies baseball cap shaded Luke's eyes, but his exposed neck burned in the relentless July sun. He longed for the deep quiet shade of a square back in town. On the phone, Tully told him to meet her at the marina and bring a weekend bag. She hadn't said much else.

Now Luke stood in the marina parking lot, his conscience sweating as much as his skin. Alex Wynn's behavior ruffled him. So what if the guy didn't like him? Plenty of people didn't like him. But the way the man became so animated when talking about a hitman, had Luke bothered.

Then he remembered the receipt from Easton's pocket and the conversation that went on a little too long in that parking lot, and a sour feeling hit him in the gut. What had that slimy dope slinger found out?

And then there was Tully. Thad was right. Did any of this matter? He was chasing his tail hoping the evidence he needed would materialize in front of him. If he kept pursuing this, would the real guilty even feel justice? Or would all the wrong people be crushed by it?

Easton's wife and daughter. His fellow officers. Tully. All this time and he still couldn't escape from making that choice.

He heard her before he saw her. From a hundred yards away the thumping of old-school country music reached him. An old beat up green Blazer screeched around the line of parked cars and headed for him. The windows were down and Tully's hair whipped around her face. She rolled into the parking space next to him, cut the ignition, and swung open the door.

His conscience would have to wait. Whatever Tully had cooked up was all he wanted to think about. Luke forgot his agitation and the sweat rolling down his back. He pushed up his sunglasses to hide his stare.

Tully's frayed cutoffs fell below the curve of her butt exposing tanned legs. A white tank top skimmed her chest. She'd traded her favorite motorcycle boots for cowboy boots, and a windswept mess of dark blond fell around her oversized aviators as she slid to the ground.

"Hey there, G-man." She smiled at him.

Luke dropped his bag on the sticky blacktop and grabbed her around the waist.

"Is that a .45 in your pocket or are you happ...," she teased, but he cut her off when he pressed his lips hard on hers.

"Wow," said Tully, straightening her glasses. She reached into the back of the Blazer and pulled out a worn brown leather bag with a gigantic silver buckle. Then she pulled her boots off and tossed them in the back before slamming the tailgate. From the bag, she pulled out a pair of cheap flip-flops and threw them on the ground.

"I couldn't touch you for three days." Luke came up

behind her and kissed her neck as she slid the flip-flops over her toes.

She lay her head back on his shoulder and leaned into him. "How does two straight days of it sound?"

"I'm interested," he murmured.

"Then let's get the party started right." She reached into the bag again and pulled out a mason jar containing clear liquid and a single lemon slice. With a sly smile, she thrust it into his hands and walked away.

Tucking the jar into his chest, Luke grabbed his bag and followed. "Where are we going?"

He saw her smile, but she kept walking.

"Alright, I'll play your little game."

"What's the matter, G-man? Hate not being in charge?"

"Yeah. Unless someone makes it worth my while."

She stopped and whipped to face him so fast he almost dropped the jar. Her lips were so close to his that he could taste her sweet breath, but she stopped short and hovered. "What makes you think I'm not?"

Then she turned and walked down the dock without looking behind. He looked at her swaying hips for so long he had to run to catch up.

Like a lost puppy, Luke tailed her to a pier marked '5'. Two slips from the end of the pier she dropped her bag and leaped onto a white speedboat. The blue stripping down the side twisted into the words 'Savannah Blue'.

Snapping off the cover, she wadded it up and threw it below deck, then turned to Luke hesitating on the pier. He knew as much about boats as he did about open-heart surgery.

"You comin, G-man?"

He grinned and tossed his bag at her. She looked surprised but caught it easily and dropped it on the deck.

Then with fake confidence, he jumped onto the boat as she unwound the mooring ropes.

"Ready?" She smiled that awkward smile at him.

"Ready." This felt so good he no longer cared if it was right.

At a flick of her wrist, water sloshed as the engine roared to life. She pushed the throttle forward and the boat lurched. They puttered down the narrow waterway and through the mast pillars marking the marina entrance.

As they reached the mouth of the river, the buoys demanding 'no wake' fell behind and Tully pressed the throttle. Luke grabbed the seat to keep his balance as the nose tipped up and the boat shot forward.

The spires of the Talmadge Bridge faded into the background and marsh spread out in every direction. The wide river snaked back and forth cutting through the endless tidal creeks and grassy flats.

Luke made his way to the back seat and fell into it. He grew up in the mountains of Colorado. Here in the reeds, spires of dead trees, and the fishy smells he was a stranger. But it was beautiful the way the sun glinted off the water.

Startled by the engine, a flock of cranes rose into the sky. A quick flash caught Luke's eye, and he turned in time to see a scaly tail slip into the murky water.

Tully stood at the wheel, her hair streaming in the wind. For a second, he didn't recognize her profile. Her shoulders were relaxed, and she held her head high. For the first time in their short history, she looked calm, happy even. Luke forgot any apprehension about their destination. This week could only get better.

They followed the river for an hour. Every now and then Tully would cut the engine and point something out to him. She knew every inlet, outlet, and animal on this river. As soon as Luke was sure they were too far to ever find their way back, they rounded a wide bend and he saw it. It was perfect.

In front of a scraggly patch of trees on a low island, a small cottage rose up on wooden pylons. A long pier stretched across the front and down to a covered dock on the edge of the island. There was nothing else in sight but the marshy lowlands and the river stretching toward the Atlantic.

Tully let off the throttle and turned the wheel. The boat swung around, and she slipped it into reverse. She backed the boat into the dock. Cutting the engine, she hopped onto the bow, threw out the bumpers, and lassoed the pier.

Once she had tied the boat off, she smiled at Luke. "We're here."

"I'm not sure where 'here' is, but I like it," Luke said, taking in the water lapping around the barnacle-crusted pylons. He heard the low hum of a generator providing power to the remote house. "Where do you go if you need milk?"

"Taken care of." She jumped onto the pier. He followed her carrying both bags. They climbed a short flight of stairs that connected to the long walkway running across the front of the cabin. The last three stairs brought them to the screened porch.

Wicker rockers and a hammock piled with pillows furnished the porch. Tully put her key into the front door and turned it. Immediately a blast of hot humid air from inside hit Luke. He hesitated. Maybe he could sleep on the porch.

Without hesitating, Tully swept inside and began opening windows. Luke pretended to check out the porch, letting the hot air clear before following her into the living room.

An overstuffed couch and two chairs were grouped in

the center of the room. The brick fireplace seemed ridiculous in the oppressive heat.

"Open those for me." Tully pointed behind him to two more windows facing the front porch. She crossed the large open room into the kitchen and opened two more.

As soon as she was satisfied that all the windows were open, she walked back into the living room and flipped a switch by the front door. In the attic, a fan started with a low hum. A steady breeze rushed in through the screens and back to the unseen fan. Immediately the sweat on Luke's forehead evaporated along with worries about his overnight prospects. He looked around.

Old wood paneling that Luke suspected was original had been painted over in fresh white. A dark blue rug covered the wide planked wooden floor and two coordinating throw pillows sat on the couch and chair. Clear signs of a woman's domain.

Three portraits hung on the wall over the fireplace. One was a grainy color photo of a smiling man in sheriff's brown with dark brown hair, a mustache, and Tully's unmistakable blue eyes. The other two were black and white. The last looked like it had been taken around the First World War.

Tully was in the kitchen. She'd flipped on an ancient radio and started unloading two boxes full of groceries as Johnny Cash wafted out of the speakers. They were from different worlds, but she had good taste in music.

Luke followed, intending to help. She grabbed one box and hoisted it onto the counter with a grunt. He lifted the other and placed it beside hers. She smiled and before he could stop himself, his arms were wrapped around her waist and he pulled her close. They danced slowly to the music.

"Is that chapstick in your pocket or are you happy to see me?"

"Bitch," he breathed.

She giggled and twisted out of his grasp and turned to the boxes.

"You own this place?"

"Papaw Meara left it to me," Tully said. "I'm named after him. And Papa Meara got it from his daddy."

"Do these places last that long? Seems like the water would take its toll."

"It does. Takes a lot of upkeep. William Meara built this place in '25 to run his whiskey out to the coast. Back then the Savannah River was the only patrolled river in the area. That's where all the steamers came in. Only moonshiners and locals were on the Bull River, most of them down on Tybee. For forty years this was the only structure sitting on the river. I can't let it...what?"

"I should have known you came from a family of boot-leggers." Luke grinned.

"You better wipe that shit eatin' grin off your face, or I'll do it for you."

"Thank you for proving my point." He ducked as she threw a loaf of bread at him. "It's pretty impressive, actually. Outlaw to third-generation cop in only four takes." His grin faltered at her smirk.

"You didn't go back far enough."

"Huh?"

"William Meara was the Sheriff of Wilkes County for most of his adult life."

Luke's mouth fell open, making Tully giggle again.

"And he was the best distiller in the region. He needed this place because his whiskey was in such high demand in New York City. The waterways were the safest and cheapest way to move it up the coast. Papaw always bragged about Congressman LaGuardia being a big fan, but no one can seem to verify that for me."

"Wow."

"It's part of the reason I moved to Savannah after Momma died. I love this place."

She rarely said a word about her family and when she did, it was accompanied by unhealthy amounts of liquor. He had begun to avoid the topic entirely. Now she spoke of them with a smile.

The thought hit Luke at the same time the coffee can did. It bounced off his chest and careened toward his big toe. The top popped off, but the foil seal saved the day. He smiled in spite of his throbbing foot.

"You come out here a lot?" Luke set the can on the counter and eyed his attacker. She mouthed the word 'sorry'.

"I do now. Momma was never a big fan of this place." Tully opened a drawer next to the sink and pulled out a dishtowel. "She only came out because Dad loved it, and she loved him. I came with Granny and Papaw as often as I could, but she never came again after Daddy died."

"Mom wasn't a big fan of mosquitoes, huh?"

"Don't you start. They're not that bad."

"So that's how it is? Put on bug spray and shut the hell up."

"Or just shut the hell up."

Luke grabbed the dish towel from her and began to twist it in his hands.

"Do it and die," she warned as he bladed to snap it at her. He let it loose and it cracked her on the hip. She howled and jumped on him and they fell to the floor.

By the time they ate dinner, the bed was rumpled, and the sun was going down. They tried watching TV but spent the hour arguing. Tully declared all science fiction 'total bullshit', while Luke maintained that aliens were just as believable as a princess kissing a frog, but that girls didn't have trouble getting into those stories. That earned him a pillow to the head.

That conversation led to a related argument about what to watch. Luke kept stopping on every sci-fi movie he could find to wind her up more. He settled on a baseball game because when he stopped on it, Tully stopped arguing and watched.

An argument soon broke out over the playoff prospects of her beloved Braves, and they agreed to turn the TV off and move to the hammock.

An hour later, they were curled up on the hammock with her head nestled in his arm. The breeze off the river, combined with the porch ceiling fan, canceled the humid air and made the dark space pleasant. Bullfrogs croaked softly and a crane cried out somewhere down the river. Soon Tully was sound asleep on Luke's arm.

He watched her as she slept. She had freckles. He'd noticed them before, but they stood out now, at home on her pretty nose. He could barely see the scar she hated so much. Back in the real world, she carried it around like a pack mule. Out here it seemed as normal a feature as ears or eyebrows.

Nothing sarcastic or harsh had come out of her mouth in the last few hours. She still felt the need to argue every-thing with him, but she had giggled the whole time. Today was the first time that sound came out of her mouth since he met her. He was going to have to get to know her all over again.

She snored softly, her breath lifting a strand of hair. Hair always found its way onto her face, usually from tossing and turning. Eyeballs darted around behind her closed lids, but for now she was still and peaceful. She only stirred to burrow further into his chest. Life had been brutal to this woman, and she still found a way to let him in.

The Marshall men were a little more stubborn when it came to love. His dad hadn't married until he was thirty-six. When he did give up the ship, it was to a hot mess. Marshall bravado made it impossible to resist playing hero to the damsel in distress, or something like that. His mother turned tail and ran as fast as she could away from her demons. Away from Joe Marshall and her two young sons. Luke was in college before they found out what happened to her.

Here he was doing the same thing. Tully Meara was the absolute wrong call. Then again, Marshall men couldn't resist a bad idea.

26

July 17th
0815 Hours

The next morning Luke woke up to blurry light in the window. Rain plinked on the tin roof. The dim bedroom and soft sheets lulled him back to a doze.

He rolled over expecting to bury his face in a mess of hair that smelled like flowers. Instead, he felt a cool pillow. Tully was gone. He reached for his watch. Seven-thirty.

Slipping out of bed, he pulled on shorts and padded into the living room. It was empty. Outside, past the porch screening, something flashed then disappeared. Luke looked again and saw a fishing pole rise and fall.

A few moments later, dressed in a tank top and shorts he stepped onto the porch. Hanging next to the screen door he spied a worn Boonie hat complete with decorative fish hooks and lures. He grabbed it and headed out. The rain felt good. It cooled him while the marshy air prodded him awake.

Tully sat on the pier where it crossed the water to the

dock, legs dangling over the side. Her tattered t-shirt and rolled up quick-dry pants were soaked. She had a fishing pole wedged between her legs and slouched underneath a hat like Luke's but with fewer hooks and lures.

He grabbed the extra pole lying next to the tub of night crawlers. Fishing he could do.

Awkwardly, he tried to maneuver into a sitting position without falling into the river. The lure snagged his shorts as he twisted. It made Tully laugh.

Like the night before, it struck him how different she was. Beneath that floppy hat, with her feet swinging from the pier, she looked young and innocent. Not hard and brittle the way he'd grown to know her. This place drew the poison out of her. Maybe she could stay like this if they never went back. Maybe they both could.

"Morning." She smiled at him.

"Morning. You're up early."

"They don't bite as good when it gets hot."

"It's even too hot down here for the damn fish," joked Luke. He brought the pole over his head and cast.

She looked pleased at his ease with the rod. "You fish a lot?"

"Used to go all the time growing up. Ski in the winter, hike and fish in the summer."

"Then you're gonna love it here."

"I believe you. I have a sneaking suspicion your Mom didn't like fishing. There's not much else to do here."

Tully laughed. "She hated it. Mom always got so bored. But out here, you do nothing. It's kinda the point."

"Works for me."

"Hiking the Rockies sounds fun, though." She eyed him sideways.

"Yeah? I'll take you some time."

"I'd like that." She smiled.

He couldn't help himself and leaned in to kiss her. "Is this why you brought me out here?" He said when they broke apart. "To fish?"

"Why do you think I brought you out here?" She pulled her lips away from his.

"Either fishing or you're going to make me disappear. I'm still not sure you've totally forgiven me. Maybe this is all a ruse to make me pay for my sins."

Tully laughed. "I'm not gonna lie, it crossed my mind." She leveled her blue eyes on him. "This place has nothing but good memories for me. I didn't think you'd change that. That's all."

"You still thinkin' it?"

"It depends."

"On what?"

"If you keep talkin." She picked up a worm and flicked it at him.

"Fine, I'll shut up."

"Just kidding. Talk as much as you like. I like hearing your voice."

"You seem...happy out here." Luke wasn't sure if he should bring it up, but it was too late now.

"I am."

"Not like 'on vacation' happy. I feel like I'm meeting you for the first time in a parallel universe."

She rolled her eyes then grew serious. "Nobody stares at me out here." She reeled in an empty hook choked with soggy grass and frowned at it.

"Why does it bother you so much? Most people show off their scars."

"Idiots," she huffed.

"Why are they idiots?"

"Anyone who makes fun of their scars is lying, and anyone who thinks they're cool is a knuckle dragging buffoon. They fail to grasp a basic concept. Or maybe they're too shallow to care." She stabbed a nightcrawler with her hook.

"What concept is that?"

"Most people get to tuck away their past and bring it out when they're ready. In private, surrounded by people they trust. But when you can't hide it, the most painful moment you've ever lived through is advertised like a billboard." She swung and her bait hit the surface with a plunk. "Out here I'm, I dunno, normal. Like everyone else."

"You mean 'normal' the way everyone pretends to be. We all go around saying we're okay when we're not. It's exhausting, but no one will admit it until they're forced to. Why would you want to pretend?"

"Why? To be able to face the world and not have them know my deepest and darkest. To make my past my own, not a public spectacle, that's why. When people see a scar they know something terrible happened."

"What's wrong with that?"

"It's none of their fucking business. I wonder every day what my life would be like if I didn't have this scar on my face. Who would I be if I never had to endure the pity?" The words poured out of her, matter of factly, lacking any emotion.

"But you have the chance to break free of it," Luke said. "To live honestly, with no pretense. You don't wear the chains the rest of us do. It didn't beat you. That's what's on display. You don't have to pretend."

"I'd rather pretend. Pretending would be a relief."

"Trust me. It's not." The words came out before he could stop them.

Tully's head came up and her eyes narrowed as she studied him. This place was working its purging voodoo on him now. Was he really about to tell her this? Not even the men that made it out of Iraq with him knew what happened. Why was it so important that she know?

Never mind that she didn't know what he found in her partner's pocket; she might turn tail as soon as she found out he was a coward. It wasn't until she shifted uncomfortably that Luke realized he'd stopped talking. His bobber dipped below the water, but he paid it no attention.

"We were pinned down in the bombed-out shell of a little tobacco shop outside Mosul."

Tully had to turn her ear toward him to hear him. His voice barely rose above the pattering rain.

"It was early in the war. We were picking off the high value targets one by one. My team was tasked with capturing Muharib Al-Asir. He controlled that particular patch of hell and coordinated most of the roadside attacks in that region. Intel had him holed up in a compound about sixty miles outside Mosul in a small village. They were right, and we had him in our sights. But it turned out they were wrong about one thing. How many insurgents were between us and the target.

"It was still too hot for helos at the time, so we went in by vehicle. We had cover of dark, but our vehicle hit an IED outside town. Maybe several, I'm still not sure."

He took a deep breath. "It took out three of my guys immediately. We barely made it to cover at the tobacco store before the hadjis showed up. Although 'cover' is overstating it. It wasn't much more than a low cinderblock wall, and they had the high ground. Two more guys went down. My best friend Rob took one in the thigh. He bled out in under a minute."

Tully looked back at the hazy river to give him a little privacy.

"The cavalry got there by sunrise, but the insurgents were dug in. And only a block away from us. Any air support would have killed us too, so we fought on and off for twelve hours. By then every one of my team including me was hit, but I was the only one that could still hold a gun up. The rest of the team was out of commission or dead. The infantry unit took enough pressure off that I was able to switch our location to a more defensible, intact building across the street. As soon as it was dark, I carried them all across."

Luke paused and cleared his throat. It was a minute before he continued.

"I got the three still alive over first then went back for the dead. My last trip across the street, this li…"

Her forehead wrinkled when his voice broke. He dipped his pole several times while he composed himself. "This little kid runs out from the alley three doors down. Out of nowhere, he's kicking a soccer ball in the middle of a war zone. I'm standing in the doorway, and he sees me. I swear we stare at each other for an hour." Loathing crept into Luke's voice.

"Maybe it was the fog, I don't know, but I'm convinced he's gonna run off and tell the hadjis where we are. I didn't know how long he was there. He could have known exactly how many of us there were and how many were dead. I couldn't take that chance. I didn't take that chance."

Out of the corner of his eye, Luke saw her flinch. The rubber handle cracked as he twisted it between his hands. "It was us or him, and I made the wrong call." Luke laughed bitterly. "You asked why I didn't take the fucking medal. There you go."

The rain beat steady on the river.

"It wasn't his war." Suddenly Luke couldn't stand the feel of the rain on his skin.

Tully didn't seem to mind the rain as she intently studied the ripples beneath her feet. "Wasn't yours either."

"Doesn't matter.

"Of course it matters." She sounded defensive.

"When is it ever okay to hurt someone who doesn't deserve it?"

"You say that like you had a choice. That choice is a luxury; a question only intellectuals in classrooms and politicians behind podiums get to ask. In the real world, there is no answer."

"There is an answer. Never. It's never okay."

"But you'd be dead if you didn't," she said quietly. He looked over and found her looking at him. "You didn't make the wrong call, Luke." They fell quiet.

Collateral damage was the term. Most people could write that little boy off without a second thought. An unavoidable casualty to save more important lives. Justified.

Luke spent a lot of sleepless nights and overworked his liver trying to make himself believe what Tully and the rest of the world seemed convinced of, but he failed. Justified? Justice isn't supposed to punish the innocent. When it does, it isn't justice.

Two years before, he caught two separate high-profile cases he couldn't square with his post war vows. He walked away from both when it became clear that all the wrong people would pay. So what if an accountant embezzled 50 million dollars? God forbid the rich get justice while a little girl with MS lost her only parent to the federal correctional black hole.

He never offered an apology or an explanation and never would. The first time he got slapped on the wrist. The second time Joe Long demoted him and shipped him to this steamy purgatory where Steve Simon could watch him. It was the perfect excuse to get him out of Washington so he couldn't make any more waves.

Tully didn't know any of that and she never would. And she didn't know that she would be directly responsible for destroying him.

Last night he fell in love with his savage, fragile beauty. Any stability she retained hung on by a whiskey-soaked thread. What this cluster fuck would do to her made him physically ill.

Now her fate would rest on his conscience like all the others. Last night on that hammock he realized he would have to choose his downfall. He could have Tully or a career. Not both.

"It's not about wrong or right for people like us." Tully broke through his racing thoughts. "It's about surviving long enough to claw your way out of the hole that life kicks you into. Survival isn't right or wrong. You do what you have to. Period. People who bray about right or wrong have never faced their own extinction."

The rain picked up.

"It doesn't have to be that way. I don't have to be that way."

Tully gave him a bitter scowl. "What? Are you gonna save the world, like some damn superhero?"

Luke ignored her scathing tone and kept his voice even. "Probably not. Doesn't mean I can't try."

"That's exactly what it means." Tully's fishing pole jerked as she twisted to confront him, agitated. "That's a lie we tell ourselves to feel better about our meaningless existence."

"Is everything a lie? Do you believe in anything?"

"Yeah, I believe in something. I believe in making yourself strong enough to stand up when you should get knocked down, and smart enough to win when you should lose. Nobody's coming to help."

Luke kept his voice low. "Just because everyone in your life has failed you, doesn't mean I'm wrong."

Tully's pole landed on the boards with a crash. She leaped up and half ran to the porch door.

Luke was on her heels. When she whirled, he was ready for it. He reached up and caught her wrist in mid-swing. The rain fell hard now stinging their skin.

"You don't know anything about me," she yelled at him. She tried to sound mocking, but tears welled in her eyes. "Are you gonna be my hero? Are you gonna save me?" She tried to rip her hand back.

Luke wrestled her arms down and placed his lips by her ear. "Only if you'll do the same for me."

Tully stopped fighting and bowed her head. Luke released her and lifted the brim of her hat from her eyes. "Why did you automatically assume I was talking about you?"

She avoided his gaze.

"I don't have all the answers, Tully, but I don't think it's that complicated. Good and bad exist together. They have to. Look, I know life is shitty, but maybe if we end up with more good than bad, we can make it be enough." He hoped he sounded convincing. If she could believe it maybe he could too.

"Look at this place. At you. A location was all it took to change you into someone I don't even recognize. You don't feel the need to throw yourself in front of bullets out here. You're my proof the answer is simple."

She squeezed her eyes shut to stop the tears. It was a minute before she composed herself enough to speak. "How?" It was a whisper.

"Sorry?"

"How do you make it enough?"

He pressed his lips to her forehead. "I'm not sure yet, but I think I'm getting warmer."

Tully's damp hair fell over his shoulder as he picked her up and carried her through the door leaving the pounding rain behind.

27

August 3rd
0125 Hours

John Cade flinched and glanced around as a dog barked somewhere down the street. He walked past a weedy lot flanked on three sides by one-story cinderblock houses with peeling green paint. The remnants of a chain-link fence surrounded a patchy common area littered with toys and trash.

A tiny convenience store with bars on the windows and the cinderblock houses lined one side of the street. On the other side, a decaying motel advertised rates by the half hour. Cade left his BMW parked in the motel lot. He prayed it would still be there when he got back.

Cade had gone into the motel to inquire about a room at ten pm, exactly as Wynn directed him to, and paid the clerk to hold onto his cell phone. Another item he wondered if he'd see again.

The hotel was mercifully vacant on a random Tuesday. He paced the smelly lobby until he saw Wynn pull past and park. He couldn't get out of there fast enough. The scent of cleaning solution and body odor lingered in the fabric of his three-hundred-dollar linen shirt as he walked down the street.

Ahead, parked among a hundred other vehicles crowding the shoulder, he saw Alex's ridiculous car. Cade couldn't believe he drove that thing. So much for blending in. Then he remembered the way the toothless motel attendant looked at him and scooted down the cracked sidewalk faster.

A cigarette soared out of the slit in the driver's window as Cade approached. It sent up a stream of sparks as it hit the ground. A woman walked by loaded down with grocery bags oblivious to him or the man in the car. Her face dripped with sweat.

Once she passed, Cade grabbed the handle of the steel gray Ferrari 458 and swiftly pulled the door closed behind him. He adjusted the vent pouring out cold air. It wasn't just the humid summer night that had him sweating.

Without looking over, Wynn shifted into drive and screeched out of the parking spot.

"Alex, I know...," Cade started.

"Why the bloody fuck is the FBI coming to my office? And asking about a dead cop no less. I would love to know how he made that particular connection."

Wynn kept checking the mirrors as he took several left turns to make sure they weren't followed.

"I...I don't know," stammered Cade.

Wynn pulled the car into a grocery store parking lot. He downshifted, and the car lurched forward to a stop. Then he twisted in his seat so he could confront the cowering Cade. "Like hell you don't know. How did he end up at my office?"

Cade seemed to forget his nervousness for a minute and glared at Wynn. "He found a fucking phone, Alex."

The doctor looked surprised for a moment, then his face

hardened. "Is that so?"

Cade could tell this was news to Wynn. It emboldened him. "The question you should be asking is why did he find a cell phone in Twomey's pocket? I gave you specific instructions to take care of that little item. We're here because of your mistake, not mine."

Wynn recovered quickly and offered a dark smile. "You really think that matters, mate? If that FBI dick knows about the reporter, then it's you he's coming after. Not me."

Cade's fear returned, but he wasn't nervous this time. His eyes grew wide with terror.

Wynn sat back in his seat and lit another cigarette. "I'm not a danger to him. He's got plausible deniability on me. But you. You have the headlines to sink his considerably profitable ship. And if the FBI is poking around, he's going to plug all the holes if you know what I mean."

Cade shook his head violently. "He wouldn't do that. Not to me."

Wynn flicked ash out the window. "You really believe that? No one knows better than you what he's capable of, Johnny. Did you really think you're his only coda?"

Cade said nothing but his chest heaved.

"You need to have your server checked, Johnny. By people you trust. And your phone too. He probably knows you're out running around right now. Why do you think I made you leave your phone at that rancid motel? It doesn't look good. Especially when you're already a threat."

"I'm not a threat. He knows that. He only got where he is because of me."

Wynn took another puff. "That makes you a bigger risk. Somehow that fat arse got hold of your email and that was enough to have him silenced. I can't imagine the details you have on the prick. He's not about to let anyone torpedo his campaign. *Anyone*."

Cade grabbed his knees in near panic. "I'm not a threat to him," he repeated in a whisper.

"Everyone folds when they're under enough pressure, Johnny. You haven't exactly got a steel-clad constitution. I've seen you crack under less than this. You're an idiot if you think he doesn't know that."

"What do I do?" Cade wasn't asking Wynn in particular. He was just asking.

"Don't do anything stupid. If the FBI agent had anything, he would have already made an arrest. There's been one inquiry on my bank accounts, and my phone records were pulled. If you were paying attention, he's probably pulled yours too. If he doesn't know about the offshore accounts, we've nothing to worry about. Sit tight and it will blow over. All you have to do is control your nerves. A tall order, I know."

"But he knows about you."

"We're college mates. That's a good enough reason for us to be in touch. He has the disadvantage here. He has to prove his case, and he can't prove bugger all."

"That doesn't really help me does it?"

"Not my problem, mate."

"Alex, you have to help me." Cade grabbed his old college friend's arm.

Wynn yanked away. "No, I don't. This partnership is over. We have to let things cool off a bit. I've got my own problems to deal with, don't I? This is our last collaboration."

"No, you can't.... I don't know what to do."

"Get your shit checked. If I get hacked, I know about it immediately. You'd do well to follow suit. I hope you have a plan B, mate. Now get out." Wynn flicked his cigarette onto the pavement.

"You're not going to take me back to the motel?"

"Get out of my car. Don't ever call me again."

28

———

August 5
0830 Hours

The quiet office soothed Luke's racing mind. Sleep had been elusive the past few days. He had to make a decision, and he knew he couldn't postpone it for much longer. Kicking this ridiculous job to the curb and running away with her was what he wanted, but it wasn't that simple. It was never that simple.

For the last two nights, Luke stayed in his hotel room instead of with her to clear his mind. He knew that any decision he made in her presence was not a rational one. He was still lucid enough to realize that.

By the time he heard anyone moving around in the office, he'd already been there for three hours. At 8:30 the hall lights flicked on and he knew Susie had arrived. Soon, doors begin slamming and conversation drifted down the hall. If he stayed in the office, he wouldn't have to see anyone except Thad.

No one ever came to the broom closet and that suited him just fine. He preferred to be left alone. Especially now that Greg bumped shoulders with him every chance he got. Not to mention Thad's rapidly souring attitude. Not that Luke blamed him.

Luke leaned back in his chair with his hands clasped behind his neck and listened to the sound of the AC over the voices down the hall. It was a much nicer sound, but he was starting to wonder if the whoosh wasn't actually the sound of this case sucking the life out of him.

Twomey didn't kill himself. There was no denying it now. But the only evidence he had was on a dead man. The questions kept piling up with no answers. How far up this went was anyone's guess. If this broke, it would make the last administration's scandals look like an ice cream social.

With the woman he loved caught in the middle.

Maybe with a little maneuvering, he could still close the case quietly and protect her from the worst of it. Right now, the truth was his exclusive turf, and it was what he said it was. Besides, he would probably never have enough evidence to do more than implicate Easton and cast doubt on the other players. Cade was up to his eyeballs in this mess, and more players were surfacing. The more shoulders to bear the blame, the softer the blow. In theory anyway.

Luke took out his phone and pulled up the photo of the receipt from Easton's pocket. He zoomed in on the date and spent the next few minutes staring at it, in deep thought about something else.

The door flew open and Thad breezed in taking off his jacket. When he saw Luke, he started. These days he almost always beat Luke into work.

"Oh hey, boss. You're here early."

Luke set his phone on the desk.

"Hey, have you talked to Susie?"

"No. I haven't even been out for coffee…," Luke was interrupted by the buzzing of his cell phone. Before he could reach out to flip it over, Thad's eyes flicked to the glowing screen. It read 'Tully'.

Thad froze. "What the hell?"

Luke mashed the silent button.

"Tell me that wasn't who I think it was."

Luke set his mouth and avoided Thad's gaze. Now it was Thad that started pacing the broom closet. Luke sat still looking at the phone cradled in his hands. Time to face the music.

"Dude, what are you doing? Please tell me you haven't been spending all this time with her."

"She's sorry about trying to break your nose. She feels bad actually."

"You know that's not what I'm talking about. We pulled a search warrant on her partner, and you're sleeping with her? Were you sleeping with her then?"

Luke said nothing.

"Oh my god," said Thad. He threw himself into his chair.

"We don't have anything we can move on," hedged Luke. He knew it sounded pathetic.

"You're the one that said we follow every lead, boss, no matter how weak. Not that the receipt in his pocket is exactly weak." Thad snapped out of his stupor. Now he was angry. "Or do the rules not apply to your love life?"

At Thad's challenge, Luke glared. "Leave her out of this. She's not involved," he growled.

"That's not what I asked you." Thad calmed down, but he didn't back away from Luke's menacing glare. Instead, he pointed at him. "They were close. Very close. How can you be sure she didn't know about this?"

"We can't assume that." Luke was suddenly defensive. That question occurred to him a million times, but hearing Thad say it out loud grated his conscience.

"Really? 'Cuz we've been assuming an awful lot in this

investigation. What are you gonna do if her dead hero partner turns out to be a political assassin? What are you gonna do if she knew about it?" Thad jabbed a finger in Luke's direction again. "If it comes down to choosing between blondie and the cold hard bitch truth, which one you gonna pick?"

Luke's lip curled when Thad called Tully 'blondie'.

"Never mind. Stupid question." Thad sat back sounding defeated.

"I'm sorry," growled Luke.

"You heard me." Thad whirled in his chair to look at the morning sun streaming through the window, leaving Luke glaring at air. "Since when does a woman do this to you?"

When Luke said nothing, Thad plowed on, undeterred. "Christmas came early last year when Steve told me I was working with you. But two months ago, a different Luke Marshall walked through that door. I don't know what happened."

Luke didn't have an answer. He didn't know either. He ran his hands over his face then through his hair.

Thad was right. What was he doing? Tully probably wanted to know if he was coming over after work. He should walk away. Delete her from his phone and never speak to her again. Even as the thought slammed into his mind, he knew he would be knocking on her door at five. Earlier, if he could help it. Thad wouldn't understand, but she wasn't just some woman.

Thad sighed. "And now Cade's spooked."

Luke straightened. "What?"

"Susie said he came in about thirty minutes before me. He asked for you, but Greg pulled him into his office. She said Cade bolted three minutes later."

Luke snatched up his phone and punched in Cade's

number from memory. It rang once and went to voicemail. He dialed again. Straight to voicemail.

"John, it's Luke Marshall. You came to see me an hour ago. I assume you want to talk, and you can talk to me directly. Call me back on this number. I'll meet you somewhere neutral. I promise I'll work with you as much as I possibly can. We can come to an arrangement. Call me back. I'll be waiting for your call."

"And now he won't pick up the phone, great. Luke? Where are you going? Luke."

Luke didn't hear Thad as he threw the door open and started down the hall. Standing by the file cabinet in his office, Greg didn't seem surprised to see Luke when he turned around.

He looked pleased at the fury on Luke's face. "Your suspects are as skittish as you are. How you ever earned your little nickname is a mystery to me. All you do is tiptoe around trying to keep from offending the local fuzz."

Luke stood rooted in the doorway, his ears buzzing.

"I know what you came here to say. But you're going to mishandle this one too, Marshall, and you don't need my help to do it. But you can take comfort in the fact that it will be your last failure at the Bureau. We need real agents, Marshall, not washed up PTSD patients that can't handle their shit."

Luke didn't mean to do it, but a moment later he heard Susie scream behind him and saw Greg Lawrence looking up at him from the floor. Blood gushed from Greg's broken nose onto his blue shirt. A bruise was already darkening his left eye socket.

Luke spun and stalked past a cowering Susie out the front door. Halfway down the block, Thad caught up to him.

"What was that? You punched him?"

Luke kept walking.

"Where are you going? Stop walking and talk to me," Thad yelled at him, making people turn and look.

Luke pulled up and faced him. "I'm going to find Cade. Make him talk. This ends now."

"And do what with it? Are you gonna charge anyone? Who can you charge? Do you even know what you're doing anymore? What we're doing?"

Luke didn't answer immediately, and Thad threw his hands up.

"Keep your phone on you," said Luke as he turned and started to the car. "And stay out of the office. I'm going to find Cade and find out what's going on. This ends today, one way or another."

Thad jerked his head upward once then turned and walked down the street. "Oh, I seriously doubt that," he said under his breath

Luke could tell Thad was pissed, but he didn't really care right now. As fast as he could without running, Luke walked to the parking lot and pulled the Impala keys out of his pocket. His phone buzzed again. He pulled it out of his pocket expecting to see Cade's number flashing.

It was Tully again. He saw he had missed two calls from her while he was punishing Greg for his transgressions. Something was wrong. She preferred texting to calling. Now she'd called three times in a row.

Luke mashed the answer button. "Hey," he said in a low voice.

Silence greeted him from the other end.

"Tully?"

He could hear breathing, and then a sniff, maybe? But no one spoke.

"Tully, what's wrong?"

Luke forgot about Cade. "I'll be right there," he said into the phone. He got no answer.

29

309 E. Gaston Street # C
August 5th
1023 Hours

Luke rapped on Tully's door and turned to look at the courtyard. The morning sun found a path through the canopy and sparkled on the stagnant water in the forgotten fountain. It even made the overgrown garden beds look cheerful. A beautiful, forgotten place.

Tully's gray-haired neighbor was out, as always, obsessively tending her small garden, the only one that received any care. Even in oppressive heat, she was outside stooped over flowers that never reciprocated the love they received.

The courtyard was far too shady for them to thrive still, she tended them faithfully. She looked up when Luke entered the courtyard but turned back to her sparse rose bushes without acknowledging him.

Luke envied her. She knew that tomorrow would be much like today. Stable, predictable. Meanwhile, his personal rabbit hole kept getting deeper. What he wouldn't give to curl up on the couch with Tully and watch TV, with none of this mess weighing him down. A mundane activity that he no longer hated the thought of. Now he ached for it.

As Luke stood contemplating the old woman, he realized Tully still hadn't answered the door.

He knocked again. What if she changed her mind? She'd been moody since their weekend at the river house, but she'd had sullen periods as long as he'd known her. He was getting used to them. It always translated to rough sex, not ghosting him. Something felt wrong.

Luke tried the door handle. It turned. Making a mental note to yell at her for leaving the door unlocked, he pushed it open. When he stepped inside the thick smell of ethyl alcohol hit his nose. His senses heightened instantly.

"Tully?"

In the kitchen, he skidded to a stop. Not much of a cook, Tully's kitchen was usually spotless. Now it was an unholy mess.

Broken whiskey bottles lay in the sink. Shards of glass were strewn over the counter, their former contents dripping onto the floor.

She wasn't there. Luke drew his gun and held it at low ready.

"Tully? Tully?" He yelled her name as he ran across the room, glass crunching under his shoes. Pushing through the door into the bedroom, lit by the morning sun. His eyes flew around looking for any sign of her. Nothing.

The bathroom door was ajar, and the light was on. He crossed to it. Peeking through he could make out the neck of a glass bottle and the hand clutching it. Gently he pushed the door open.

The bathroom was also in shambles. The shower curtain and rod lay across the tub and towels were thrown everywhere. In the middle of the chaos, Tully sat on the floor leaning against the wall. Her phone lay on the floor next to her. The bottle in her hand was empty, and she didn't move when he came in. She kept looking straight ahead.

Luke holstered his gun. At the click, she flinched but still didn't look up. He knelt down trying to process the dueling relief and worry. She was safe, but she was not okay.

He expected her to be drunk; she usually was. But when he got closer, he saw her eyes were clear and bright, and her breath was sweet. She hadn't had a single drink.

No tears threatened, but the look on her face ripped to his soul. Luke guessed she had sat on the floor all night long.

Everything he could think to say sounded stupid and clumsy, so he sat down beside her. They didn't say anything for a long time.

After a while, she turned her head away from him. "It's my fault he's dead," she whispered. She clutched and released the bottle like a security blanket. Like she needed to feel it in her hand. It chinked on the tile as she rocked it around. "He was trying to help me. He was just trying to help me. All he ever did was try to get me clean. This is my fault."

Without thinking he turned and cupped her cheek in his hand. She didn't fight him as he pulled her face around, but she squeezed her eyes shut so she didn't have to look at him.

"Maybe he succeeded," said Luke.

Her eyes opened and searched the tile. Since they got back from the river house, she had made a valiant effort to open up. She even spoke briefly about her father. Maybe it was why she had been so moody.

Little by little she had exposed her wounds to him, still raw behind the cocky disguise. But now he saw the other side of Tully Meara in all its ugliness, peeking out from behind the beautiful one. He was sure he wasn't meant to see this much, but he had and now they couldn't go back.

He pulled her onto his lap. Her rigid body relaxed, and she let go of the bottle. It rolled to a stop next to the tub.

Tully buried her face in his neck as he stroked her hair. Between ragged breaths, her mouth moved like she wanted to speak but thought better of it.

Luke's arms tightened around her as a sharp memory hit him. The memory of a young boy peeking through a crack in the door as Joe Marshall gently picked up his wife from the bedroom floor and laid her on the bed. Her demons had bested her too.

For twenty years, Luke struggled to understand how his father loved a woman that had betrayed him. Betrayed them. As he sat on the floor with Tully, it made sense. Love strips away logic and replaces it with recklessness.

A tear reached through his shirt and jerked him back to the present. The woman in his arms was disintegrating. Everyone she'd ever cared about was gone. He should be gone too, but there he was on the bathroom floor, in desperate love with her.

Enough.

Pete was dead and damned if he would let Tully follow her partner down that path. They could start over and do it right this time.

Tully stirred and sharp pain in his back reminded him they had been on the floor for a long time. He stood up and lifted her in his arms. She reached for his neck and pulled herself closer as he carried her into the bedroom.

Sweeping one hand out, he knocked the throw pillows to the floor and laid her on the bed. She burrowed into his chest and soon her breathing evened out. An hour later eyelashes stopped batting against his neck.

Luke couldn't fall asleep so easily, but the struggle was over. He would sacrifice a thousand reputations if it meant saving her. She wouldn't be the one to pay. Not while he had the power to stop it.

The next thing he knew, Luke woke up. He'd fallen asleep. From the light, he judged it was late afternoon. He sat up and looked at the clock. It was six o'clock. Work flitted through his mind. He had skipped an entire day of work, after punching out his boss, but he had more pressing concerns. Tully was gone.

He jumped out of bed and peered into the great room. She sat at the table wearing a white tank and her favorite ratty sweats, arms wrapped around her knees. The kitchen was once again spotless, and every vestige of her meltdown had vanished. Even the smell of liquor was gone. He walked to the island and leaned against it.

"I'm sorry." She avoided his gaze.

"No apology is necessary, but an explanation would be nice."

"You don't want that, trust me."

"You scared the shit out of me."

"I'm sorry," she repeated. "I don't...I don't want to do this anymore."

"I gathered as much." Luke grabbed the throw from the back of the couch. Wrapping it around her hunched shoulders, he kissed her hair.

She wrapped her arms around herself and finally looked at him. "I don't want to drink anymore. I can do that. The rest of it won't be so easy." She looked out the picture window.

Luke thought of the pill bottles he'd found in her medicine cabinet. Yeah, that part would be a little harder. Sensing she might need a minute, he walked to the kitchen and made a scene of looking for the coffee. He rifled through the pantry with no success.

"It's in the freezer."

He gave her a sheepish smile then reached into the freezer and grabbed it. Behind him, he heard her speak softly.

"It's time. Time to move on. There are some things, and people, I need to leave in the past. Where they belong."

Luke turned around. She was looking off into the distance, her eyes bright and clear like the sky scrubbed clean after a storm. He put the coffee can on the counter and forgot it. "You breaking up with me?" He kept his voice light, but he honestly didn't know what the answer would be.

She looked confused. "What? No."

He walked over to her and fell to his knees beside her chair. The blanket had fallen off her hunched shoulders. He settled it back into place.

"Why would I do that? You're the one thing in my life that isn't physically killing me or breaking my heart. That's why I have to change. So I can keep you."

Luke reached up and kissed her forehead but let her continue.

"I'm just...I don't...really know...how to do this. I'm sorry." Flustered, she shielded her face with her hands. "It's just that...how am I supposed to undo my mistakes and become a different person?"

He wrapped his hands around hers. "I don't think people really change. I think they screw up the courage to tell the past to go fuck itself, or they don't."

She relaxed a little and sighed with pleasure as his warm hand covered her icy ones and returned his smile. "I dumped a lot of baggage on you all at once, and there's more. If you ran for the hills, I wouldn't blame you."

"Yeah, that was awesome of you." He broke into a grin relieved to know she still wanted him. He reached up and brushed the hair back from her face.

"Some people are harder to love than others," she whispered.

"I don't know. I thought you were pretty easy."

She laughed out loud and sniffed.

Luke got to his feet and held out a hand. "Don't change too much."

"You'd rather be with a raging alcoholic?"

He shrugged. "How do I know if you're any fun sober?"

"How much fun would it be if I punched you in the nose?" She said.

He grabbed her in a bear hug. His lips came down hard on hers and she leaned in. Luke bent and swung her up into his arms. Once again, he found himself carrying her into the bedroom. Only this time he was smiling.

Once she fell asleep, he could slip away and do what needed to be done.

30

FBI Satellite Office
August 5th
2341 Hours

It was half-past eleven when Luke let himself through the front door by Susie's desk. He'd left a note on the pillow telling Tully that he would be back before breakfast, and to pack a bag. It didn't matter where they went, but they were leaving.

He came to type up two documents. The first was his final report officially closing the case due to insufficient evidence. The second was his resignation letter. He would email it tonight, call Steve in the morning, and move on with his life.

Then he would pack up whatever personal possessions he had in the broom closet and never come back. With any luck, he could do it before Greg or Thad made it to the office.

As he passed the break room, Luke saw light coming from the broom closet. Thad must be in. Either that or Greg was rifling through their office. Greg didn't give a whit about this case unless he could use it to damage Luke. Luke wasn't going to give him that chance.

Before he barged in, Luke peeked around the corner. He saw Thad sitting in the office pouring over a stack of papers and a spreadsheet.

He would have to face Thad. The kid deserved that at least. Luke swallowed hard and rounded the corner.

Thad swung around to see who it was. "What are you doing here?"

"What do you mean? I work here." Luke tried to joke but it fell flat.

Thad didn't smile. "Boss, I think he's gonna press charges."

"I'm not worried about that."

"You're not?"

Luke shrugged and turned the conversation away from him. "Why are you here?"

Thad shrugged trying to look like he wasn't completely stressed out. "Gotta work at some point. I stayed out of the office all day to let things cool down. Might as well work while it's quiet. Not like I'm gonna be able to sleep."

Luke leaned against his desk. "What are you working on?"

"Are you gonna tell me about Cade?" Thad slapped the spreadsheet down on the desktop and whirled in his chair, telegraphing irritation.

"I didn't find him." Luke spoke in a clipped voice.

Thad's eyes narrowed. "Nowhere? You checked his house? The country club?"

Luke nodded toward the stack of paper. "What is that?"

"What do you think? The same thing I've been working on for the last two months. All these reports trickling in from all the little podunk agencies." He gestured out the door to the other side of the T that branched off the main hall.

There was no broom closet on that side. It was a dead end. The fax machine was rarely used these days, so it got banished to the dead end. "There's one or two every few days. Hell, I think I heard it beep since I've been sitting here. And don't change the subject." Thad eyed him with suspicion.

Luke took a moment before he went on, then decided to rip it off. "You can stop. We're finished. I'm closing the investigation."

"What?" Thad's eyes went from slits to wide orbs.

"I'm shutting it down. No more chasing ghosts."

Thad's surprise quickly mutated into anger. He jumped up from his chair and threw his hands in the air. "Are you serious? Just like that we're quitting?"

"We've exhausted our leads. And our suspect is dead. What do you want me to do?"

Thad muttered something as he elbowed past his chair and walked to the window.

"You want to say that again." Luke squared off to him.

"I said," Thad exaggerated the words as he slowly turned back to face Luke, "I hope your girlfriend is happy."

Luke's lip curled into a snarl, but Thad wasn't done. "You've been muscling this investigation whichever way you wanted it to go this whole time. Why stop now?"

With great effort, Luke kept his voice low. "We don't have a case. You agreed that we have nothing more than circumstantial evidence."

Thad bristled. "I fucking said that in Atlanta. This belligerent expedition to swamp town was your idea. We are here because you insisted we would find something. You said we were staying until we did. But now all of a sudden, you're listening to me. Now that you've got something to lose, you're ready to listen to reason."

Luke pushed off his desk and took a step closer to get in Thad's space. The kid didn't even have the good grace to be nervous about talking to him like that. "If you have something to say, say it," he growled.

Thad didn't back down. "Okay. How 'bout this? First, you never leave the office, then you start coming in late. You sleep with a witness but keep investigating her partner. You punch out Greg for tampering with your investigation, then close the case ten hours later.

"You're all over the place. Nothing I've heard about the great Luke Marshall has been true since we got here. Nothing. Except maybe your tendency to drop cases whenever it suits you."

Thad's barb hit its mark. Luke clenched his jaw and he bumped Thad's chest with his. "You think you know everything about me?"

"Obviously I don't. But I do know Cade walked through that door this morning to see you. I'm pretty sure he didn't want to have a beer and talk baseball. He's always been the missing link in this case. You've waited for this moment for months, and now you wanna quit because your girlfriend might get her feelings hurt."

Luke spoke through gritted teeth. "I'm closing the case because we have nothing to move forward on."

"Please," scoffed Thad. "You don't even believe that bullshit. And it's certainly not going to convince anyone higher up the food chain. Did you even try to find Cade, or were you with her all afternoon?"

"You done?" Luke wasn't going to answer Thad's questions. He wasn't after answers from Luke anyway. Thad had clearly thought up a slew of comments since finding out about Tully that morning, but she was just the straw that broke him. He had wanted to vent for a long time now.

Luke let him talk. Thad could get it off his chest then he could move on too.

"No, actually. I'm not done. I want to know one more thing." Thad sounded calmer.

Luke backed away to de-escalate but said nothing.

Thad turned his back to Luke and headed to his chair. "I sat in here every day, next to you, sifting through a haystack for this needle. And the whole time I thought we were on the same page. But all this time you were out canoodling the pretty witness."

He eased himself into his chair with a sigh. "I get it, you don't care how it compromises you. But did you ever once think about how it would compromise me?"

Luke felt himself deflate. Thad was right. "No. And for that I'm sorry."

Thad put his hands up to his forehead and leaned back. "You left me hanging. You don't trust me?"

"I do trust you."

"Then what the hell, man?" Thad threw his hands in the air again.

"I didn't tell you because I knew it was wrong. I didn't," Luke paused and studied his hands, "I didn't think it would last this long." He walked to his chair realizing how exhausted he was and fell into it.

Thad's anger subsided. "But it has lasted this long. You're walking away from this case for her. Don't bother denying it."

Luke hunched forward in his chair, unable to keep the pain out of his face.

His expression threw Thad off balance. He'd never seen his partner like this. "What is going on with you?" Thad's voice softened.

"You ever had something you couldn't win at? Something you couldn't beat?"

"Yeah, but probably not what you're talking about."

"I can't explain it, Thaddeus. I've put you and Steve in a bad position, and I know that. I can say I'm sorry, but I would do it again. And I could lie and say I'm trying to save her, but the truth is it's not her I'm trying to save."

Thad looked at him, gauging his words. He said nothing, but Luke saw compassion dueling with the anger on his face.

"I'm done, Thad. Maybe I won't find the answers with her, but I can't throw away the chance to try."

Thad pursed his lips and bounced his fist off the armrest a few times. "You really did it, didn't you, old man? You went and fell in love."

"I know I have to give up something."

"You'll be giving up your reputation. That's what you'll be giving up."

"My reputation has never brought me a second of peace. She has. But I can't be here and with her. It won't work."

Thad gave a grunt of amusement. "Finally, something we agree on," he said. Then he grew serious. "Luke, you know I've got your back, right? I didn't mean...I'm not gonna...," he trailed off. "This does explain a few things. I know this can't be an easy decision for you. Okay, now I'm done."

Luke felt a surge of concern toward his young partner. Thad stood to lose something in this mess too. He hadn't considered it until now. Thad's fate would be on his shoulders as much as Tully's. They'd talked for too long. Time to move.

"Let's clean up the office and get out of here. I don't want you to submit a report. I'm calling Steve tomorrow after I send him mine. I'd rather your name not be on any paperwork associated with this case."

"Psssht. I don't care about that." Thad waved him off.

"You should, kid. You've got a bright future here. Don't let the Gregs of this agency tell you otherwise."

"They'll probably send me to the mailroom after this," Thad said eyeing Luke for a reaction. He saw Luke smile. "Alright, Boss. It's done. Let's pack it up." Thad hoisted himself out of his chair and grabbed an empty box in the corner. He started throwing in everything he could reach.

Luke had no box, so he looked around for something to hold the small number of possessions he'd accumulated over two months. He spied an empty trashcan in the hallway and went for it when he heard a loud buzzing in the office.

Hurrying back so he wouldn't miss Tully calling him, he saw Thad pull his phone out of his pocket and study the caller ID. Thad pressed the answer button and put it to his ear. Luke glanced at his own phone sitting next to the computer. It was dark.

"Hey, girl. What's up?... Yeah..."

Luke watched Thad's face twist with surprise and horror. Thad looked up at Luke, his eye wide.

"Are you kidding?...When?...Okay. We're on our way. You got somebody responding?... Okay, tell them not to shoot us. ... No, we know where he lives...Thanks." Thad's phone hand fell to his side, his face a mask of shock.

Luke dropped the trash can and took a step toward him. "Thaddeus?"

"SPD communications just got a 911 call from Cade's house. The nanny was screaming hysterically that someone had a gun. That's all they could get out of her. They're sending their people out now. What is happening, Luke?"

A sick feeling welled up in Luke's gut. "Let's go."

31

---

309 E. Gaston Street #C
August 6th
0017 Hours

She was born May 27, to Samuel and Alice Meara in Prickett, Georgia. They lived a contented life in a small farm town. The kind of place where everyone waved to each other and front doors were never locked. Where mud pies were an acceptable form of currency for a popsicle, and crawfish from the creek made it to the table.

Life was insulated and happy. Evil lived in a far away fairy tale, not Prickett. Or so she thought.

Tully was seven years old the night she found out evil didn't have a zip code. More than one life was destroyed the night her father died, but none as completely as hers.

Her mother lapsed into a protective depression. For the next ten years, Tully cleaned the house, shopped for groceries, got herself ready for school and did her homework, all while caring for her bed-ridden mother.

Her mother's death had been calm and peaceful,

surrounded by people loved ones. Cancer was a far gentler executioner than the one that took her father.

Tully thought she left it behind when she left for college the next year. But she no sooner started her first year when the past began to crush down on her.

That's when she met Alexander Wynn. A popular professor, he was handsome and smart. She showed up late to his first class and had to sit in the front. He approached her at the end of class and every class after. It seemed to Tully that he always knew what to say. What she needed to hear. She thought it was a miracle when he showed up at her door the night she reached the end of her rope.

At first, he was gentle. Every whisper sounded like gospel. It took very little to convince her to kill for the first time. A life for a life. Charlie Hayward took her father's life so she would take his. Her first lesson. She learned a lot that freshman year. Like how quickly gentleness can tarnish into abuse. And how unforgiving the wrong choice can be.

For the next fifteen drunken, wasted years she managed to arrange his manipulation into something that resembled security. Who else did she have? Alex protected her. Now and then she would wake up from a guilt-induced bender and try to break free of his domination.

Alex would fold her entire life into one tidy, threatening paragraph and throw it at her. It worked every time.

Until two months ago. She left the phone in the senator's pocket as an act of rebellion. A loud warning to Alex that she had the power to take him down if he didn't let her go. She was determined to see it through this time, even if it killed her. It probably would, but she didn't care. She would be free of him.

Then everything went wrong. She knew Pete had started to suspect her ever since she saw him talking to Nick. Nick put it together and came to extort money from her. As he always did, Pete stood between her and the threat, and now he was dead. It should have been her.

Out of the haze of that night, Luke showed up and soothed every torment she'd ever felt. Those brown eyes cut through the rot in her soul and laid bare something beautiful. Something she'd forgotten was there. Something she had forgotten she wanted.

An hour ago, he left. She pretended to be asleep while he scribbled a note and left it on his pillow. This morning she nearly told him everything on that bathroom floor. And she didn't know if she would have the courage to do it when he got back. His note said pack a bag, but the baggage she carried around would destroy both of them.

Tully flipped the covers back and padded into the kitchen, her feet taking her to the liquor cabinet without her brain even checking in. Not until she reached into the empty space did she remember she stopped drinking. She sighed and went to the couch.

She'd been so wrapped up in the way Luke made her feel, she forgot the reason he was there. He was looking for her. He was hunting her, and he would find out the truth eventually. Would he throw the cuffs on her and call it a day? Could he forgive her? He always talked about running away. Would he still want her bags packed and waiting if he knew the truth?

A framed picture of Sam Meara in his official deputy brown, the American flag behind him, sat on the end table. She picked it up and pressed her forehead to the glass. In the end, it didn't matter. Luke Marshall's legacy would be what no other man had managed to do. She kissed the glass.

She would tell Luke everything. If by some miracle he could forgive her, she would never look back. And if he couldn't, she would still be free of Alex's repulsive control. That would be enough.

Tully's head jerked at a soft rustle outside. She craned her neck to see the front door and listened. Nothing.

"Hello?" She wiped her face dry and listened. Silence.

Tully jumped up and yanked the door open. A yellow manila envelope lay on the doormat. Her eyes darted around looking for movement. She snatched it up and ran through the courtyard in her bare feet, her father's portrait still clutched in the crook of her arm. She flew through the tunnel and onto Gaston Street searching for the courier. Nothing.

She looked down at the envelope in her hand. That was strange. She expected to hear from him, but Alex usually called her to guilt her back into submission. Opening it, she pulled out a 4 x 6 photograph.

For a moment she was drowning, her lungs unable to take in oxygen. She let go of the photo and her father's picture. The frame shattered on the concrete sidewalk. She staggered backward into a parked car as both photo and envelope wafted away from her. Her legs refused to support her and Tully slid down the car. On all fours she crawled to the photograph.

It was a snapshot of her and Pete standing in their favorite shady spot where they drank their coffee every morning. They were laughing, unaware their picture was being taken from across the street.

Tully wretched. Short choppy breaths sent pain searing up her back. The dark street dissolved as her vision blurred.

"What would he do if he found out? If you went to jail would he even visit you?" Alex always used Pete to keep Tully in line. He knew Pete was one of the few people whose approval she still sought. He was all Tully had left.

Alex was a brutal lover and mentor, but he'd never threatened her partner's life. He threatened to kill Tully, to expose her, but even Alex knew that Pete was a clearly marked boundary. So, he kept her in line with threats of Pete's disapproval, and it worked.

So that was his move. This was the final control tactic. When Tully left the phone behind, she had drawn a line in the sand. This was Alex's answer. The mind games were over, and the message was clear. She'd tried to walk away, so he wound up Cummings and set him loose. Alex sent Cummings that night. He'd come for Tully, but Pete stopped him. The message was clear. Now he would kill her.

Alex had already bled away fifteen years of her life, and the only thing her father had left her, a conscience. He devoured them until there was nothing left. Now he had taken Pete.

Rising to her feet, she picked up the broken frame and the 4x6. She trudged back to her apartment, not feeling glass cut into her bare feet. Halfway there she broke into a run leaving a trail of bloody footprints behind.

Running into her bedroom, she traded her sweats and tank top for jeans and a T-shirt. Then she threw open the closet door and ripped through the top shelf until she found a small ceramic jar. She emptied its lone item into her hand and stuck it into her jeans pocket. Then she pulled on her boots and jacket and grabbed her truck keys.

She knew where he would be tonight; he was there every night. Alex Wynn would get nothing else from her.

32

———————

August 6
0108 Hours

The city lights faded as Luke sped over the Talmadge Bridge, the Savannah River below them. The moonlight reflected off the smooth black surface sending spikes of light shooting off the surface. Thad watched the river through the window as Luke pushed the car to its limit.

The knot in Luke's stomach tightened. John Cade's house was ten miles outside of town. A quick drive at the speed he was demanding from the car, but would it be fast enough?

The timing was all wrong, and he'd bet his last dollar it had something to do with Cade's visit this morning. He had himself convinced it was nothing until Thad got that call.

Cade had his finger in the dike, and now he was waving a gun around.

"Luke," yelled Thad pointing through the windshield.

Luke squinted. Outside the cone of the headlights, a figure frantically waved them down.

A plump woman of about fifty ran up to the car before

Luke could stop. Her short graying black hair was wild, and she wore an old-fashioned nightgown with a ruffled collar. Her eyes were wide with fear, and she clutched a portable phone handset to her chest.

Thad hopped out of his seat as the car rolled to a stop.

Breathless, the woman began yelling in rapid Spanish.

"Calm down, ma'am. No, no, ma'am, I need you to take a deep breath." Thad put his hands on her shoulders and spoke firmly.

Luke made his way to the car hood and leaned against it with his head bowed, listening. The woman took a jagged breath then started babbling again.

"Deep breath, ma'am," Thad coached.

She took another breath and gained enough composure to remember her English. "Meester Cade, he is crazy. I don't know what...." She started sobbing.

"What happened?" Thad prompted her.

"They came home late from party and ever...everything seem alright, but then I hear shouting from the leeving room...."

"And?" Thad shook her gently.

"I went into the leeving room and he had a gun and he was shouting and the gun was so loud. I run away. I was so scared. I left poor Mees Helen." The woman dissolved completely and slumped to the ground.

Thad made no attempt to catch her.

At her words, Luke sprang off the hood and jumped into the car. Thad slid in beside him, pulling out his phone to relay the update to his dispatcher friend.

Luke hit the gas and sped the three hundred yards to stone pillars marking 504 Riverside Lane. A rooster tail of gravel spewed behind as Luke gunned it down the long tree-lined driveway.

Moments later, the driveway split, circled an elaborate

water fountain, and joined itself again in front of the house. Tall pine trees rose up on all sides except in the back yard where a gentle grassy slope led down to the river.

The massive white home rose two stories with Grecian columns supporting a double veranda that wrapped around the house. In the center of the antebellum facade hung heavy wooden double doors. One of them stood open.

Before they reached the circle, Luke pulled the car off the driveway. The men slid out into the hot night. It was quiet except for a humming air conditioner and chirping crickets. Light blazed in every window on the ground floor.

Luke left his door open and knelt beside it. Metal scraped on Kydex as he drew his gun. A scrape on the other side of the car told him Thad had done the same.

Luke sprinted to the corner of the house with Thad on his heels. Moving fast, they hugged the railing on the way to the porch stairs. Once they were safely on the veranda, they pressed themselves against the wall beside the doors.

Luke turned and questioned Thad with a thumbs-up and received one in answer. Luke inched to the open door and stopped, listening.

Nothing.

Pushing his Glock out in front, Luke pivoted and stepped through the door into an imposing foyer. It was empty.

Dueling staircases curved up each side of the two-story foyer. They met on a second-story landing lined with a hand-carved banister. The first-floor hallway cut under each staircase and ran the width of the house. Straight ahead was a wide doorless arch into a great room.

Luke could see an imposing stone fireplace on the far side, and a large oriental rug covering the heart pine floor.

Luke froze, unsure of where Cade was. There was precious little cover out here if the bullets started flying. He felt the cold grip of his gun warm in his sweating hand.

Then he heard the muffled crying of a woman coming from the room ahead. That must be where they were, but he didn't hear Cade.

Luke edged closer to the great room, every muscle in his body coiled to act. He tiptoed to the archway and pressed his shoulder against the wall. Beside him, Thad did the same beside him.

On the far right side of the room, Luke could see Cade rocking on the edge of an overstuffed leather chair. His shoulders were hunched, and he clutch a large silver pistol in his right hand. It rested on the fat leather armrest, but it twitched violently in Cade's hand.

Luke couldn't yet see the wife, but it looked as though Cade had her hunkered in the corner.

Luke turned to Thaddeus and pointed toward the whimpering. Then he pointed in Cade's direction while miming a gun with his thumb and index fingers pointed. Thad nodded and readjusted his hands around his weapon.

Luke leaned out from the doorway. "John. It's Luke Marshall."

He got no answer, but Luke saw Cade's head turn and bleary eyes flick toward him then back to the corner. Cade's designer tuxedo was rumpled and an untied bow tie hung limp from his collar. Cade's shoulders heaved with every breath.

"What are you doing, John?"

Cade shifted the gun on the armrest and kept rocking. He said nothing.

"I know things seem a little out of control right now, but this isn't going to fix anything," said Luke.

Finally, Cade spoke. "There is no fixing anything." He sounded defeated.

"John, you need to let Helen go. Don't drag her into this."

At Luke's words, the distraught man leaped out of his

chair and began pacing back and forth, alternately sobbing and screaming. A crystal tumbler of brown liquid in Cade's left hand sloshed everywhere. His gun came up and pointed at the corner. It was a chrome-plated Desert Eagle .50 caliber. A canon of a pistol and Cade handled it like a novice.

Luke tensed. His finger flicked from the rail of his own gun down to the trigger.

Cade sobbed and dropped his weapon to his side. Luke didn't relax. Cade had a twitchy finger wrapped around the trigger of a gun he couldn't handle.

"I'm taking the fall," whined Cade. "This wasn't my idea. Do you hear me? This isn't fair." He sniffed and pointed his gun at the corner again. He seemed to talk to his wife more than to Luke.

Luke stepped from behind the doorjamb, his gun pointed at Cade. Cade saw the movement and spun.

"Drop your gun," he screamed. He jabbed the hand cannon in Luke's direction. It shook violently.

Slow and deliberate, Luke holstered his Glock. From the corner of his eye, he saw Thad shift and take his old spot to cover Cade from the hall.

Luke stuck both hands out. "Alright, no gun. See? Will you talk to me now? Before you do something you can't take back."

Cade sniffed again. "Ok." He calmed a little and seemed grateful to have someone besides his wife to listen. "It's not fair." He sounded like he would start crying again.

Sirens sounded in the distance as Luke stepped into the great room.

Cade's panic kicked up at the sight of the FBI agent coming closer. "That's far enough," he squeaked, wagging his gun around. Now that he had two targets to cover, he wasn't sure where to point it.

Luke scanned the room. To his right French doors led out to a stone terrace overlooking the river. A woman cowered next to them. Her red silk dress was torn at the shoulder revealing angry red scratches on her pale skin. She had been pretty once, but now her bleached hair and botoxed face gave her a stretched out, secondhand look. Mascara ran down her cheeks as she lifted pleading eyes to Luke.

Luke's stomach hit his feet.

In her arms, Helen Cade clutched a young boy. He couldn't have been older than ten. He wore superhero pajamas, and his head rested on his mother's chest with his eyes squeezed shut. The boy must have run down to investigate the commotion after the nanny left. Without thinking, Luke took a step toward him.

"I said that's far enough," John screamed, hysterical.

Luke stopped and put up his hands. "John," he warned, "let your son leave."

John shook his head, but doubt crept into his expression.

"You're wrong, John." Luke pointed to the corner, his voice hard. "Tell me to my face he bears as much blame as you or Wynn, and I will walk out right now and let you shoot him."

Cade flinched at Alex's name. Then he looked at his son.

"Say it. Say it to me," Luke roared.

The Desert Eagle dipped, and Cade looked back to Luke. His nod was almost imperceptible.

"Noooo," wailed the woman. There was no relief on her face as she rocked back and forth clinging to her son, terrified of being left alone.

"Brice, come here," Luke commanded. He took another step toward the boy. Brice Cade struggled to obey as his mom clung to him.

"No, no, no," she whispered over and over, her eyes locked on her husband. Suddenly she released the boy and covered her face with one hand like she couldn't bear to look at him anymore.

Brice pulled away hard, breaking her grip. He hesitated beside his mother, but she had already curled into a tight ball. Luke grabbed him by the arm and yanked him toward the door.

Sirens wailed to a stop outside the door. Luke guided the boy to the arch and shoved him out into the foyer. He saw Thaddeus' hand reach out ready to shuffle him outside. Luke turned back.

Cade's face had grown less panicked and more uncertain as boots pounding on the porch made the walls shutter.

"Now Helen." Luke kept his voice even.

"No." Cade raised his gun and pointed it at her. This time his voice was steady. "She doesn't go anywhere," he said.

She cowered obediently.

"John," Luke said, "be reasonable. Let's work this out."

"She's not going anywhere." Sweat beaded on Cade's upper lip. He rubbed his forehead sloshing more liquor. "She's...she's...this is all her fault."

"You bastard, don't you dare blame this on me." Helen Cade forgot her fear and came out of her fetal position shrieking at her husband.

"You told me to go to the FBI," he yelled back.

"He hacked us, John. He was tracking you and me," she yelled back. "And you didn't even know it." She stopped yelling but her voice oozed disdain. "And you thought he was your friend. I was trying to save us. I am still trying to save us."

Cade shook his head vigorously trying to clear it.

"This is why he never had any respect for you." Helen struggled to her feet.

"Fuck you," Cade screamed jabbing the gun in her direction making her back against the wall. His head swiveled to Luke. "He lied to me. After all I did for him. They told me he was reading emails and texts. Spying on me." He didn't sob, but tears welled in Cade's eyes. "He wouldn't have known Twomey hacked him if it wasn't for me." The tears broke loose and dripped down Cade's nose.

An indignant huff came from the alternately terrified and enraged woman. "Don't play dumb. You were a means to an end," she barked. "Why don't you grow a pair and tell him the truth?

Her voice turned pleading. "We can fix this. Together. We've got an ace to play. We can get immunity for testimony or something. You're a fool if you don't use it."

"Shut up," Cade screamed.

Helen Cade wasn't done berating her husband. Her sneer returned. "We're done if you don't man up."

"Shut up," Cade screamed as he continued to cry.

"Henry's not going to be a Senator now so you can stop blowing him for your precious cabinet position. Twomey ruined everything when his spooks hacked Henry's email. It's only a matter of time before everyone knows about that reporter."

Luke couldn't believe what he was hearing. Henry. Henry Onessa blackmailed the Washington elite, and Congress, with the dead soldiers. Not Cade.

Helen turned to Luke who couldn't tear his eyes away from her. "Twomey hacked Henry's email in April. He found out Henry knew about the reporter and then leveraged it to collect campaign money and favors. Twomey threatened to expose him, so Henry made John order a hit on...."

"SHUT UP." Cade dropped the crystal glass and

wrapped his free hand around the shaky one clutching the gun.

"He's cleaning house, John, which means us too. He knows you went to the FBI today. Why else would you get an anonymous call saying I'm an FBI informant? You know perfectly well I'm not. He's trying to wind you up. We have to do this, John. It's the only way now."

Cade shook his head. "No, I can't. He'll kill me."

"Please, John. He was going to kill us anyway if you didn't do it first." Helen now shared his panic as she tried desperately to persuade her husband. "You know as well as I that shrink and his little cop aren't the only...."

At the mention of Wynn, something snapped in Cade. His finger tightened on the trigger as his hand clenched.

Luke's hand flew to his hip. In one smooth motion, his finger pressed the holster release and he drew smoothly. He brought his Glock up to plane and his finger found the trigger in one smooth movement.

It took a millisecond to draw, but it might as well have been a year. The blast of his own gun married with the louder report from Cade's.

Helen cut off mid-sentence and staggered backward, her face frozen in surprise. She hit the wall next to the French doors and sunk to the floor, eyes round and vacant.

A wide cone of blood droplets splattered the stone hearth as Luke's round entered Cade's temple and exited out the other side. John Cade died before he hit the Persian rug.

The scene suddenly exploded with noise. The Savannah Police Department SWAT team stormed through the front door, swarming past Luke into the living room. Luke heard thumping, but whether it was boots or his heart pounding he didn't know.

In slow motion, he looked over at Thad. Thad gaped

back at him, his own gun hanging limp. He heard everything.

As the SWAT team cleared the room several and administer aid to Helen Cade, two turned and eyed Luke. He realized his finger was still pressed on his trigger.

"Luke, you okay?" Thad's voice was shaky.

Luke didn't answer. All he could manage was holstering his gun. He turned, dazed, to the front doors making his way stiffly past the men in OD green fatigues. Out in the sticky night, he trudged to the car and sunk into the driver's seat cradling his head in his hands.

Minutes later, footsteps crunched on the gravel next to him. "I called Steve," said Thad. "He's coming to work the shooting. He doesn't trust Lawrence."

When Luke didn't answer, Thad shifted his weight. "We're gonna have to tell him everything."

33

The Executive Club
E. Jones Lane
August 6th
0139 Hours

Tully stood in a dark alley that ended in an ivy-covered retaining wall. Three men leaned against the wall, smoking and laughing with two topless blonds in g-strings. Smoke breaks here were clothing optional.

The alley led to the basement door of a Georgian mansion, a soft thumping from inside the only advertisement. There was no sign. If you didn't know about the Executive Club, you didn't belong there.

Tully didn't look the part of aspiring stripper in motorcycle boots and a leather jacket, but her t-shirt cut low enough to give it a go. She smiled at the two burly bodyguards flanking the entrance.

"Can I help you, Darlin?" The black bouncer said. Right on cue, his eyes locked on her chest.

"I'm here to see Mr. Jackson. He's expectin me." She glanced over at the white bouncer. His muscles were more grotesquely swollen than his partner's. He looked skeptical, so she winked at him and put her hand on her hip sticking her chest out. "You wanna search me?"

He grinned. "We don't do that here," he said, pulling the door open for her.

Inside, Tully planted her back against the wall to let her eyes adjust to the dark. "You should," she muttered. The throbbing beat swallowed up her words. Across the dark room, she saw a solitary door. Her destination.

The large room was filled with sumptuous leather nail-head chairs grouped around raised platforms. A pole rose from each platform with a naked woman wrapped around it. Topless waitresses ferried expensive drinks from the bar.

The alternative upstairs offered poker, scotch, and networking if that was more agreeable; or if a customer needed an alibi. Down here, the business was pleasure, and business was booming.

No one noticed her skirt the room as she made for the door. She pushed it open and slipped into a wide hallway with the same dim lighting. More doors led off the hall. A shiny brass number marked each door.

Number 9 was at the end of the hall. Tully tried the handle. Locked. She pulled the key from her pocket and eased it into the lock. The handle yielded this time. All these years, he never changed the lock. More loud music escaped through the crack and a blast of cold air hit her face.

He liked it cold. He liked how uncomfortable it made the women. Another calculated control tactic. Without seeing it, she knew the scene. Alex would be sitting in the overstuffed leather chair, a cigar smoking in the ashtray next to the scotch he favored on the table next to him. He'd be on his phone ignoring the woman foolish enough to be in there with him.

Tully took a deep breath, surprised at the sudden tremor in her hand. She pushed the door open. Alex's head came up, and he straightened in the chair. A sly smile quickly replaced the surprise on his face. He set his phone on the table and leaned back, his eyes never leaving her face.

The naked dancer stopped mid-leg raise and flipped her hair back. "Um, we're a little busy here." She wagged her head.

"Get out," Tully said as she locked eyes with Alex.

"This is my client, bitch."

Tully turned to the young woman and gave an unnatural, guttural laugh. Walking over, Tully grabbed a fistful of dark hair and yanked her head down bending her in half.

"Trust me. Even your soul is worth more than he's paying." She heaved the woman out the door and slammed it shut.

As soon as Tully flipped the lock, her cheekbone slammed into the wood. Alex jerked her around. His hands slammed into her chest, and the back of her head bounced off the door.

"Come to relive the glory days, Baby?"

She threw her head forward and connected. He jerked away, his hand over his nose. Tully paced in a half-circle getting her back away from the wall. "Why did you do it?"

"Why did I do what?" Alex sneered.

Enraged, she flew at him, her fists pounding. "You sent... Nick to...kill...Pete," she huffed.

He was ready this time, and her blows didn't make it past his block. Her punches were hard but wild. She realized too late she was out of control, emotional. The one mistake she couldn't make now. Not ever. She hesitated.

Alex noticed and pushed her hard. She stumbled back, catching herself before she fell.

"The fuck are you on about, Tully?" Alex gingerly

touched his nose, assessing the damage.

She set herself, ready to attack again. But she didn't. "Why?" Tears brimmed her eyes.

"Why what?" The tears bought nothing but more contempt.

"I told you to leave him out of this."

"What are you talking about?"

"It was the only thing I ever asked from you," shouted Tully. "And now Pete's dead because you sent that crackhead. You wound him up and set him on Pete."

"What? No, I didn't, you psychotic bitch. Now, will you cut this shite out before they revoke my membership."

Tully faltered. Why wouldn't he admit it? He never denied anything. Then she remembered he was a liar. She pulled the crumpled photo from her pocket and threw it at his feet.

Alex looked down surprised. "What the fuck is that?"

She began circling her prey, coiled to attack.

Alex moved with her, making sure he kept her to his front. "You think I sent you that?"

"Who else?" Tully snarled. "Who else would know to send it to me?"

"How should I know? I don't send you paper. It's bloody careless. Besides he was your supplier, not mine. I didn't associate with that gutter rat. If you're looking for someone to blame, it's your fault your partner is dead. Not mine."

Before he finished speaking Tully charged him, her hands stretched out to grab his neck. She envisioned smashing his conceited face into her knee.

His hands came up between hers and batted them to the side. Air rushed from her lungs as he landed a punch to her diaphragm. As she gasped for air, he grabbed her throat and twisted using her momentum to slam her against the wall.

Alex put his face next to hers. His breath felt hot on her

skin in the cold room. "No doubt he found out about you and saw dollar signs. Don't forget, Baby, you're the one that left a tidy trail of crumbs pointing to your partner. Something I doubt was accidental."

Tully flinched. "You're lying," she croaked as he squeezed her throat tighter. She felt a hot tear let go and roll down her cheek.

His lip curled at the sight of it. "No, Baby. It doesn't mean I'm lying simply because you don't like the truth." He released her windpipe but grabbed the back of her neck and yanked hard. "Somebody else sent you that. But then, you made this mess. It shouldn't be a surprise that someone wants to clean it up." He yanked hard.

Tully stumbled forward and slammed into the stout side table beside the tufted leather chair. She bounced off and rolled to a stop on her back. Scotch and cigar ashes splattered her as the bottle and the heavy crystal ashtray hit the floor.

Alex was on top of her instantly, straddling her. "You've been in this position a lot lately, haven't you?"

He leaned forward, resting a forearm on her Adam's apple. With the other hand, he grabbed her hair and slammed her head into the floor.

Stars erupted in her vision.

"To be honest. It's not your best one," he said letting the pressure off her throat.

Through the spotty haze, Tully saw something on the floor. The bottle of scotch she knocked over in her fall. She blinked to clear her vision.

Alex took her hair again and forced her to face him. "We both know you're not here because your drug dealer killed your BFF. You're here because of that dreamy FBI agent running around town."

Tully dropped her hand to the side feeling for glass.

Alex laughed. "I knew you were riding him the second he walked into my office. You start fucking the other side and suddenly you want to walk the straight and narrow, but I've got some bad news, Baby. Agent Marshall will find out about you."

Alex tightened his grip on her hair. "He's not especially bright, but you served both of us to him on a platter when you left that phone. And when he puts it all together, he will do his job. Men like him always do." Alex laughed again. "Did you think he was gonna get down on one knee? Girls like you don't get a happy ending."

The bottle was just out of reach. Tully's fingers grazed the lip, but she couldn't grasp it. She forced herself to hold his gaze so he wouldn't notice her reach.

It made her shiver. There was no trace of the gentleness he baited her with so long ago. His emotions were controlled and calculated. In the beginning, he hid it well. He made no such attempt now.

His smile turned ugly. "Nice touch, by the way, leaving that phone behind to put the pressure on me. You want out. Message received. But you forgot one very important thing, you little dope fiend. Without me you're nothing but a crooked cop. The most decorated officer in the history of the Savannah PD is a killer. It's quite the headline."

Tully jerked, hoping it seemed like a reaction to his words. It was enough. Her fingers closed around the prize. As hard as she could, she swung the scotch bottle up. Alex threw up his hands, but he was too late.

The bottle shattered against his temple raining glass on them. Tully threw her hips up pitching Alex forward. In a flash, she flipped onto her stomach, pulled her head through his legs, and rose to her feet in an agile move.

Tully took a deep steadying breath. Every inch of her body hurt, her face bleeding, but it infused her with purpose. Pain made her stronger. So much of it had come from Alex, but it had always served her well no matter the source.

Now she would use it one last time. The sharp awareness of it brought back the control her emotions had stolen. Coldly she eyed her kneeling opponent.

Alex's hand covered the bleeding knot forming on his head. Slowly he pulled himself to his feet and looked at the blood smeared on his palm. "Kitty finally grew a pair of claws."

He tried to sound smug, but she heard the anger. He was beginning to understand.

"I told you I was done," she said, calm for the first time.

"Yeah, yeah. Just like last time. And the time before that."

"Did you really think this would never happen?"

He whirled to face her. "Actually, I thought it would happen a long time ago."

Blood smeared on his shirt as he wiped his hand across his chest. "You were the only one I never had to paddle to keep in line. You were so sweet and compliant. I never had any problems with you. I only had to tell you I loved you."

Tully exhaled. She, the salvaged fool, saw it so clearly now. It threatened to take her to her knees, but the pain overpowered the shame. Instead, she stood taller. After years of lies, he finally told the truth. He was afraid.

"Then again, you had a bigger debt to pay," Alex continued quickly when he saw her listening.

"You're the monster that destroyed me. I owe you nothing." Her instinct kicked into high gear, and she dropped her eyes to his chest so she could see every movement.

Alex's face twisted with rage. He jammed his finger toward her. "I pulled your daddy's gun away from your pretty little head and made you a formidable talent. I made something out of you. I took your pathetic life and gave it purpose. And a pretty handy income too."

"You should have let me die," she said calmly.

"You call me a monster, but I have always been the only thing between you and absolute ruin. Me. Not him." Spit flew from Alex's mouth as he yelled.

"I used to believe that, Alex. But he is something you'll never be."

"And what's that? A hopeless romantic?" Alex's sneer was ugly.

"Real."

Alex's eyes grew dark. He took a step forward and his shoe clinked on the crystal ashtray. Leaning over he grabbed it and brandished it at her. "Then maybe I'll suicide him next."

He barely had time to react before Tully slammed into him. They fell to the floor, Tully on top raining down blows. Alex swung the ashtray aiming for her face, but she knocked his hand back. Blood spurted from his nose before he gave up trying to make contact and threw her off.

Tully rolled away springing lightly into a crouch.

This time Alex rose to his feet slowly. He was still dangerous, but she was younger and lithe from constant training and a hard life.

His indulgences had weakened him. Alex straightened his collar and wiped his bloody nose. "I appreciate the spunk, but you're not leaving me. Without me you're nothing. Somebody else's penis isn't going to change that. You belong to me."

"No."

Her decisive tone sent him into a rage. His face twisted into a snarl, and he advanced on her. She took a step back and felt hardwood beneath her boots. The stripper pole touched her back. Reaching up she grabbed it with both hands and brought her legs up. She aimed a devastating kick at his chest.

Alex reeled backward and caught himself on the armrest of the chair. This time she didn't hesitate.

But he was ready. As she attacked, Alex dropped to one knee and drove a braced elbow into her bad hip. Something popped and again stars exploded in her vision. She staggered sideways.

Alex rose and caught her. Pushing her backward he slammed her against the pole, pinning her arms around the pole behind her. She shook her leg trying desperately to get it to respond.

Alex rested his chin on her heaving shoulder. "God, you fight the same way every time, you know that? You're so predictable. Other than FBI Agents, it's your biggest weakness."

Tully struggled to draw a breath through the searing pain. "I would have done anything for you." She didn't know why she said it. One last pathetic plea for his approval.

"You did everything I needed you to do, like the good little experiment you were." His voice was cold. "If it's any consolation, you were my best." He spread her wrists and planted a kick in the small of her back.

Unable to get her bad leg underneath her, Tully fell next to the chair. She crawled behind it desperate to put something, anything, between them. Bending her right leg under, she threw her weight down hard. Her hip popped back into place. More stars.

She pulled herself up clutching the backrest for support. Sweat beaded on her forehead despite the cold room, and she swayed as she took one hand off the chair.

Alex was menacing as he paced in front waiting for her next move. "I'm not the kind of man you tell goodbye."

"I'm not saying goodbye, Alex." Tully pulled her father's

Nightguard out of the waistband of her jeans and aimed it at him.

The blast hit her ear hard but dissolved into the thumping base.

Alex staggered back and looked in disbelief at the red stain growing on his shirt. He fell to his knees then to one elbow. A groan escaped his gaping mouth as his head hit the floor. Tully watched his chest rise once more, then stop.

Tully walked over and knelt beside him. She ran her hand over his face to shut his eyes, then bowed her head and sobbed bitterly.

Someone pounded on the door. Everyone heard the shot. A key scraped on metal, but Tully opened the door before they could unlock it.

Brent Jackson held the key in his bony hand, eyes gaping. Behind him the brunette Tully tossed out and several men crowded the door gawking at the scene behind her. Blood dripped from Tully's face onto her white t-shirt. Wynn's blood smeared her gun hand as she pointed it at them.

A path appeared through the mob as they retreated from her wild, raw expression. She moved across the main room not bothering to stay in the shadows. The music still thumped but no one moved. They were all watching her.

Two steps from the front door it opened, but she was ready. She ducked low between the two bouncers that let her in. Coming up beside the white bouncer, she buried the butt of her gun in the side of his wide neck. He fell to his knees. She leveled it at the black bouncer who raised his hands and backed up.

Tully turned and fled into the night. Feet slapped the pavement as they gave chase, but she easily outpaced them. Their heavy breathing faded and disappeared. She turned right and kept running. She didn't have long.

34

FBI Satellite Office
August 6th
0301 Hours

Luke made Thad drive back to the office. He needed to think through this. The dam had broken and by morning this story would be swamping news feeds. Nothing could stop it.

Henry Onessa built his reputation and career on the corpses of dead American soldiers. America's sweetheart politician was a swindle and a fake. And now he was a murderer.

And Twomey found it. He found everything. Politics as usual had him searching for something to blacken his opponent's eye. Instead, Twomey found a scandal that would reach as far up as the Presidential Cabinet and Congress.

With Cade smack in the middle. It didn't matter what he intended to tell Luke that morning when he came to the office. After tonight, search warrants would flow freely. Luke's only limitation was how fast he could get search warrants to a judge before the involved parties wiped their servers and powered up their shredders.

No one would be untouched by this.

And Tully. He needed to get to Tully and make her tell him what she knew. Force her to tell him about her partner. Tell him everything.

Luke stopped lying to himself the moment Helen Cade spoke those words. If she knew, there was no way Tully didn't know. Shielding her would not be enough. Now he had to keep her out of jail.

Thad was right. Blinded by emotion and desire, he was willing to sacrifice everything to keep his girlfriend happy. Maybe he could still protect her if he moved fast enough. There would be plenty of blame to spread around, but he had to get to her and soon.

He looked down at his phone. The screen was black. He had dialed Tully three times to wake her up. She hadn't answered.

Thad flew into the deserted parking lot by the FBI office and screeched to a stop. Without a word both men jumped out of the car and ran into the office. Thad continued on to the broom closet, but Luke stopped in the break room. He needed a minute alone. And he needed Tully to pick up the phone. The words 'call ended' flashed on the screen again. She still wasn't answering.

What was he even going to say to her? How did he start this conversation?

Hey, babe, I need you to tell me what you knew about this massive conspiracy and your homicidal partner. I was gonna run away with you, but now you may be going to jail. Wanna get married?

She lied to him. Every time she spoke so reverently of her partner, she had lied. Could he trust what she said now? Still hyped on adrenaline from his shooting, the rustle behind made him wheel.

It was Thad, winded as though he had sprinted to the

break room. Sweat beaded on his upper lip, but it couldn't be from exertion. The broom closet was ten paces away.

"What is it, Thaddeus?"

Thad closed the distance and thrust a stack of papers into Luke's hand like it was on fire. "This was on the fax machine."

He backed away running a shaky hand over his mouth. "Remember how I told you the smaller police agencies were trickling in? Well, this one must have trickled in right before we left."

Thad threw himself down on a break room chair. "It must have been the one that came before we went to Cade's house." Thad cursed under his breath.

Luke looked at the paper in his hand. It was a photo-copied handwritten police report dated April 4, 1989. Wilkes County, Georgia. He skimmed down the distorted lines until a name snagged his attention. Samuel Meara. This was the official report of his death. Luke knew this. Why had Thad sent off for a copy of this?

Luke glanced back at Thad who now had his forehead mashed against the tabletop. His blood ran cold. Thaddeus hadn't known. He just found out about Tully. He knew nothing of her past.

Shuffling to the last two pages, Luke read faster. On the bottom was a typed police report in a newer format dated ten years ago. Same town. The name Charlie Hayward was typed in the 'victim' block. Luke knew that name too. A quick check of the old report confirmed it. Charlie Hayward killed Samuel Meara in 1987. His throat went dry.

Charlie Hayward served fourteen years for the murder of the Wilkes County Deputy. He was released a few weeks before the second report was taken. He had been diagnosed with terminal prostate cancer and released to die at home.

They found Charlie Hayward shot through the head

in the backyard. Cocaine in the bloodstream of a non-user and no alcohol. Toxicology was the same as Twomey and the Labor Boss. And God only knew who else.

The room went out of focus. It wasn't similar. It was exact, but crude. The report noted there were signs of a struggle. The victim had been so hated that nobody cared to investigate further.

Luke leaned against the wall struggling to comprehend what he was reading.

No one ever noticed. There was no national database for suicide specific toxicology. No one would ever notice the pattern unless they were looking for it.

She knew that. She knew this pattern would remain undetected for a very long time. Forever maybe. She knew a lot of things it seemed. Not least was how to manipulate him.

The paper yielded as Luke's hand clenched down so tight his knuckles turned white. He threw the paper at the wall.

"Luke. Luke, this whole thing is messed up...." Thad trailed off, his voice steady now. "Say the word and this whole thing disappears. Nobody knows but us. If we say the senator killed himself, that's what happened. We can come up with an explanation for Cade.

Luke kept staring out the window. He couldn't look Thad in the eye. Moments ago, he was trying to save her. Now his partner was trying to save him.

Luke looked at his favorite square aglow in the familiar orange streetlights, only now he hated the sight of it.

He was a fool. She seduced him as thoroughly as he'd fallen for it. The truth crashed over him. He was the reason this case never went anywhere. It was right under his nose, but he was too distracted to see it. Humiliation and fury churned inside him, and he heard someone yell. It sounded like him.

A sharp pain seared through his hand as he punched the wall over and over. He didn't stop until he felt the drywall give way under his bleeding knuckles. The crumble satisfied his rage for the moment. He shook his hand. Pain spiked up his wrist and into his forearm, clearing his mind.

His time playing the fool was over. That woman had no idea the depths he would send her to. He would pay hell itself a visit if that's what it took to drag her there.

"No," Luke said over his shoulder. "This ends tonight."

The menace in his partner's voice made Thad's head swing up. Worry clouded his face, and he opened his mouth to speak. Luke cut him off.

"Get on the phone to Steve. I'm gonna need everybody from the Atlanta office that he can spare. Especially the Forensic I.T. guys. I don't care if he has to steal a chopper to get them here. And I want our Tactical Response Team mobilized and here asap."

"Why do you want TRT?"

"Just do it."

Thad nodded at the same time his phone chirped. He pulled it out of his pocket. "Yeah." His face was vacant as the voice on the other side jabbered.

"Where? Ok, thanks, Mary." Thad hung up. "Alex Wynn is dead, Luke. They ID'd his body. He was shot at a member's only club on East Jones Lane." Thad fiddled with his phone as Luke stared out the window.

"Luke, it was Tully. They've got like ten eyewitnesses that put her on the scene while we were at Cade's place. SPD has been there for about forty minutes."

A perverse sense of relief flooded Luke. This would make it easier to run down that lying bitch.

He turned to Thad, calm. "Let's go."

35

The Executive Club
E. Jones Lane
August 6th
0347 Hours

The alley teemed with police and pulsed with red and blue flashing lights. Luke stopped when the yellow ribbon warning 'Police Line - Do Not Cross' grazed his belt. He watched the scene.

Patrons and dancers in borrowed men's jackets paced in a corner of the alley, corralled by a uniformed officer. Through the open door, Luke could see more men and women inside overseen by more uniforms. His gaze traveled over the brick mansion towering two stories above them, a look of disgust growing on his face.

At the other end, Captain Timothy talked to three plain-clothes detectives in a tight huddle. His rumpled gray polo and khakis had been selected in an obvious hurry. All four wore guns, badges, and stunned expressions. Luke's eyes narrowed when he saw the Captain pinching his nose.

Thad approached the officer manning the tape line and

pulled out his credentials. She nodded and lifted the crime scene tape so they could cross. Luke ducked under but stayed at the top of the small hill by the road. Thad didn't leave his side.

Captain Timothy clapped one of the detectives on the shoulder and said something to him. The detective nodded. The Captain turned and looked over the scene with a tight expression. His eyes stopped on Luke at the top of the alley. Luke saw him sigh and start toward them.

Luke spoke first. "Was she hurt?"

Thad glanced uncomfortably between the men, but the Captain seemed to be thinking the same thing. "We're not sure. There's not much blood and most of it looks like his. But witnesses say she was bleeding and limping. They...."

"Where is she?" Luke cut him off.

"I don't know. We're getting a search warrant for her apartment right now." The Captain's eyes narrowed as something occurred to him. "How did you find out about this? It only happened forty-five minutes ago."

Luke wasn't going to answer that question. He put his face next to Captain Timothy's and growled, "Did you know?"

"Know what? I don't even know what happened, or why she was here. She didn't even know the victim." Realization and dread dawned on his face at the same time. "Did she?"

Luke laughed bitterly. "Oh, she knew him, alright."

"What? How?"

Luke wasn't laughing anymore. Every word out of his mouth was a hiss through gritted teeth. "He was her handler."

Captain Timothy looked confused. "What do you mean 'her handler'? I don't underst...."

"She's a killer, Captain. Your precious Tully is a killer."

The Captain took a step back as if Luke had physically hit him. He shook his head slowly, but his brow furrowed.

"Did you know?" Luke roared at him. The entire alley stopped and turned to watch.

"How...how could I know?" Captain Timothy's gaze dropped to the pavement. His shoulders slumped as he began to grasp what Luke was saying.

It made Luke angrier. "The same way I should have known," Luke hissed, his voice low again. "None of us were fucking paying attention."

"I've known her since she was a girl. I knew her father. It's not...it's not...," he trailed off and his eyes glazed over.

Luke knew he was remembering the red flags. The small things he had always dismissed now made sense. A list that would forever make him question himself.

Luke knew because he had his own list. "Not what? Possible? Anyone is capable of anything and it's our job to know it. That line is not going to work anymore. Now tell me what you know."

"Okay." The Captain pinched his nose and exhaled loudly through pursed lips. Finally, he met Luke's accusing glare. "She had a problem with the pills and booze. Everybody knew that," he whispered. "She took a bullet on the job for god's sake. I thought that...."

Luke stepped so close their chests bumped. "Did you cover up Atlanta for her too?"

"What do you...Atlanta?" The Captain was confused again.

"She killed Cecil Twomey. Assassinated him actually. What? You didn't know that either?"

Captain Timothy's eyes grew wide in disbelief. Or fear. Luke couldn't tell.

"Oh, that's right. It's not possible. Savannah loves their

pretty little hero, even if you roll her over and find maggots underneath."

The Captain seemed to rally when Luke slurred Tully. He brought his hand up and gestured at Luke like a man used to giving orders. "Listen, we'll handle this. She's...."

Luke didn't give a shit if he was the ranking officer on the scene. "She is an assassin. How the hell are you supposed to 'handle' this? She was one of yours. She gaslighted you worse than she did me."

Luke's accusation punished Captain Timothy into silence. He couldn't seem to find any words to rebuff the onslaught which suited Luke just fine. Less interruption for his tirade.

"Here I am beating myself up for not figuring it out after a couple of months, and you've known her for her entire life. I guess it was easier to look the other way. Well, you can't anymore. So, it's my turn now."

The Captain's face turned red. "You listen here. We're going to take...."

"No. You are not." Luke jammed a finger in his chest. "You will stay out of my way, or I will take this city apart brick by brick."

Luke didn't wait for a reply. Spinning, he yanked up the crime scene tape and strode into the street so fast Thad had to jog to catch up.

"I want our evidence team in that building. Yesterday. And mobilize the tactical unit.

"Uh, to where?"

"I don't know yet, but I want them in the chopper on their way here. They can hold at the airport. When I find her, I want them ready to go. Got it?"

"Luke, wait."

"Discussion's over, Aulden." Luke walked toward the car.

"Where are you going?" Thad threw up his hands.

"Her apartment."

"Then I'm coming with you." Thad moved to follow him, his cell phone already in his hand. "She could still be there."

Luke stopped at the car and put his hands on the roof. He bowed his head, afraid his face would betray him. "Do what I asked please, Thaddeus," he said quietly.

Thad took a step back. He wasn't sure if he should follow anyway or try to talk Luke out of it. He decided against both.

"Alright, Boss. I can get TRT here in forty-five minutes. ERT will take longer. They're all in bed."

Luke got into the car and slammed the door. Tires squealed as he hit the gas.

"Sure, I'll get a ride back," Thad muttered.

Ten minutes later, Luke's tires scraped the curb and he jumped out. Once more he found himself standing on Gaston Street. It was four in the morning and everyone was asleep.

Luke stood outside the tunnel and let regret sear through him. Twenty-four hours ago, the woman he loved couldn't keep her hands off of him. Now he hunted her like an animal.

Several feet away a glint caught his eye. On the sidewalk by a parked car, shards of glass reflected the streetlamp. He walked over.

Under the front tire, he saw a manilla envelope. He picked it up and examined it. It was blank and empty. Luke put it in his pocket and looked around to see where the glass came from. The car window was intact, so he knelt to pick up a piece and saw it. The trail of bloody smears leading from the glass toward the arch.

At the sight of the blood, Luke took off running through the tunnel.

At her door, he stopped and drew his weapon. What he

would find inside he didn't know. He twisted the knob. Of course she hadn't locked it. He pushed the door open.

The apartment was dark. Luke stepped into the foyer and pressed his shoulder against the wall. The familiar smell of gardenia made the hairs on the back of his neck stand straight up.

"Tully?"

No answer came and he couldn't bring himself to say her name again.

Leading with his gun, he stepped into the living room. The first thing he noticed was the large framed photo of her father missing from the couch end table. He cleared the living room and the kitchen then ran to the bedroom.

Clothes draped out of dresser drawers that had been haphazardly pulled open. She'd been here and left in a hurry. The closet was open, and the light was on, but the hanging clothes appeared undisturbed. The top shelf, however, had been tossed.

Luke holstered his gun and sat on the bed. He hadn't expected her to be there. He certainly hadn't expected his raging anger to transform into confusion. Why was he confused? The mission was crystal clear now.

He picked up her pillow and buried his face in it. It smelled like her. Memory after memory soured like a mouthful of vinegar in his stomach. He drew another deep breath allowing himself to hate everything it brought to mind. Luke threw the pillow on the floor and looked at the closet shelf.

The left side looked more jumbled than the right except for a void against the wall. He tried to remember if he ever noticed a bag there but came up with nothing. Luggage was not on his mind during the hours he'd spent there.

He walked to the closet and examined the shelf closer. A blue ceramic dish lay upended, empty. A cardboard box sat beside it. He couldn't see into the box, so he pulled it off the shelf. It contained the lid to the blue ceramic dish, a blank notepad, and a brown Stetson with a gold star on the front. Her father's hat.

The notebook didn't look as old as the other pieces. In fact, it looked new, except that several pieces had been torn from it. The half-circle remnants of the top pages were still caught in the spiral spine. He tossed it and the box on the bed. Then he turned his attention to the desk.

Pulling open the drawers he rifled through the papers inside. Nothing but medical paperwork, bills, and old receipts.

Luke opened the laptop sitting on the desk and ran his finger over the mouse pad to wake it up. The password prompt appeared. Luke typed in every word and date he could think of that she might use, but each time 'password incorrect' flashed on the screen. Luke tried the date her father died.

Password Incorrect

The laptop flew across the room and Luke let out a roar of frustration. Drywall pieces flew onto the carpet as the computer bounced off the wall and fell to the floor. She was in the wind. Every good assassin has an escape plan.

He fell onto the bed meaning to clutch his head in his hands. The box corner crunched under his holster as he sat down. He grabbed it and meant to throw it across the room too, when he spotted the notebook again. Why was it hidden away in the closet with her father's hat?

Luke leafed through every page. Blank. He was about to toss it into the box when he thought of something. Flipping to the first page he turned the notebook on its side and held it up to the light, looking across the surface.

Gotcha.

It was faint, but the paper was indented. Something had

been written on the page above and torn off, a tale-tail impression left behind.

Luke stepped to the desk and grabbed the small lamp. He snapped it on and held it so it shined across the surface of the paper. Sure enough, the oblique light accentuated the indented writing well enough to make out some of it. He grabbed a pen and a scrap of paper and began copying the letters he could make out.

It was a list.

Cape Ak_itas
Pacon
Edi_h
*Ulsa_*
Triumph
Mes_ina
_rge_t Fr_esia
Atl_nta
Nord Hak_ta

So that was her out.

Luke dropped the lamp and grabbed the list he wrote. He strode through the apartment and out the door for the last time. The urge to look back was strong, but he resisted. It was time to close this chapter, not relive it.

By the time he cleared the tunnel, Thad's phone was ringing. Luke heard jet engines whine in the background. Thad was at the airport.

"She's headed for the port," he said.

Thad sounded stressed. Luke imagined him running around organizing a vehicle convoy to accept the Tactical Response Team and their inevitable piles of equipment.

"Sorry, what?" Thad yelled over the ruckus on the tarmac.

"You got an ETA?"

"TRT is about twenty minutes out," yelled Thad.

"As soon as they touch down, get everyone to the Port of Savannah. Go straight there. She's leaving on a cargo ship. I'm headed over there now. I'll let you know when I find her."

36

Georgia Ports Authority Ocean Terminal
August 6th
0441 Hours

The burning anger Luke felt at Tully's apartment had evaporated. The thought of seeing her made him numb. Whether denial or a fault of his senses, it seemed like a long time ago that he found out about her. As though ages had passed.

Luke glanced at his watch after he passed a sign announcing the Port of Savannah entrances. Early morning traffic was light, and he'd blown through every red light. It hadn't been ages. It had been twelve minutes. He couldn't trust his perception or judgment. Once again, she had the advantage.

Maybe it would be better if he was too late to stop her. He would look like a buffoon, but it was no more than he deserved. She could disappear into legend, and he could retire into obscurity. Didn't sound so bad. But even as he thought it, Luke mashed the accelerator down harder.

The guardhouse appeared in his headlights much

quicker than he anticipated. He slammed on the brakes to avoid the reflective gate arm.

Security at gate one was a small windowed building between the entrance and exit lanes. Steel arms stuck out from both sides blocking the road. An 8-foot chain link fence ran in both directions with barbed wire spiraled on top. The drowsing security guard's feet dropped off the counter as the Impala screeched to a halt. The guard slid off his stool, all traces of sleep gone.

"Where do I find a schedule of ships departing today?" Luke yelled at him before he could make it to the gatehouse door. Luke stuck his credentials out the window hoping to speed things up.

The guard's name badge said 'Chris'. Chris wore a white polo with the blue Georgia Port Authority logo and black pants. He had a fat plug of tobacco in his lower lip and looked confused at the man shouting at him. His regulars were bored dock workers dreading the day's shift, which wasn't due to start for another two hours.

He squinted at the badge Luke held out. "Watchoo want departures for, sir? What is that?" Chris gestured to Luke's badge.

Luke ignored the first question. "FBI. Where is the office?"

"What office? Can ya be more specific? We got a lotta offices here." With a little more swagger now, Chris spat onto the patchy grass by the guardhouse.

"I need to see the schedule of ship departures."

"Should I get the perimeter units here?" Instead of answering Chris grew excited. "I got a couple of guys that can...."

"Son, answer the question and let me through this gate," Luke said loudly.

Chris's face fell as his hopes of getting in on the action

were dashed. He shrugged. "You don't need it. Ain't but one departure this morning. Container ship weighing anchor in about forty-five minutes. The Argent Freesia. There's a couple container ships being offloaded now, and more coming in but they won't be ready to go...."

Luke recognized the name from the list. "Where's the Argent Freesia?"

"She's docked at berth 5."

"What's the destination?"

"Don't know that, sir. The administration offices'd have that information. They're down by the Garden City Terminal, near the 1-2-3 stacks."

"The what?"

Chris pointed down a shadowy, unlined paved road. "Just follow that road past the three white buildings on the left and the rail yards'll be on yer right. After that the road veers right, and you should see the admin building straight ahead. They oversee yard operations and keep copies of all the scheduling there. Don't open till 8 tho, so I don't kn...."

"Good. Listen, there's a bunch of agents coming right behind me. Let them in and tell them where I went. Alright, Chris?"

Chris nodded and spat, his eyes wide.

"Stay here. Don't wander around," Luke ordered, indicating the conversation was over.

Chris bobbed his head again as he stepped back and hit the button to raise the arm.

Luke inched forward and saw the road split. To the right down a short spur, he saw a wide, multi-lane road running past warehouses and into a container yard. Stacks of stories high patchwork colored containers were visible from everywhere in the port, brightly lit for around-the-clock crews. As Chris instructed, Luke's road went left and stretched into darkness.

He flew past the 'Authorized Personnel Only' sign, and soon he saw the three buildings ahead on the left. As he approached, he could see the rail yard across the road from the buildings. The rail yard was very dark, the partially loaded rail cars lit only by the container fields beyond.

The cluster of three buildings had dull white siding and flat roofs. A shared parking lot wove around them and each building had weak lights illuminating their multiple entrances. The first building was marked #100. The second building was #110.

As Luke glanced at it, the black metal digits weren't the only thing he saw in the dim light. A familiar rusty green tailgate was parked behind #100.

Luke kept going until he passed building #110, then cut the headlights and slammed the brakes. Wrestling the steering wheel left, he entered the parking lot of the third building and swerved behind a parked tanker. He cut the engine and left the door open as he slipped out.

In the distance, he heard a helicopter. If Thad was flying TRT over from the airport, they were going to have words. Talk about advertising their presence. Luke cringed. It sounded like something Thad would do.

Sheltering behind the tanker, Luke surveyed the parking lot. Doubt washed over him, and he shot a glance over his shoulder at the dark railyard.

Why was her truck here, six thousand yards from the river's edge? She could be in the rail yard, but that was a slow way to escape. Slow was not her style. Something wasn't right.

He drew his weapon and darted into the blackness along the fence line. He sprinted the length of the parking lot until he was even with #100, then he knelt in the darkness watching. Seeing no movement, he crept to her truck and peered inside. Nothing.

The building provided pitiful cover, but he pushed his back against it anyway and followed it around pulling every door handle. The building was locked tight.

At the corner, he gauged the distance between him and #110. The roughly one-hundred-yard sprint offered no cover. He scanned the windows and the roof before sprinting across and fell against the rough siding listening for any sound. Nothing. He tried the back door. Locked.

Once more, Luke inched his way around the perimeter checking doors. He inched up a short handicap ramp beneath an unremarkable bronze sign that said *CMS-CMG Shipping Lines, International.* He pulled on the glass door expecting a deadbolt to catch. Instead, he pulled it open.

Luke let go of the door and pressed his back against the building so he could pull out his phone. He tried typing a text with one hand, then cursed and gave up. He holstered his weapon and hammered out a quick text to Thad.

Building 110. Set up on rooftops. Gate 1 will direct you.

He drew his gun again.

Five minutes out, came the reply.

Luke slipped the phone into his pocket and reached for the door. He swung it open and crossed the threshold with his gun up.

The room he entered was a sparse lobby. The lights were off, but daylight would not have made the white Formica countertop and plastic chairs any more welcoming. A single window let in the weak light leaking from the container yards. To the left was a large cluttered desk and chair, on the right a keypad door.

Luke tried the door. It was locked so he kicked it in.

This room was no more cheerful than the lobby. A row of modular desks sat along the far wall and a copier/printer unit in the back of the room. Another beat-up metal desk piled high with paperwork sat along the front wall of the building.

Behind the desk, a plate glass window replaced most of the front wall. Through it, he saw the dark hole of the rail yard and the glow of the container stacks beyond. The harsh industrial lights were losing their oomph as the sky lightened from inky blue to a soft gray.

Another door in the corner of the room led out to the front lot. A familiar leather bag sat on the floor beside it. Keeping his eyes on the door, Luke stepped into the room.

Something hard crashed down on the back of his head and the room dissolved into a blurry haze. He staggered forward and blacked out.

The linoleum was cold on his cheek when Luke came to. He sat up and reached to touch his throbbing head, but something clinked and his hand stopped. Opening his eyes, he saw his right wrist cuffed to a modular desk leg with his own handcuffs. He slid the cuff to the floor and touched his holster hopefully, but his fingers closed around air. Instead, he used his left hand to rub the knot forming on his neck.

"Looks like you keep getting the jump on me."

Gray light backlit a familiar shape between the desk and the window wall. She was wearing her favorite jacket, she loved that jacket. Her face raised toward the sky. "You keep letting me," Tully said quietly.

Luke saw the outline of the gun in her hand. "No argument there," he said.

She wasn't watching him, so he scanned the immediate area around him. The desk leg was flimsy enough to break, but not before she could put two in his chest. He saw his gun laying on the desktop, her back to it.

Boots thudded above them. The cavalry had arrived. Luke's eyes flicked toward the ceiling when he heard the noise. As though she'd expected it, Tully didn't flinch.

The loud whumping sound Luke heard earlier grew louder. It was now loud enough to drown out the ruckus above them. Unlike the stomping boots, it made Tully's head turn.

Luke's eyes followed hers to the plate glass window. The chopper he'd heard minutes earlier was touching down on the road out front.

Through the window, Luke watched three TRT officers approach the chopper pilot, guns aimed at his chest. The man raised his hands in surrender and was unceremoniously yanked from the cabin and hustled away.

"Now what? You sail off into the sunset?" Luke meant to sound apathetic, but it came out angry.

Her laugh was hollow. "The boat was my backup plan. My pilot was supposed to be here thirty minutes ago."

"Wow, your getaway kinda blows. I'm a little disappointed," Luke sneered at her. "But I gotta give credit where it's due. Even I'm impressed with how well you played me. Like the professional you are."

Tully turned her head enough to see him, but not look directly at him. She offered no defense against his tirade.

"They're going to study you for years to come, babe," Luke said. "You constructed the perfect disguise. The wolf in a sheepdog's uniform. But you got sloppy, didn't you? Leaving the cell phone behind."

"I wasn't sloppy," she said quietly.

"Oh yeah?" Luke's voice was mocking. "You left a critical piece of evidence at the scene. What the hell do you call it? I call it a rookie mistake."

"I did what I had to." Her voice was firm like she was done talking about it.

Luke scoffed. "What does that mean? Were you bored? And I was the entertainment."

Tully took a deep breath and straightened. She still

wouldn't look at him.

"And your partner. Tully, you framed your partner. That man saved your life."

"No." She sounded choked. Her head dipped and her shoulders heaved like she was struggling to breathe.

Luke didn't care. Her reaction was enough to light a fire in his gut. "You planted a receipt in his bloody uniform to throw me off your scent. You worked when he was out of town. Just enough, Tully. Just enough breadcrumbs that if anyone ever came sniffing around they would focus on him, not you."

"No," she cried out, not able to keep the pain out of her voice this time. She whirled to face him, and the look on her face tore at him. "I didn't plant that receipt."

"I don't believe you." Luke said it, but he did believe her. Still playing the fool.

"I don't care what you think. I didn't even know he had it until after he died. That's when I found it missing." Her voice barely rose above the turbine engine noise leaking through the front door. "He must have found it in my gym bag when I left it out."

"You left it in your gym bag? On purpose? First the phone, then proof you were in Atlanta when he was killed. Tsk, tsk, that's not very professional," Luke mocked. "Maybe Thad was right. Maybe you are just a sociopath after...."

"It was for someone else, okay." She cut him off. "I was going to plant it on someone, but not Pete."

"Who?" Luke asked the question, but he already knew the answer. He'd known it the second Captain Timothy told him the dead man's name at the Executive Club.

"Don't make me say his name." Tully turned to face the window so she wouldn't have to look at Luke. "I saw Pete talking to Nick. I knew he had suspected me for a while, but that's when I realized he was checking up on me. He must have found the receipt after that. I think he made up his mind to confront me about it the night Nick killed him."

"You expect me to believe that you didn't willfully implicate Easton, but you worked when he was out of town. Why?"

"So he wouldn't find out." She whispered to hide the waver in her voice.

"His blood is still on your hands," Luke growled.

She didn't answer. Didn't turn around.

"Did it help?"

No answer.

Enraged at her silence, he sent a kick at the desk leg, the only thing he could reach. "Did it help?" He roared at her.

"What?" She sounded choked again.

Luke ripped at his cuffed hand violently making the desk shudder. "All those scars. You've been stitched up more times than there are days in a month. Did all those ridiculous heroics soothe your conscience when you were out killing for money?"

Tully stayed still and silent.

"All that lying and now you have nothing to say." Luke gave up and let the handcuff clink on the floor.

"I never lied to you." Her voice was strained, but she was calm.

"Don't." Luke jammed a finger in her direction. "Don't pretend you're broken up over this. Of all that horse shit, what was true? Tell me."

"You messed everything up when you came here," she said. "You were never supposed to happen. Not you."

"You knew what would happen when you left that phone. Maybe you missed that day in hitman school, but you don't get to choose your FBI agent. At least you were lucky and drew a clown that fell for your BULLSHIT." Luke yelled the last word.

He needed her to cry, scream, curse. Anything to show that it had mattered.

But she didn't. She looked out the window. The darkness hid most of her face, but he knew she was sad by the way her shoulders hunched and her arm wrapped around her waist.

Even now he had no defense against it. "You win. I see now that I was just a complication while you were trying to offload your boyfriend."

She flinched.

Luke sighed heavily and sat back. "You told me you loved me. Was it true?"

He watched her shoulders heave. When she answered it was a forced whisper. "No."

Luke laughed bitterly, his nostrils flared, and his mouth carved into a twisted smile. "Here I was thinking I was riding in on a white horse to save you. Turns out I was the donkey that got taken for a ride."

Tully turned and looked straight at him. She had a sad smile on her face. It scared him. He could forgive her. He already had, but it was too late for any of that to matter.

The sun crested the container stacks, and light began to fill the room. Luke could see her hand clench and loosen around the butt of her father's Nightguard.

"A white horse?" She shook her head and smiled again. "I don't get a happy ending." She brought the revolver up and her eyes fell from Luke to the snub nose.

"Tully, no." Luke knew the words were useless before they came out. "It's not too late. Turn yourself in...to me and we...we can work it out."

Her thumb worked the release and the cylinder swung open. "Work it out," she repeated. She sounded calm and peaceful.

"Yes." Luke, on the other hand, couldn't keep the mounting fear out of his voice.

"You mean an insanity plea."

"If that's what it takes, yes. I don't know. We'll figure it out."

"I'm not insane."

"You don't want to spend the rest of your life on the run."

"You and I both know that is not going to happen."

The gun tipped in her hand and bullets plinked on the floor a moment later.

"Tully, stop. I can help you." Luke abandoned all pretense and begged. "Please let me help you."

Her smile was heavy. "You want the truth, Luke? The truth is there was never any other choice for me." Her wrist flicked and the cylinder locked into place, empty. She tucked the gun into her waistband in the hollow of her back and pulled her jacket over it.

"Tully, please." Luke strained against the cuffs. "Tully, no."

She took a deep breath and drew her shoulders back. Ignoring her bag, she walked to the door and rested her hand on the bar.

"Tully. Tully, wait." Luke was yelling when saw her stop. Thinking she had listened, he fell silent.

She turned to look at him. "Pete had nothing to do with this. He was a good man. I know you don't owe me any favors, but please don't make his family pay for what I did."

She pushed the door open and descended the three stairs to the parking lot.

The whine of the idling turbine engine filled the room then faded as the door closed behind her. When her boots hit the pavement, a piercing voice cracked out of a bullhorn. "Stop. Turn around and put your hands up where we can see them."

Luke saw Tully walk toward the helicopter. She didn't hesitate.

He spun and kicked the desk leg as hard as he could. It cracked but didn't give. He kicked it again and again until he heard wood splinter and the leg bent. He looked up.

Tully was halfway across the parking lot. She walked, paying no attention to the bullhorn.

This was taking too long. He had to get to her. What she was planning couldn't be undone. Luke's foot slammed into the leg and he was rewarded with a satisfying crunch.

The metal leg fell to the floor. He slid his cuff off and launched himself at the door praying he wasn't too late. He slammed into it and burst onto the pavement. What he saw made him feel like a bomb went off next to him.

Twenty agents had taken positions on top of all three buildings. The roofs bristled with rifle barrels aimed by men in full tactical gear.

Luke knew the rest of them were hunkered down behind the scattered vehicles. The bullhorn boomed again ordering Tully to put her hands up.

Tully stood at the open door to the helicopter. She turned and faced down every FBI agent and TRT member in eastern Georgia, her shoulders squared, unyielding. The morning sun had broken the horizon and haloed the scene in golden light.

Her eyes found his, calm, even as he heard himself yell her name over the frenzied orders from the bullhorn. Luke broke into a run.

Tully never wavered. Never taking her eyes off Luke, she reached behind and pulled out her father's empty gun. Bringing it around, she pointed it at the mass of FBI agents sweating behind cover.

Gunfire drowned out the engine. The air in front of Luke filled with whizzing and the sound of bullets plinking off the fuselage. She stumbled and dropped the gun, but he was still fifty yards away. He ran faster.

On the roof, Thaddeus screamed into his radio for a cease-fire as soon as he saw Luke sprint into the hail of lead. When that didn't work, he began hitting agents on the back and waving frantically at the team leader on the other roof. The firing tapered then stopped.

Tully took a step forward and fell to her knees gasping.

Luke threw himself down beside her and caught her before she hit the blacktop. Instinctively he wrapped his arms around her and cradled her.

He looked down. Blood bloomed on her white shirt beneath the jacket, and her tanned skin was pale. She opened her eyes and took a ragged breath. Hot blood ran down his forearms. He held her head up with his hand as she struggled to speak.

"Luke." Her voice was hoarse.

"I'm here, Baby."

"I'm...sorry." Her expression was labored with the effort of speaking. A tear escaped and lingered on her scarred cheek.

"Shhh, don't talk." His own tears blinded him.

"You were r...right, you know." She convulsed in his arms and licked her lips like they were dry. She tried to smile but lacked the strength to hold it.

"It...was enough...I was with you. wasnough," she slurred, fighting to speak again. "I forgot what that felt like."

He shifted her limp body in his arms to bring her face close. She stiffened in his arms as a small red bubble formed in the corner of her mouth. Her head lolled back, and she grew heavy in his arms.

Luke pulled her tightly to his chest as footsteps pounded on the pavement.

37

———————

Norcross Tigers Minor League Stadium
Suwanee, Georgia
November 7th
1435 Hours

The red, white, and blue banner proclaimed 'Onessa for Senate' above the jumbotron declaring "WE DID IT!" in 10-foot letters.

As the newly minted U. S. Senator Onessa and his polished wife strode onto the stage holding hands, the crowd of thousands went wild. The couple waived happily to the crowd who cheered louder.

In the middle of the congregation stood Luke. Around him, a sea of American flags waved and signs bearing 'Onessa for Senate' bobbed up and down.

At the sight of Onessa, screams and shouts erupted all around Luke, but he never moved. He stood tall and silent, hands by his side. His eyes never left Henry Onessa.

The Senator took his place behind the podium for the victory speech and pointed at someone in the front with a big smile. Henry Onessa gripped the podium and smiled, waiting for the cheers and whistles to fade.

"Ladies and gentlemen. My fellow Americans. Friends. We did it!" Henry Onessa raised his hands high with a big smile.

The crowd erupted again. Onessa scanned the throng with a satisfied smile, his gaze snagging on the single static figure in the frenzy.

His smile faltered, and he dropped his hands when he saw Luke. The politician recovered quickly and continued waving.

Luke turned and pushed through the crowd. Tully was right. No one was innocent. But if she paid, they would all pay.

Washington would burn.

Luke Marshall will return in *The Orchid File*

Reviews are critically important to authors. If you enjoyed this novel, please leave a quick review to share your experience with other readers. Thank you for supporting independent authors.

ABOUT THE AUTHOR

R. J. Strong is a veteran police officer and Crime Scene Investigator who married into a family of police officers. When she's not writing characters who do bad things for good reasons, she travels, lifts weights, and cleans up dog hair. She lives in Northern Virginia with her husband and son.

This is her first novel.

Catch up with her at rjstrongbooks.com

www.ingramcontent.com/pod-product-compliance
Lightning Source LLC
Chambersburg PA
CBHW020336010826
48970CB00012B/1313